Eloisa James

Not That Duke

PIATKUS

PIATKUS

First published in the US in 2023 by Avon Books,
An imprint of HarperCollins Publishers, New York
First published in Great Britain in 2023 by Piatkus

1 3 5 7 9 10 8 6 4 2

A CIP catalogue record for this book
is available from the British Library.

ISBN 978-0-349-43441-4

Printed and bound in Great Britain by Clays Ltd, Elcograf S.p.A.

Papers used by Piatkus are from well-managed forests
and other responsible sources.

MIX
Supporting
responsible forestry
FSC® C104740
FSC
www.fsc.org

Piatkus
An imprint of
Little, Brown Book Group
Carmelite House
50 Victoria Embankment
London EC4Y 0DZ

An Hachette UK Company
www.hachette.co.uk

www.littlebrown.co.uk

*For all the befreckled, bespectacled women
in the world
and the men who love glasses and freckles,
especially Alessandro.*

Not That Duke

Not That Duke

PART ONE

PART ONE

PROLOGUE

February 20, 1816
12, Mayfair Place
The Duke of Huntington's townhouse

"I've found your duchess." Determination was stamped all over the dowager duchess's face. "Lady Stella Corsham is perfect for you: the granddaughter of a marquess, with a sizable dowry. Able-bodied, well-bred, and original."

In an act of profound self-control, Silvester Parnell, Duke of Huntington, did not roll his eyes.

Or otherwise indicate that in demanding her son marry a version of herself—a short, opinionated woman, albeit with spectacles rather than a monocle—his mother had lost her mind.

"'Original' is not a characteristic that interests me," he said instead.

His mother's eyes sharpened. "I suppose you are looking for a girlish nitwit who will entertain ladies for tea and never embarrass her children."

He pretended to think about it. "Does she have to be a nitwit?"

"Yes," the dowager snapped, adding: "Because you want her to swill tea all day long."

When his parents first married, rather than redecorate the ducal country house as did most new duchesses, Her Grace had redesigned the chimney on her husband's first experimental steam engine. In the years since, she had delighted in flouting society with everything from her clothing (unconventional) to her entertainments (*Julius Caesar* performed by trained rats was a notable example).

Silvester and his sisters had grown up with the full knowledge that "polite" society considered his mother—and by extension, her family—to be eccentric, if not mad. Once sent to Eton, where he routinely engaged in fisticuffs in his parents' defense, Silvester came to the conclusion that although he adored his mother, a less divisive duchess would be preferable.

"Do you think I am unaware of how much you and your sisters wish that I would blend into the wallpaper like most of the noodling nobility?" she demanded now.

"I am proud of your chimney," Silvester said, meaning it. His mother's clack box feed pipe for locomotives had survived four iterations of ducal steam engines and was still in use around the country.

"Lady Stella—"

Silvester interrupted. "Which doesn't mean I want to marry Lady Stella."

To be clear, he didn't mind Stella's lack of height or her spectacles. Certainly he appreciated her rather glorious bosom.

The eccentricity? That he minded.

Rumor had it that she'd read the entire encyclopedia, which explained the fact that their conversations were often startling. And interesting.

He liked arguing with Stella; he just didn't want to marry her.

"Want to? *Want* to?" The dowager pounced like a robin on a worm. "What does *want* have to do with it? You need a duchess. Lady Stella is suitable."

"My fiancée will be of my choosing, Mother. I would like to be in love with my wife."

She snorted inelegantly. "Romance is a fool's game, nothing to do with marriage. You're making a laughingstock of yourself mooning about after Yasmin Régnier."

Fool he may be, but Silvester intended to marry Yasmin. She had charm, hair the color of old ducats, a naughty giggle . . . More than that, he and Yasmin were friends, never mind the fact that he'd love to bed her.

He felt the pull of her in his bones, deep in his gut.

Perhaps even in his heart.

"Moonblind." The dowager waved her monocle at him. "Lady Yasmin is not for you." His mother was small in stature, but she made up for it with gargantuan willpower.

"I intend to ask Yasmin to marry me," Silvester told her.

His mother replaced her monocle and eyed him. "You'd better open the Dower House. Lady Yasmin won't want to live with me."

A full renovation of the master bedchamber and Dower House at the ducal estate, Huntington Grange, was already in progress. "You will come to love Yasmin," he said, not at all sure, but it was worth a try.

Her Grace snorted again. "Every Season, one woman attracts all the men like seagulls on a gutted fish."

"A lovely metaphor," Silvester commented.

"A lady who tolerates fools will make a dreadful wife."

"Why?" Silvester inquired, though he didn't really care.

"Because she *tolerates fools*," his mother repeated. "She has no bollocks!"

"No woman has bollocks, as they are male appendages," Silvester said. "May I point out that Stella has as many suitors as Yasmin?"

"Fortune hunters and third sons," the dowager said contemptuously. "You'd be the only duke. My point is that Lady Stella braves ballrooms in spectacles, although society dictates that ladies should blunder blindly around the dance floor."

"An idiotic rule," Silvester agreed.

"Don't you see?" his mother demanded. "You need to find a woman who has backbone, not just a woman at the center of a crowd."

His mother was a brilliant tactician. She delivered that line with just the right amount of scorn. If women were allowed to debate in the House of Lords, the opposition would wither.

Luckily, he had a lifetime's worth of experience thwarting her demands.

"No," Silvester stated.

From the moment he entered Eton at the age of eight, he had carefully shaped a reputation for easy charm to counter his family's reputation for eccentricity.

That didn't mean he hadn't inherited his mother's steely core. Or his father's entitled ferocity.

"I will never marry Lady Stella."

The best debaters know when to retreat. His mother bounded to her feet and headed for the drawing room door. "You won't marry Lady Yasmin, either," she said over her shoulder.

He opened his mouth to retort—

But she was gone.

CHAPTER ONE

March 24, 1816 (just over a month later)
THE DUKE AND DUCHESS OF TRENT'S ANNUAL BALL

ℬearing the weight of a man sounded interesting . . . until it happened.

Mind you, Lord Belper was a particularly healthy specimen. Stella found herself pinned to the floor, gasping for air.

She had made an error while dancing a quadrille and bumped her partner, who collided with her bosom and toppled like an elm tree struck by lightning.

"Lord Belper," she rasped, pushing ineffectively at his shoulders. From above came a swell of alarmed voices, along with more than a few giggles.

"Wha' happened?" he asked groggily. Perhaps his head hit the floor when he fell. Hers certainly had.

"I can't breathe," she gasped.

"I can," he informed her.

His weight suddenly disappeared as someone hauled him upright. "Belper, you dunderhead," a deep voice said. "Are you in the whiskey again?"

Stella took a desperate gulp of air and realized that her vision was blurry. "Does anyone see my spectacles?" She should sit up and look for them, but her head was spinning.

"Drink had nothing to do with it," Lord Belper said, sounding sulky. "She tripped me!"

"Lady Stella, are you injured?" She knew that voice, she thought fuzzily. Deep, low, confident . . . Without her spectacles all she could see was a circle of blurry heads standing out against a bright haze of chandeliers.

"Can't see where she goes . . ."

"Blind," someone else remarked.

And then, worst of all: "Bounced on her like a feather-bed." With a laugh.

Just to top off the disaster, a drop of hot wax fell from a candle far above and landed with an audible plop on her cleavage.

Stella squeaked and slapped a hand over her bosom just as a man bent closer. She instantly realized who had spoken earlier. This particular duke smelled like late autumn: apples, spice, a touch of starch, a hint of snow in the air.

Altogether delectable.

Her head cleared abruptly. She was lying on the floor, and her rumpled gown was pulled above her ankles. Her aunt would have hysterics.

"My spectacles?" she asked again, rolling to the side and yanking down her skirts before she came to her knees, peering between the feet that surrounded her.

The Duke of Huntington crouched down beside her. "I have them, Lady Stella. They are undamaged."

His Grace had astonishingly beautiful eyes: as gray as a winter day to go along with that . . . that autumnal odor of his. Stella blinked up at him before she snatched her spectacles and put them back on her nose, threading the sides around her ears.

He put a strong hand under her elbow. "Are you uninjured?" Silvester asked, once she was on her feet. She thought of him as Silvester because the name suited him. It was a fancy, elegant name for a fancy, elegant man.

"I'm fine," she mumbled.

Stella thought of her body as capable of walking and dancing, most of the time. Luckily she was sturdily constructed, since her bones never broke, no matter how often she tumbled to the ground.

But around Silvester? With his broad shoulders, the handsome curve of his jaw, the easy swing of his muscled body, his gray eyes, even his commanding nose . . .

His smile.

Around him, her body became her enemy, serving up shaking knees and quickened breath. Desire that flared straight down her back after a glance at his lower lip. Or the touch of his hand on her arm.

He went to Stella's head like potent wine.

The very sad, very secret, truth was that she was captivated by a frivolous aristocrat.

"Stella!" Her aunt pushed through the crowd. "What happened?" Her eyes were wide with alarm.

Mrs. Thyme's eyes were often wide with alarm, since Stella didn't seem to be able to maintain the refined tone on which her aunt depended. On which *civilization* depended, if Mrs. Thyme was to be believed.

Stella often said the wrong thing. She argued with gentlemen. She regularly dropped things to the floor, including, at times, herself.

She was unrefined, to say the least.

"We fell," Lord Belper said, displaying a remarkable ability to synthesize facts.

Silvester nodded at Stella and melted into the crowd.

"I'm glad neither of you were injured," said a cheerful voice as an arm wound around Stella's waist. "By next Season, we'll all be far more proficient at the quadrille. For now, we shall retire, dear."

Their hostess, the Duchess of Trent, was one of the few women in London whom Stella thought of as a friend. Perhaps because Merry was an American, she was happy to talk about subjects considered inappropriate for a lady.

"There's no need—" Stella began.

"Your gown is creased," Merry said firmly.

"Given that you insist on wearing those spectacles, I just don't understand how you fell!" Stella's aunt cried after they were ushered into the duchess's own bedchamber.

"I was confused by the quadrille," Stella explained.

Lady Jersey had recently introduced the dance, and it had taken off like wildfire. But prancing back and forth in little quadrangles while circling at precisely the right moment wasn't easy.

"I expect it was Lord Belper's fault," Merry said. "He drinks to excess. He walked into a lamppost at Vauxhall a few weeks ago."

"No, it was my fault," Stella confessed. "I misjudged the distance between us and turned too early."

"I don't understand," Mrs. Thyme wailed. "You've had the best of dance masters. Your uncle and I have shirked no expense. And yet social indiscretions follow you everywhere."

"Me too," Merry said kindly, if ungrammatically.

Mrs. Thyme waved her fan in the air as if she were conducting an orchestra. "Last week, Stella knocked over a glass of red wine that poured into Lord Pettigrew's lap. He was wearing pale yellow breeches. I was hopeful he'd come up to scratch with a proposal, but now he's dancing attendance on Lady Lydia. Moreover, my butler tells me that the table linen, woven in Venice, will never be the same. Never!"

"Here's a robe, Stella," Merry said. "Lucy will sponge and press your gown, and you'll be back downstairs in no time."

While Mrs. Thyme amused herself by recounting all of Stella's mishaps since the Season began, the duchess's maid eased Stella's gown up and over her head.

"Please send up a tray of champagne and some canapés, Lucy," Merry said.

"Lord Belper was stretched on top of her," Mrs. Thyme moaned, returning to her previous lament. "Everyone will think the worst!"

Merry shrugged. "The worst being that Belper took some pleasure in the act? I doubt it."

"He took advantage!"

Her Grace winked at Stella. "Dear Mrs. Thyme, may I suggest that you return to the ball and make certain that no one has vulgarly suggested Belper chose to leap atop Stella in the middle of my annual ball? I will keep your niece company, as I would welcome a chance to rest my feet."

Stella sighed after the door closed. "My aunt is convinced that every man who dances with me is a wolf. As well as those who don't dance with me."

Merry grinned at that. "I encountered a wolf or two in my first Season in London. My husband among them." Responding to a quiet knock, she rose and went to the door.

Stella would not have called Merry's husband wolfish. The Duke of Trent was dignified and handsome in a distant sort of way.

Yet her aunt was convinced that all men were lustful marauders. Hounds straining at the leash, eager to destroy a lady's reputation for sexual or financial gain. Her greatest fear was that a man would climb into Stella's bedchamber from the conservatory roof, but since Mr. Thyme religiously nurtured seedlings over the winter, he flatly refused to tear down the greenhouse.

Practically from the moment Mrs. Thyme took on the unexpected burden of raising her orphaned niece, she had made a point of informing Stella that men want more than a kiss.

Worse than a kiss.

But lo these many years later . . .

To Stella's mind, the evidence just wasn't there.

Lord Belper had taken no pleasure in bouncing on her like a featherbed. She had never experienced the press of a male thigh or even the brush of a knee during a waltz. No one offered her illicit kisses in the shrubbery.

Stella's conclusion?

Male lust was wildly overestimated.

CHAPTER TWO

Merry carried a silver tray across the room and set it down. "One of the irritating things about being a duchess is that the title supposedly renders one incapable of labor. I had to wrestle this out of my butler's hands."

Stella leaned forward and tapped one of the champagne glasses before wrapping her hand around it. Even wearing her spectacles, she had trouble judging how far away an object was.

"Bottoms up!" Merry said cheerily. "That's an American toast, by the way. I heard it on my last visit to Boston."

Stella took a gulp of champagne before returning to the subject they had been discussing. "I haven't seen much evidence of gentlemen who scheme to damage a lady's virtue. I haven't experienced it, I mean."

Merry opened her mouth, but Stella added hastily, "It could be, of course, that my red hair and freckles, not to mention the spectacles, are enough to curb their lust."

"Pooh!" Merry retorted. "Your hair is beautiful. One of my dearest friends, Mrs. Cleopatra Addison, has fiery red hair, and I assure you that she had most of the male population at her feet when she debuted.

What's more, to be frank, your bosom is a thing of beauty."

Stella generally thought of her breasts as annoyingly large compared to the rest of her but she smiled a thank-you. "My aunt has warned me many times that unmarried men will attempt to kiss me. They haven't."

"Is there someone you would like to kiss?" Merry asked. She was pouring herself another glass of champagne, so she topped up Stella's glass as well. "I hope you don't mind if I get tipsy. I forgot to eat today because of all the last-minute preparations for the ball."

"From what I see, hapless sentimentality overrules lust," Stella told Merry. "Dowries aside, unmarried gentlemen are either in love or looking for love."

"A utilitarian quest that masquerades as romance," Merry said, poking through the small squares of toast that had been sent up with the champagne. "Must needs be done, though. The world must be peopled. I think that's Shakespeare. Being an American and ill-educated, I'm never entirely sure."

"Benedict, in *Much Ado about Nothing*," Stella said. "*The world must be peopled. When I said I would die a bachelor, I did not think I should live till I were married.*"

"You had that stored in your head until just the right moment?" Merry asked, looking impressed.

Stella shrugged uncomfortably, realizing that she'd once again broken her promise to Mrs. Thyme to keep irritating knowledge to herself. "My point is that the bachelors we meet in ballrooms are not lustful, as my aunt insists. They are looking for love."

"They could be doing both," Merry said, a nostalgic look in her eye suggesting that her husband had managed that feat.

Stella didn't answer. Many men had an eye on her dowry, but as far as she could see, not a single one of them had designs on her virtue.

They were looking for *lovable* women.

Stella would be the first to admit that she failed on that front. She was too awkward, too outspoken, too argumentative. Too peculiar. Too much hair.

Not to mention the spectacles.

Her own family had shown little propensity to love her, so why should some random stranger with whom she had danced a few times?

Men looking for love were selective. Their eyes skated over Stella as if she were invisible, after which they plunged to their knees before bird-boned and delicate ladies, tender girls with silky ringlets.

Silvester was a good example. He scooped Stella off the dance floor—but he promptly slipped away to bow before Lady Yasmin.

"Just decide who you want and inform him of your choice," Merry advised her. "You must try this salmon paste. It's quite delicious."

Stella had to stuff a piece of toast in her mouth to suppress a humiliated squeak at the very idea of her "informing" Silvester that she had decided to marry him. "Is that how you found your husband?" she asked, once she swallowed.

"Well, no," Merry said. "That is, I chose someone, but he turned out to be the wrong person."

"After which, you chose the duke?"

"No, he chose me," Merry confessed. "My advice doesn't match my experience."

That didn't surprise Stella. Merry's husband had likely pursued her with the fervor with which Silvester was pursuing Lady Yasmin. Stella hadn't formally met Yasmin, but she had a shrewd idea that the lady didn't get into arguments with her suitors.

Lady Yasmin was Silvester's equal in the marital sweepstakes. Their children would be exquisite, rich, and titled. They would gracefully dance without ever falling over.

Silvester wasn't looking for a woman who had memorized Shakespeare plays but someone slender, beautiful, and undeniably charming. Stella's legs were sturdy even without having children, and charm was in short supply. Her eventual husband would propose with an eye to her dowry, not her allure.

Lucy popped back into the bedchamber with Stella's gown over her arm.

"I suppose we must return to the ballroom," Merry sighed, finishing her champagne. "Lucy, poor Lady Stella is in the midst of the horrors of her first Season. Can you think of any advice?"

Lucy gave Stella a grin. "Men like to be listened to, and they all think they have something worth saying." She tossed Stella's robe onto a chair and dropped a billow of sweet-smelling silk over her head.

"They want to be charmed," Merry said, unsurprisingly. "The easiest way to do that is to convince them that *they* are charming. Watch Miss Fitzwilliams for a few minutes. She's adorable. Tedious, but adorable."

Stella was not adorable.

"Adorable" came from the Latin word *adorabilis*, which meant "worthy of worship." Stella knew that because the summer before her debut she had read straight through the first four volumes of the 1773 *Encyclopedia Britannica*.

The definition might seem irrelevant, but it wasn't.

Gentlemen entered ballrooms looking for a woman to *adore*.

To worship.

Stella didn't qualify.

Back in the ballroom, Stella saw Julia Fitzwilliams bouncing across the floor with Lord Mornay, snaring his attention with shyly admiring glances. Stella had danced with him earlier, but she had been riveted by his toupee and hadn't exchanged more than a greeting.

"Julia's waltzing with Mornay," Merry said, *sotto voce*. "What *is* that toupee made from? It's the mystery of the evening!"

"Horsehair," Stella whispered back. "I couldn't take my eyes from his forehead throughout our dance, so I'm fairly sure that he didn't find me charming."

"You don't want *him*," Merry said. "Oh, there you are, dear." Her husband bowed before them and said something in a low, rough voice.

Merry laughed. Later, when Stella was standing with her aunt's cronies, learning about rhubarb purgatives, she puzzled over his comment. He was leaving in the morning for Wales so he wanted his wife to—

Suddenly she caught the word "spectacles" and realized that a cluster of people nearby was discussing her vision, as if blindness was a reasonable choice.

She quickly looked the other direction. Her fingers curled tight in her gloves before she forced herself to relax. A rush of whispers followed, but she knew with sickening certainty that those voices would rise.

Sadly, she had come to understand that *she* was the real audience for discussion of her spectacles and other shortcomings. Ladies enjoyed enumerating her unlovable features, more so if she could overhear. Anticipation squirmed in her stomach, sending a pulse of misery up her spine.

The size of her dowry, combined with her noble grandfather, ensured she had many suitors. Unfortunately, as fortune hunters besieged her, prettier and sweeter ladies resented it.

Sure enough, Miss Brothy tittered something about "spots."

Those would be her freckles.

Stella's mouth had twisted, so she flattened it into a slight smile. Lack of reaction was the only claim to dignity she had left.

Behind her back, a male voice said firmly, "I find spectacles quite attractive."

It took a moment to sink in.

Her aunt pinched her arm. "That was Giles Renwick, Earl of Lilford!" she hissed. "Why didn't I think of him? By all accounts, he's intellectual, so he won't mind your reading."

Mrs. Thyme did not share Stella's fondness for the encyclopedia, and had seriously entertained the idea that unladylike reading had leaked through her niece's pores and alienated potential suitors.

Stella blinked at her. "Renwick . . . The same earl who gave that speech about *habeas corpus* last week?"

Her aunt rolled her eyes. "If my sister was alive, I'd give her a piece of my mind for having those spectacles made. If you'd never learned to read, you'd be betrothed already, freckles or no. I don't know him well enough to introduce you, but I'll ask our hostess to do it. Don't you dare mention *hibius cibius*."

Shortly thereafter, Stella found herself curtsying before a tall, serious man. Giles Renwick, the Earl of Lilford, had high cheekbones, a chiseled jaw, and a haunted expression. His eyes lit with interest when she brought up the impending act affecting judges' use of *habeas corpus* in criminal trials.

When Mrs. Thyme moaned, his lordship courteously asked if she was feeling well before turning back to Stella. They discussed the law throughout the next dance.

The earl didn't loathe her spectacles. He didn't seem annoyed by her interest in jurisprudence. He could love her. Or perhaps—just perhaps—he was smart enough to realize that love was poppycock.

Perhaps he would choose a wife based on mutual respect and intellectual interests, rather than coy glances.

Stella was thinking about that when Silvester bowed before her. Her heart skipped a beat, and she forgot about the earl.

"I trust you have recovered from your tumble, Lady Stella?" he asked.

"Yes, thank you," she said, dropping a curtsy.

"May I have the pleasure of this dance?"

"It's another quadrille," Stella said, clearing her throat. "I'd rather not."

"Poppycock," he replied, pulling her onto the dance floor without waiting for an answer.

When they joined another couple, Silvester promptly took the lead, spinning her firmly in the right direction. "Belper is a duffer," he remarked, after they completed a few more figures without disaster. "You're doing fine."

"It was my fault," Stella said. "I turned the wrong direction."

"I've done it myself. Damn—excuse me, dratted—dances get more complicated every year."

His admission was untruthful. She'd watched the duke circle the dance floor any number of times, including this very evening when he gracefully negotiated the steps of the new *Dance Ecossoise*, just arrived from France. It was even more complicated than the quadrille.

The dance parted them again, so Stella gave herself a firm lecture. Silvester was kind enough to fib about his dancing skills, but he didn't know what *habeas corpus* was, or likely even that there was such a law.

Not that it mattered, since he would never consider her for a spouse, but she had determined to marry the most knowledgeable man she could find, not just someone who was good at dancing.

Back together for a final turn, Silvester murmured, "Did you see that Belper just bumped into the lady behind him? If I heard correctly, she called him a barbarian."

She smiled at him, touched that he was still trying to make her feel better. "Before I debuted, I believed in the distinction between barbarians and gentlemen."

To her horror, the sight of his powerful neck, head thrown back as he laughed, prompted an image of her running her tongue down its length.

When he bowed in front of his next partner, she couldn't stop herself from ducking behind her fan to ogle his arse in tight silk breeches.

Her aunt would be appalled. *Appalled.*

Not because Stella admired Silvester: that was

practically obligatory for young ladies. The Duke of Huntington was the most eligible man in England, possessed of a large estate, decent stature, and all his teeth. Ladies' eyes followed him everywhere.

But she doubted that other debutantes had explicit daydreams about how they'd like to . . . to lick him. Do breathless, depraved things that Stella couldn't quite envision.

Late at night, she spun stories under the sheets, during which he did things that she was certain no other lady had even imagined. Obviously, all those men looking for love didn't engage in dissolute thoughts about the women at whose feet they worshipped.

It was her humiliating secret.

Doubly humiliating because Silvester was so far above her.

All of which didn't stop her from enjoying the way he bowed, one powerful leg extended. His fashionable pantaloons strained over a muscled thigh that would overshadow even sturdy legs like her own.

A low thrum in her blood informed her that she would cheerfully follow him into the shrubbery or a secluded room.

In fact, it could be that Mrs. Thyme's warnings about male lust disguised a more serious danger, not in men but women.

To be blunt, *ladies* want more than a kiss.

Worse than a kiss.

At least, Stella did.

CHAPTER THREE

THE BREAKFAST ROOM,
THE DUKE OF HUNTINGTON'S TOWNHOUSE

"**I** have directed your sisters to break their fast in bed," the dowager duchess announced as soon as Silvester seated himself in the breakfast room. "We have important matters to discuss."

His legs tensed. His man of business was—

"Don't even think about running away," his mother snapped, pointing her butter knife at him. "I haven't seen you in three days, other than across a ballroom floor."

Their butler, Wickford, bent down at Silvester's shoulder. "Cold pork, Your Grace?"

"Yes, thank you," Silvester replied, resigned to his fate. "I like your new wig, Mother."

"It's not a wig," his mother said, picking up a small loaf of bread and lavishly buttering it. "I renewed my hair with the juice of a walnut. Actually, many walnuts. Eighty-seven in all."

The dowager's hair was now coal black, though her eyebrows remained white. She wore a black-and-white-striped gown that might have graced a zebra with a propensity for silver buttons.

"It's very attractive," Silvester murmured, accepting a healthy portion of eggs and two slices of ham, as well as some stewed mushrooms and a few sausages.

His mother eyed his plate. "I presume you are preparing for exertion, rather than impending famine?"

"In fact, I'm meeting Giles Renwick at Gentleman Jack's boxing salon."

His mother made a face. "The Earl of Lilford and the Duke of Huntington dressing in absurd garments the better to pummel each other. Of course, you do have reason."

"We do? Thank you, Wickford, mustard would be very welcome."

"Giles Renwick is at the head of the line stretching in front of Yasmin Régnier," his mother said. "I've seen her looking at him."

Sadly, that was true.

Yasmin was smitten by Giles. Yet all the things Silvester appreciated—Yasmin's delicate femininity, her French gowns, her giggling sense of humor—Giles would despise.

Did despise.

His friend's lip curled if anyone mentioned Yasmin in his presence.

If Silvester had a horror of eccentricity, Giles had a profound dislike of scandal. Darling Yasmin had arrived from France trailing rumors about her virtue, not to mention factual accounts of her mother's flagrant *affaire* with Napoleon.

If Giles paid more attention to Yasmin, he would realize that she was virtuous, if not prudish. But he hadn't and wouldn't. Silvester had no intention of enlightening him. What's more, if Giles was hiding infatuation behind his disparagement, Silvester certainly didn't plan to lose Yasmin to his old friend.

"I won't speak to the absurdity of the way *you* look

at *her*," the dowager continued. "It's painful to watch. I could endure your infatuation if I thought the lady in question felt more than fondness for you. She doesn't."

Silvester's jaw clenched.

"I hope that the truth doesn't offend you," his mother said, her tone cheerfully indifferent.

"Giles paid Lady Stella marked attention last night," Silvester remarked, getting his own back.

That brought on a glower. "It would serve you right if the earl scooped up the woman I chose for you."

"Was there an important matter you wished to discuss?" Silvester inquired. He had no intention of engaging in another discussion of Stella, whom he devoutly hoped had managed to catch Giles's eye. They were perfect for each other: serious and studious.

Although she'd surprised him with that quip about barbarians last night. And her bottom lip hinted at a sensuality that would likely shock Giles to the bone.

"Harold has arrived in London."

"Harold?" Silvester repeated.

"Harold Rowson. Your cousin Harold, from America," the dowager said impatiently.

"Hardly my cousin. He must be two or three times removed," Silvester pointed out.

"Irrelevant. He spent the night at Germain's Hotel, and he will move here this morning." She turned to the butler. "Wickford, pay attention, if you please. Tell the housekeeper to open the green suite. It has the largest wardrobe. As I recall, Harold never travels with fewer than three trunks."

The butler bowed. "Yes, Your Grace."

Silvester flicked him a sardonic glance. He knew perfectly well that Wickford not only paid attention to all conversations, but made a habit of listening at doors, the better to gather material to sell to gossip columns.

Which explained why his sisters, who hadn't yet debuted and were allowed to attend only events hosted by their mother, regularly appeared in the newspapers.

"We'll take him around society with us," the dowager continued. "His mother writes that he plans to marry and move to Paris, where he will open a laughing gas salon."

"A what?"

"Surely you've heard of it. A gas made from iron filings and nitric acid."

Of course, his mother knew the formula. "I remember fools trying it at Oxford," Silvester said. "It made them giggle like dairymaids. But a 'salon'?"

"His mother says that the gas is offered at parties nowadays."

"Not parties that I attend," Silvester said. "I suppose Harold is looking for a large dowry to finance his scheme."

"Of course," the dowager replied. "His mother quite rightly refuses to allow him to draw funds from the estate. Moreover, he needs a lady to act as his hostess and read aloud poetry and such." The duchess was uninterested by most social gatherings and had only the faintest idea what took place in them.

"It's a *laughing gas* salon, not a literary salon," Silvester pointed out.

"After the Scavenger Hunt tomorrow, I shall send Pansy and Holly to visit my sister in the country," the dowager said thoughtfully. "My daughters will not marry a giggler, and Harold is remarkably pretty for a man."

"The last time he was in London, he followed Beau Brummell around like a duckling, albeit one in frills and lace."

"His mother complains that Harold is fashionable and expensive, not unlike Brummell," the dowager said. "Wickford, this milk has gone quite cold."

"Yes, Your Grace." Wickford looked regretful.

"Fetch hot milk from the kitchen," Silvester ordered, when the butler showed no sign of moving.

After the door closed, he added, "We have to let that fellow go. He's not only lazy, but he's making a fortune selling lies to the gossip columns."

"Hmmm," his mother said vaguely. Domestic duties did not interest her. "I believe Wickford has corns, and it's quite a walk to the kitchens."

"Harold is presumably following Beau Brummell to Paris," Silvester said, returning to the matter at hand. "Brummell fled the country last month, leaving a raft of gambling debts."

The dowager pursed her lips. "I never liked Brummell. Though his edict regarding the brushing of teeth has improved the air quality in ballrooms."

"I suspect the laughing gas salon will offer opportunities for gambling, rather than poetry readings."

"I shall bring Harold to that Boodle woman's tea party this afternoon. She can be counted on to limit her invitations to young ladies with substantial dowries."

Silvester finished his ham. If his cousin wanted money to back his salon, he'd have to venture into the lion's den. Lady Boodle would be guarding the cave.

"You will accompany us," his mother continued.

"No, I will not."

"I need you to get us through the door. Your sisters aren't out, so I can't use them as an excuse. Lady Boodle won't have invited gentlemen, but she'll make an exception for you. She would like her daughter Blanche to be a duchess." The dowager's voice had a clipped edge of distaste.

Silvester was used to being eyed like a piece of prime beef, but that didn't mean he allowed lionesses to snap at his toes. Moreover, Blanche was one of those young ladies who fancied themselves clever thanks to an ability to make unkind comments. Like Lady Lydia, her best friend. "Never."

"The sooner Harold finds a fiancée, the sooner he'll take her off to France," his mother said, waggling her eyebrows. "Until then, you will have to escort him to your club. To that boxing salon. To Almack's. It's the least you can do." More eyebrow waggling.

"I suppose I could accompany you to the Boodle tea party," Silvester conceded.

She threw him a smug look. "I'll also expect you to attend my annual Scavenger Hunt tomorrow, as well as my *Bucolic Supper with Riparian Entertainments.*"

Silvester loved his mother. He did. But . . . "What's a 'riparian entertainment' when it's at home?"

"At home? Riparian . . . riverside," his mother clarified. "I blame Eton for the deficits in your vocabulary."

"I shall be desolate to miss it, but—"

She cut him off with a raised finger. "The Earl of Lilford, Lady Yasmin, *and* Lady Stella have accepted my invitation. That should prove entertaining. Unless, of course, you want to leave the field clear for his lordship."

"Well played," Silvester said, reluctantly.

"The earl's sister, Lady Lydia, will also attend. Perhaps Harold could marry Lydia, if she speaks French. Oh, and Lady Stella's aunt, Mrs. Thyme, who is just the sort of nincompoop whom I most despise."

"Lovely."

His mother ignored that sour comment. "I'll invite the American Duchess as well. I gather the duke is traveling, but I find her so refreshing."

Silvester nodded. He liked Merry, as the Duchess of Trent insisted on being called.

"I expect she knows Harold. America isn't very large, after all. Once one knows one American, one feels one has met them all."

CHAPTER FOUR

En route to a tea party given by Lady Boodle
for select debutantes and their chaperones

Until Stella debuted, she didn't realize that the Season was a competition that ranked ladies as winners and losers.

The losers were women like her. It didn't matter how many suitors she had; everyone knew that the men were actually courting her dowry. The winners were exquisite ladies like Yasmin, drifting around the ballroom trailing smiles and French perfume.

"I would quite like to be a wallflower and thereafter, a spinster," Stella said abruptly.

Her aunt was gazing at the small glass she carried in her reticule, while reapplying the "rosy glow" she felt signaled youth. "You would?" Mrs. Thyme's question was polite but disbelieving.

"If I had charm, exerting it to dazzle man after man would be exhausting," Stella pointed out. "Not unlike being a courtesan. Though, of course, those ladies are paid for their charm and other . . . skills."

"Stella!" Her aunt's eyes widened with horror. "If we weren't in a moving carriage, I should leave the room. Thank goodness your uncle is in the country."

Mr. Thyme had a singular passion for growing gourds. He regularly won prizes at the county fair, having discovered that gourds could be coaxed to bulging glory by being nurtured with warm manure and regularly turned toward the sun. In short: they needed his supervision.

"A concubine entices a man for the evening in exchange for coin," Stella mused. "A lady is supposed to entice a man as well, and she doesn't even get paid for it."

Ladylike comportment dictated that Mrs. Thyme always sat bolt upright, even in a carriage, but now she collapsed back against the velvet seat, a trembling hand on her heart. "My sister is turning over in her grave," she moaned.

Stella was of the opinion that rotation in the grave was unlikely. "The prize for not being a wallflower is, of course, marriage. But is that truly a prize?"

"Yes!" Mrs. Thyme snapped upright again. "It is."

Stella sighed.

"What else will you do with your life, Stella?" her aunt demanded. "You're too odd to become a governess."

"I—"

Mrs. Thyme interrupted. "You have a home with me. But after my husband's brother or his son inherits the estate, what will you do then?"

Stella knew the answer. "Use my dowry to live in the country. Anywhere with a bookstore nearby."

"You have no idea about the dangers that women face. You could never live alone. You would be pitied, but worse, murdered or *ravished*."

Stella was fairly certain that a woman of means could hire grooms to fend off random criminals, but she'd learned long ago that Mrs. Thyme's England was crisscrossed by hedgerows thick with lustful men.

"Only the most wealthy noblewoman can afford her own household. No, you'll become a lady's companion, Stella. Companions are allowed to be eccentric. Governesses are not. You'll spend your life sitting in the corner, winding balls of yarn and fetching tea when the footmen are too busy."

"I wouldn't be very good at that."

"You wouldn't be happy. Moreover, the tea tray would regularly crash to the floor."

"I haven't dropped anything since that wineglass," Stella said defensively.

"I have been offering up special prayers." Her aunt cast her gaze soulfully at the roof of the carriage before lowering her chin and narrowing her eyes at Stella. "Thanks to divine intervention, you didn't break your leg after tripping up Lord Belper."

"I never break my limbs," Stella replied. She felt dispirited, and anxiety pinched the back of her neck.

"More to the point, you must marry," her aunt stated. "You need a house of your own, and a husband who will not flinch as the family crystal is demolished." The hint of bitterness in her voice spoke to the demise of a vase bought on her wedding trip to Venice.

Stella liked the idea of a husband as much as any other woman, but if there was one thing the Season had taught her, it was that no one wanted *her*. Not the way she was.

And there was no becoming someone else.

She couldn't magically turn into Yasmin, who likely never dropped a glass in her life, always turned in the right direction during a quadrille, and knew how to giggle so that a man's eyes softened, causing him to fall in love.

"Don't despair," her aunt said, leaning forward and patting Stella's knee. "Your uncle told me last night that he plans to double your dowry."

The fierce humiliation that swept down Stella's spine was nearly unbearable. She parted her lips and forced herself to say, "I am most grateful for his generosity."

Her aunt nodded. "When your father provided for you, he didn't take the spectacles into account, let alone the red hair and freckles. Besides, Mr. Thyme told me the money will come from my dowry, which is, of course, unentailed. He understands that it's more prudent to put the money forward now, than face the problem when it's too late. A lesson for life, my dear."

When would it be it too late? Two years from now, when she was twenty-two? Or when she was twenty-four? Just how many Seasons did she have to endure?

"Even if you would rather be a wallflower, Stella, you *must* make an effort to engage your suitors. Your mother would wish it. Your uncle will weed out degenerates and the like, but it is up to you to push gentlemen from courtship to actual proposals. To be blunt, dear, your face has a tendency to look pouty. I think it's the formation of your lips."

Stella swallowed hard. "I can't give up my spectacles, but I . . . I'll try. More than I have been trying, I mean."

"Smile more often," her aunt advised.

The carriage began rattling over cobblestones, jolting both of them up and down. They must be getting close to the Boodle residence.

"That is all I can ask," she added. "Last night I heard that the Earl of Lilford is definitely looking for a wife. He is taken with you, and he won't mind your reading. Plus, your dowry will now be large enough to attract a man at the very top of society."

She pulled out her glass again and pinched her cheeks. "You have a sweet nature, Stella. If you would just try to be more refined. *Never* say the word 'courtesan' aloud. It makes me shudder to mouth the syllables."

"I won't," Stella promised. Desperate to change the subject, she said, "I thought the Duke of Huntington was the very top of the marital sweepstakes. A duke is higher than an earl, no?"

"He doesn't count," Mrs. Thyme said. "He's chasing after the Régnoir woman, and likely he'll have her. Much good may it do him."

"Yasmin is beautiful," Stella said. "She's kind too. She is never part of the smirking circles."

"'Smirking circles.' Well put, my dear. No, Lady Yasmin is not a gossip. I discount the duke, because we must be reasonable about your prospects. With a doubled dowry, some of your suitors will come up to scratch, but unless you can snare the Earl of Lilford, they will be second sons or foreigners. Americans, and the like."

Stella nodded. She'd always known Silvester was like the man in the moon: so far above her that a silvery glow—

That was too stupid to even put into words.

"But the Earl of Lilford is a real possibility," her

aunt said encouragingly. "You would be a countess, Stella. A *countess*."

"A countess in spectacles."

"Noblewomen make fashion, they don't follow it."

Stella took a deep breath and reminded herself how lucky she was. Many an orphaned girl had no dowry at all, let alone affectionate relatives who cared what became of her, even if they couldn't bring themselves to approve of her.

Somehow the thought wasn't very comforting.

The carriage was slowing down. Stella glanced idly out the window and then let out a shriek. "Stop!" She banged on the roof to catch their coachman's attention. "Tweed, stop the carriage!"

Her aunt looked about wildly. "Have we lost a wheel?"

The vehicle came to an abrupt halt. Stella pushed the door open and jumped to the ground, nearly falling to her knees before she caught herself. She picked up her skirts and ran back along the street, her eyes searching the road.

The little shape she'd seen whirling away from the carriage wheels lay motionless in the gutter. Behind her, her aunt was calling out shrill commands to their coachman, Tweed.

Stella crouched down beside the corpse. It was a white kitten, striped in dark gray. Sadly, it had probably been only a month old. She adjusted her spectacles and then realized that its narrow rib cage was moving.

"Oh, sweetheart," she breathed, scooping it up. As far as she could tell by gently stroking its legs, no limbs were broken. The kitten shuddered all over and blinked open dazed blue eyes.

"You can't see me clearly, can you?" Stella breathed.

"What is it?" her aunt shrilled, arriving at her shoulder. "Thank goodness you have your gloves on." She gasped, hands flying to her heart. "Stella, that's a rat! They come in white, you know. Drop it, this moment!"

"It's a kitten."

The cat let out a near-soundless meow.

Mrs. Thyme bent down and squinted. "What an unattractive animal. The stables at our country house are populated by red felines. Do put that creature down, Stella."

Stella came to her feet, nestling the kitten in her cupped hands. "Look, she has dark rings around her eyes, as if she wears spectacles."

"A fanciful interpretation," Mrs. Thyme said.

Stella dropped a kiss on the kitten's nose.

Her aunt sighed. "I suppose the mews can always use another cat to keep down the rat population. Give it to Tweed. The Boodle residence is only a block from here, and we're already late." She turned and started back for the carriage, calling over her shoulder, "Do come along, Stella!"

Stella brought the kitten up to eye level. The stripes that spread over its forehead gave it a worried look. "You are a darling," she crooned. "Are you a girl or a boy?"

She—or he—opened its mouth and meowed again, displaying tiny needlelike teeth. "You look like a girl to me, which means you can come to a ladies' tea party," Stella whispered.

Her reticule was too small, but she wore a sizable pocket tied under her skirts as she often carried a book.

She glanced over her shoulder to make certain her

aunt was safely in the carriage before she eased the kitten through the slit in her skirts into her pocket. She kept a comforting hand on the cat as she walked back to the carriage.

"Are your gloves soiled?" her aunt demanded once Stella was seated and the carriage started up.

Stella spread her hands, displaying spotless white silk. She didn't dare to glance down at the lump nestled beside her. Thankfully, the kitten showed no signs of wanting to claw herself free.

Mrs. Thyme sighed with relief. "We'll tell Tweed to feed the animal with a milky cloth. It's too small for minced beef."

"Thank you!" Stella responded.

"Speaking of food, given Lady Boodle's status in the ton, it would be most unfortunate if any of her china broke. I suggest that you refuse a cup of tea."

"At a tea party?" Stella ventured.

"They'll assume you're on a reducing diet," Mrs. Thyme said.

Stella casually spread her hands over the seat on either side of her. "I can certainly avoid tea. Thank you for the suggestion."

She'd been dreading the party, but she didn't mind so much, now that she had a secret companion.

"I'm happy to see you smiling," her aunt said. "I know that polite society can be intimidating, Stella, but truly there is nothing to worry about. Just think of your dowry and hold your chin high!"

Stella's fingers curled around the warm creature nestled by her leg.

"I shall do my best."

CHAPTER FIVE

Walking into the Boodle drawing room beside her aunt, Stella saw Blanche Boodle and seven or eight young ladies clustered together on one side of the room, chattering as if a flock of sparrows had landed in the same tree. Lady Boodle and the older women were seated on the opposite side of the room, which meant she couldn't hide amongst them.

Curtsying gave her an excuse to hold up her skirts, her hand carefully positioned to disguise her pocket. As quickly as possible, she slipped into an armchair next to Lady Lydia Renwick, the Earl of Lilford's sister. If his lordship was indeed looking for a wife, Lydia might be her sister-in-law. Smiling at everyone, she casually rearranged her skirts to disguise the kitten curled into a tight ball by her leg.

Across the room, her aunt was presumably informing the other chaperones of Stella's enlarged dowry. For their part, the young ladies were intently dissecting the marital prospects of every debutante not invited to the tea party.

Lydia was among the most talkative and seemed to have strong opinions about those deemed unfashionable.

Which begged the question: Why on earth had Stella been invited? This was a party for winners, not losers.

By the time a footman offered to replenish teacups, the conversation had shifted to a looser topic that could be summed up as *what gentlemen want*.

"They want to fall in love," Stella offered.

Lydia snorted. "They want a large dowry and blue blood. You are a marquess's granddaughter, Lady Stella, but your dowry is even more important."

Well, that explained her invitation.

"They admire the feminine arts," Julia Fitzwilliams put in. Her father was reportedly considering three proposals, so all eyes turned to her. "Singing a ballad is effective, but French songs make you seem knowledgeable without being a bluestocking."

Stella thought Julia's shudder at the word "bluestocking" was overly theatrical, but it was nothing Mrs. Thyme hadn't warned her about a million times.

"My mother won't allow me to learn any French songs, as she considers them improper," one young lady said.

Julia rolled her eyes. "I can teach you a French ballad. That way no one can consider it improper."

"The music for *Plaisir d'Amour* is on the pianoforte," Blanche Boodle remarked.

"I love that song!" Julia cried, clapping her hands.

The young ladies promptly traipsed off to surround the pianoforte, where Julia began flipping through sheet music. Since Stella knew any number of songs in French and German, and more importantly, didn't want to disturb her kitten, she remained seated, as did Lydia and Blanche.

"Do you understand the French language, Lady Stella?" Lydia asked.

Stella was nibbling a ginger biscuit and thinking about how much she'd love some tea. But her aunt was right about the danger. The table was too far away to touch with her knee, which would have helped her judge where to replace a cup.

"I do," she said, nodding. "I had a French governess."

"French governesses abound, but that doesn't mean their charges learn the language," Lydia said with a titter. "Blanche and I had years of French instruction in one of the very best seminaries for young ladies, but the only thing I remember is *adieu*, which is either goodbye or hello. I forget now."

"Yet you sing in French?" Stella asked Blanche.

"That's easy enough," Blanche replied. "You needn't understand the words. In fact, it's better not to. French sounds so improper that a claim of ignorance is an excellent defense."

Lydia shook her head. "Lady Stella isn't a featherhead like you and me, Blanche. What is Julia singing about now, Stella? You don't mind if I call you Stella, do you?"

"Of course, you may. *The pleasure of love lasts only a moment*," Stella said obediently. "*The grief of love lasts a lifetime*."

"Love is a mere jest," Lydia said, her voice sharp.

"I agree," Stella said, rather surprised to find that there was anything they agreed on. Lydia often flaunted sweetness, like a strawberry about to go soft at the height of summer, but her eyes were hard.

"Are you invited to the Duchess of Huntington's Scavenger Hunt tomorrow afternoon, Lady Stella?" Blanche asked.

"Yes," Stella replied, wondering if it would be rude if she offered Julia some pointers on the French language. Miss Fitzwilliams clearly had no grasp of pronunciation.

"We decided that we should speak to you before the event." Lydia's expression indicated a delicate mixture of regret and hesitation.

Stella didn't trust it. Didn't trust *her*. Those strawberries were rotten at the core, just as sympathy often hid maliciousness.

"I see," she said. "May I ask the subject?"

"We want to help," Blanche said, leaning forward.

Julia was singing the refrain about the pleasure of love again. All the chaperones had begun listening, and she was capping every line with a cascading arpeggio.

Overdoing it, in Stella's opinion. Julia's performance felt strained, as if she were producing girlishness on command.

"I failed last year, in my first Season," Lydia continued. Her voice grated, and bitterness shadowed her eyes. "I even tripped over chairs the way you do."

Stella blinked. "I'm sorry to hear that."

"I did not fail," Blanche stated, "but I didn't receive proposals that my father deemed acceptable."

"Blanche is expected to marry into the aristocracy," Lydia put in.

"More importantly, I was at the Duchess of Trent's ball when she introduced you to Lydia's brother," Blanche said.

Stella molded her lips into a smile. "Did I do something wrong?"

"No, but for your own sake, I shall speak with perfect candor."

"I wish you wouldn't."

"We only want to help," Lydia said, her voice sympathetic. "I don't want you to flee London in tears at the end of your first Season, the way I did."

Stella never cried, but that didn't seem like the right point to make.

"When our hostess introduced you to the Earl of Lilford," Blanche said, "I was standing not far from the Duke of Huntington and his current mistress, Lady Yasmin."

Stella's eyes rounded. "His mistress?"

"Of course," Lydia said. "Why do you think Lady Yasmin refuses all those marriage proposals?"

"*If* the proposals are actually made," Blanche said. "They might be mere rumors."

Lydia shook her head. "I overheard Lord Peterkin telling a friend of his that Lady Yasmin's grandfather wouldn't even allow him to propose. His Grace said that Peterkin didn't have the stature or wealth for his granddaughter. Even though *everyone* knows Yasmin is little better than a streetwalker." Her voice was sour but matter-of-fact, as if she were merely sharing a fact.

Stella cleared her throat. "I've watched Lady Yasmin, and—"

"My point is that Lady Yasmin and the duke were seated together on a couch, and I happened to be standing just behind it," Blanche interrupted. "His Grace began talking about you."

Stella's face pulled tight, and her throat felt as if it was closing. "I'd rather not know what he said," she managed. She curled her hand around the warm kitten.

"It is painful to hear distressing truths," Lydia said,

"but it's better to *know*, don't you see? Besides, it's not as if it matters what the Duke of Huntington thinks of you. Even I, the daughter of an earl, recognize that he will never look to me. He has no need for a dowry, and you and I aren't beautiful enough to catch his eye."

"I don't like listening to gossip," Stella said, suddenly feeling a faint vibration under her palm. The kitten was purring.

"It's for your own good," Lydia stated.

Lydia was a horrible person, Stella realized: mean while miming kindness. There was no way to silence her. Even if Stella walked away, Lydia would follow.

"All right," she said, giving in. "All right."

"The Duke of Huntington pointed you out to Lady Yasmin," Blanche said. "He said you weren't a fribble, the way they are. That's good, because some men genuinely admire bluestockings, Lady Stella. Though not His Grace, obviously. He added that you don't give a damn about appearances, along with something about your spectacles."

Stella cleared her throat. "Unfortunately, I can't see without—"

"My point is what His Grace said next, which was about you and Lydia's brother, the Earl of Lilford," Blanche cut in. She lowered her voice to a manly drawl. *"The earl could always instruct the family portraitist to pretend the spectacles don't exist. I'm sure he expects perfection in his wife—or at least will want to pretend he's found it."*

Lydia tittered. "I expect you know that after you were presented, the Queen herself remarked that your hair reminded her of a bonfire."

Stella had to admit: when Lydia decided to be

mean, she committed totally. Her expression revealed nothing more than concern and sympathy. It was only the depths of her eyes that shone hot and fierce, like something in a nightmare.

"That's why I wanted to speak to you," Lydia continued. "I suspect the duke was warning Lady Yasmin that she wouldn't get anywhere dangling her wares in front of the earl, that is, my brother. But the more important point is that men seeking brides *are* looking for perfection."

Stella's stomach was burning with humiliation. It was one thing when random gossips made fun of her spectacles and her freckles. But Silvester—

Silvester had said that her husband would be ashamed of her spectacles?

"The duke said you use your intelligence like a hammer," Blanche added.

Stella's lips had gone numb. She felt as if pieces of her had frayed, as if she were an old piece of flannel. She had known Silvester wouldn't consider her as a wife, but she'd interpreted their dances and friendly conversations as indicating something.

Not affection, but respect. He seemed kind when he saved her glasses after she fell during the dance.

She had been wrong, obviously.

Behind her back, he enjoyed making fun of her as much as the rest of "polite" society did.

"Then the duke said that *he* was looking for generosity of spirit and spiritual virtue in a wife," Blanche added. "Oh, and he said something about a big bosom as well." She glanced down at her breasts, which were certainly generous.

Blanche would clearly like to be a duchess.

"'Virtue' must have been an inside jest," Lydia said. "I think the duke plans to marry Lady Yasmin. But the important point, Stella, is that His Grace merely said what everyone has been thinking."

"But you can improve your appearance," Blanche said earnestly. She actually seemed to have the idea that she was helping.

"I understand," Stella said. One of her legs was jittering. She forced her feet together, flat on the floor.

It didn't matter what Silvester thought of her. He was a nasty person, laughing at her while chattering to his beautiful mistress.

"You merely have to do something about the freckles and the—the way your hair is pulled back, as if you don't care a fig for appearances," Blanche continued. "Your appearance is far too natural, if you'll forgive the observation."

"I can change my hair," Stella said, her hand curling tighter around the sweet, purring creature in her pocket. Her red hair was pulled back because her aunt thought that a looser style rendered the color too startling.

"I suggest boiling onions in water," Lydia said self-importantly. "Let the water cool and then soak your head in a pail until that red turns gold."

"How is she supposed to breathe with her head in a pail?" Blanche asked, raising an eyebrow.

"Hold her breath, of course," Lydia retorted.

Julia had dragged out the French ballad with trills and arpeggios, but it was finally over. Everyone was clapping enthusiastically, and Julia had turned a pretty shade of pink.

Surely Stella could walk away now? Yet she didn't

want to make an enemy of Lady Lydia. Every instinct warned her that Lydia was enjoying this conversation. If the lady felt snubbed, her advice disregarded . . .

If Lydia decided to make someone's life a nightmare?

She would do just that. An edgy malice shadowed her supposed kindness.

Stella cleared her throat. "If I change my hair color, what will happen when I am married, and my husband discovers my hair is actually red?"

"Plant an onion field," Lydia advised. "Only you and your maid need know the truth. A lady must preserve a sense of mystery."

"It could be that deception is essential in marriage," Blanche said. "Certainly my parents keep secrets from each other."

"Incidentally, did you see that the Dowager Duchess of Huntington has dyed her hair black?" Lydia asked. "A sign of mental decay, obviously. The woman is growing ever more eccentric, even though she's been the strangest person in the ton for decades."

"When you're a duchess, it doesn't matter how strange you are," Blanche observed.

"Since you are *not* a duchess, Stella, you need to change more than your hair," Lydia continued. "You'd better stop using your intelligence like a hammer, because gentlemen don't like it."

"Thank you for the advice," Stella said.

"You mustn't give up!" Blanche said encouragingly. "Your hair is pretty, even though it's red. Look, I bought you this."

She took a small bottle from her reticule. Stella quickly slipped her hand out of her pocket and accepted the gift.

"It will cover up your spots. I asked the apothecary for a formulation that would suit a ginger complexion."

Stella turned the bottle over in her hands. Irrationally, the gift made tears press on the back of her eyes.

"You are really *too* kind, Blanche," Lydia shrilled. Her tone was bored. The fun was over. She put a hand on her friend's arm. "Darling, as the hostess, you must join the others. We'll leave you here to contemplate our advice," she said to Stella.

Which made it clear that Stella shouldn't consider herself their friend, merely the beneficiary of kindly instruction. As if Stella would dash after the two of them, begging for more insults.

Stella watched them go, frozen as a rabbit when a fox sniffed around her burrow.

She felt sick.

It was . . . it was merely the shock of it.

She had pictured Yasmin and Silvester like Greek gods with their amber hair, their pedigrees, their easy grace. The rest of society milled below them at the foot of Mount Olympus: the ladies desiring Silvester, the men in love with Yasmin.

She had thought that the way the two of them laughed and sparkled in each other's company was evidence that they were *good*.

Kind.

Decent people.

Obviously, they were not, any more than the Greek gods had been. Meanness hurt more when it came from the very top.

When the judgment came from Zeus, in short.

Lydia and Blanche joined the girls thronged around

the piano, where Julia was leafing through sheet music again, still chattering about French melodies. The silence on Stella's side of the room felt thick and musty, but she couldn't bring herself to stand up.

At her side, the kitten rolled to her back and stretched its limbs. Stella gave her a tummy rub through her gown, desperately wishing that she was home.

"Stella!" Her aunt's disapproving voice proceeded her. "You mustn't sit over here by yourself."

Stella was certain that her aunt had never been offered advice from the likes of Lady Lydia. Stella's mother and her sisters had been noble progeny. In the family portrait, all three of them stood tall and exquisite . . .

Though now Stella thought about it, the portraitist might have improved on reality.

From some angles, her aunt seemed to have no chin, as if her face simply got tired and turned into her neck. Presumably Stella's mother had used a lorgnette to identify her dance partners, since she had been as nearsighted as Stella, but there was no sign of it in the family portrait.

Nodding to her aunt, Stella casually draped her right hand so as to disguise the kitten.

"What did those girls say to you?" Mrs. Thyme asked, sitting down, her eyes narrowing.

Stella cleared her throat. "Lady Lydia and Miss Boodle told me . . . gave me some guidance about how to better present myself. Miss Boodle gave me this."

"Pear's White Imperial Powder." Her aunt's suspicion turned to happiness. "How kind of her! That's just what I would have suggested, dear, if only you'd been amenable."

"If I wear that, the man I marry will think I don't have freckles. What happens on our wedding night?" Stella asked. "Or the following morning, if I wash my face after he retires to bed? I have them all over my body."

Mrs. Thyme turned visibly pink. "Really, dear, that's not an appropriate question! I am surprised that you even had such a thought."

"Well, I have," Stella said bluntly. "I can't imagine a man would be very happy to wake up to a wife covered with freckles he never imagined existed."

Mrs. Thyme sighed. "Marriage is shocking on so many fronts. Believe me, freckles are the least of it."

"Then why does everyone make such a fuss about them?"

"Fine, clear skin gives assurance of the inherent residence of three admirable graces to beauty," her aunt said promptly. "Wholesomeness, Neatness, and Cheerfulness. You have *all* those qualities, of course."

Stella didn't think she was very cheerful. And she wasn't sure about wholesome either. Wholesome ladies didn't fantasize about horrid dukes. Not that she would ever do that again.

"It's not just about freckles. People feel you aren't trying," her aunt added.

"The Duke of Huntington doesn't *try*." She spit that out, a rough truth that plopped into the space between them.

"He's a man."

"Lady Yasmin doesn't—"

Mrs. Thyme raised her hand. "Lady Yasmin is effortlessly charming, but her costumes? Her French gowns and dampened petticoats? Her lip color? I'm not convinced her hair is natural. I expect she uses lemons to lighten it."

Stella didn't agree. Yasmin's hair was a tarnished gold color, like a lantern burning low. One couldn't get that by soaking one's head in boiled onions, or lemons either.

"I promised Lady Boodle that you would sing for us," her aunt said. "In French, of course."

"Oh, I wish you hadn't," Stella said.

"Some guests here today have sons, Stella," her aunt said firmly. "You must put your best foot forward." Her aunt and uncle had hired numerous music masters when it became clear that singing was among Stella's few ladylike graces.

"I am trying," Stella said.

Mrs. Thyme lowered her voice. "I warrant your accent is fifty times better than Julia Fitzwilliams's. I hardly remember a word of the language, but I know that 'amour' shouldn't rhyme with 'bower.'"

CHAPTER SIX

$\mathcal{M}$rs. Thyme towed Stella across the room to the pianoforte, scattering girls to both sides. "My niece will now sing to us in French," she said loudly. "She has an excellent voice."

Lydia snickered and said, "A family trait."

Stella frowned at her, because no matter how wary she was of Lydia, her aunt and uncle had taken her in without complaint when her parents died. They didn't love her, not the way they would have loved a child of their own, but they had done their best with the cuckoo that landed in their nest.

She managed to position herself in such a way that her right leg and its lumpy pocket were sheltered by the pianoforte. Since there was no escaping a performance, she took off her spectacles so that she didn't have to see her audience.

She chose to sing a French ballad about the moon. It was sad, and she felt sad. But also it showed the range of her voice, just in case some gentleman wanted a soloist along with a dowry.

Her voice filled the drawing room with all the confidence she never felt when she was dancing or holding a teacup or the hundred other things that required knowing precisely where one was in space.

A moment of silence was followed by a burst of applause. Stella hastily put back her spectacles so that the faces around her came into focus. All around her ladies seemed to be chattering with genuine admiration.

"One more song," Lady Boodle commanded. "I wish my husband was here. He loves the French language."

Blanche was clapping. "You truly know French," she exclaimed.

"Was that an improper song?" Lydia asked.

"Not at all," Stella said. "It was about the moon."

"It sounded quite suggestive," Lydia mused. "I think because you gave the words the right intonation, whereas Julia just sounded as if she were singing English words I hadn't heard before."

To the rear of the drawing room, a butler opened the door and announced, "The Dowager Duchess of Huntington, accompanied by the Duke of Huntington and Mr. Harold Rowson from Boston, Massachusetts."

Twittering like blackbirds, all the ladies turned toward the door in unison.

Blanche and her mother trotted over to greet their new guests, followed by a flock of hopeful maidens. Stella remained where she was, flipping through sheets of music. The kitten seemed to have fallen asleep again. She didn't want to bump her awake by walking across the room.

Nor did she want to greet Silvester, if truth be told.

Despite herself, she finally turned to look at him. Silvester was objectively beautiful, but it was like looking at an empty room while remembering snippets of conversation.

His hard-cut mouth was *hard*. The shimmer she

thought she saw? The rough masculine strength that made her feel safe? Fool's gold.

Her heart didn't speed up, even as she watched him give Lady Boodle his warmest smile while introducing his relative.

Mr. Rowson was clearly related to the duke, though he was slimmer, his forehead higher, his eyes lighter gray. She would have expected an American to be rugged, but he was sleek and fashionable, his hair glossy and his eyes untouched by wrinkles.

Lydia was laughing and chattering, so Mr. Rowson must be important. Perhaps he had an estate with a river. Earlier, Lydia had informed them that since Gervase Park in Surrey didn't include a river, Lord Carew had only a negligible claim to a country estate.

Stella turned back to the sheet music, a mistake that allowed her to be ambushed. A crowd suddenly formed around her, chirping about her ability to sing. She looked up just in time to be confronted by Silvester.

"Lady Stella, I believe you know my mother."

Stella dropped into a deep curtsy, plucking up her skirts to disguise her pocket. "Your Grace."

"May I introduce my cousin, Mr. Harold Rowson?" Silvester added.

Harold Rowson's smile showed an orderly array of white teeth. He bowed with a male version of Julia's arpeggios: his hand flourished in the air.

Silvester's amused eyes met hers, and just like that, the heart-slamming attraction was back.

But this time she was steeled against his dazzle.

There was nothing magical about a gentleman who enjoyed making fun of those he considered to be absurd. He probably mocked his own cousin behind closed doors.

"Just think!" Lady Boodle shrilled. "Mr. Rowson tells us he is moving to Paris! You must, you simply must, sing another song in that language, Lady Stella. It will make him feel at home. I shall accompany you myself."

Without waiting for a reply, Lady Boodle sat herself at the pianoforte. Stella edged around the instrument until her right leg was out of sight again, removed her spectacles, and sang the song her hostess suggested.

To her surprise, a drawn-out, albeit faint, meow trailed off when she finished singing. Thankfully, the kitten lapsed into silence when applause broke out.

After she replaced her spectacles, she discovered Harold Rowson beaming at her. Perhaps her command of French could win her an American estate with a river or two. She couldn't bring herself to care.

"*Ravissante!*" the American cried.

Behind his back, Mrs. Thyme's joy was so bright that Stella fancied it could be seen around her aunt's head, like one of those medieval halos painted in gilt.

"Who wrote that lovely song, Lady Stella?" the Dowager Duchess of Huntington asked.

The dowager was short and kindly, and Stella rather liked her black hair color, even given its greenish undertone. "It was composed by Élisabeth Jacquet de la Guerre, a lady who lived in the court of Louis XIV, Your Grace."

"Do you know Madame de la Guerre's pastoral duet?" Mr. Rowson asked.

When she nodded, he stepped toward her. "May I beg your indulgence? My voice does not match yours, but I would take pleasure in singing the duet with you."

"Of course." This time Stella didn't take off her spectacles, just fixed her gaze on the far wall. Mr. Rowson sang quite well. His accent was acceptable, albeit with an American twang. Her tutor, Madame Escoffier, wouldn't have been offended.

In fact, singing with him was surprisingly pleasurable. His voice wound through hers, and even Lydia stopped whispering behind her hand.

After the last stanza, he frowned and glanced down at their feet.

"You have an excellent voice, Mr. Rowson," Stella said quickly, pretending that she hadn't heard a kitten caroling with them.

"That was lovely," Silvester said. He made no attempt to hide his amused surprise. Apparently, short, plain women weren't supposed to have talents of any kind.

She was done with him, done with the duke.

"Thank you," she said, turning away to talk to Lady Boodle.

She didn't notice that Silvester had stepped toward her until a deep voice said in her ear, "I particularly enjoyed the troubadour in your pocket, Lady Stella."

He strolled away, laughing.

CHAPTER SEVEN

Later the same day, in Stella's bedchamber

"I'm sure it has fleas!" Mrs. Thyme peered at the kitten, who was splayed upside down in Stella's lap, playing with a piece of string. "Please tell me that you haven't allowed that creature onto your bed, Stella."

Stella and the kitten had just enjoyed a refreshing nap, but for the sake of domestic harmony, she shook her head.

"I accept the new fashion for small dogs," her aunt said, seating herself. "Julia Fitzwilliams tucks a canine into her reticule, after all. But a cat will never do, Stella. You couldn't possibly train it to walk on a leash."

"I could try," Stella said, tickling a tummy rounded by milk.

"The animal belongs in the stables," Mrs. Thyme said. "Not in the house. I could not believe my ears when I was informed of its presence. I'm certain that I instructed you to hand it to Tweed."

"She will keep down the mice," Stella suggested.

"There are no mice in my house!"

The cook would not agree, but Stella held her tongue. Her aunt was happiest when sheltered from the inconveniences of domestic life.

"It is rather sweet," her aunt said. She extended a finger, and the kitten promptly batted at it. "Those markings remind me of the shoeblack stage actresses put around their eyes."

"I'm calling her Specs," Stella said.

Her aunt sighed. "I know it's difficult being the only lady in spectacles. If only your mother had lived, she would know best how to manage the situation."

Stella had few memories of her mother, since she had still been in the nursery when her parents died after a pleasure boat overturned on the Thames. Unfortunately, most of her memories were tied to the horror of Stella's freckles.

They had appeared when she was a baby, and shortly thereafter, spread like a plague over her body. The whole household had been recruited to prevent further spotty spread, and after Stella was orphaned, Mrs. Thyme had taken on the battle with fervor. In fact, Stella thought she was such an avid reader because she was never taken to the park as a child.

"It would be easier if I wasn't the only person in a room wearing spectacles," Stella agreed.

Her aunt nodded. "I do understand that you cannot go about without them. I told everyone at the tea party the difficulties you have even *with* spectacles, and they were most sympathetic."

Stella groaned silently.

"I ventured to say that in time, many women will wear spectacles. I don't believe it, of course, but we must look ahead to your daughters."

The idea of shepherding daughters, bespectacled or no, onto the marriage market filled Stella with horror, so she bent over Specs and gave her a kiss.

"You must wash that animal if she's to live in my house," Mrs. Thyme stated. "I shall ring for a bowl. You may not use your own washbasin because of the fleas."

A short time later, Stella lowered Specs into a large bowl of warm water. After the shock—during which she scratched Stella's arms in a frantic bid for escape—Specs accepted her fate.

"She's enjoying herself," Mrs. Thyme said with satisfaction.

Stella didn't agree, but Specs was certainly brave. She was energetically swimming around the bowl, her sopping head barely above water. Stella scooped her out and wrapped her in a towel, dropping a kiss on her wet fur.

Specs glared up at her as Stella gently rubbed her dry. No, she did not enjoy that swim.

"She's even more ratlike when wet," Mrs. Thyme said, shuddering. "I suppose she may remain in your bedchamber, Stella, though she really belongs in the stables. It's most unusual, but then, you *are* unusual, aren't you? Your husband will have to accept your eccentricities."

"What if I don't find a husband?" Stella asked, sitting down so she could dry Specs's stomach. "By the end of the Season, I mean?"

"I have a plan," her aunt said, seating herself as well. "We'll travel to Paris. Now that that horrid Napoleon is in exile, Paris is itself once again. The French are all eccentric, so we'll be welcomed there. You will return next Season with Parisian flair, Stella. An entirely new wardrobe."

Stella put Specs on the floor. She meowed, rose up on her back legs, and batted at Stella's calf.

"I believe she is requesting that you pick her up," Mrs. Thyme said, bending over to see the kitten more closely. "Look how fluffy she is after a bath! You must bathe her every day, Stella."

Stella reserved judgment on that.

"Would you like to see something funny, Aunt?" Stella sang the first line of her favorite hymn. *"Amazing grace! How sweet the sound, that saved a wretch like me."*

Still standing on her back legs, front paws on Stella's leg, Specs opened her mouth and caroled along with her.

Mrs. Thyme broke out laughing. "Her voice isn't as deep as yours, but it is energetic for such a small creature. Mr. Thyme will love hearing it, though darling, please don't sing that hymn. He can't abide the words."

Stella raised an eyebrow.

"A *wretch*?" her aunt said. "He is scarcely a 'wretch,' and neither am I. And then the *'Shout, Shout, Hallelujah'* is quite energetic, so improper. In this family, we don't *shout*. I believe the author was a Protestant, which explains everything, doesn't it?"

"Specs is catholic in her musical tastes," Stella said. "Would you like to hear her sing in French?"

Mrs. Thyme chuckled. "Yes!"

So Stella and Specs sang the first lyric from *"Plaisir d'Amour,"* after which Mrs. Thyme said that she would instruct the cook to make a special beef broth for Specs.

"But no taking her to tea parties," she added. "I thought Lady Boodle's pianoforte was wheezing, but now I gather that was your kitten's musical contribution."

Specs was trying to climb the ruffle on Stella's

gown to reach her lap. "Perhaps I might bring her to the dowager duchess's 'riparian entertainment'?" Stella asked, disentangling Specs's needlelike claws and picking her up. "If Julia Fitzwilliams is invited, I'm certain that she will bring her dog."

"But what *is* that entertainment?" Mrs. Thyme asked, her brow darkening. "I find Her Grace so irritating when she taunts us with her large vocabulary."

"'Riparian' simply means by the river," Stella said. "I don't think she meant it to be superior, Aunt."

"Dukes and duchesses never do, but somehow they always impress their superiority upon us anyway," Mrs. Thyme said moodily. "Her son, the Duke of Huntington, seems to feel that his smile will make us forget his rank. But that is not the case."

Even thinking about Silvester made Stella feel sick.

"I suppose you might bring Specs along, if you are able to keep her on a leash," her aunt continued. "You wouldn't want her to dash into the river, given how much she enjoyed the bath."

"Would you like to hold her?" Stella held out the fuzzy kitten.

Mrs. Thyme accepted with a dubious expression, but after Specs licked her finger with a minuscule tongue, she broke into giggles. "I have a pink ribbon that would suit her white fur. Or perhaps blue would be even better, to accent her gray stripes."

"I could make her a halter from ribbons," Stella suggested.

"Keep her out of the kitchens," Mrs. Thyme ordered. "Not because she's unclean, because just look how fluffy she is now. But what if someone tripped and spilled hot broth on her? You stay here with us," she crooned, lifting the kitten up in cupped hands.

Specs licked her nose.

Just like that, Specs was no longer a rat who belonged in the stables.

She was a member of the family.

CHAPTER EIGHT

Afternoon
THE DOWAGER DUCHESS OF HUNTINGTON'S SCAVENGER
HUNT

The Dowager Duchess of Huntington's annual Scavenger Hunt was one of the most anticipated entertainments of the Season, sending aristocrats charging through London to find absurdities like a button depicting a ship or a green chamber pot.

After a decade of such hunts, Silvester was heartily tired of the event, but its saving grace was that competitors broke into pairs, albeit with a maid in attendance if chaperonage was needed. He intended to claim Yasmin as his partner and discard the maid.

The drawing room was already crowded with giddy aristocrats by the time Yasmin and her grandfather were announced.

He had just started toward Yasmin when his mother climbed onto a low table with the support of a footman. She was wearing her monocle and looked like a stout dictator from a hapless country.

"Hear ye!" she bellowed.

He caught his baby sister's eyes. "I couldn't stop her," she mouthed.

His brows drew together as his mother began dictating the couples who would compete together, even though she had never before bothered to pair off her guests. Sure enough, Silvester and Lady Stella were the first partners announced by the dowager.

Pushing away the irritation that surged through his body, he made his way to Stella and bowed. It wasn't Stella's fault that his mother had identified her as a future duchess on the basis of mutual blindness and shared eccentricity.

On the other hand, Stella's singing definitely set her apart from his mother, who tunelessly bellowed hymns on Sundays, considering melody something attended to by tradesmen and their wives.

Stella's voice was everything she wasn't. She seemed practical, without a sensual bone in her body. Her clothes were utilitarian and prim, generally ruffled up to her chin. But when she sang, her voice stroked a man's skin like deep velvet.

For some reason, she didn't look quite as serviceable today.

Perhaps his knowledge of her singing voice made her look more sensual. Or perhaps it was the fact that she had smuggled a singing kitten into a tea party. He frowned, realizing that she had painted out her freckles, which was unfortunate. Unpainted, her skin was lovely.

Not that his opinion of her allure mattered one way or the other.

Lady Stella bobbed a curtsy. "Good afternoon, Your Grace."

"Did your kitten accompany you this afternoon?" he asked, eyeing the line of her skirts. Though it was manifestly ungentlemanly to notice, her hips were delightfully ample. He didn't see any indication of a surreptitious guest.

"I left her at home."

He grinned at her. "Tea parties would be a good deal more tolerable if everyone brought a dog or cat."

He saw a reluctant smile in her eyes, though she didn't seem to be in a good mood.

"Do you have a dog?" she asked.

He shook his head. "As a boy, I had pet rats, but they are not a long-lived species. I secretly brought my favorite rat, Pete, to the drawing room for tea several times. So we have more in common than I had imagined, Lady Stella."

Stella didn't seem enthusiastic about that revelation. "Did Pete live in the mews?"

"Certainly not. In the stables, he might have been lured away by his wilder brethren. He lived in the nursery. Is your kitten residing in the stables?"

She cleared her throat. "In my bedchamber, somewhat to my aunt's dismay."

"Does this feline have a name?"

Stella turned a little pink. "I have named her Specs, as she has dark circles around her eyes."

He laughed. "Charming. I should like to meet her. Perhaps you might bring her to the next ball."

Stella's brows drew together. "Your Grace, I suppose we must partner during the scavenger hunt, but I would be grateful if you would refrain from asking me to dance in the future, as my aunt might be affronted if I refuse."

Silvester blinked. In a wilderness of young ladies, he had always found Stella refreshingly conversant and interesting, so he never missed a dance with her, and often asked her for two.

"Are you offended because I laughed about Specs being smuggled into tea?" he asked.

"Certainly not," Stella stated. Her expression was composed. She had poise, if not height.

But then Stella never greeted him with a longing simper; she had too much dignity for that. He felt a surprising pang at the idea she had taken a dislike to him.

He didn't want to marry her, but he genuinely enjoyed her company. He couldn't think of any other woman who would bring a yodeling kitten to a tea party. Of course, it was for the best. If Stella refused to dance with him, his mother would have to give up her marital ambitions. The dowager couldn't ignore it if the lady had taken a strong dislike to him.

"If I may inquire, how have I offended you?"

Stella hesitated and then said, "I don't approve of looking down one's nose at others. Though I do realize that, for a duke, the opportunity must be nearly irresistible. After all, society considers everyone from an earl to a tinker beneath you."

At that moment, the dowager duchess announced that Yasmin was paired with Giles, which was simple malice on his mother's part.

"I like to think that I'm not particularly haughty, even given my rank," he said.

"I expect one never does," Stella replied.

Silvester didn't have time for a lengthy discussion of his faults. Some deep instinct told him that he couldn't allow Yasmin to jaunt off in a carriage with the Earl of Lilford.

Giles didn't want to marry Yasmin. But at close quarters, experiencing the dazzling potency of Yasmin's smile, the shimmering beauty that caught you behind the knees, informing you that there was no other woman like her?

Giles would succumb. Any man would succumb.

Or perhaps he had already succumbed. Silvester couldn't help suspecting that his old friend's obstinate dislike of Yasmin hid deeper feeling.

"Look here, why don't we form a partnership with another couple so we can win the prize?" he asked, dropping the question of his arrogance.

Stella cast him an unfriendly look. "Are you certain that you should engage in the scavenger hunt, since your mother made up the clues?"

"Why not?"

She pursed her lips. "Fairness."

Silvester's eyes caught on Stella's plush mouth, and he felt a flutter of disquiet. For God's sake, he was in love—almost in love—with another woman. He had no right to be noticing Stella's lower lip.

"I had nothing to do with creating the list," he said. "My sisters are in charge and have been since they were young girls. Come along."

Silvester threaded his way through gentlemen bowing before their partners and couples eagerly scanning the list of items, Stella at his heels.

"If we were in Ireland, I could find a rosary," someone commented.

"Do you suppose they have an ostrich egg in the Tower of London Zoo?" another fool asked.

On the other side of the room, Silvester found Giles and Yasmin standing silently beside each other. He felt a pulse of satisfaction at Giles's stiff expression. Being paired with a scandalous woman for several hours' entertainment was the earl's idea of hell.

Meanwhile, his mother had gotten around to announcing the prizes. One year she gave away a silk stocking filled with guineas. Why a stocking? No one knew.

Now she took something from a footman and held it high. "A vulture crown!" she shouted, waving it around. "Likely worn by a female pharaoh."

"Only if that pharaoh was born a couple of years ago," Silvester said, stepping forward to stand beside Yasmin. "My mother is taking the opportunity to get rid of some ill-advised jewelry acquired during her craze for Egyptian art."

Giles's mouth was a tight line, while Yasmin was hiding her infatuation as best as she could. Silvester felt a stab of tenderness for her. In a different world, he would hope that Yasmin got her heart's desire: in short, Giles.

As it was, he was certain that he could become her heart's desire. Giles was too grumpy for such a light-hearted woman.

"Lady Yasmin, may I introduce Lady Stella?" he asked, setting off a flurry of curtsies and bows. He was pleased to see Giles ease into a smile. Stella would make him a good countess.

His mother was waving around a wooden box and promising that it held something every gentleman in the world would be happy to own. Silvester took that with a grain of salt. At Christmas, she'd given him one of the new silk top hats, swearing that men would soon wear them every night. It made him look as if his head had sprouted a chimney. That was a style that would never catch on.

"I thought perhaps we should join forces. Four heads are better than two, after all," he suggested.

Giles threw him an irritated look. "Your mother just announced that all pairs must tackle the list on their own. Gifts are for the winning couple only."

Yasmin's elbow dug into Silvester's side. "Of course, we won't break the rule," she said, smiling at Stella.

Who looked as peevish as Giles.

His mother was in the middle of reeling off the rules. "The couple who finds the most objects—or obtains one of the first three items—wins," she called. "Number two is the Bishop of Norfolk, by the way. I haven't seen my brother in ages, so if anyone manages to snag him, he must come for tea before he trots back home. Just so you know, he *is* in London."

"How could we locate a bishop?" Yasmin asked.

Silvester glanced at Stella. "I might have an idea."

"Wouldn't that be cheating, since he is your family member?" she asked dryly.

"It isn't based on intimate knowledge," Silvester explained. "I read in the morning paper—"

"Don't forget to take a chaperone," his mother shouted, sending her guests surging toward the drawing room door. "Carriages are waiting!"

"Excellent," Giles clipped, pulling Yasmin away without ceremony.

"That was quite rude," Stella remarked as Giles and Yasmin disappeared into the throng around the door. "Also, I gather, very disappointing for you."

Silvester frowned at her. "You're remarkably blunt."

She shrugged. "In the scavenger hunt known as the marriage market, I have no interest in winning your attention from Lady Yasmin, so why not be honest about it?"

Silvester was taken aback. No marriageable young lady had ever expressed disinterest in his attentions. His brows drew together at the realization that only a pompous ass would believe every eligible lady wanted to marry him. Hopefully he hadn't become as haughty as Lady Stella clearly thought he was.

"We might as well try to win," he said, changing the subject.

She eyed him. "Do you always want to win, no matter the game?"

"Yes."

"Even when the stakes are small?"

"What do you mean?"

"A wooden box? When you could have had several hours with Lady Yasmin?"

Silvester eyed her in return.

"The current stakes are very small," she said, adding pointedly, "When the Earl of Lilford 'wins,' he instigates a law that changes the nation."

"True enough," Silvester said. "Giles and I are boyhood friends, but I am frequently surprised by our differences."

"Yes, I can imagine the comparison must be galling," Stella agreed.

Silvester's jaw clenched. It was true that Giles was a mainstay in the government, a man whom the prime minister often consulted.

The PM didn't ignore Silvester, but almost no one

outside those interested in currency markets had any knowledge of their conversations.

Harold walked up, towing Blanche Boodle, who sported a bird's nest of yellow spun sugar atop her head. "Good afternoon, Lady Stella, Duke."

Blanche gave them a smile. "Lady Stella, may I say how much I like your new hairstyle?"

"Lady Stella's hair is a flame, like laburnum blossoms in spring," Harold said.

Silvester groaned silently. Harold had obviously discovered the lady whom he wished to transport to Paris. Stella deserved better. Harold was handsome, of course. He had the slim figure that showed to best advantage in pantaloons. And he wasn't unkind.

But he wasn't right for Stella.

"You are both too generous," Stella said, dropping a curtsy. "Since laburnum is golden, I suggest that Miss Boodle's hair deserves the compliment, not mine."

Silvester had the sudden conviction that Stella had been made to feel inferior by Blanche Boodle and her like.

He stole a quick glance at both ladies, keeping in mind his sisters' endless discussions of female beauty. "Lady Stella is remarkably fortunate to have such thick eyelashes. Hair can, of course, be embellished with woolen pads, but thick lashes cannot be falsified."

"Of course they can," Stella contradicted, looking entirely unimpressed by his compliment. "Ladies regularly glue strips of mink fur to their eyelids."

By now, virtually all of the guests had left the room. He was prickingly aware of his mother, tucked on a couch with Yasmin's grandfather, undoubtedly wondering whether he would fall madly in love with Stella's eyelashes.

He was tempted to switch partners with Harold just to irritate his mother, but he didn't want to spend two hours with Blanche. Stella may have taken against him, but even so, she was better company than Blanche. In fact, better company than most of London.

"Shall we begin the hunt?" he asked her, nodding toward the door.

"You may have noticed that many pairs have exchanged partners," Harold said. He waved the scroll he held. "I would be happy to take the opportunity to escort Lady Stella to a print store where we can buy the sheet music listed here: 'A composition by Beethoven.'"

"My mother considers Beethoven's music too invigorating for young ladies," Blanche remarked.

Stella's eyes widened.

Before Blanche could offer more absurdities, Silvester said, "I never trade partners. My mother wouldn't countenance it. Good afternoon." He caught Stella's arm and marched away without further ado.

"*Invigorating?*" Stella repeated. "What on earth is she talking about?"

"Young ladies are restricted to girlish melodies," Silvester said. "Naturally, my mother insisted my sisters learn Beethoven's later work by heart."

"But 'invigorating' implies . . ."

"Music that rouses the wrong sort of emotion," Silvester said. "Passion is, after all, supposedly a dangerous emotion for women."

He glanced to the side and found that Stella had a disquieting smile playing around her lips.

"I shall make a point of investigating Beethoven's work," she said, laughter in her voice.

"Do you play the piano as well as you sing, Lady Stella?"

Typically, he was coming to realize, she didn't bother with maidenly modesty. "Yes, I do."

They passed through the door of the drawing room. Thankfully, Harold and Blanche weren't nipping at their heels.

"I believe my mother's brother can be found at Lambeth Palace," Silvester said. "According to the paper, the bishop took part in a special liturgy given by the Archbishop of Canterbury this morning. He may refuse to return to my mother's house—he is often disconcerted by the pleasure she takes in vigorous debate—but I can pull the favorite nephew card. Actually, I am his only nephew."

He saw a shadow of distaste in Stella's eyes.

"If you wish."

She truly did belong with Giles: they both had the same poker-straight, narrow view of right and wrong. Ignoring her indignant expression, he escorted her down the hallway toward the entry.

A light scent, something flowery that didn't float on the air, reached him as they walked. Glancing down, he could see what Blanche meant about Stella's hair: she had allowed it to curl around her face, rather than pruning it back like a rosebush in winter. That must be why he found her sensual today, rather than practical.

All in all, Giles wouldn't be unlucky to win Stella, and Harold would be extraordinarily fortunate.

Just now, the air around Stella practically breathed

disapproval, which made him want to poke at her, like a schoolboy pulling a girl's pigtail.

When they reached the entry, no maids were in sight. "Where's Mrs. Thyme, your chaperone?" he asked.

"Mrs. Thyme has no interest in scavenger hunts, so she is visiting a friend," Stella said. "She plans to return later this afternoon, since your mother promised all young ladies would be accompanied by maids."

Wickford approached with a pained expression. "Your Grace, I regret to say that there isn't a maid left in the house. Even the kitchen maids have been dispatched." Clearly their butler disapproved of this reckless misuse of household staff.

"I think we can all agree that His Grace will not attempt to compromise me," Stella said. "I fail to see how a trip to Lambeth Palace differs from a drive in Hyde Park, which would be considered quite acceptable. In fact, it could be argued that a visit to the residence of the Archbishop of Canterbury has the odor of sacrality."

"'Sacrality'?" Silvester repeated.

She rolled her eyes. "I'm sorry if I confused you. Stench of the sacred?"

"You may count on me to act like a gentleman," Silvester said, wondering whether Giles and Yasmin had left with a maid. Likely not. Damn it to hell. His instincts had been right.

He caught avid interest on Wickford's face and frowned. He wouldn't put it past the blighter to sell information about any pair who climbed into a vehicle unchaperoned.

"We'll take my curricle," he said to Wickford. "I

wouldn't want to allow anyone to think that I escorted Lady Stella in a closed vehicle because I had designs on her virtue."

She threw him a jaundiced glance.

The butler bowed. "Just so, my lord."

After Wickford bustled off, Silvester asked, "What was that look about?"

"No one would ever think *you* have 'designs' on *my* virtue. You are right to defend yourself, but you needn't clothe it in an elaborate conceit that you are protecting me."

Silvester blinked. Was she insinuating that he ought to defend himself against her seductive wiles?

She read this expression and turned red. "Not me!" she hissed. "I meant you obviously must protect yourself against attempts to compromise you. You're a duke. Surely some lady has cornered you in a library."

"Not so far," Silvester said. "I gather you're assuring me—yet again—that you have no interest in my hand in marriage, whether obtained through fair means or foul?"

"That is correct."

The finality in Stella's tone was only surprising because he had become accustomed to more-or-less blatant indications from young ladies that they would like to be a duchess. Did that make him a pompous ass? He wasn't sure.

"Me, my title, or Yasmin?" he inquired, after Stella put on her pelisse. They were standing side by side, waiting for Wickford to return to the house and announce that the curricle had been brought around from the mews.

"What are you talking about?"

"You seemed to tolerate my company two days ago when we last danced; now you're all twisted up with dislike. Why? Are you one of those righteous maidens who consider Yasmin to be the devil?"

She glowered at him from behind her spectacles. "To the contrary, I have observed that Lady Yasmin is far more prudish than many in polite society."

"That is my conclusion as well," he said, feeling more cheerful. Yasmin and Giles were together in a carriage, but nothing would happen. Yasmin was prudish. "In that case, I presume you've taken a dislike to me."

"Do you find that a novel experience?" she asked, her tone distinctly cool. "Admittedly, the hordes do seem charmed by your jolly smiles."

Silvester caught back a grin. She was certainly observant: of Yasmin *and* of him.

"If you'll forgive me for my bluntness," Stella continued, not even pretending to sound regretful, "I feel growing distaste for the way in which gentlemen, not just you, take themselves so seriously, while doing nothing serious."

Silvester felt a stab of enjoyment. Female adoration had long since become boring. His mother and Yasmin appeared immune to his charms, such as they were, and it seemed Stella had joined that group. "I gather you think that I do nothing but consider my cravats all day?" he inquired.

She raised a perfectly arched eyebrow. "Don't you consign that all-important task to your valet?"

"Leaving me with nothing to do but contemplate my nails?"

She opened her mouth, apparently thought better, and shut it again.

Silvester stretched out his hand. His fingers were wide-knuckled and broad, certainly not gentlemanly. His knuckles were bruised by the rounds he'd gone with Giles at Jackson's salon.

"My valet despairs because I refuse to wear gloves soaked in cream to bed."

Stella's eyebrows flew up yet again.

"You don't slather your hands in cream?" He picked up her hand and pretended to examine it. Her hands were as small as the rest of her, but they weren't petite or frail.

"My fingers are too stubby to be ladylike," Stella said. "My maid polishes my nails with Graf's Hyglo paste, but there is no disguising my short fingers, which might explain why she hasn't attempted to beautify them."

Silvester grinned at her. "I find your hand delectably small, Lady Stella. Refined, I would call it."

"A connoisseur of ladies' hands, are you?"

"Since I have nothing else to do," he said promptly. Succumbing to the impulse to annoy her, he raised her hand to his lips and kissed it. Sure enough, her eyes sparked with irritation.

"My valet wants me to wear Hessian boots with tassels, and I am giving it a serious thought," he said. "I tried to dampen his interest by acquiring an ebony tasseled cane, but that blandishment failed; he is determined that I must have tasseled boots. What do you think of that, Lady Stella?"

She had remarkable eyes: wide-set, a green-blue color, more blue than green. Like a winter sky, because her skin was like snow. Her mouth turned down as she thought about his absurd question.

That bottom lip? If Stella wasn't so . . . so who she was, men would be dreaming about that mouth.

"You are making fun of me," she said, her voice sharp. "Not for the first time, but it's never kind to do so, is it? You don't care for my opinion; you find me unfashionable and claim that I use my intelligence as a hammer. Why would you care what I think of your boots?"

A hammer?

Wickford opened the front door and announced, "Your curricle is rounding the corner, Your Grace."

Lady Stella marched outside, her figure practically quivering with indignation, and Silvester sauntered after, trying to remember when he had compared her to a hammer.

Nothing came to mind. He didn't remember saying anything of the sort.

What's more, it wasn't true.

She was no blunt weapon. If he had to describe her—

To his surprise, he realized that he could not.

Lady Stella Corsham was too complicated to be summed up with ease.

Irritatingly beautiful might do it.

Because she was irritating.

He was reluctantly coming to the conclusion that she was beautiful, especially when her eyes snapped fire at him.

Not that it mattered.

CHAPTER NINE

Stella walked down the steps of the ducal residence and looked about for something interesting that she could pretend to study until the curricle drew up before the gate. She could feel Silvester's presence looming behind her.

She sneaked a glance and sure enough, he looked offended.

Honestly, it was as if no one had ever pointed out that insults were certain to make their way back to the slighted person.

Fairness made her admit that probably no one had. Likely dukes were never confronted with the consequences of their actions.

Or perhaps he was cross because she had impugned his feckless existence, which actually wasn't fair of her. Why *should* a duke consider more than the fashion for tasseled boots? It sounded as if his valet was eager to take even that gentlemanly task off his hands.

The ducal residence was as grand an establishment as Stella had ever seen. The building was made of soft white stone, with willowy columns and equally delicate windows. Whereas most townhouses stood shoulder to shoulder, Silvester's was pushed back from the street and surrounded by tall gates embellished with iron leaves and curlicues.

Like the velvet tablecloth that set off a precious vase, a dense, glossy lawn stretched to the gate. It must cost a fortune to maintain such perfection.

She walked over to inspect it more closely.

The lawn resembled bank notes, if notes had roots. And were green. When Silvester joined her, Stella's skin prickled all over, but she kept her gaze on the grass.

"If I have insulted you in any way, Lady Stella, I heartily apologize," he said. "I do not think of you as a hammer, and I can't imagine how you gained that impression."

"Because you said it," she replied, before she remembered that her aunt had told her over and over never to contradict gentlemen, no matter the circumstance. She didn't look at him, keeping her eyes fixed on the lawn. "I accept your apology," she said, not allowing disbelief to leak into her voice.

"When did I say it?" Silvester asked.

She arched a brow. "Really? Are you contradicting me?"

"I wouldn't—" The duke stopped short, his brow furrowing.

"I imagine you thought it was a private conversation," Stella conceded.

"I do remember Blanche Boodle hanging over my shoulder at some point while I was conversing with Lady Yasmin." His voice was grim.

"I have the impression that Blanche plans to marry into the nobility," Stella said, starting to enjoy herself.

Silvester seemed to be grinding his teeth.

"Not to me," he said shortly. His expression would probably make a small child cry. In fact, he looked completely different from the endlessly charming nobleman who reigned over polite society. "I apologize." His ferocious scowl was clearly directed at himself, though she thought Blanche was lucky to be out of sight. "That was an unkind characterization of you, and untrue."

"It's not *very* untrue," Stella admitted. "My aunt thinks that I've warped my mind by reading too much."

"You don't use your knowledge against others," Silvester said. He shot her a tight, frustrated look. "Whereas my deplorable attempt to make Yasmin laugh gave Blanche Boodle a hammer to wield."

Stella shrugged. His mention of Yasmin made her feel suddenly awkward again. Not to mention his acknowledgment that society viewed her as a figure of fun. She looked back at the lawn. A bird was singing, and out of the corner of her eye, she could see a splash of flowers.

Silvester took a step closer, so his shoulder brushed hers. "Does the grass seem healthy?" he asked, his voice rumbling in her ear.

"Certainly. If bank notes were green, they would look like your lawn."

"I suppose one might view grass, London grass at least, as an indication of wealth."

Might?

Her father had owned a middling estate, with a house in London and a country estate—without a river. Their London house had been cramped and narrow, with a tiny patch of grass outside the front window and a kitchen garden in back. It had been entailed, so her eldest cousin lived there now, but she still remembered her mother's dissatisfaction with that front garden.

Just like having a river in the country, a lawn signaled prestige.

"My curricle has arrived," Silvester said, slipping his fingers around her elbow and drawing her through the gate to the street.

It wouldn't be polite to pull her arm away, even though his touch was unnerving. Instead, Stella reminded herself that she felt only dislike for the duke.

And yet his charm, that deep, cool voice and deceptively thoughtful air, slid over her like sunshine. Even more: he had admitted that he'd made a stupid remark while chasing Lady Yasmin's attention. His apology was sincere.

His Grace's curricle was an elegant version of his lawn. The body of it perched on huge wheels, hanging between them like a nest blown free by the wind. It was painted midnight blue, so dark as to be almost black, picked out in silver and hitched to a matched pair of silver-grey horses.

Together, the vehicle looked wildly expensive and fragile. A ducal toy, something that no one with pretentions to *gravitas* would ever drive.

"Your curricle looks unsafe," Stella observed.

A groom set a low box beneath the door, which wouldn't make the slightest difference to her inability to vault herself into the seat.

She looked at Silvester. "Is that a jest?" She nodded to the box.

"Bring Her Grace's mounting box," he ordered.

The groom trotted away, returning with a much

taller box, presumably used by Silvester's mother, though Stella couldn't imagine the dowager duchess climbing into a beehive on wheels.

She picked up her skirts and hopped onto the box, then looked up at the shining leather seat. She wasn't entirely sure how far away it was, but she was certain that she would misjudge, bounce off, and thump down onto the cobblestones.

"If you'll allow me," the duke said behind her.

Stella glanced over her shoulder.

"May I boost you to the seat?"

She nodded.

Large hands curled around her waist. Silvester lifted her without an audible grunt—which she much appreciated—before taking himself around to the other side and leaping onto his seat.

Behind them, a groom pulled himself up onto a narrow ledge between the wheels and took firm hold of an iron bar. "Are you certain your groom is safe?" Stella asked.

"Binder? The man can cling to a straw in a storm." Raising his voice: "You're all right, aren't you, Binder?"

"Couldn't be better, Your Grace," the man shouted back cheerfully. "They're nice and fresh; give 'em their heads and they'll take us at a nice clip!"

Silvester lifted the reins, and his horses merged smoothly into traffic. Stella ran her finger over the vehicle's shining, navy blue paint.

"The curricle is new," he said, adroitly steering around a milk wagon. "I chose the color myself. What do you think of it?"

"A bright color would be vulgar. Black would be common. I believe you achieved your goal. The dark blue declares itself quietly, and yet the silver trim glitters enough to inform the unobservant and ignorant that you are wealthy."

He burst into laughter.

Stella couldn't stop herself from smiling at him. Lord knows what he would say about her after this afternoon's excursion. Mrs. Thyme would definitely advise that Stella limit herself to comments on the weather.

"You think me a very shallow creature," Silvester said a moment later.

"Not at all," Stella said, trying hard to sound sincere. "Curricles are important, after all. I mean, the color of curricles. Just like lawns! Very, very important."

"But not compared to the achievements of the Earl of Lilford, who influences the laws of the land?"

She cleared her throat. "I'm sure you have ducal responsibilities, have you not?"

"I pay my gardeners' salaries."

"As a young lady, I have no responsibilities other than to be charming enough to attract a husband," Stella said, in the spirit of fairness. "It's not fair of me to criticize you. Sometimes I feel my entire life is bounded by a tea tray."

"Not all laws originate in the House of Lords or Commons," Silvester said, an odd note in his voice.

Stella had decided that although the curricle was high off the ground, its balance and springs were excellent. The seat scarcely swayed though they were bowling along at a fast pace. She relaxed and turned her body partly toward him. "What do you mean?"

"Money governs which laws pass and fail in this country," Silvester said. "For example, England just passed a coinage act that established a gold standard for the pound. Do you know of it?"

"I read about the Coinage Act," Stella said. She was fairly certain that Mrs. Thyme would gasp in horror if she knew that Stella revealed as much, but it wasn't as if the duke was one of her suitors.

"The act is an exemplar of laws invoked by commerce rather than by those who govern. The Royal Mint is regulated by laws enacted by the Houses of Lords and Commons, but the content of those laws? Politicians don't have the knowledge or, if you'll forgive me, the intelligence."

Stella thought about it. "So, are you a banker? When you're not being a duke, I mean."

"No," he said. "Bankers spend too much time fiddling about."

She narrowed her eyes. "But you do things with money, don't you? With gold, I expect, since you brought up the new act."

"I do." Silvester slowed his team to a walk as they threaded their way through a crowded street. "During the war with France, the Mint issued bundles of paper notes. Now the Prime Minister needs to redeem them."

"But not with silver coinage?" Stella watched intently as the sophisticated aristocrat peeled away as if he had never existed.

This man, the one sitting beside her, breathed a different kind of power, one brewed of intelligence and daring, if she had to guess.

"Silver coins have been debased and will be used only for small denominations."

Stella didn't understand why, but she wasn't inter-

ested in particulars at the moment. The complexities of
the man who sat next to her were far more absorbing.

"What did you have to do with the decision?" she
asked. "Who was behind the law? The Mint? The
Prime Minister? The House of Lords?"

"Lords are born to a position that gives them a
voice," Silvester said. "It doesn't give them the ability
to understand complicated fiscal policy."

"But you have that ability," Stella guessed.

"I watch the markets. For several years, the market
price of silver has been lower than the Mint valuation.
The financial stability of the country depends on balance. Using a gold standard will solve that problem."

"I see." Stella watched him from under her
lashes. Silvester was guiding his team with noncha-
lant ease even though the street was crowded with
masses of shoppers, barking dogs darting from one
side to another, not to mention a child wielding a
broom in the center of the crossing.

Generally speaking, she had found people to be
precisely whom they appeared to be. Mrs. Thyme presented herself as a matron who spent her energy hon-
oring the elaborate rituals of society and fearing the
disreputable passions of men. And that was precisely
who she was.

On the opposite extreme, Stella had thought Silvester was kindly and discovered he was occasionally unkind. She had thought he was foolish, and it seemed
he was the opposite. Nor was he lazy.

In fact, he was Machiavellian; her favorite author
would think him a fine candidate for a prince. Put that
together with the fact that Silvester couldn't bear not
to win . . .

"I would guess you bought gold in large amounts in the last six months," she hazarded. "You thereby influenced the price that the Mint puts on that coinage."

She saw one side of his mouth curling up. It wasn't the big, charming smile he offered to society. It signaled genuine amusement.

"How did you come to that conclusion?" he asked.

"I guessed. You are unlikely to be satisfied with an advisory role, no matter how carefully you watch the markets."

"I thought I was so bumbleheaded that I could scarcely be trusted to pay my gardeners?"

"Do you want me to pat you on the hand for doing something other than capering in a ballroom?"

CHAPTER TEN

Silvester threw back his head and laughed. Every time he thought he understood Stella, she surprised him again.

"My mother thinks that I should leave these matters to the Bank of England," he said. "You're the first to understand that trading currencies is crucial to financial futures, hers and others. May I call you Stella, by the way?"

"No, you may not," she stated.

"Specs?"

She scowled at him. "Specs is my kitten."

"I like your spectacles. My mother wears a monocle, except on occasions when she is compelled to use a lorgnette. But those are few and far between."

"When does she use a lorgnette? And by the way, if you ever address me as Specs, I shall throw something at you."

His eyes were light with laughter. "I shall keep that in mind for moments when I am asked to play the bowler in cricket. Practice is always helpful when it comes to catching."

He adroitly guided the curricle around a corner. "As for my mother's monocle, she never brings it to the queen's drawing room, as Her Majesty thinks a monocle is unladylike. The queen does not mind a gold-encrusted lorgnette on a long stick."

"I would guess that the golden lorgnette was your gift," Stella said. "Because you knew that Britain would go to the gold standard sooner rather than later."

"Our drawing room glints like a dragon's hoard," he agreed.

"That was cheating."

"What?"

"You knew ahead of time, before the Currency Act passed. The newspaper mentioned that the price of gold had risen immediately. It's just like this scavenger hunt. You know that your mother's brother, the bishop, will accompany you, and only you, home for tea. I expect your sisters knew that as well, when they put him at the top of the list. The entire hunt is rigged."

"Until I read the paper this morning, I didn't know he was paying a visit to the archbishop," Silvester objected.

"A shoddy excuse," she said, scowling at him. "If you hadn't read that article, we'd be tooling off to the bishop's residence, wherever that is. Even if others read the article, you are the only person who can talk your uncle into a carriage."

Their vehicle had become mired in a crossing, surrounded by a mess of vehicles. With a glance backward and a jerk of his head, Silvester sent Binder into the middle of the street to direct traffic.

"I won't disagree." Then he said, "You are wearing your hair differently, as Miss Boodle mentioned. You usually pull it back, but you've left curls around your face."

Stella gave him a cool look. "I am as uninterested by ladies' hair as you are in tassels. To return to our former subject, I am curious about why you want to win the scavenger hunt so much that you would cheat."

He opened his mouth, but she held up her hand. "In essence. I admit there are no rules against it."

"You are harsh," Silvester said, frowning at her.

"You were harsh about me, and yet you don't care to hear an evaluation of yourself?"

"I apologize—"

She shook her head. "You already apologized, and I shouldn't have brought it up again. So why *do* you want to win the wooden box your mother is offering?"

"In truth?"

She nodded. "You have everything that a man could wish to buy, from this extravagant vehicle to a tasseled cane that likely cost as much as a month's rent. Why the contents of that wooden box?"

Silvester was surprised to discover that Stella was pricking his conscience by insisting that he shouldn't try to win the scavenger hunt. Damn it. And why the hell had he told her so much? He had never told Yasmin of his involvement in the currency markets.

"It's because I don't know what it is," he confessed. "It's likely something absurd. But I cannot resist a mystery."

"And your mother knows that," Stella exclaimed, a smile in her eyes. "That's why the prize for the lady is visible to all, but that for the gentleman is a secret. She wanted to make certain you enjoy the game."

"Yes. My mother actually cares very little for polite society. She likes to put on her entertainments, sometimes for many and sometimes for a few. But she really does them to amuse herself and her children."

"I suppose that's acceptable," Stella conceded.

Having cleared the crosswalk, Binder leaped onto the back of the curricle. Silvester raised the reins and his pair sprang forward. "Why do *you* want the vulture crown?"

"I don't."

He caught her eyes. "Yes, you do. Otherwise, you wouldn't be in this carriage, not with your finely tuned ethical sense."

"You make me sound like a hypocritical prig."

He waited.

"To be honest, I'm curious," Stella confessed. "I have read about the Egyptians, and I would love to see that crown up close."

"Curiosity isn't priggish. My mother took a deep dive into Egyptiana when the craze hit. She sprinkled Sun God scarabs all over the house, supposedly for good luck. Do you know what a scarab is?"

Stella nodded.

"My mother commissioned scarabs in the form of a brooch for each of my sisters, the insect's body decorated with a large emerald. She was curious about the scarabs' positive influence, so she wanted them worn at all times."

Stella chuckled. "I am imagining a bulbous emerald brooch. Did your sisters agree?"

Silvester glanced at her, unsettled by how much her deep chuckle pleased him. "No. Pansy began wearing a cross to counter the Sun God's influence. My mother was frightfully disappointed: she complained that she alone wearing the scarab wasn't a large enough sample to prove or disprove the promise of good luck."

Stella laughed. It was the first laugh of hers he'd heard, and it was a good one, clear and joyful, not high and tinkling. "Did Her Grace experience good luck?"

"It's difficult to know. She tumbled down the hill while skiing. Pansy attributed that to not wearing a cross, while my mother insisted that she would have broken her neck had she not worn the scarab."

"What is skiing?" Stella asked, her eyes alight with interest.

"A practice my father brought back from a visit to Norway. We strap long pieces of wood called skis to our boots and slide down hills in the country."

"It sounds marvelous!"

"You must try it," Silvester said, just catching himself before issuing an invitation. One did not invite an eligible young lady to one's country house unless a proposal was imminent, and obviously, it wasn't.

"I couldn't," Stella said.

He frowned at her.

"My spectacles get horridly foggy when it's cold outside. I've tried skating but I bump into people."

"I understand," Silvester said. "One mostly falls over, anyway."

"I already know how to do that!" Stella said with another deep chuckle.

"You are not clumsy," Silvester said. "You dance extremely well, Stella."

"Nonsense!"

"Allow me to disagree."

"Only when you aren't being foolish."

He laughed at that. "I'm not foolish. Do you know how many ladies trod on their partners' toes? Whereas I have had the pleasure of waltzing with you several times, and you follow me perfectly."

"In a waltz, I can trust my partner to whirl me about rather than having to guess where we're going, or how close the other couples are." She grinned at him. "The waltz is the only dance I truly enjoy."

Silvester had a sudden memory of curling his arm around Stella and holding her tightly to him as they whirled into a waltz. He would be very sorry not to partner her again.

"Do you still hate me so much that we can't waltz together?" he asked.

She wrinkled her nose at him. "Promise that you won't say mean things about me in the vicinity of Blanche Boodle or Lady Lydia."

"I'm horrified that I ever said anything unkind about you," he said evenly. "I will never do so again."

They drew up in front of Lambeth Palace, and Binder dashed around to the horses' heads.

"In that case, I'd be happy to waltz with you," Stella said, her voice warm. Warmer than he'd ever heard it.

Silvester watched his uncle stroll out to meet them, trying to grapple with the fact that her voice felt like a gulp of whiskey: luxurious and too sensual for—for Stella.

That was not important. *Not important.*

His uncle was wearing a cassock under a magnificent loose cloak of white silk covered in gold embroidery. Silvester jumped down, leaving Binder standing at the horses' heads.

"Your mother sent a groom informing me to expect you," his uncle said by way of greeting. He caught sight of the curricle. "You can't expect me to climb into that abomination. 'Twould be blasphemy! I'm wearing my cope, you heathenish nephew!"

"Your sister longs to see you," Silvester said, kissing his hand. "You know what Mother is like."

"Yes, if I don't go for tea, she'll chase across town and interrupt me at supper," the bishop said mournfully, walking toward the curricle. "Your mother is far too vigorous for comfort, my boy."

Binder placed the high box reverently before His Excellency's feet.

"Who's waiting up there?" the bishop asked, peering at Stella.

"Lady Stella Corsham," Silvester said. Then he called: "Lady Stella, may I introduce my uncle, Bishop Luverde?"

Stella slid along the seat and peered over the edge. The wind had tousled her curls and they stood out around her head, the color of rubies gilded by firelight. She looked truly delightful, her spectacles not detracting in the least from her curved lips.

"I am honored, Your Excellency," Stella said, giving his uncle such a lavish smile that his elderly relative blinked.

That mouth of hers.

Most gentlemen focused on the spectacles and missed what was under their own eyes.

Sure enough, after that his uncle puffed his way

onto the curricle seat, where he plumped down between Silvester and Stella and proceeded to chatter with her all the way home about the role of Nonconformists in parochial churches.

"How on earth do you come by all this information?" Silvester asked Stella, peering around his uncle's considerable bulk.

The rumor that Stella was reading an encyclopedia turned out to be true. "So far, I've read the first four volumes, but of course, the Anglican religion appears in the first volume. Which reminds me, Your Excellency . . ."

Having no interest in lay-led voluntary societies—whatever they were—Silvester found himself brooding over Stella's future. Normally, ladies didn't go around leaking knowledge like a sieve.

Frankly, it reminded him of his mother when she was in the height of her Egyptian craze and claimed to know more about hieroglyphic writing than the men running the Museum of London.

It would be hard for Stella to find a gentleman who would allow, let alone encourage, his wife to read encyclopedia volumes and engage in lively conversation on obtuse subjects.

Possibly life was different in America. Harold had talked about Stella all the way home from the Boodle tea party. But Silvester didn't like the idea of the two of them together.

Giles wouldn't be a good husband for Stella either. Giles was serious all the time, whereas Stella had a hidden sense of fun. She smuggled a *kitten* into a tea party. Giles would squelch her, and she would turn into a sober bluestocking, peering at everyone through her spectacles. Giles rarely danced, so she would likely stop dancing as well.

Whereas Stella should be waltzing around a ballroom—and yes, going down a snowy slope—tight in her husband's arms, laughing all the time.

Still, it wasn't his business.

CHAPTER ELEVEN

By the time they reached the duke's residence, many of the guests had returned and were standing over heaps of miscellaneous objects, like hens protecting oddly shaped eggs.

The moment Stella, Silvester, and the bishop entered the room, there was a general groan.

The other two objects in the top three, those that guaranteed a win, were a hat worn by Napoleon and the Queen's coronation crown, and obviously no one produced either of those.

To halfhearted applause, the dowager duchess proclaimed the winners. She handed her son the wooden box and Stella the vulture crown, which turned out to be a plain circlet of gold supporting a great beak carved from ebony that jutted over the forehead of the female ruler. The beak shone with a dull gleam that might well have sent an awestruck populace to their knees.

Silvester opened the box, gave a bark of laughter, and shut it again.

Stella remained awkwardly at his side, accepting resentful compliments and fervently wishing that her aunt would arrive to escort her home, especially after the dowager duchess blithely bid her guests farewell and disappeared with her brother.

Lydia sidled over. "May I see the crown?"

"Of course," Stella said, turning to her. To her relief, Silvester drifted away.

"It's ugly. Still, that wasn't a fair hunt," Lydia said broodily.

"I completely agree," Stella said, which seemed to assuage her.

"Of course, you had nothing to do with it. It's not as if His Grace chose you as his partner. It's just that Lord Pettigrew and I found quite a few things on the list and may well have won."

"His Grace certainly did not choose me," Stella stated. Blanche was heading toward them, so she was glad that Silvester had moved to the other side of the room. He might snarl at Blanche for eavesdropping.

"Oh, there you are, Blanche," Lydia said. "Did you and Mr. Rowson have an enjoyable afternoon?"

"We drank a great many cups of tea while the dowager duchess told us about a chimney she designed. We couldn't attend the scavenger hunt, since there were no maids to serve as chaperones."

"We had the same problem," Stella said idly. The circlet of the vulture crown was etched with Egyptian hieroglyphs. Perhaps if she brought it to a museum, they could decipher them.

"Did you venture outside without a chaperone?" Blanche asked.

"In an open vehicle," Stella clarified. "His Grace wanted to be certain that no one would consider either of us compromised."

"That would explain what happened to your hair," Lydia said acidly. "Better you than me."

There was a moment of silence as Stella and Blanche

silently registered that Lydia would kill to go anywhere alone with the Duke of Huntington, and what's more, she would have arranged to be compromised. Probably she would have thrown herself into his arms in the open street.

Lydia laughed into the silence. "Of course, the duke had to be prudent. Stella as a duchess? I don't think so." She stepped closer and whispered, "Have you seen how angry he is? Or perhaps the right word is 'heartbroken'?"

Stella blinked at her. "What do you mean?"

"You're frightfully unobservant, even with the spectacles," Lydia said disapprovingly. "I expect that's why you took a tumble in the ballroom. He's over there."

Stella turned. Silvester was glaring out the window. His shoulders were rigid, and he looked perilously close to an eruption of anger.

"Could he be cross because his mother forced him to accompany you?" Lydia asked.

Stella shook her head. "He didn't seem to care."

"*You* are the unobservant one," Blanche said to her friend, shaking her head. "Do you see your brother anywhere, Lydia?"

Lydia turned pale. "No!" She wheeled and stared around the room.

"At this very moment, the earl is shaking the sheets with Yasmin Régnier," Blanche said. "Stole the duke's mistress from under his very eyes. No wonder the man looks so enraged."

Stella looked at her with exasperation. "Lydia looks quite sick with nerves. Was that necessary?"

Blanche blinked. "No." Rather surprisingly, she

turned to Lydia. "I'm sorry. That was a vulgar remark, and I apologize."

"What is *vulgar*," Lydia snapped, "is Yasmin running off with my brother!"

Stella excused herself and walked over to Silvester, who was gazing at the street, jaw clenched. "You mustn't stand around looking bleak. Everyone's talking about you."

In the carriage, he had smiled at her like a friend, but now his eyes were chilly. "May I be of assistance, Lady Stella?"

That was the Duke of Huntington speaking, rather than Silvester.

Stella ignored it. "They will return," she said, meeting his eyes. "Stop watching for their carriage. I told you: Lady Yasmin is punctiliously virtuous."

He blinked, and his brows drew together. "That obvious, am I?"

"Yes. But you shouldn't worry. You and Yasmin make sense." She answered the question in his eyes: "Golden girls and boys."

"If you're quoting Shakespeare, those golden girls and boys 'come to dust,' if I remember."

"As will we all," Stella said. "My point is that the two of you match: beautiful, shimmering, everyone watching you."

"I'm not beautiful," Silvester said, but she could see hopefulness in his eyes. He was hoping that Yasmin would saunter in and nestle down on the couch beside him.

Stella couldn't suppress a pang of longing for his wide-knuckled, big hands, for the way his gray eyes turned warm with laughter, even, shamefully, for the width of his thighs when he sat beside her in the curricle.

Yasmin must be cracked if she chose the Earl of Lilford over a duke.

This particular duke.

"You *are* beautiful," Stella retorted, keeping her voice flat so he understood that she wasn't flattering him. "Cheekbones, jaw, shoulders—aristocratic, all of it. Oh, and you have hair and all your teeth. That's what's made you what you are."

He raised an eyebrow.

"The most eligible gentleman on the marriage market," she explained. "Just think, you won that title without anyone knowing that you're up to your knees in ill-gotten gold."

His eyes darkened to steel gray, but Stella didn't care. She was getting her own back, just a little, for the way he told Yasmin that her portrait would have to be repainted.

Thinking of that, she leaned closer and breathed, "If you tell anyone that you called me 'Specs,' I will tell the world that you are speculating in gold because you had advance knowledge of the Coinage Act."

"It's not illegal," he said instantly.

"It sounds illegal. More: it sounds unethical."

"You've made that point already. Your definition of immorality and mine diverge on several points."

Stella grinned at him. At least Silvester didn't look sad any longer. His brows were knit, and he was glowering. She preferred him frustrated to embittered.

Then, from behind his shoulder, she caught sight of Lydia leaning toward another lady and whispering, her eyes on Silvester. Undoubtedly, Lydia was making fun of him for showing emotion.

Even in the short time she'd been in London, Stella had learned that gentlemen were supposed to show no emotion, never mind the fact that so many were floundering about, desperately in love.

Abruptly realizing she could easily draw Lydia's attention from Silvester, she lifted the vulture crown and put it on her head. It settled firmly in place, the long beak looming over her spectacles. "How do I look?"

Silvester cleared his throat. "Regal." He grinned. "Am I to take it that you would have donned my mother's scarab brooch?"

"If my mother were alive to give me a gift, even an Egyptian deity, yes, I would wear it," she said flatly.

He winced. "I apologize."

All around the room, not just Lydia, but everyone else was turning to peer at her. Voices rose into a joyous refrain. Too late, Stella realized that while her ploy to draw Lydia's attention from Silvester was effective, her aunt would have hysterics when she heard of it.

No pharaoh would quail before English society. Stella straightened her back and smiled around the room. Her hair had been blown about in the curricle, and the headpiece was the final straw: she could feel coils tumbling over one shoulder.

"Take it off," Blanche mouthed, eyes alarmed, making her way toward her. When she was close enough: "You look absurd with that beak towering over your forehead."

Stella shrugged.

"I'm glad I didn't win that hideous thing!" Blanche said. "Here, give it to me and I'll pretend to examine it."

Silvester had turned away and was delighting a circle of ladies with that charming grin of his. Anyone who thought he was lovelorn was changing their mind. Likely they had decided he had been angry at being paired with her, and now that she had put on the crown, they sympathized with him.

Stella handed Blanche the crown.

Lydia joined them. "I'm so tired of listening to people squeal about how handsome the duke is," she said. "Are they ignoring his nose?"

"It is rather large," Stella admitted.

"I prefer a less authoritarian nose. A quieter nose. Like Lord Pettigrew's."

"A fine nose," Stella agreed. "I had an interesting talk with Lord Pettigrew about his dogs."

"Yes, one does," Lydia agreed.

"Hopefully you like dogs?"

"I do."

"A good nose and a shared love of canines. That's enough for marriage," Stella said cheerfully.

"You are *so* odd," Blanche said.

CHAPTER TWELVE

Four days later
March 29, 1816
The Dowager Duchess of Huntington's
Bucolic Supper with Riparian Entertainments
Green Park, London

Dressing for the Dowager Duchess of Huntington's bucolic supper was challenging, because Stella's aunt insisted on overseeing the process. "Perhaps the blue costume would have been better," Mrs. Thyme said now, biting her lip.

Stella was wearing a high-waisted green gown with a spray of white ruffles around her neck. Unfortunately, high waistlines were designed for ladies with long necks and stork legs.

The *modiste* had claimed that the ruffles on top and bottom would make Stella look taller, which was not the case.

Her aunt had approved of the excessive ruffling around the neck because it hid Stella's cleavage. Mrs. Thyme considered exposed breasts to be tantamount to a red cloak before a bull: any hint of breasts would make lustful men leap from the shrubbery.

In Stella's opinion, the gown made her look like a thimble with a head on top.

"You were worried that I couldn't sit on the ground due to the blue dress's narrow skirt, and my red pelisse looks best with a green gown," she reminded her aunt. "We mustn't be late for Her Grace's 'entertainments,' whatever they are."

She turned from the mirror. "Specs! Where are you?"

Specs bounced out from under the bed and trotted toward her.

"She looks like a dust ball," her aunt observed. "A fluffy one. Are you putting on a leash? Julia Fitzwilliams carries her dog in a reticule, but she changes its leash to match her gown."

Stella knelt down and fitted a halter made of pink ribbon around the kitten's fat tummy, much to Specs's dismay. The kitty hissed, but didn't claw her, the way she had the day before. They were making progress.

"Doesn't she like it?" Mrs. Thyme asked.

"Not yet. But she does like being taken about. Yesterday she was in my pocket throughout my visit to the Pantheon Bazaar. She likes to look around." She pulled open the slit in her gown, and eased Specs into her pocket. The kitten immediately hooked her claws into Stella's dress from the inside and popped her head out.

"I must say, she is quite adorable," Stella's aunt said.

"She'll likely sleep during the afternoon. She's been dashing about all morning, jumping to the bed and back to the floor."

"I still feel animals shouldn't be allowed on a bed," Mrs. Thyme said, in the fretful way of someone who knows an argument is lost. "We must go. Tweed complains so much if the horses stand about in the street."

"I'm ready." Stella checked to make sure she had scraps of cheese in her reticule. Experimentation had proved that a bellyful of cheese sent Specs straight to sleep.

"I loathe picnics," Mrs. Thyme moaned. "Sitting on the ground like the meanest of peasants, with ants for company. But no one can say that I haven't done my best to find you a spouse!"

"Certainly not," Stella murmured.

If she didn't marry, every person in polite society would accept that her failure stemmed from spectacles, spots, and general ineptitude.

"I nearly forgot! I would never suggest lip color for Almack's, but I think that you can risk a slight frivolity at an outdoors event without being considered *fast*," her aunt said, dropping a small box on the dressing table. "I am persuaded that we must counteract the freckles with any cosmetic means possible."

Stella wrinkled her nose. "Lip salve tastes like fish oil." Her mouth was already too wide. Emphasizing it made her resemble a carp.

But she obediently rubbed on the crimson color.

A thimble topped with the head of a carp. Lovely.

"You needn't worry about the flavor," her aunt said. "Even if the Earl of Lilford asks you to marry him this afternoon, he won't be so improper as to kiss you. But that said, stay within my eyesight at all times. A betrothed woman is at particular risk of losing her virtue."

Stella rolled her eyes. Typical: her aunt imagined the earl overwrought with lust, whereas she had a hard time imagining Giles, as she now thought of him, kissing anyone, fishy flavor or no. To be blunt: the earl was rather stodgy.

Yet since he and Yasmin never did return to the scavenger hunt, perhaps he wasn't as stodgy as he appeared. Last night at a *musicale*, Blanche had repeated a joke she overheard about Giles, Yasmin, and a four-legged frolic, after which Lydia burst into tears. Blanche had immediately apologized again. Stella found her an odd mixture of sarcastic and remorseful.

"Have you reviewed your notes?" Mrs. Thyme asked, as they walked down the stairs.

The morning after Stella had first danced with the Earl of Lilford, her aunt sent a footman out for all the newspapers, dumped them on the breakfast table, and told Stella to take notes on important topics.

After a month of regularly engaging Giles in serious conversation, Stella felt optimistic enough to idly imagine a wedding in St. Paul's Cathedral. She would wear a long veil embroidered with gilt angels that had belonged to her mother.

Giles would wait for her at the top of the aisle, his haunted expression replaced by . . . satisfaction. Not love.

She couldn't imagine him in love with her. But she could imagine the earl concluding that she would be a suitable countess. As long as Yasmin—

Well, as long as Yasmin actually returned home after the scavenger hunt, rather than inviting Giles to her bedchamber.

Since the Huntington residence didn't back onto the Thames, the dowager duchess's "riparian entertainments" were taking place in Green Park on the banks of the Tyburn. When Stella and her aunt climbed out of the carriage, they discovered two striped pink-and-white tents set up on the riverbank, shading sofas and chairs presumably transported from the ducal household.

"No blankets on the grass," Mrs. Thyme said happily. "Be sure to remain under the tent at all times, Stella. I don't want to see more spots on your face. And don't remove your cloak or the sun will strike your arms."

The duchess's grooms had scythed the long grass on the banks of the river, so the smell of cut grass wafted toward them, along with the hum of bees and the ripple of water. The dowager duchess was sitting with her son under one tent, and the other held a cluster of guests. Laughter drifted to them on the breeze.

A quartet at the curve of the river was playing Mozart, and a butler was offering a silver tray of champagne glasses. The scene was like a watercolor that sprang to life with the smell of spring grass and the chirping of ladies.

"Very nice," her aunt said approvingly, as they walked toward the tents. "Her Grace seems to have conceived of an elegant entertainment, for once."

Stella ignored that; her aunt had an absurd dislike of the dowager, based on some girlhood slight. Or perhaps the fact that Her Grace obviously didn't give a bean for Mrs. Thyme's precious social rules.

She felt a little giddy. The tents were so pretty, and the music sounded like prisms of light glinting off river water. Hope sprang up in Stella's heart. Perhaps this afternoon the Earl of Lilford would smile at her unreservedly.

Would offer a ring, so she could be *done* with

courtship and the Season. It wasn't the most romantic reason to long for a proposal, but Stella felt a passionate wish for the humiliating charade to be over.

The dowager duchess merely raised her hand as they approached, but Silvester strolled out to greet them.

His mouth curled in a way that suggested he was amused by something, hopefully not Stella's ruff. Mrs. Thyme curtsied with a breathless titter; even matrons couldn't resist the duke's jaw. And the rest of him.

Stella stopped herself from an absurd impulse to arch her throat and try to look a bit taller. She and Silvester were now friends, or at least she thought they were. The cheerful grin he gave her suggested he felt the same.

It didn't matter if a friend thought you looked like a thimble.

After Stella and her aunt had curtsied before the dowager, Her Grace motioned Mrs. Thyme to sit beside her. "Take Lady Stella to the other tent," she told her son. "We elders will chew our cud here in peace. Oh, and give that cloak to a footman, Lady Stella. It's likely to give you heatstroke."

Stella didn't dare look at her aunt, who certainly did not consider herself elderly and wouldn't appreciate being compared to a cow.

After handing over her cloak, she took Silvester's arm and headed toward the other tent, where Giles stood beside Lydia and Yasmin.

Lady Yasmin turned to greet them. She was wearing a ravishing gown that made her legs look twice as long as Stella's. Almost all of her bosom was exposed, and her translucent sky-blue overskirt blew in the light breeze, emphasizing the shapeliness of her legs.

But her smile was so kind that Stella couldn't hate her for being so enchanting. If she were a man, she'd probably be trying to push Silvester and Giles out of the way and court Yasmin herself.

Stella had scarcely finished her curtsies when Lydia pulled her to the side. "I only came in order to speak to you," she whispered. "I shan't stay. Lord Pettigrew will escort me to Gunter's later this afternoon."

Stella tucked her lips into a smile, hoping that Lydia hadn't come up with more advice.

"My brother takes my opinion very seriously. I am seriously considering whether I should inform the earl that he should marry you."

Stella's eyes slid over to the Earl of Lilford, who was looking down at Yasmin with an unreadable expression. She couldn't imagine that he would allow his sister to command his choice of wife. "That's very kind of you," she managed.

"It's my duty as his only family member," Lydia reported. "It would be helpful if you could look more ladylike. My brother is quite proper. The spectacles, for one thing, but you should also rethink that lip color. Your mouth is somewhat large, isn't it?"

Stella realized that although she was beginning to cautiously like Blanche, she didn't feel the same about Lydia, whose blue eyes were flat, somehow, and mean. "I can't see without my spectacles. I might topple into the river."

Lydia frowned. "They do give you the air of a

bluestocking, which is good. Giles needs someone who can discuss the news of the day." She hesitated. "I try, but I can never think of anything to ask."

Stella *always* had questions. About everything. "That isn't a problem for me."

"I had hoped that he would take a *penchant* for Blanche. But she can't be bothered to read the *Times*," Lydia explained. "When she does, she doesn't understand it, which is practically the same thing, isn't it?"

"I see," Stella said, wondering if she was supposed to comment on Blanche's claims to literacy. She had a suspicion that Blanche pretended to be far more ignorant than she truly was. In short, Stella should be imitating her.

"You may be just what we're looking for in a countess," Lydia mused.

Stella cleared her throat. "Because I know how to read?"

Lydia nodded. "You have excellent breeding, and you're not courting scandal like Lady Yasmin." There was a jittery dislike in her comment. "Not that her departure from the scavenger hunt in the company of my brother was indicative of illicit behavior, no matter what people say. Giles assured me that he escorted the lady to her home. She was fatigued and bored. They don't have events like that in France."

"I haven't seen Lady Yasmin do anything imprudent." Stella had watched Yasmin flutter away if a man pressed her hand too tightly or leaned in too closely. In fact, the only time Yasmin had ever courted scandal was when she didn't return with the earl.

"The woman dampens her petticoats and worse," Lydia said with a curl of her lip. "We can't have *that* in the family. Giles is far too intelligent to fall for her wiles. He dances with her once a night merely from politeness, but I have asked him to refrain from the practice in the future."

"I see," Stella murmured.

"There's been enough gossip about the two of them. *Your* reputation is pristine," Lydia said.

Because: *male lust is wildly overestimated*.

But Stella kept her mouth shut. She had, after all, seen Lydia slip from the ballroom on occasion, in company with a young man. It suggested that Lydia prompted lust, even if she didn't.

A depressing conclusion.

"I suppose we'd better return to the tent," Lydia said. "You mustn't get any more freckles." She tucked her arm through Stella's as if they were the best of friends, drawing her back to the group.

Yasmin was seated on a sofa, chatting with Harold Rowson, who had just arrived with his fellow countrywoman, the Duchess of Trent. Lydia seated herself beside them, and Stella walked over to stand beside Merry, gratefully accepting a glass of champagne and nodding to Silvester and Giles.

"Hello, darling," Merry said, giving Stella a kiss rather than a curtsy.

"We have been discussing our most memorable summers," Giles said.

"These two knew each other as boys and spent one summer careening about the country on ponies," Merry explained.

"Not ponies," Silvester said with a deep laugh that made Stella's skin prickle. "We were eleven years old. We were on proper horses by that age."

"We should have been at Eton for summer term, but they had an outbreak of smallpox, and everyone was sent home," Giles said in his grave voice.

"Thankfully, without pox," Silvester said. "My mother was terrified that we would end up permanently spotted."

"How fortunate," Stella said, giving him a bland smile. "One hates to think that such young noblemen might have suffered such a cruel fate as being *permanently spotted*."

After a momentary silence, Silvester let out a bark of laughter. "You've made me feel like an ass yet again, Lady Stella."

Stella grinned at him. "You deserve it. Noblemen with perfect skin should be careful with their aspersions."

"I find Lady Stella's freckles to be charming," Giles stated.

He didn't mind her spectacles—*or* her freckles? "Thank you," Stella said, fighting to look composed rather than surprised.

"As do I," Silvester said, his tone rather sharp, a look in his eyes that she couldn't decipher. "I can't imagine why people dislike them."

"Fine, clear skin gives assurance of the inherent residence of three admirable graces to beauty: Wholesomeness, Neatness, and Cheerfulness," Stella informed him, breaking into a laugh at the revolted expression on his face.

"Personally, I would love to have freckles," Merry said. She wound an arm around Stella's waist. "We should all have them. Just look at the duke."

They all looked at Silvester.

"Wouldn't he look marvelous with a spray of freckles over his nose?" Merry said, giggling.

"My nose is not my most delicate feature," Silvester said with a chuckle. "Adding decorative flourishes would be a mistake."

"It is imposing," Stella said, throwing him a mischievous glance.

"My nose had already grown to this size at the age of eleven, when Giles and I were jaunting around the countryside. My profile resembled your vulture crown, Lady Stella."

Stella choked with laughter. "Well, my freckles poured over me as a toddler."

"But your complexion is charming, and my profile was and is not," Silvester said, his eyes resting on her face, an unmistakable ring of truth in his voice.

"The duke is not exaggerating about the size of his nose," Giles put in. "We used to call him Beaky at Eton."

Stella met Silvester's eyes and mouthed "Beaky," barely holding back a peal of laughter.

He narrowed his eyes and mouthed back at her: "Specs."

CHAPTER THIRTEEN

After that, the picnic was delightful. By an hour later, Stella had drunk three glasses of champagne and was having trouble controlling the trills of happiness that kept going up her spine.

Silvester was lavishing attention on Yasmin, as he always did. But a few times, when Stella said something that made the group laugh, he would glance at her with approval.

Which shot through her blood like champagne.

She tried to tell herself that it was Giles's attention that made her happy. For a while, he and Lydia stood on either side of her, like twin cypress trees. She felt sheltered by their height and, after she rubbed the lip salve off on a napkin, sanctioned by Lydia.

Yet truthfully, it was Silvester's smile that turned the afternoon delightful, made the air feel soft and gold. His amused eyes dusted over Stella's face on the way to admiring Yasmin's perfect features.

She'd take what she could get.

She was engaged in a battle of wits with Silvester about the nature of truth—naturally, he thought it was variable and she thought it an absolute—when an ear-splitting shriek interrupted their banter.

Stella whirled around to find Lydia was screaming,

her eyes rounded with horror. The musicians stopped playing, so Lydia's voice broke a startled silence.

"Your leg! There's something crawling up, up your leg, up your *leg*!" Lydia screamed again, pointing at Stella. "A rat!" She threw herself on a couch and pulled up her feet.

Stella squeaked and looked down at the wiggling lump under her skirts.

It was Specs, of course. Stella had been so engaged in trying to convince Silvester of his inaccuracies that she'd forgotten all about the kitten.

Specs was not only awake; she was climbing Stella's gown from the inside. Stella couldn't help giggling as she caught up Specs's squirming body and eased her into the open. "It's merely my kitten, Lady Lydia! Voila!" She held Specs in one cupped hand. "She's a mere baby but definitely a feline, not a rodent."

Lydia was pressed back against the sofa, her breath coming in sharp gasps. Giles moved to seat himself beside his sister, an arm around her shoulders.

"I'm sorry I didn't introduce you to her earlier, but she was asleep," Stella added. "I didn't realize that she'd woken up."

Specs looked around, twitching her ears, and meowed in greeting.

"That's . . . that's disgusting," Lydia cried. "You had a wild animal in your pocket. Next to your skin. It . . . It touched your undergarments!" She drew in another sobbing breath.

Silvester stepped forward. He picked up Specs and said reprovingly, "Lady Lydia, this is no wild animal."

Stella thought she'd never seen anything more

adorable than the duke's huge, somewhat battered fingers curled around a tiny striped cat.

"I love the way the tips of her ears are touched in black," Merry said, stroking one of Specs's ears.

The dowager and Mrs. Thyme arrived at their tent out of breath.

"Oh, that's just Stella's cat," Mrs. Thyme said, patting her bosom. "I thought we had experienced a rat infestation! One never knows at a picnic."

"*Cats* do not belong in polite company," Lydia insisted, her voice shaky.

Rather to Stella's surprise, Mrs. Thyme said, "*Our* kitten certainly belongs in polite company. She is better trained than Julia Fitzwilliams's dog, which snaps at people."

The dowager peered closely at Specs through her right eye, the one with a monocle. "The Egyptians thought a great deal of cats," she reported. "I believe they domesticated them, much as we do dogs. Does it care to walk on a leash?"

"Not yet," Stella admitted, realizing that Specs wasn't wearing her halter. She plucked a frayed mess of pink ribbons from her pocket. "I made a halter with a leash, but she seems to find it an indignity."

Silvester threw her an amused look. "You'll need something stronger than ribbons." Specs rolled over on her back and batted Silvester's fingers.

"She is so adorable," Merry said. "Do come look, Lady Lydia!"

Specs caught Silvester's forefinger with her front paws and started scrabbling at it with her back paws, pretending to attack.

"My turn to hold her," Merry begged.

After a while, Lydia relented and came over to see the kitten more closely, though she refused to hold her, claiming that cat paws were revolting.

"You may bring that animal to my tent later," the dowager announced. "I should like to make a closer examination in order to compare it to Egyptian hieroglyphs of felines. We elders will repose ourselves before the entertainments begin. A nap is called for."

Silvester took his mother's arm to escort her back to her seat. Stella caught her aunt's martyred glower as she turned to follow. Mrs. Thyme truly was doing everything in her power to ensure that Giles had unchaperoned conversation with Stella.

Yasmin seated herself on one end of a sofa. The earl ushered his sister to a chair, and Stella sat down in the other, Specs on her lap. Harold and Merry seated themselves on the opposite sofa. After which Giles sat down so close to Yasmin that their legs were touching.

He glanced down at Yasmin without a trace of the deep affection with which Silvester regarded the lady. But Yasmin didn't lean away from him, and Stella could have sworn that she never allowed a man to sit so close.

In fact, Stella had the distinct impression that her aunt was going to be disappointed about that proposal.

She fed Specs a piece of cheese, trying not to watch Yasmin and Giles. It wasn't as if Giles was Stella's property. He hadn't declared himself, obviously. He often escorted her to the supper dance, and gossip columns paired their names, but that didn't mean much.

In the marriage market, Stella was a loser and Yasmin a winner, so Yasmin had her pick of the available men. That was simply the way it was. It wasn't the first time that Stella had learned to live with unpleasant facts.

"After the ladies repose themselves, the entertainment will begin," Silvester said, returning to the tent. His eyes flew to Yasmin and Giles, and his lips tightened.

"I assume you will give a speech in Parliament tomorrow regarding the Corn Act," Stella said hastily to Giles. "On which side lie your sympathies?"

"The act will prohibit imported grain, will it not?" Yasmin asked.

"It will prohibit imports at moments when domestic prices are high," Stella explained. "That will protect the interests of landed gentry, obviously."

"Those are my interests," Giles said flatly.

Stella looked at the earl, surprised. "Surely you must look farther than your own interests. Unless foreign exports lower the price of grain, the poor are unable to afford bread."

"We must look out for the unfortunates of the world," Harold put in, rather pompously.

That was rich, given that the American was obsessed with his Parisian salon that would welcome—so he had told her—only the *very* highest in society.

"You aren't to be let off so easily, Giles," Yasmin said cheerfully. "French farmers sell their grain to the English, as I remember it."

Lydia's eyebrows flew up. *"Giles?"*

Yasmin blinked. "Formal address is so old-fashioned among friends," she cried. "Silvester and I have been addressing each other by our given names for months, so please, can we all be more informal?

Stella, your name is French, so naturally I adore it. Mine is Yasmin, which is *not* French, but a version of my mother's favorite flower, jasmine."

"I prefer informality!" Merry said, clapping her hands. "My name is Merry, as in Christmas. I know you say Happy Christmas here, but back in Boston, we are merry instead."

Stella was fairly sure that Mrs. Thyme would consider Yasmin's suggestion a sign of moral degeneration. She was aware that her aunt's first name was Lillian, but she couldn't imagine being asked to use it; her own uncle addressed his wife as "Mrs. Thyme."

Still, Lydia murmured assent, so Stella agreed. She could hardly be the only one to insist on propriety, no matter how affronted her aunt might be.

"These days, no country should act as if it is an independent entity," Merry said, returning to the conversation.

"An excellent point," Giles said, looking intently at Yasmin. "I shall certainly bring up the impact on foreign relations." He began plying Yasmin with questions about French farmers, not that she seemed to have many answers.

Stella tried to have all the facts—at least, those in the papers—at her fingertips, the better to help Giles make decisions, but Yasmin just laughed, teasing him for supporting the landed gentry and his own interests.

"No, I have no idea who grows French grain," she said impudently. "Any more than I know who the English prime minister is!"

"Because you are a lily of the valley," Silvester said, sitting down on the arm of the sofa next to Yasmin. He was close enough that Stella caught a whiff of warm man and river water, along with a touch of lime and apple.

Humiliatingly, the scent made her nipples tighten, and a ripple of heat wash through her body. It was mortifying to recognize (again) that her body didn't care about Silvester's adoration of Yasmin. Just the nearness of him sent a pulse of heat between her legs, something she was certain no true lady experienced.

Stealing another glance at him under her lashes, she caught a glare that went between Giles and Silvester that stripped the heat from her body. She would have described the earl's gaze as savage.

Giles? Mild-mannered Giles? Stodgy Giles?

She must have been mistaken. If the earl *was* feeling savage, Silvester wouldn't have smiled back so cheerfully.

Would he?

Suddenly, Stella had the unnerving feeling that she was too naïve to understand the games played by dazzling people like these three. She turned away and fed Specs another piece of cheese.

Lydia had been looking more and more bored. Now she jumped up and said, "Brother, I have another appointment, so I must return home." She glanced at Yasmin, and added, "Immediately." Dislike filtered through her voice like sediment through muddy water. "You may remain here, naturally, but I would ask you to escort me to our carriage."

"Certainly," Giles replied, standing.

Stella thought that he showed remarkable patience, given that his younger sister sounded like a minatory governess.

Silvester promptly took Giles's place next to Yasmin, who greeted him with a melting smile. It was like a game of musical chairs that Stella had once played as a child.

Or perhaps a better analogy was to compare Yasmin to a cat. The other day Specs had caught a mouse in the fireplace, and until Stella intervened, she played with it, allowing it to run away only to catch the poor creature again.

Yasmin was a kindly cat, but then, she had two mice to play with.

CHAPTER FOURTEEN

The sun was hanging low by the time the dowager woke from her doze and announced the "riparian entertainments" she'd promised, sending a troupe of grooms around the curve of the river.

Silvester suggested that they all go down the slope to the water, but Stella shook her head. The sun would slant into her face. If she ended up with more freckles, Mrs. Thyme would be horrified.

"I prefer to stay here," she said, knowing she sounded absurdly prim. "The sun . . ."

"We understand," Silvester said briskly. "Yasmin and I will broach the evil sunlight, won't we, darling?"

"Don't call me 'darling,'" Yasmin said, swatting him. But she allowed him to draw her down to the reedy riverbank. Merry had been chattering to Harold about acquaintances they had in Boston, and they readily set off together.

Which left Giles and Stella alone. Except for a kitten, chewing busily on the ribbon that substituted for a leash.

"I shall remain here, if you permit," the earl said. "Even given my great respect for the dowager duchess, I have low expectations of her 'riparian entertainment.'"

Stella felt a pang of irritation at his courtesy. Giles

would never leave a lady alone. Wouldn't it be better to simply admit it?

Then it occurred to her that he might actually take this opportunity to propose. Perhaps her instincts were wrong. After all, Yasmin had traipsed off with Silvester without a backward glance.

She went rigid with . . . something. Anticipation? Fear?

Emotion curled into a hard knot in her stomach.

She tried to fix on the image of herself walking down the aisle toward Giles, but it slipped away with the conviction that she wished, desperately wished, that a different man would wait for her at the altar.

A man who had no interest in her.

Yet she had to marry. With sudden energy, Stella turned to the earl and gave him a wide smile. "I cannot get more freckles," she confessed.

Giles raised an eyebrow.

"I am covered with them already." She might have drunk too much champagne, but why worry? This afternoon was golden, the kind of experience that the Season is supposed to offer. The kind a schoolgirl imagines when she pictures life as an adult.

"As I said earlier, I like your freckles," he commented. "They're charming."

It wasn't a declaration, but close.

On the other hand, he didn't appear to be on the verge of proposing marriage, not unless a man would do that while obsessively watching Lady Yasmin, who was caught in a ray of late afternoon sunshine, radiant, her hair glossy and soft.

Her face unspotted, Stella thought sourly.

"Here they come!" the dowager bellowed. She

walked over to their tent. "Get up, both of you! You're too young to hide in the shade like Mrs. Thyme. Give that kitten to your aunt, Lady Stella. I shall inspect it after the entertainment." She stumped off down the slope.

Her command pulled Giles's attention from Yasmin, back to Stella.

"I do believe that the sun is low enough that the brim of your bonnet will shade you," he said. "Shall we?" He stood, holding out his elbow.

Stella felt a spurt of defiance. Her aunt wanted her to marry an earl, so she could scarcely refuse his lordship's request. They brought Specs to the other tent, where Mrs. Thyme cheerfully took her in her lap. There wasn't a speck of disapproval in her eyes. It seemed that a possible betrothal did indeed outweigh the menace of new spots.

As Stella and Giles strolled down the bank, a flock of ducks appeared around the bend of the river, quacking noisily.

Giles's chest rumbled with low laughter.

"Are those *hats*?" Stella asked, just as they reached the others.

"The straw hats worn by Italian watermen," the dowager duchess confirmed.

"The hats are tied under their chins," Stella said, astonished.

"Their bills," Silvester corrected, glancing at her. "Beautiful detail with the floating ribbons behind, Mother. If ducks have a nationality, these definitely would quack in Italian."

The dowager nodded, her eyes crinkling. "Your father and I went to Venice back in '97. The watermen push long boats called gondolas. Their hats were trailing ribbons of red, green, and white, celebrating their new flag. Your father . . ." Her voice trailed off. "The watermen sing. I thought the ducks would be a good substitute."

Stella thought that was rather sad, but sweet.

The birds had stopped swimming and were milling about.

"Come over here," the duchess bellowed at them, waving her walking stick in the air.

"I'm afraid that ducks don't speak English," Stella said.

"*I'm* afraid they're hungry," Silvester said.

Sure enough, the birds paused just long enough to munch their hats before they indignantly sailed on down the stream, quacking an unlyrical, outraged chorus.

The following silence was broken by Yasmin's peals of laughter. She was standing on the edge of the river, hanging on to Silvester, risking a short but steep drop-off into shallow water.

Stella had to repress a nasty spasm of envy. Yasmin touched Silvester so easily and vice versa. One of his broad hands was holding her, his fingers curling around her delicate waist.

She didn't have to look down at her waist to know that his fingers wouldn't wrap around her the same way.

"Are you very disappointed by those greedy fowls?" Silvester called to his mother.

"How dare they eat their costumes!" the dowager grumped. "I wanted a hat as a keepsake. Someone fetch a groom to haul me back up the slope to the tent."

Merry was already walking back toward the tents with Harold.

"No, look," Stella called, pointing at the river. One duck was paddling toward them, her hat intact.

"I want that hat. Bread!" the dowager commanded her son.

Silvester nodded and started up the bank.

"You're going to topple," Giles called to Yasmin, sounding exasperated. Without a backward glance at Stella, he strode to the river's edge.

Though the earl didn't touch Yasmin as improperly as had Silvester and, in fact, merely touched her shoulder to direct her to back away from the water, Stella was struck by the idea that there was something even *more* intimate in the way they looked at each other.

She began sorting through her impressions of the afternoon: Lydia's sharp eyes, with that disconcerting sizzle of possessiveness toward her brother. Yasmin blurting out Giles's first name. Harold, enthralled by his laughing gas salon, ignoring Merry's claim that the "very best" people would not sniff gas in public. Silvester, balanced on the riverbank, adoring his golden Cleopatra. Yasmin next to him, smiling kindly.

The expression in Yasmin's eyes when she looked at Giles.

And then Stella.

The thimble, awkward and short. Standing apart from the rest, as if separated by a pane of glass, except for the rare moments when she and Silvester got into an argument. The realization made her feel invisible, like a puff of air that drifts through a room unnoticed.

Suddenly Stella realized that if she married Giles, she would spend her entire life on the wrong side of the window, watching two men in love with one adorable woman.

Of course, she could remove her spectacles. Paint her face every day to conceal her freckles. Put on the kind of stays that hoisted one's breasts into the air paired with a gown that exposed her bosom.

She could chirp and giggle.

But—she didn't want to.

And she highly doubted that the disguise would somehow, miraculously, make her "adorable."

Silvester returned with a piece of toast, which he gave to his mother. As Stella watched, a glaring match between Giles and Silvester resulted in Silvester escorting Yasmin to the tent.

Giles turned to Stella, but she shook her head, wanting nothing to do with either of Yasmin's suitors. "I'll wait for the dowager duchess." When he looked as if he might (reluctantly) remain at the shore, she waved him back up the bank.

Her Grace was tossing crumbs into the river. The solitary remaining duck paddled closer, hat tipped at an outlandish angle because she kept bobbing her neck to pick up the toast.

"Greedy bird," the dowager muttered. She cast a look at Stella. "Are you enjoying your first Season, Lady Stella?"

"No," Stella replied. The duck's legs were lazily paddling in the blue-green water, her eyes fixed on the toast in the dowager's hand. She must have been too hungry to join the rest of the fowl, who had quacked their way down the river, legs pumping vigorously.

"I didn't care for mine, either," Her Grace remarked.

"I don't remember it very well now, thank goodness. All the little humiliations fall away with years."

Stella doubted that, but she held her tongue.

The duck quacked loudly, wanting more bread, and the dowager stepped toward the water. "Come closer, duck!" she commanded. "I need that hat back. I sewed the band on myself."

Given her monocle, Her Grace's vision was as imperfect as Stella's, which meant that she wasn't good at judging distances. "I think you're—"

Too late.

The dowager slipped, but managed to land on her feet, albeit up to her calves in green, muddy water. The duck backed up at the splash, but kept her beady eyes fixed on the remaining bread, dampened but still in hand.

"Hell and damnation!" the dowager exclaimed. "I've lost my monocle!" She kicked up a billow of mud.

Stella came to the edge of the river. "May I help you out, Your Grace?"

The dowager shook her head. "Not yet. I'll have that hat if I have to swim for it." She floated the remaining toast onto the surface of the water. The bird swam toward her, and the dowager quickly snatched the hat, pulling it over the duck's beak.

"Bravo!" Stella couldn't help laughing.

The dowager grinned at her. "The water is a pleasant temperature, but I suppose I must clamber out. Lady Stella, if you would be so kind?"

The veteran of many disasters, Stella prudently kicked off her slippers before she stepped to the riverbank and leaned forward—and then plunged into the river when the dowager tugged harder than she expected.

Cool water splashed her face as she fell to her knees in the mud. Gasping, she slapped a hand over her glasses.

"Bloody hell," the dowager exclaimed, backing up. "I do apologize, Lady Stella."

"I'm quite all right," Stella gasped, managing to scramble to her feet while still holding on to her spectacles.

Her gown was soaked to her hips.

Lady Yasmin regularly dampened her petticoats, which made them cling to her slender thighs. Stella's were not slender. She looked down at herself, fruitlessly plucking drenched fabric from her stout legs.

"We're a pretty pair," the dowager commented. "Wet as hens, and no one to notice our plight. My son is so wrapped up in longing for a woman who doesn't give a bean for him that I could drown out here before he'd notice."

"Oh," Stella said. What could she say? It was true.

"He'll get over it," Silvester's mother said moodily, shooing away the duck, who was edging closer in case more bread was to be had. "But not before she breaks his heart, drat it. Being a mother isn't always fun."

Stella scooped up her skirt and began to wring it out before she realized the idiocy of that gesture. "Will you take my arm, Your Grace? The bank is slippery, but surely we can climb it together."

"I ought to try to find my monocle first, though I mustn't lose the hat." The dowager slapped the duck's hat on her head and serenely tied the soggy white ribbon under her chin, leaving the red and green ones drooping over her shoulder.

Stella burst into laughter.

Smiling, the duchess pointed a dripping hand. "You're one to laugh! I heard about you wearing that wretched Egyptian crown. I tried it on once in private, and I resembled an old eagle. We could have a contest to judge whose millinery is the least attractive."

"I believe you have the advantage," Stella said, giggling. "The duck's hat looks like the cupola on an ill-designed pagoda, if you'll forgive the presumption, Your Grace."

"Likely you looked as pretty as you do now, even in an Egyptian crown," the dowager conceded.

Stella stopped breathing from pure surprise.

No one had ever called her pretty. Ever.

At the top of the slope, under the tents, the butler was circulating, handing out cups of tea. Stella couldn't read anyone's expressions from this distance, but she guessed that not a single one of the dowager's guests cared about her absence. If they even noticed.

Merry would notice if she was gone long enough.

As would Mrs. Thyme, who would be vexed that Stella fell into the water without Giles nearby to play the knight in shining armor.

The dowager was amusing herself by stirring up mud. "Since my slippers are ruined, I kicked them off. I'm trying to see whether I can feel the monocle with my toes. Drat it, I won't be able to see a thing at dinner."

"Why haven't you tried spectacles?" Stella asked. "I assure you that it's better to see through two eyes than one."

"They look daring when you wear them," the dowager said. "I'm afraid that I would just look old. But then, I *am* old, so why not look it?"

"You do not look old," Stella said firmly.

Daring?

She thought of her spectacles—everyone thought of her spectacles—as an impediment. Ugly.

But perhaps she ought to begin thinking of them differently. Perhaps even thinking of herself differently.

Categorizing herself as a loser and Yasmin as a winner didn't do her any good. It may be reality, but it also made her miserable.

I'm pretty even wearing a vulture crown, Stella told herself. A giggle escaped her lips.

"What's funny?" The dowager was still kicking with the energy of a small boy.

"My aunt threatened to faint if I donned the vulture crown again. I believe she consigned it to the attic."

"Well, but your aunt—" The dowager decided not to finish her sentence, much to Stella's relief. "I suggest you stop paying so much attention to fashion. You would look best in a gown with a proper waistline, like what I'm wearing."

The dowager's gown did indeed have a closely fitted waist. It made no concessions to *la mode*: it had no ruffles, no pearl adornments, no bobbles or fringe.

"Just look at the top half of you," the dowager added, nodding.

Stella looked down. After being splashed with water, the starched ruffles around her bodice had collapsed like a sail without wind, exposing cleavage approximate to Yasmin's. Her aunt would die of mortification.

"Not to be vulgar but . . ." Her Grace paused. "Why *shouldn't* we be vulgar? Vulgarity isn't a crime. Your top half is bait for a marital mousetrap, as are your hips."

"I see," Stella managed. So the dowager duchess's sartorial advice included a generous display of bosom. She couldn't stop herself from laughing.

Her Grace looked at her, surprised.

"You and my aunt are diametrically opposed in your attitude toward the male sex. Or at least, toward the Season and courtship." She felt herself turning pink. "As regards what men are looking for."

"Which of us married a duke?" the duchess asked, kicking again. "Your aunt and I debuted together, you know, even though I'm older than she. They called your mother and your aunt the 'two lilies.' Slender, reasonably good-looking, proper. Played by the rules: *all* the rules." She rolled her eyes. "If you'll forgive me, child, oh so proper and boring."

Stella cleared her throat. "Perhaps we should return to the tents."

"I can tell Mrs. Thyme had the dressing of you," the dowager said, ignoring that suggestion. "When you first got out of the carriage, I thought that ruffle made you look like the Biblical Holofernes."

Stella blinked.

"Think of those portraits in which his head was carried about on a platter," the dowager explained.

The laughter that bubbled up from Stella's stomach couldn't be controlled. "I thought of a thimble, with a carp's head on top."

Her Grace splashed over to Stella and held out her elbow. "I see nothing piscine about your head, but I suppose you know your anatomy better than I do. Why a carp? Why not a salmon? They do have a vaguely pinkish tone, after all."

Stella knit her arm into the dowager's. "Salmon

would do as well. I was wearing lip color, which has a fishy taste, and makes my mouth look very wide. Piscine, in fact."

"I applaud your vocabulary," the dowager said as they made their way to the bank. "I'm not sure I can climb it," she observed when they reached the side of the river. "Slippery as hell, isn't it?"

She threw Stella an impish look.

"Hell is reputed to be scorching rather than slimy," Stella pointed out.

"We'll have to wrench my son from his inamorata," Her Grace said blithely. "Back up, dear, and look helpless. I shall force Silvester to enter the river so he can push me up that bank. He's getting altogether too fussy about his clothing, and it will do him good."

"I see," Stella said faintly, swallowing hard at the idea of Silvester picking her up the way he had when she entered his curricle. Holding her, the way he had held Yasmin.

"My butler tells me that my son has ordered boots with tassels, which strikes me as quite ill-bred. Too bad he's not wearing them this afternoon."

The dowager's smile could be described as mischievous, if not downright wicked. "Watch this." She raised her hands to her mouth and hollered, "Help! We've fallen in, and we may drown!"

Stella laughed. "Drowning would be difficult. Everyone knows how shallow the Tyburn runs. I've heard some say they might brick it over and create a sewer."

"It certainly is dirty. I hope the water didn't go into your mouth?"

"Only a few drops."

Silvester began striding down the hill. Even though his face was indistinct to Stella's eyes, there was no mistaking those broad shoulders.

"He could at least run," his mother observed. "At this rate, the tea tray will have to be floated across the water to us."

She waved. "Get up to a gallop, Duke!" she bellowed.

CHAPTER FIFTEEN

As soon as he heard his mother's shout, Silvester wheeled about.

Thankfully, the dowager wasn't in danger. She was standing in green-tinged water just above her knees. Stella was in the water as well.

"Oh, no!" Yasmin cried. She turned to Giles, who was standing far too close to her, in Silvester's opinion. "Both of you, go! You must rescue the ladies immediately."

"Certainly," Giles said, not moving. Obviously, he had come to the same conclusion as Silvester as regards the dowager's peril.

"Your pantaloons will never recover if you enter the river," Harold said with evident horror. "I suggest that you dispatch the grooms."

In the other tent, Mrs. Thyme was on her feet uttering faint screams, a hand over her heart.

"Fetch all the blankets we have in the carriage," Silvester told the grooms, who were staring open-mouthed down at the river. "Harold, would you be so good as to calm Mrs. Thyme? No need for both of us to get wet," he said, turning to Giles. "My mother's entertainments are clearly over for the day. I would be grateful if you would escort Yasmin to her grandfather's house."

He was tired of the day's battle over Yasmin. The hell with it. If Giles wanted to propose, he might as well give him an opportunity.

"I would be honored," Giles said, bowing.

Silvester watched out of the corner of his eye as the two of them walked toward the carriages. They weren't holding hands, but there was something in the way they walked beside each other . . . He could be wrong.

Hopefully he was wrong.

He started down the slope, thinking of Yasmin. Then his eyes landed on Stella, and he froze in midstep.

Her gown clung to her body, and what a body it was. Her arse, to be blunt, was as beautiful as her bosom: round and generous. Her thighs were deliciously plump. A man would never feel as if he were bedding a stork. He could pull her across a bed and drop on top—

Jesus.

What was he thinking?

Behind him, Mrs. Thyme was indulging in a full-blown fit of hysterics. He glanced over his shoulder. Harold was vigorously fanning the lady.

So the prickly girl who had turned into a friend had a luscious body. That didn't change anything.

Stella was still—Stella.

As he walked down the slope, his mother splashed water at Stella, who threw back her head in laughter and splashed her back. Splashed a *duchess*. Another arc of water caught the sunlight before splashing onto his mother's bosom.

"How dare you!" the dowager chortled, flinging handfuls of water at Stella's chest.

Merry ran past him down the slope. "Is it cold?" she called. "I'm miserably hot."

"Reached that time of life, have you?" the dowager called back.

"Not yet," Merry said cheerfully.

Before Silvester realized what was happening, Merry hopped off the riverbank, landing with a splash.

Silvester sat down and began wrenching off his boots.

Hooting with laughter, Merry splashed Stella, after which sprays of water began flashing through the air between the three ladies.

By the time he put his boots to the side, the water fight had calmed.

"Best remove your stockings, dear," his mother called from the water. "The river bottom is muddy."

Merry nodded. "It's soft and gushy. My children will love this. The Thames runs at the bottom of our garden, but the current is too strong for swimming. I shall bring them here." She looked delighted, presumably intending to plunge back in the water accompanied by offspring.

Silvester peeled off his stockings as he listened to his mother inquiring about the American Duchess's children.

"You must come to one of our garden battles," Merry said. "We drape togas over our clothing, and everyone is required to declaim in Latin." She struck a pose, one dripping fist raised in the air like a statue swept away by a flood. *"Non ducor, duco!"*

"I am not led, I lead," Stella translated, rather to Silvester's surprise.

But then, the woman was endlessly surprising. Here

she was, knee-deep in muddy water, calmly chatting with two duchesses. Most drenched ladies would be as hysterical as Mrs. Thyme.

He began struggling out of his coat, silently cursing his valet for the fact that it fit like the proverbial glove.

"How do these battles progress?" Stella inquired.

"With wooden swords," Merry explained. "No strong blows allowed, but two strikes signal a warrior's demise. We have a laurel wreath for the winner, which sadly is inevitably worn by my eldest son, Thomas."

"Is there a reason he oughtn't to win?" the dowager inquired.

"Given that one day he will be Duke of Trent, it's important to remind him that he's a mere human. He invariably comes back from Eton swollen like a bullfrog."

The dowager let out a peal of laughter. "I face the same battle to this day, my dear. Why do you suppose that my son will soon plunge into the river? They grow more bullfroggish as every year passes. A mother's work is never done."

Silvester muttered a curse under his breath and tossed his coat to the side.

"*Palmam qui meruit ferat,*" Stella said to Merry.

"Which means?" his mother asked.

"*Let he who earned the palm, wear it,*" she explained, grinning. "You'll have to earn the palm yourself to take it away from your son, Merry. Perhaps you should take fencing lessons."

"You are both invited, nay, *required* to attend our next battle," Merry said gleefully. "My Latin vocabulary is pretty limited at the moment."

"I think I would like to swing a wooden sword,"

the dowager announced, which didn't surprise Silvester at all.

"I'm going in, and then I'll lift each lady to you," he told the two grooms who had arrived with blankets. Mrs. Thyme's groom looked shocked by the antics of the nobility, but his was bored.

"Perhaps I will take a fencing lesson first, the better to dethrone Thomas," Merry mused.

"You could imitate the dowager duchess. Just bring your son to Green Park and push him into the river," Stella suggested.

Bloodthirsty wench.

His mother and Merry convulsed with laughter, naturally.

Silvester slid down the bank into the water, his toes curling into the mushy riverbed. "Who would like to be first to leave the water?" he asked briskly.

"First in, first out," his mother announced. "I hope you don't strain your back hoisting me into the air, dear."

Silvester splashed toward her. He had the odd sense that his mother had brought about this debacle deliberately, though he had no idea why. But then, he often didn't understand his mother.

Perhaps she had been overheated and wanted to bathe. Or tired of Mrs. Thyme's company.

As Silvester lifted the dowager toward the bank, one of their grooms caught her hands and helped her up. A second groom wrapped her in a blanket. She took his arm and started back up the slope.

"I'm next," Merry said, striding through the water to Silvester's side. "I promised the children I'd be home hours ago."

Once on the bank and wrapped in a blanket, she waved goodbye and set off after the dowager.

"I can climb out if you would steady my arm," Stella said, looking prickly.

The sound of her laughter seemed to hang over the river. Plus, her horrendous ruff had wilted, revealing perfectly shaped breasts that turned dusky pink when she caught his gaze.

"I've already lifted you in the air once," Silvester reminded her, wrenching his gaze away from her bosom.

Damn it.

That dress was clinging to the soft curve of her hips. With just a long step, he could wrap his arms—

He stopped himself with an internal shock. What in the bloody hell was he doing? He never thought about ladies in such improper terms.

"I didn't like your gown at first," he heard himself say. "That ruff . . ."

She curved her lips into something of a smile. "May I have your assistance up the bank, Your Grace?"

Silvester frowned. "I didn't mean it that way. And we're on a first name basis, remember?"

"Of course," Stella said, ploughing through the water until she was just below the spot where a groom waited with yet another blanket. "Perhaps you could help me?" she asked, looking up at the fellow.

Irritation shot through Silvester. No groom was going to touch Stella, not when she was wet like . . . like this.

"No," he said sharply.

She looked at him, green-blue eyes framed by river water, and he lost his breath for a moment.

Obviously, it was due to the shock of sending Yasmin off with Giles.

"I only meant to say that your dress looks better without the ruff," he said briskly. "Now, if you'll turn toward the bank, I'll hoist you up."

It wasn't until he saw the pink in her cheeks turn red that he realized "hoist" wasn't a flattering word. But Stella turned without a word. His eyes fell to her plush, indecent arse, fabric clinging to every curve.

No wonder women wore layers of clothing. They had so much beauty to hide.

When his hands touched Stella's waist, he felt a little shudder go through her body. In a flash, he realized that she would be an equal partner in bed. Her husband, whoever he would be, would be the luckiest man in the Goddamn world, because Lady Stella's body was . . . And she was that too.

All that.

In a swift jerk, he tightened his hands just above the flare of her hips. The dizzying shock of touching her went straight to his loins but he managed to raise her into the air.

Mrs. Thyme's footman caught Stella's hands and wrapped her in a blanket. She started up the slope without looking back.

Silvester stayed in a whirl of muddy water, waiting for his cock to subside. Hell, waiting for it to stop throbbing as if he was about to lose control.

"What are you doing?" his mother shouted from the tents. "My monocle is lost. You'll never find it."

Silvester reached up, caught the side of the bank, and pressed up in one smooth, furious movement. He was losing his mind.

Yasmin—

He meant to ask her to marry him. His mind was made up. He'd informed his mother and taken a diamond ring from the ducal safe.

Obviously, the way Yasmin looked at Giles—which unfortunately bore no resemblance to the way she looked at Silvester—had given him an internal shock so strong that he almost lost his sense of decency.

If Yasmin wasn't betrothed to Giles on the morrow, perhaps he should pop the question and get it over with. Find out whether he won or lost.

When Silvester entered his mother's tent, boots in hand, his mother was still mummy-like in a blanket, although the duck's hat she wore was an unlikely accoutrement for a mummy. Stella was wrapped in a green cloak, holding Specs.

Mrs. Thyme was reclining on the sofa, a white handkerchief clutched in her hand. The lady glanced up, then down at his bare feet, and let out a horrified yelp.

"Really, Duke," his mother said in a distinctly mocking tone. "You ought not to affront the sensibilities of ladies by displaying bare toes. Male toes are too large and virile. They might excite any woman in the vicinity to unseemly thoughts."

Stella made a choked sound that suggested she had suppressed a laugh.

Mrs. Thyme threw the dowager a bitter look. "*Most* ladies are delicate and tender by nature, and I certainly include my niece amongst those who deserve respectful restraint. God forbid she should be labeled 'indelicate.'"

Silvester sat down and pulled stockings over his

damp feet. His valet would not appreciate the mud, but he could always threaten to jump in the river wearing boots the next time. Tasseled boots.

"In fact, I feared a scandal would come of this . . . this river incident," Mrs. Thyme said in a quavering voice. "One that might destroy Lady Stella's reputation, but dear Mr. Rowson explained that it was merely wholesome play."

Stella's aunt was clearly hoping that Giles would come to his senses as regards Yasmin, but obviously she would be happy to pair her niece with an American adventurer. Never mind that Harold was moving to France with an idiotic notion of setting up a salon for sniffing illicit substances.

Stella deserved a man with a sense of humor and a good brain, not a man who wanted her dowry. Well, her dowry and her French accent.

"Duchesses will be duchesses," Silvester's mother said briskly. "No one bothers to be scandalized over my antics, Mrs. Thyme. Mostly because I don't care. You should try it. It's a far more wholesome way to live than plaguing yourself about the opinions of a set of acidulated dowagers."

Silvester stamped into his second boot, giving silent points to his mother for crushing use of vocabulary.

Mrs. Thyme closed her eyes, as pained as if she'd been offered a candied grasshopper. Cutting in before the ladies could engage in more charming banter, Silvester beckoned Mrs. Thyme's footman, who stepped forward and assisted the lady to her feet.

"Thank you very much for this lovely picnic," Stella said, bobbing up and down in an awkward version of a curtsy since one hand kept her cloak closed in front and the other held a cat.

Specs, startled by the dip, meowed loudly.

"Thank you, dear," the duchess said. "This was one of the most diverting afternoons I've had in ages."

"I agree," Stella replied, looking confused and pleased. "Your riparian adventures were truly entertaining."

His mother squawked with laughter. "*Riparian*, indeed! I woke up this morning feeling ancient and missing my husband. You made me happy by not treating me like an old stick. You and the American Duchess."

As Stella said goodbye, Silvester couldn't see her breasts, hidden as they were behind that cloak—but it didn't mean he had forgotten how luscious they were.

In fact, maybe *he* should grab a blanket and wrap it around his waist. Even without looking down, he knew that his front was veering far closer to immodesty than were his bare toes.

"Do you forgive me for whatever idiotic thing I said this time?" he asked her, noting that Stella nodded, without the beaming smile she gave his mother.

"Certainly," she replied. She was fibbing, devil take her.

"I shall escort you to the carriage," Silvester stated.

"I hardly need to be escorted across a meadow."

"Specs does." He took the kitten and popped her on his shoulder before he offered Stella his arm. They set out after Mrs. Thyme, who was already clambering into the carriage.

At least someone liked him: Specs nudged his cheek with her nose and then wrapped her tail around his neck.

"What did I do this time?" Silvester asked as soon as they were out of earshot of his mother.

Stella glanced at him from under her lashes. "Nothing."

He stopped short, dropping his arm and catching her hand in his. "Stella. I won't let you go until you tell me."

"Oh, very well," she said crossly. "If you must know, you said, quite rightly, that you'd have to *hoist* me up on the bank."

He stared at her.

The silence was broken only by the twittering of birds. She didn't meet his eyes. Her hair had fallen from its topknot and rippled down her back.

That lower lip? She wasn't even pouting. That lush lip was all hers.

He cleared his throat. "Has anyone ever told you that you're extraordinarily quick to take offense? Where no offense was meant—and indeed, no sane person would think that an insult was possible?"

"You said you'd 'hoist' me," she repeated, shooting him a cross glance.

"My mother had just asked me to 'hoist' her up on the shore." A grin broke over his face. "You don't like that word, but you're hoist by your own petard, because I was merely quoting my mother."

She wrinkled her nose.

"Actually, I think that 'petard' might be a word that shouldn't be uttered in front of a lady," he added.

She was pink now because he irritated her, not because she was feeling hurt. "No, 'petard' refers to a bomb. The quote is from *Hamlet*."

"As if Shakespeare wasn't the master of bawdy

expressions. I gather you didn't like the implication that I would need a team of oxen to lift you out of the river, the way they hoist marble blocks into the air?"

Stella narrowed her eyes at him. "I suggest you stop while you're ahead."

He took a step closer, so close that he could see the way her skin was dusted with cinnamon sugar. "I already lifted you into my curricle," he pointed out. "You're being an idiot."

Her cheeks reddened even more. "What would you know about it?"

"About what?"

"About being . . . being *me* when the other ladies are willow-twiggy?"

"Do you remember when you informed me that I was a fool to believe I could mock people in public without my insult being repeated far and wide?"

"Yes."

"You're being just as much of a fool." His voice had taken on a throaty edge. Stella's fault, because she was so damned desirable up close. "Your curves are perfection. Willow-twiggy may be good for hanging a gown on but not necessarily for—"

He broke off and stepped back abruptly. "You'll have to take my word for it. Word of a duke."

"As if a title ensured rectitude," Stella muttered.

But she didn't sound hurt. Silvester held out his elbow, and they walked across the field toward the carriage without another word. Her groom had placed a box before the open door, but Silvester stepped forward and wrapped his hands around her waist.

"Duke!" she hissed.

He had a point to make. He lifted her and held her

in the air for a moment before he put her into the carriage.

"*You!*" she said crossly, twitching out of his hands and turning around. "I'll take Specs, if you please."

The kitten had anchored herself to his jacket during their walk, so it took a moment to work free her claws. "Was that 'you' a question?" Silvester asked, schooling his voice to innocence. "Or perhaps it was simple recognition that I was right? Am almost always right, in fact."

Stella took Specs from his hands and shook her head. "Neither."

He glanced over her shoulder into the carriage, but Mrs. Thyme was paying no attention; she was staring intently into a small mirror and powdering her nose. "Your claim of an insult hangs on the specious belief that your curves are not desirable," he said in a low voice.

She leaned forward and whispered, "Actually, I win this round."

"The evidence is lacking."

"The *evidence* is that you are courting Yasmin, as are most of the other bachelors in London." Her grin was triumphant as she backed inside and sat down. "Goodbye, Your Grace," she caroled as the groom shut the door.

Silvester watched the carriage leave, thinking not about Yasmin's slender form, but about Stella's expression. She didn't give a bean that he was courting Yasmin. There wasn't a trace of jealousy in her eyes.

Which was good, of course.

Because he planned to marry Yasmin, unless she had betrothed herself to Giles on the way home.

After he and his mother had climbed into the ducal town coach, he said, "I gather a 'set of acidulated dowagers' is your summary of polite society, Mother? *Acidulated?*"

"I should demand the tuition that we paid back from Eton," she said. "'Acidulated' means vinegary. Acid. Court bouillon is acidulated by adding lemon juice." She looked him over, head to foot. "As is the court and all its noblewomen. I take it that Lady Yasmin's yearning looks at the earl have acidulated you."

Silvester frowned at her.

"They aren't yet betrothed," his mother continued. "You might still win her hand from your childhood friend, if that's how you care to define success."

"This isn't a contest," he said sharply.

"Isn't it?"

After that they sat in silence, but for the drops of water falling from their clothing and rolling across the floor.

CHAPTER SIXTEEN

All the way home, Mrs. Thyme held forth on the offensive character traits of the Dowager Duchess of Huntington, while Stella sat quietly, trying to stop herself from thinking about Silvester's thighs outlined by drenched silk.

Not to mention . . .

That bulge couldn't have been what she was thinking it was.

It didn't seem possible.

Not to mention . . . *petard*? There could be only one interpretation of why he thought that phrase was indelicate. If it referred to anatomy.

Male anatomy.

"I do not blame you for falling into the water," her aunt concluded. "No one can blame you, no more than I blame you for winning that disastrous Egyptian crown."

Stella managed a smile, because her aunt was trying to be kind. She clearly did blame Stella for entering the river, as well as donning the crown.

"We'll avoid the dowager in the future," Mrs. Thyme announced. "Thank goodness no one important attended the picnic, other than the earl, of course. I'm sure that other chaperones turned down the invitation, realizing that the duke was hopelessly infatuated with Lady Yasmin."

A little silence fell in the carriage.

"I don't suppose you noticed . . ." Mrs. Thyme began, but didn't finish her sentence.

"I noticed," Stella said tiredly. "The Earl of Lilford is also in love with Lady Yasmin. I believe the feeling is mutual, though, of course, the Duke of Huntington would rather it were otherwise."

"She'll make a precious countess, unless she chooses to be a duchess," Mrs. Thyme muttered. "Thank goodness *she* didn't fall in the water, because her gown would have melted like spun sugar."

Stella nodded.

Presumably, she ought to be devastated by the prospect of losing the Earl of Lilford, her only suitor of high rank, but in truth, she didn't care. If he asked, she would marry Giles, and in time presumably come to care for him.

But gaining Lydia as a sister-in-law?

It was almost a good enough reason to refuse his proposal.

Oddly enough, though Mrs. Thyme was certain that Yasmin's betrothal would appear in the morning paper, no such announcement was made, in writing or through gossip.

Nor the day after, nor the rest of the week.

In fact, Lady Yasmin stopped dancing with the Earl of Lilford altogether. For the entire Season, he had always claimed her first waltz, a dance that everyone watched with keen interest.

Now he didn't even glance her direction on entering a ballroom.

"She turned him down," Mrs. Thyme concluded. "Of course, a duke *is* higher rank than an earl. She wants to be a duchess."

Lydia was triumphant and told Stella repeatedly that her brother would *never* cavort with such a scandalous woman, let alone marry one.

Stella wasn't so certain.

Yet the facts seemed evident: Yasmin and Giles now ignored each other, and Giles danced with Stella, if anyone. He didn't offer to escort Stella to any events, but Mrs. Thyme concluded that was due to the earl's punctilious care for his little sister. Even now that Lydia was engaged to Lord Pettigrew, her brother continued to act as her chaperone, as when he accompanied Lydia to the country to visit Lord Pettigrew's parents.

By the end of April, Stella was in the habit of dancing twice with Giles every evening, and often going into supper with him. Her other suitors still flocked around her, especially as the news of her enlarged dowry spread, but they wooed without conviction.

Only Harold refused to accept that a fortune hunter could never win a lady's hand when an earl was in the offing. It was simple mathematics to Mrs. Thyme. Just as Yasmin chose a duke over an earl, Stella would never consider an American over an earl.

Silvester danced with Stella too—always a waltz, and often two. She was happiest in those moments, whirling around the ballroom in his arms, with no worries about falling down or losing her balance. He held her so tightly that their thighs brushed together, his arm circling her, his big, warm body only inches from her own.

They talked straight through each waltz, about everything from Specs to the currency markets. Sometimes he stayed at her side through the following dance, the better to continue a conversation.

Unless, of course, the next dance was promised to Yasmin. In that case, Silvester kissed her hand and was gone.

He even paid her morning calls, claiming that he loved to listen to Specs sing. Yet not even Mrs. Thyme at her most optimistic suggested that the duke was courting Stella.

"Lady Yasmin has him on a leash," Mrs. Thyme said darkly. "I can't imagine why they haven't announced their betrothal. She glances across the ballroom, and he leaps to her side. It's not manly."

"But you've always said that gentlemen—"

"Not *that* way," Mrs. Thyme said. "Not the way he looks at her. Husbands shouldn't look at their wives that way. It's almost indecent."

"Desirous?" Stella hazarded, confused.

"Affectionate," Mrs. Thyme stated. "More than affectionate. It's like seeing a husband and wife dance together." She shuddered. "It just isn't done."

Thankfully, day after day of Stella reminding herself that Silvester was merely a friend—albeit, perhaps her closest friend—began working.

She stopped blushing when they met. She couldn't stop her body from delighting in the feeling of being surrounded by him during a waltz, by his wintery soap, by the way he laughed. But she applied herself to rejecting the idea that he was desirable.

Let alone the most desirable man of all.

Luckily, Specs was always there to distract her during

moments in which Stella felt battered by jealousy of Yasmin. Specs was growing into a lithe, beautiful cat, who loved to play as well as sing.

"I don't know what we ever did without her," Stella's aunt said one morning. She was reposing on a settee in the morning room, a damp cloth on her forehead, suffering from a headache. Rain was splattering against the windows, so Mrs. Thyme had announced they would spend the day indoors.

Stella was tossing a crinkled ball of silver paper across the room so that Specs could scamper after it. Sometimes the kitten even brought it back to her, though most of the time Stella had to retrieve it.

The butler opened the door. "Madame, the Duke of Huntington has sent in his card. Are you at home? I would remind you that I shall be unable to serve tea, as I am escorting James to the dentist."

James was their footman. Being terrified of the dentist, he had waited until his cheek was swollen, a look that Mrs. Thyme found so grotesque that she had ordered the butler to make certain that the offending tooth was pulled.

"I suppose so. I wouldn't normally be at home to any of your suitors, Stella, not when I can scarcely raise my head, but His Grace doesn't count."

The butler bowed and took himself away.

"You may bring out the chessboard, if you wish. The game isn't precisely ladylike, but the duke obviously considers himself the older brother you never had."

Silvester strolled into the morning room while Stella was still trying to figure out if he did indeed think of her as his sister. It was a wretched thought.

He was courting Yasmin, so her aunt was probably

right. Stella had lively battles with Silvester, and they liked to play games, both of which were said to happen in nurseries. As an only child, she had to rely on hearsay.

This morning Silvester was head-to-foot a nobleman. His short coat was graced with a double row of silver buttons and barely touched his breeches, flaunting a waist that appeared to be as muscled as his thighs. His cravat fell in immaculate pleats; his buttonholes were embroidered with silver thread; his boots shone like mirrors.

Combine that with rumpled curls, gray eyes, and the smile playing around his mouth as he met her gaze?

No wonder she couldn't get him out of her head. She was a human being, after all. Even Specs raced across the room to roll on her back at his feet, demanding affection.

Stella deliberately slowed down, strolling to the door and then dipping into a curtsy. "Good morning, Your Grace."

As the butler pulled the doors closed, Silvester scooped up Specs and popped her onto her favorite place on his shoulder. The little cat rubbed her head against his cheek and purred.

Stella was dismally aware that she would purr in the same way if given the chance.

"I recognize that gown from our riparian adventures," Silvester said, grinning. "I'm amazed your maid managed to starch those ruffles up to your ears again."

"I only wear it when we are not home to callers," she confessed, striving for a careless little-sister tone.

"I am honored to be allowed through the door."

"You are privileged for my entertainment. My aunt is irritated if I read in her presence, but she declares me too fidgety without a book," Stella said, giving him a lopsided smile. "She has not been at home to any of my suitors today, as she has a headache, but you have slipped by her guard as the brother I never had."

He laughed. "Brother?"

"Bow to me, you lummox," Stella said, not sure what to make of his tone. "My aunt is watching, and even brothers must observe the proprieties."

Silvester put a hand on Specs, fell back a step, and swept into a deep bow.

"*I* feel honored," she remarked, looking at him from head to foot. "Why all this sartorial splendor so early in the day?"

"I'm escorting Yasmin to a charitable luncheon for orphaned rabbits," Silvester replied, looking markedly unenthusiastic.

Stella laughed. "Orphaned girls, not rabbits. We had meant to attend, but the rain and my aunt's headache will keep us at home."

"Lucky you," Silvester grumbled. "I am counting on beating you in a game or two of chess to put me in a properly charitable frame of mind."

"Nonsense," Stella said, grinning at him. "You can't bear the fact that I had such a triumphant victory on Saturday. It's been bothering you ever since, or you would be sitting in Yasmin's drawing room, not ours."

"Yasmin is not a lady who welcomes an early caller," Silvester said. "She takes her *toilette* very seriously."

"I gather she wouldn't wear a gown that made her head resemble Holofernes's on a platter, even at home?" Stella asked, beginning to walk back toward her aunt's settee.

Silvester raised an eyebrow. "Your ruffles may be unflattering, but I wouldn't consider the gown worthy of Biblical, not to mention murderous, associations."

"Your mother suggested Holofernes," Stella told him.

"Ah. Well, I disagree. After all, Holofernes's head is generally depicted with a morose expression—naturally so, given his demise—and your quite lovely smile disqualifies you. What's more, I have fond memories of that gown doused in water."

Stella barely took that in before they arrived at Mrs. Thyme's side. Her aunt raised her head and peered out from under the damp cloth draped over the upper part of her face. "Your Grace, you must forgive me, as my wretched head prevents me from rising to greet you. My hair is so dowdy that I'm embarrassed to let you see me."

"You are exquisite as ever, even while suffering," Silvester said, one hand cupping Specs again while he dropped into a bow.

"I trust your fraternal kindness," she said. "I certainly couldn't trust any of Stella's suitors."

Silvester cleared his throat. "Of course."

"Do play chess on the other side of the room," she begged. "The two of you laugh so much. It makes my head ache."

"Are we never to laugh, or should we restrain ourselves only when your aunt is poorly?" Silvester inquired as they walked to the other side of the room to set out the chessboard.

"She finds laughter saucy at best, and vulgar at worst," Stella clarified.

Silvester groaned. "At what age were you orphaned?"

"I was eight years old." Stella flipped open the games table.

"*Now* I am in a properly subdued frame of mind for luncheon, ready to express my pity for female orphans with a shower of sovereigns."

His tone was sardonic, but the quick glance he gave her settled warmly into her stomach.

"I am lucky to have had relatives," Stella said, feeling a stab of disloyalty. "Mrs. Thyme cares for me."

"Obviously. What a pity that she doesn't like evidence of your happiness. Or trust you around your suitors."

"She does trust me," Stella protested. "Here we are on the opposite side of the room, where she cannot hear our conversation. You could be saying provocative things." She felt herself turning pink. "Not that you would, because you don't feel that way, but—you know what I mean."

"It's because she trusts *me*," Silvester said, matter-of-factly. "She knows I'm courting Yasmin, so I am neutered."

Stella frowned.

"Castrated," he amended.

Her mouth fell open.

"Since you read the first four volumes of the encyclopedia," he said helpfully. "Unless that was an exaggeration? Did you avoid reading definitions that your aunt would term unladylike? Which begs the question how a lady can possibly be offended unless she already knows the offensive reference?"

Stella couldn't stop herself from gurgling with

laughter. "I've often wondered the same thing! My aunt reproves me for not blushing when indelicate topics are introduced—but how can I blush unless I know they are indelicate? And if I do know the referent, why would I blush?"

"The same reason that your aunt is offended by the sight of male feet even though presumably she has seen your uncle's toes any number of times," the duke pointed out. He cast her a wicked look. "It's the product of intrinsic female delicacy. Of course, there's a chance that you simply don't have that attribute."

Stella was pretty sure he was right, but she was absolutely certain that her aunt would have an attack of vapors if she heard this conversation, so she changed the subject.

"You may play White," she said, beginning to set out the chessmen. "You might want to put Specs on the ground, as she will never be able to resist the chance to leap to the table and scatter the pieces."

Silvester sighed. "It goes against my grain to accept White and make the first move, but I need every possible advantage in order to win." He put down Specs, who promptly ran out of the drawing room.

An hour later, Stella was fighting off a brutal attack by Silvester's queen when a scream erupted from somewhere upstairs.

Across the room, Mrs. Thyme started awake. "Shall I have no rest?" She sat bolt upright, her face draining of color. "An intruder knew that we were left alone in the house, and he has gained access!"

"I'm sure it's nothing so horrifying," Stella called, coming to her feet and running across the room to pat her aunt's hand.

Another scream echoed down the stairs.

"The butler is out," Mrs. Thyme gasped. "You mustn't go upstairs, Stella. Stay here with me! Lock the door!"

"It's far more likely to be a mouse," Stella said reassuringly. "That is Lily screaming. She has a particular dislike of rodents."

"There are no mice in my house," Mrs. Thyme said, but without much conviction.

"With your permission, I shall accompany your niece upstairs," Silvester said.

A flurry of emotion crossed Mrs. Thyme's face as she weighed the possibility of a lustful intruder against that of a lustful duke. Stella practically saw her aunt conclude that the Duke of Huntington, who was in love with an exquisite Frenchwoman, had no interest in seducing her awkward, short niece.

"I trust you to remain in the hallway, Duke," Mrs. Thyme conceded. "I expect it is some foolishness." As another scream rang out, she collapsed back against the pillows. "Stella, your maid could show a modicum of concern for my frail state. People judge me able to surmount every challenge that life throws at me, but that is not the case."

Stella dropped a kiss on her beleaguered aunt's cheek and ventured up the stairs followed by Silvester. When a fourth scream emerged from her bedchamber, Stella pushed open the door and peered in. As she had guessed, no nefarious intruder had entered the window.

Silvester bumped into her from behind. "Forgive me," he said, steadying himself by curling his hands around her waist.

Lily was sobbing gustily on the far side of the room.

"What is the matter, Lily?" Stella asked.

Silvester had apparently forgotten that he was holding her.

How could he forget? Their bodies were as close as in a waltz. She could feel the warmth of his large body just behind her. She couldn't help wishing that she'd donned a longer corset, one that nipped in her waist.

"A gift for you, I presume?" he said in her ear.

"What?" Stella asked, twisting to look at him.

When their eyes met, his hands dropped as if scalded.

"You needn't be so fearful," she said, scowling at him. "I have no wish to compromise you."

"As you have told me repeatedly," Silvester said. Still, he fell back a step.

Stella poked him in the chest. "Don't be an idiot."

"Strong words!"

"You might as well have 'Property of Yasmin' etched on your forehead." She turned around and walked into the room. "Lily, what—"

Her question broke off as she saw what had upset her maid.

Arranged in the center of her favorite lacy pillowcase was a fat, brown mouse. A very dead mouse, given its broken neck. Specs was seated upright next to the corpse, tail curled around her body, looking highly satisfied with herself.

Stella groaned. "Not on my pillow, Specs!"

"A gift of food," Silvester commented, staying where he was, in the doorframe. "How kind."

Stella walked over and handed her maid a handkerchief. "Lily, will you please fetch a groom from the mews to remove the mouse? I would be most grateful if you didn't tell my aunt what happened."

Lily nodded shakily and ran from the room, blotting her tears.

"You are remarkably tranquil," Silvester said. "One would be able to hear my sisters screaming five streets away."

"Alas, this is not Specs's first victim," Stella said. "When possible, I rescue the mice alive. She prefers cheese, so generally I can lure her away."

"A sign of good taste," Silvester remarked.

Stella bent down until she was on an eye level with Specs. "You mustn't bring me mice," she ordered. "Definitely do not leave them on my pillow. You are a bad kitty."

Specs hopped off the bed and strolled out of the room, tail high in the air.

"You've offended her," Silvester observed. "My mother wore the same expression when I refused to wear the absurd top hat she gave me for Christmas."

"Offense would imply that Specs has learned English between now and last night, when I scolded her for deliberately pushing a teacup off the bedside table," Stella said, straightening up. "She likes to see things smash."

Silvester was still leaning in the doorway, an odd expression on his face.

"You look somewhat discomfited," Stella observed. "Did the dead mouse turn your stomach?" She gave him a teasing smile. "A blow to your manly reputation, if people knew."

His eyes rested on her thoughtfully. "I can trust you not to spread that information, since you haven't yet informed all of London that you consider me to be manipulating the currency markets for my own benefit."

"Not *entirely* for your own benefit," she corrected him. "I suppose the new currency law did strengthen England's finances."

"You could say that. You could also say that I saved the country from defaulting on its debts."

Silvester walked into the room, coming to a halt directly in front of Stella, so close that he could wrap an arm around her waist and slide into a waltz.

Not that they could waltz in her bedchamber.

"If I look discomfited, it's because we are alone for the first time. I suspect your aunt has informed you that unmarried ladies and gentlemen should never be unaccompanied," he said, adding, "especially in a bedchamber."

CHAPTER SEVENTEEN

Stella blinked up at him, her entire body going still. "Of course, she has. My aunt is convinced that male scruples are overcome by the mere glimpse of sheets, all evidence to the contrary."

He raised an eyebrow. "You don't agree? I expect your aunt would not accept a dead mouse as chaperone."

Stella smiled wryly and told him the truth. Why not? He was her friend, practically her only friend. And he was in love with Yasmin.

"In my opinion, male lust is wildly overrated."

She expected him to laugh.

He didn't.

She frowned, because suddenly his eyes were searching hers, asking a question that no one *ever* asked her.

A roughened finger touched her cheek, and Stella's disobedient body flared into life. *Desire* flared to life with his touch, even as she frantically tried to command it away.

Silvester couldn't be . . .

The finger moved down her cheek to her mouth. "Do you have any idea how beautiful your lower lip is, Stella?"

She shook her head, mute. Rain was no longer

splattering on the windows; it was falling in sheets. Other than that, the house was silent.

Her heart was beating so fast that she felt dizzy. She felt as if her senses had woken from a long sleep. The expression in Silvester's eyes didn't make sense. None of it made sense, except for a feeling of rightness as his head lowered, slowly, his eyes fixed on hers, asking silently if she wished to push him away.

"Don't be absurd," she said aloud.

He paused. One eyebrow went up. "Absurdity wasn't what I had in mind."

Unless Stella was very mistaken, she was about to experience her first kiss.

But she couldn't point that out. Or say "yes, please," which would be manifestly unladylike. She simply looked at him mutely, letting the familiar wintery scent of his soap send a wave of warmth down her limbs.

Their lips brushed together.

Was she supposed to press forward? She had closed her eyes because that's what people did when they were kissing. At least, what they did in etchings of amorous shepherds kissing shepherdesses, which were the only kisses she'd seen.

Their lips touched again. It was quite nice. Not earthshaking. Lackluster, if she was truthful.

She really shouldn't feel surprised to discover that kissing wasn't as enthralling as described. Nothing was, not chocolate torte nor the quadrille.

They were standing so close together that his snowy smell seemed to surround her. Perhaps it was soap. Perhaps she should—

Without warning Silvester's tongue slipped into

Stella's mouth, and his hands settled onto her shoulder blades, firmly drawing her closer. Just like that, a shimmer of desire turned into a forest fire.

She gasped, and Silvester made a sound in the back of his throat. A rough, needy sound that surprised Stella into opening her eyes.

His eyes weren't scanning the ballroom to find Yasmin: they were looking directly into hers, so closely that she saw that the light gray darkened to a black line around his irises. His lashes lined his eyes as vividly as Specs's coloring did.

One of his large hands slid from her shoulder to the back of her neck. He kissed her again, with a wild abandon that made heat unfurl in her stomach and spread throughout her body. Her heart was thumping as if she had run a race and her thighs instinctively tightened.

She recognized the warmth she felt from when she used to lie in bed imagining the moment when the Duke of Huntington would turn to her on the dance floor and declare his love. And other things.

That was before she knew him, before they were friends.

Longing roared down Stella's backbone as the taste and smell of him drenched her senses. He tasted faintly of coffee as their tongues slid past each other in a ravishing intimacy that she'd never imagined. His hand on the back of her head pulled her mouth even closer, as a deep growl came from his throat. The sound stripped her raw inside, made her burn for more.

Their mouths clung together, and she didn't think of anything other than the pressure of his lips, the domineering stroke of his tongue, the rough sound he made in the back of his throat when she nipped his lower lip.

On the verge of pulling him closer, Stella's common sense suddenly revived.

The mouse.

The groom, presumably arriving any moment to take away the mouse.

Worse: her aunt's warnings.

Silvester was kissing her because they were alone in her bedchamber. Not because he really wanted her. He as much as admitted it when he pointed out they were alone for the first time.

She pulled away and backed to the edge of her bed, bringing one hand to her swollen lips. "Stop," she blurted out.

Silvester was looking down at her with an unreadable expression. She felt a spurt of resentment. After all, his adoration for Yasmin was nightly written on his face, so plainly that every person in polite society had registered it. But he looked at her, Stella, with all the emotion of a bishop surveying a parishioner.

"My aunt was right," Stella exclaimed, stunned.

"If you are referring to my supposedly fraternal feelings toward you, I beg to differ."

"Mrs. Thyme has told me time and again that, given an opportunity, a man will take advantage, no matter how unattractive the woman in his company." Stella still couldn't quite believe it. "I thought she was wrong. There had been no evidence—"

She broke off.

"Until I provided you with that evidence," Silvester said, clearing his throat. "I beg your apology, Stella."

"You were overcome by the lack of a chaperone? The bed?" She shook her head. "Even given the proximity of a dead mouse? It must be so uncomfortable."

"What?"

"The ravening wish to leap on any woman whom you find yourself with."

"'Ravening'? No, don't give me a definition. I can guess. I assure you that I do not feel a wish to leap on any woman with whom I am closeted."

"Since you claim to have successfully avoided being closeted with marriageable ladies, your evidence is hardly persuasive."

He moved quickly, almost a jerk. "I didn't—"

"Moreover, you are courting Lady Yasmin. No: you are in love with Yasmin. People are merely waiting until the two of you announce your betrothal. Is that a fair assessment?" Her tone was sharp, but she owed herself that.

Silvester hesitated.

Stella narrowed her eyes at him.

He nodded.

"I like your mother. But I can't imagine where you get your moral sense from," Stella said flatly. "You are virtually promised to Yasmin and should not be kissing another woman."

His jaw clenched. "I agree."

"As for evidence regarding unbridled male lust, have you ever found yourself in a bedchamber with Lady Yasmin?"

His eyes darkened to an icy gray. She already knew that His Grace didn't like being served any sort of corrective. "Certainly not."

"Which suggests I am the only marriageable

lady you have encountered in a bedchamber," Stella pointed out. "As I said, your evidence agrees with my aunt's assessment of male restraint: to wit, they don't have much."

He broke into a bark of laughter. "You claim that I always want to win, but you are no better, Stella." He reached out and tugged one of the curls hanging by her ear. "That kiss was not merely a matter of propinquity."

She frowned.

"I know big words too," he told her, one side of his mouth tugging up.

It struck her again: the smiles he gave her were so different from the beaming smiles with which he charmed the ton. Polite society saw him dazzle, whereas she got these wry twitches. Half a mouth. One eyebrow.

"I know what 'propinquity' means," she told him. "Closeness to a bed or in this case, a mouse."

"It doesn't mean *this*. Whatever it is." Silvester pulled her into his arms with no questioning preface. One hand curved around her head, under her hair. This kiss was deeper and longer than the last, their tongues stroking against each other in a way that made Stella's common sense evaporate like a soap bubble in the sun. The kiss was desperate, urgent, accompanied by Silvester's rumbling growl and her gasp.

Stella came back to herself to find she was trembling against him, the imprint of his hand between her shoulder blades prickling with sensation. Her arms were wound around his neck, and she couldn't even hear the rain over the sound of her heart pounding in her ears. A hungry ache had sunk into her bones.

"*Damn* it!" she cried, pulling away again and drawing in an unsteady gulp of air. "It wasn't just my aunt. I was also right!" She was shocked to hear a hoarse note in her voice.

"You were correct when you decided that male lust was wildly overestimated?" This smile, the one in Silvester's eyes, was a far cry from that with which he entertained polite society. It was hungry, animalistic, and his voice was hard. "I can assure you, Stella, that male lust is alive and well."

"Obviously. No, not that."

He raised an eyebrow.

She'd been honest with him so far, so she might as well continue. "I deduced that women's desire is as dangerous as men's, if not more so. The proof of which being that you and I are kissing in . . . with—"

"With no more chaperonage than a rodent," Silvester said. "So you kissed me merely because of propinquity and a bed?"

"You are the only man who's ever tried to kiss me," Stella said. She certainly was not going to confess to how she felt about him.

Not that she understood her own feelings.

His eyes had warmed; now they cooled again, glittering at her from under lowered lids. "I would not advise that you bring another man into your bedchamber to test your self-restraint."

Stella was staring at him, thinking hard. "I owe my aunt several apologies. Not that I argued with her, but inside my head, I concluded that . . . that . . ."

"That Mrs. Thyme's warnings were foolish?" Silvester retreated to the door of the bedchamber. "Or that she was incorrect about male desire? She is foolish at times, but not mistaken when it comes to her niece's desirability."

Stella rolled her eyes.

"I have never been attracted to a portrait of Holofernes," Silvester said thoughtfully. "But *you*, Stella? You?"

"Me?" she squeaked.

"You might want to avoid bending over a bed if you don't wish to drive a man into a frenzy."

"Oh." She locked that away to think about later: not just what he said, but the raspy note in his voice when he said it.

More importantly, kissing him was wrong. Yasmin was a lovely person, and while Silvester's ethical sense seemed to be rather flexible, hers was not. At least, she hoped it wasn't.

"Be that as it may, Silvester, you are betrothed to Yasmin." If his voice had been raspy, hers was firm.

"No, I am not."

"In the eyes of the world, you are. If I might remind you, she is waiting for you to escort her to the charity luncheon."

He was silent.

"I'm not implying that our kiss requires you to marry me instead of Yasmin," she added hastily.

"For God's sake, don't tell me again how disinterested you are in me."

Stella scowled right back at him. "If you kissed me merely in order to win that particular argument, I'll kick you. Hard."

She thought his bark of laughter surprised both of them.

"Lady Stella, may I enter?"

Stella looked past Silvester's shoulder and nodded to the groom. Thank goodness Silvester had backed away far enough to register as being in the hallway. "If you would be so kind as to remove the new mouse, Walter."

Walter was holding a rag, quite likely the same rag he used after last night's offering appeared on the fireplace hearth. "If you'll pardon me, my lady, my mistress is quite upset and would like to speak to you."

"Did Lily—"

"She told the housekeeper, who informed Mrs. Thyme."

"I'll allow you to make my goodbyes," Silvester said. "I wouldn't want to intrude at such a distressing moment."

Stella eyed him and then turned to the groom. "Give me that mouse, Walter."

He had just picked it up by its tail. "My lady?"

"I need to throw it at someone."

Silvester escaped down the staircase, his laughter not mocking.

It wasn't brotherly either.

Deserving of a mouse catapult, Stella decided.

Downstairs, she found her aunt sipping a restorative glass of sherry, a handkerchief drenched in so much violet-scented *eau de toilette* that the drawing room reeked.

"Don't come near me until you have bathed," her aunt ordered. "I can smell that dead rodent all the way down the stairs." She pointed to a chair at a good distance. "I assume that the duke has departed?"

"Oh, yes, he left when it was clear there was no

intruder," Stella said. "He will escort Lady Yasmin to the charity luncheon for orphans."

"Of course." Her aunt took another sniff of her handkerchief. "His Grace is such a comfort. If I had a son of my own, I would hope he was just as genial and trustworthy. There's not a soul in polite society who dislikes him, you know."

"Yes, I do realize that," Stella said.

That was because none of them knew who he really was.

"Just look how kind he is to you, a motherless girl who hasn't had an easy time in your first Season. Not that you aren't on the verge of making an excellent match. Your mother and father would be very happy with the Earl of Lilford."

Stella nodded.

"Do you know," her aunt continued, "I would not be surprised to discover that His Grace visits so often because the earl asked him to keep an eye on you. Make sure you aren't falling for the wiles of a fortune hunter who merely wants your dowry."

Stella bit her lip before she blurted out that her aunt and uncle had deliberately created that situation by doubling her dowry.

Mrs. Thyme dropped her handkerchief. "Oh, Stella, what are we going to do?" she wailed. "The house is overrun by mice. Overrun! The housekeeper tells me that flour is no sooner brought into the house than holes are chewed in the sacks."

"Luckily, we have Specs," Stella pointed out.

"She caught one. She can hardly catch five, or ten, or one hundred!" Mrs. Thyme's voice rose.

"Yes, she can," Stella said. "She has caught three this week alone."

Mrs. Thyme turned a pale shade of green. "I wish you hadn't told me that."

"If you would allow her into the kitchens, she will catch them all," Stella said. "I believe Specs would quite like to earn her keep."

"Do you really think so?" Mrs. Thyme sat up. "I've been sitting here, thinking the most dreadful thoughts. How can I ever be at home to callers, Stella? What if a mouse ran across a lady's foot?"

"A night spent in the kitchen would be a treat for Specs."

"I will order the chef to make her chicken and giblets every day," Mrs. Thyme said. "With gravy!"

CHAPTER EIGHTEEN

Specs caught seventeen mice.

Stella waltzed with Silvester six times, Giles seven times, and Harold Rowson eleven times. Harold buzzed around her every night, still trying to persuade her that her voice would make his salon the toast of all Paris.

Mrs. Thyme ruthlessly encouraged him. "Perhaps the Earl of Lilford needs competition to bring him to the point," she said one evening. "I cannot understand why he's so slow to propose."

One night, Merry pulled her into the ladies' retiring room at a *musicale* and demanded if she was secretly betrothed to Giles.

"No," Stella said. "I don't think I shall be, Merry. The Earl of Lilford may appear to be courting me, but he doesn't care if I dance with other men."

Merry knit her brow. "Isn't that a good thing? I would find it most uncomfortable if my husband glowered at me as I hopped my way through a quadrille."

"I meant it metaphorically. If we married, I don't think that the earl would care if I found my way to other men's beds," Stella said flatly. "I mean, of course, after I provided him with an heir."

"I'm sure you're mistaken."

"Have you seen the way he looks at Yasmin?" Stella asked.

"Desirously? Everyone looks that way at Yasmin. Except my husband, thank goodness," Merry added with a twinkle.

"No," Stella said, shaking her head. "He looks at Yasmin the way your husband looks at you."

Dismay flashed through Merry's eyes. "Oh, dear."

"Remember that I told you gentlemen are looking for someone to adore? Giles has found that person. He is in love."

"He can't be. He's taking you into supper regularly," Merry said indignantly. "Also, everyone says Yasmin refused his hand. They don't even speak to each other."

Stella shrugged. "He's never shown the faintest propensity to kiss me. I believe I could lure him into my bedchamber, and he wouldn't be tempted to an indiscretion. In fact, he would be offended. He doesn't want me, Merry."

"Then he's a fool, and he shan't have you!"

"Life isn't that simple. Do you think it's better to marry a man in love with another woman or a fortune hunter?"

"Neither," Merry said promptly. "Did I ever tell you that I was betrothed numerous times? All fortune hunters, and in fact, one of them sued me for breach of promise."

Stella gaped at her. "Truly?"

"My uncle had to pay him to go away," Merry said, wrinkling her nose. "My point is that I can take you to America, darling."

"I've already found my own crowd of fortune hunters, along with one American," Stella pointed out.

"Boston is full of handsome, unmarried men, and not all of them are fortune hunters."

"Yes, but Giles is an earl," Stella said. "If he does propose, how can I possibly say no, Merry?"

"Yasmin apparently did! You could simply say: 'No, you big lummox, I will not marry a man who cherishes another woman.'"

"Easier said than done," Stella said gloomily. "My aunt would have an apoplexy."

The following night, Mrs. Thyme and Stella had no sooner entered the door of Almack's when Lydia ran to their side and said breathlessly, "You'll never believe what happened! Lady Yasmin is *gone*!"

"Gone?" Mrs. Thyme echoed.

"Left for the country with her grandfather," Lydia said, proceeding to loudly announce that one of Lady Yasmin's former lovers had appeared at a gathering hosted by the Regent. When the man approached her, Lady Yasmin blurted out the truth: Apparently, when she was a mere girl, the knave had pretended to marry her, but the elopement had been a sham, an effort to extort money from her parents.

"After that, my brother knocked him out," Lydia concluded. "Of course, any gentleman would have responded in that fashion."

Stella couldn't help thinking that should one of her former lovers appear—not that she had any—the Earl of Lilford would not avenge her with a blow to the chin.

Not even if they were married.

"The Duke of Huntington has reportedly accompanied her to the country," Lydia added, waggling her eyebrows. "I gather the reputation of his future duchess is irrelevant to him."

Wherever Stella looked, she saw clusters of people, eyes alight, chattering avidly. Despite her better interests, she began defending Yasmin. "She was a very young girl," she pointed out again and again. "Shouldn't her parents or her chaperone have been blamed for allowing such a blackguard to make her acquaintance?"

To Stella's satisfaction, Mrs. Thyme took on the battle as well. The fact Yasmin was seduced at such a young age lent itself to a cascade of scathing comments about men and their unbridled lust.

The next day, her aunt devoured the gossip columns at breakfast, fascinated by the downfall of Lady Yasmin. Stella just felt sad. At the beginning of the Season, she'd admired Silvester and Yasmin for their lavish beauty and seeming goodwill, their giddy pleasure in the ballroom and each other.

They didn't have feet of clay, as she had originally thought of Silvester, but they were real people, with real faults.

If she could hardly resist Silvester's kisses, how could Yasmin have resisted a man whom she adored, who had pretended to marry her? Frankly, Stella thought the earl should have run the Frenchman through with a rapier.

In the next days, Lydia talked feverishly of scandalous country house parties where supposedly Yasmin had hidden herself, shoring up her dislike of Yasmin as if it were a living thing that could change her brother's feelings.

Because Giles was in love with Yasmin: Stella was certain of it, and she thought Lydia knew as well.

The Earl of Lilford's cheekbones had always been pronounced, but he was beginning to look gaunt. Once he began to tell her something about Yasmin. But he stopped himself and offered her sugared almonds instead.

He wasn't the only gentleman languishing in Yasmin's absence. She had swept through London, collecting suitors as if she were playing pickup sticks. Without her, they ambled about ballrooms, flirting listlessly with less favored ladies. Blanche collected more proposals; even Stella had a few, though her uncle promptly rejected them.

The promise of a title—Countess of Lilford—hung over the family's every thought and action.

Stella couldn't imagine why Yasmin had bothered to charm anyone other than Silvester. Courting Giles was exhausting. It wasn't reading the papers and taking notes, or wearing prudish gowns to please a prudish earl (and a prudish aunt, for that matter).

It wasn't even finding herself all too often in company with his sister, Lydia, whom she frankly loathed.

It was the weariness of submitting to a process that gave gentlemen all the power over marriage. If Giles wasn't in the room, her aunt or Lydia were planning their next encounter, next dance, next supper.

Yet even when they *were* together, he was only partially in the room.

His gaze would drift away in the middle of a sentence. Something was wrong. It reminded Stella of a cloud of smoke that signaled a house was burning down a few streets away.

Frustrated by her brother's lax courtship, Lydia set up an evening at the Theatre Royal, ensuring Giles would have ample opportunity to drop to his knee and offer a ring.

"After all, what *is* he waiting for?" she demanded.

Stella shrugged.

Silvester's absence from London *hurt*. Even more so, since he was snuggled in a country house with Yasmin. She couldn't bring herself to care much about Giles.

The earl would propose or not.

It was entirely in his hands, which she loathed. The pretense of dropping to his knees was meaningless when the offer came from a nobleman. No lady could turn down the Earl of Lilford.

Except possibly Yasmin.

The theater visit didn't take place until the end of June. Stella and Giles sat in the front of the Lilford box, Lydia and her fiancé beside them. Lydia dragged Lord Pettigrew out of the box during intermission, leaving Stella alone with her brother.

No ring was offered.

The only passion Giles exhibited was when he went into a tirade about the Royal Mail service, which was apparently failing to deliver mail in a timely fashion. Perhaps misplacing or losing mail altogether.

He didn't even smile in Act V when the heroine was miraculously rescued from a marauding bear by the hero.

The newspapers took Stella's appearance in the Lilford box as verification of a secret betrothal. Stella took it as further evidence that the earl had no interest in marrying her.

Harold invited her to a Beethoven concert, although Mrs. Thyme refused on her behalf.

"Beethoven is out of the question. His music is rousing to the blood." Later, she informed Stella that even though Harold showed every sign of being able to control his baser instincts, one never could tell.

Stella thought she *could* tell.

The gleam in Harold's eye told her that her figure was more than acceptable to him. Giles evinced no such gleam. He didn't even show much sign of liking her. Giles saw her as a partner in his legislative endeavors.

"Don't bother with Harold Rowson," Mrs. Thyme said confidently. "You will be a countess, my dear. Your mother would be so happy."

Yet Stella was coming to understand that *she* wouldn't be happy, especially once Silvester and Yasmin returned to London. She missed Silvester with a piercing sadness that made her contemplate marrying Harold simply because he lived in a foreign country. The idea of seeing Silvester happily married was dreadful.

The day before Lydia's wedding, the gossip column in *The Morning Post* announced that Yasmin and Silvester were betrothed.

"I don't know why that took so long," Mrs. Thyme muttered at breakfast, after reading aloud the notice.

Stella's stomach clenched into a knot, and for a moment she thought she might lose the toast she'd just eaten.

Of course they were betrothed.

"They will have beautiful children," her aunt commented.

Numbly, Stella reminded herself that she *knew* he was courting Yasmin. Silvester had told her himself. Her . . . affection for him was absurd.

Even thinking of the way Silvester's kisses had engulfed her in burning heat made a humiliated sob press on the back of her throat. Along with a piercing sense of loneliness.

"Are you all right, dear?" Mrs. Thyme asked, peering across the table.

Not for the first time, Stella thought that her aunt could use the same spectacles she wore. "I'm absolutely fine," she said. "I'm happy for the Duke of Huntington, because although I know you don't approve of Lady Yasmin, I have seen genuine affection between them."

"For a moment, I thought . . . But he has never been more than friendly to you, has he?"

"Certainly not!" If anyone ever knew that a short, befreckled woman had been so infatuated by a beautiful duke that she let him kiss her, Stella would die of shame.

Let him kiss her? If she were honest, she might have let him ruin her.

Thank goodness for a dead mouse on the bed. Specs had saved her virtue.

"I can't wait until Lady Lydia's wedding tomorrow," Mrs. Thyme said complacently, not noticing Stella's strangled silence. "Obviously, the Earl of Lilford has been waiting to propose until his sister walks the aisle. He truly is the best of all brothers. By tomorrow afternoon, all London will know that you are a future countess!" she crowed.

The air burned in Stella's lungs. She could get

through it. She'd survived her parents' funeral, after all. An abrupt move to a new house, with an aunt and uncle whose disappointment in their lack of offspring only deepened after she joined them.

She had been alone for a long time, and if she found herself alone in her marriage, it would just be more of the same. Hopefully Giles wouldn't be so undignified as to stare longingly at Yasmin once they were both married to other people.

Stella was drifting around Lydia's wedding breakfast, trying to avoid ladies curious about her supposed secret betrothal to their host, when her aunt rushed up and clutched her upper arm. "Come."

Her heart sank, thinking that Giles was waiting in another room, a ring in hand.

Stella allowed herself to be borne away as unlucky sailors are borne away by a rogue wave: with profound helplessness and a roaring in her ears. Her aunt led her out of the drawing room and to the library.

Giles wasn't there.

Mrs. Thyme pulled Stella across the room and pushed open a door that turned out to lead to a small alley running beside the townhouse.

"Are we leaving the wedding breakfast?" Stella asked. Her aunt would never sneak out a side entrance as if ashamed of her own shadow. And yet here she was, silently marching down the alley, pulling Stella toward their waiting carriage.

The jagged, broken feeling in her chest eased. This didn't feel like the prelude to a proposal.

"Are you all right, Aunt?" Stella asked, once they were seated.

Mrs. Thyme let out a sob, hand on her heart. "Oh,

'tis the most evil, the most pernicious!" Her voice rose to a peak and broke off.

The carriage lurched into motion.

"I don't understand," Stella said. Relief was making her fingertips tingle.

"The earl is leaving for the country to find *her*," Mrs. Thyme cried. "To marry Lady Yasmin! After courting you until all of London thinks you're affianced!"

Stella's eyes widened. "Did he tell you that himself?"

"How can you be so calm!" Her aunt dashed away a tear. "You poor naïve child, you have no idea how people will pity and sneer at you. If only Mr. Thyme had accompanied us, he would have slapped the earl with his glove. The insult is such that someone ought to fight a duel for your honor!"

Stella tried to imagine her mild-mannered uncle—who far preferred growing prizewinning gourds to any activity society might offer—advancing on the earl, bloodcurdling rage in his eyes.

Impossible.

Men may avenge insults to Yasmin's honor, but not to hers.

"The earl sat beside you in the family box!" her aunt hissed. "How dare he invite you to the theater, only to make you the cynosure of all eyes?"

"Actually, Lydia invited me," Stella murmured.

Joy was washing through her, though she knew better than to express it to her aunt. Marriage to Giles would have been dreadful. The stodgy earl would have only grown more so. She, who had never been good enough to please her mother, or her aunt, or her uncle, for that matter (she had almost no memories of her father), would have never been good enough for her husband either.

Her mother had treasured the idea of a daughter with clear skin. Her aunt still treasured the idea of a daughter who was lithe and graceful, with perfect vision. Although to be fair, her mother and aunt both desperately hoped to spare her the contempt of people like Lydia.

But Giles? Giles treasured the idea of Yasmin, just as Silvester did.

"Oh, Stella!" her aunt wailed. She opened her reticule and pulled out a handkerchief as tears began to roll off her chin. "Your mother would be so disappointed in me. Are you crushed?"

"No," Stella said apologetically. "I'm afraid that I'm not very sentimental, Aunt. I'm not in love with the earl."

"*Love!* Who cares about love? Do you think I was in love with your uncle when I married him? You had the chance to be a noblewoman, to regain the status that I lost when I married Mr. Thyme." She dashed away more tears. "I failed you *and* my sister."

Stella moved to sit beside her aunt. "You did not fail me. The earl is in love with Lady Yasmin. I have a feeling that he doesn't respect the emotion any more than you do, but clearly he couldn't suppress it."

"Disrespectful sneaksby!"

"Actually, the earl was always very respectful," Stella ventured. "He never indicated by word or deed that he intended to marry me."

"No, he was not respectful," Mrs. Thyme said vehemently. "He used you as a ploy to distract society from his enduring infatuation with Lady Yasmin. I wouldn't even have known the truth if I hadn't over-heard him instructing his butler to make sure his carriage was brought around as soon as his guests were gone. I waited until he returned to the reception, and then I insisted the butler tell me where he was going."

"The butler told you?"

"After I gave him a sovereign," her aunt admitted. "He had heard it from the earl's valet. Valets always know everything."

"It would have been kinder had Giles informed me," Stella agreed. "But he never implied that he might wed me."

"That wicked varmint!" her aunt said, sniffing. "A true gentleman would never have paid you such marked attention. Now you will be known for being rejected by an earl. They'll say that he couldn't bring himself to the point because of your spectacles!"

Stella winced. "No normal woman can be expected to compete with Lady Yasmin."

"*She!* It's the fault of that wicked, evil woman!" Her aunt's voice spiraled even higher. "Must she have every man? She's caught them in her coils, all of them, as if she could marry more than one nobleman. Nay, she wants *two*!"

"Actually, I believe that Lady Yasmin will accept the earl's hand," Stella said. "She loves him, Aunt. I saw it at the picnic."

"But the paper said yesterday that she was betrothed to the Duke of Huntington. It was there in black and white."

Stella shook her head. "If the report was factual, she'll break her engagement when the earl offers to marry her."

Mrs. Thyme pleated and unpleated her handkerchief. "Should we go to Paris? Or retire to the country? Stay at home and refuse all calls?"

Embarrassment ignited in Stella's stomach at the idea of meeting Lydia's mocking gaze—but she'd be *damned* if she would run away. And thankfully, Lydia had left on her wedding trip.

"We will proceed exactly as we meant to before this occurred," Stella said. "We will not betray in the slightest that we were not the earl's confidantes. After all, the newspapers assumed that he and I would marry: we certainly didn't inform anyone otherwise."

Mrs. Thyme choked. "I might have . . ."

"We must act as if his actions are irrelevant."

"But—"

"Because they *don't* matter," Stella continued. "I don't like the Earl of Lilford much, to be honest. He's grumpy. There's something cold and impenetrable about his manner. It would have been like marrying a block of ice."

"That wouldn't matter if you were a countess," her aunt said.

"Yes, it would, because I'd have to live with him," Stella pointed out. "For the rest of our lives. Be *intimate* with him. I know you dislike frank conversation, Aunt, but you have to admit that's a challenging thought."

"He's quite good-looking," Mrs. Thyme said. But her tone was uncertain. Then she sighed. "We cannot rejoin society until people learn of the earl's flight to the country, and that will take a day or two. I can't do it. It's too humiliating. Just imagine how people will stare when his lordship doesn't appear at the Haverford ball tomorrow night to escort you to the supper dance."

Stella gave her a reassuring smile. "Perhaps we could visit the theater tomorrow instead? If we arrive on time and appear cheerful, people will notice that we are quite unperturbed."

"I suppose I could bear that," her aunt conceded.

"The Duchess of Trent's Ancient Roman Fête is coming up. The gathering will be small, and yet everything the American Duchess does is reported in the papers. Our attendance will demonstrate that I am not heartbrokenly cowering under the covers."

"I'd forgotten about that," her aunt said fretfully. "I'm not sure . . . she is *so* eccentric. What if she lures you into the river? The Trent townhouse runs by the Thames."

"The party has nothing to do with the riverbank. It's a garden battle with her children, in togas."

"Yes, but why?"

Stella gave her aunt another squeeze and moved back to sit opposite her. "What do you mean?"

"Why so eccentric? Why ducks with hats and children in togas? Why can't we simply have tea and play croquet if one insists on exerting oneself?"

"People are tired of croquet?" Stella ventured.

"You do know what the connection is, don't you?" Mrs. Thyme asked. "They're both duchesses. The American Duchess and the Dowager Duchess of Huntington. I suppose the dowager duchess will attend as well, giving me withering glances and saying things that I don't understand." More tears rolled down her cheeks.

"I shall say something very rude to Her Grace if I see her give you a withering glance," Stella said, leaning forward and patting her aunt's knee. "I shan't allow it."

"You can't. You are not a duchess. My mother could do and say anything because she was at the very pinnacle of society," Mrs. Thyme said, sobbing again.

"I don't need to be at the pinnacle of society to reprimand Her Grace if she makes my beloved aunt feel small," Stella said firmly. "And so I shall."

Her aunt shook her head. "You don't understand the way the world works, Stella. The fact you were playing in the river with those duchesses? I was terrified that someone would report it. *Their* reputations wouldn't suffer—the dowager was right about that—but *you* would have been labeled a shameless hussy. Your gown was wet in the presence of two gentlemen!"

"I promise to avoid the river," Stella said, suddenly remembering the way Silvester's hungry gaze had focused on her hips in that wet gown. And then, a few days later, he kissed her.

Clearly, he was able to feel two different emotions— lust and love—for different women at the same time. Realistically, men felt lust for many women.

But not love.

PART TWO

PART TWO

CHAPTER NINETEEN

Five days later
THE DUKE OF HUNTINGTON'S TOWNHOUSE

Silvester's carriage drew up before his London townhouse at midnight, when the city of London had fallen into a restless dusk lit by boys whose torches flickered on cobblestones slick with rain.

Wickford answered the knocker, heavy-eyed, with an unmistakable air of having quickly pulled on his livery. "Good evening, Your Grace," he said, bowing. "The dowager duchess has retired to her bedchamber."

"Of course. I am sorry to have disturbed your rest, Wickford."

"May I take your greatcoat?" The butler looked at the door. "Does your valet follow in another coach?"

"He should be along in a few days," Silvester said.

Wickford's eyelashes flickered. "Shall I assign a footman to attend you? Or I could hire a temporary valet in the morning."

"Neither," Silvester said, shrugging off his sopping greatcoat. "I shall get along by myself for a time, Wickford. If the boot-boy could polish my footwear, that'll be enough."

The butler gaped at him, but Silvester cut him off before Wickford could mention his valet's reliance on champagne to keep his boots in a shining state of beauty. "I'm off to bed. I'd like a bath in the morning."

"Will you join Her Grace for breakfast?"

"Yes," Silvester said, handing over his coat and gloves. Presumably the news of Yasmin's upcoming marriage to Giles had reached London, which meant his mother would plague him with a cascade of knowing comments. He might as well get it over with.

He was wrong. The dowager was subdued at the morning meal, peering at him over a cup of tea with an expression he'd rarely seen on her face. He would interpret it as affection or even love, but he'd been raised to consider that a puling emotion fit only for peasants.

"I'm not in a fit of black despair, you know," he said, after she offered him honey for the second time.

"I should certainly hope not," his mother replied, looking nauseated. "We do not engage in tempests of emotion in this family. However, I do acknowledge that you were struck down by Cupid's arrow. Struck through the heart. Or somewhere."

"What are your plans for the day?" Silvester asked, disregarding his mother's foray into bawdry. He had no interest in discussing his emotional state.

"The Duchess of Trent's Ancient Roman Fête," his mother said, brightening. "Finally, I am not the only person in London offering original entertainments. Guests have been instructed to wear a toga and bring a wooden sword."

"*You* plan to wear a toga?" Silvester asked, somewhat fascinated at the thought. His mother must have supplemented her hair with a cork pad, as a dark tower loomed over her forehead. Her crimson velvet gown fit snugly to the waist in a style that hadn't been worn since the Elizabethan era. "Over your gown?"

"Of course. My toga was made by Quimby's Costume Emporium deliberately to accompany this gown. My sword was purchased in the Pantheon from a children's toy store." His mother smiled with a glee that he remembered from his childhood, but which had dimmed in the years since his father died.

"I was on the riverbank during your conversation with the duchess and Lady Stella about this event. Speaking will be limited to exclamations in Latin, as I recall."

"Since I don't know any Latin, I nagged the vicar until he finally came up with *Oderint, dum metuant.*"

"Let them hate, so long as they fear?"

"Exactly," his mother said with satisfaction. "It sums up my relationship with polite society, don't you think? They all hate me, but luckily, they're afraid of me. Or least, wary of my title. That phrase was uttered by an emperor named Caligula, whom the vicar labeled a ramshackle fellow. But, I gather, a frightening one."

"I shall accompany you," Silvester stated.

She eyed him.

He accepted more hot tea from Wickford, who was listening intently.

"I don't have a sword for you. Or a toga."

Silvester glanced at the butler. "Send a footman to the toy store in the Pantheon for a wooden sword."

"Send another to Quimby's for a toga," the dowager added. "Likely they have a spare one. They outfit all the best theaters, you know. They have fascinating gowns on display. This gown was originally made for someone playing Queen Elizabeth, until the performance was canceled in favor of a modern piece. I insisted they remake it for me and then create a toga that would drape over the skirts."

Silvester nodded.

"Don't look at me like that," his mother said crossly. "Mrs. Quimby understands how tiresome fashion rules can be. Wickford, you'd best dispatch those footmen immediately. It can take an hour to cross the city these days."

After the door closed behind the butler, she said, "I am startled by your sudden urge to frequent a society event, since I haven't seen you in over a month."

"As you know, I accompanied Lady Yasmin and her grandfather to the country."

Silence followed.

Finally, his mother couldn't stop herself. "Then what happened?"

"I did not join them when they decided to visit the Addisons a few weeks ago. I traveled to our country estate instead."

"What on earth were you doing there?"

Silvester put down his fork. "I reviewed the renovation of the dower house, Mother. As you know, I intend to marry."

"You mean, you *intended* to marry. You are the most frustrating man! Do you know that your betrothal to Lady Yasmin was announced in *The Morning Post*, no less? I was quite vexed to think that you informed the papers before you sent word to your own family."

Silvester went back to eating his eggs. "The report was inaccurate. Should I become engaged,

I shall certainly inform you. As you surely know, Lady Yasmin has chosen to marry the Earl of Lilford instead."

His mother was frozen on the other side of the table, her bread and butter unheeded. "She is not the right woman for you," she offered.

"The question is moot. I shall find a different woman to marry."

"In my opinion, Lady Yasmin has made a terrible error."

He raised an eyebrow.

"You do not strut around the Parliament the way the Earl of Lilford does, but you are equally, if not more, powerful," his mother said, taking up a roll and spreading butter on it, although she hadn't finished her first roll. "You have presence, and you are a duke. *Any* woman should rejoice if you pay her the slightest attention. You mustn't feel cast down by Lady Yasmin's mistake."

"I am not."

"Some fool tried to tell me a story about her being seduced as a young girl," his mother said. "That sort of deplorable event can muddle a woman's mind, which is probably why she chose the earl over you. She will come to regret it."

"I hope not," Silvester said, rather startled by his mother's growl.

She pointed a butter knife at him. "Lilford will never leap into the river to save her from drowning, will he?"

"If you're referring to the Tyburn, you were in no danger of drowning."

"That's not the point. Lady Yasmin was a fool to

choose that block of wood instead of you. Now she's gone and broken your heart. Why did she let you escort her everywhere, if she wanted him?"

Silvester had a shrewd feeling that Yasmin and Giles had decided to marry at least a month ago. "I didn't mind taking her about. I like Yasmin. A great deal."

"She *used* you," his mother snapped. "I told Lady Stella that Yasmin would break your heart, and now she has. What if you never marry and have no children, and the line ends? I shall murder her. In such a manner that no one guesses the truth, naturally."

Silvester bit back a smile at his mother's fiery expression. "I appreciate your support, but let me say again: my heart is not broken." In fact, it had been disconcerting to realize just how much he didn't care about losing that competition.

The dowager put down her roll and patted his hand. "You know that I have never experienced such tempests of emotion. Love is not for me. But I know you felt it, and I honor you for it."

Silvester opened his mouth, but his mother held up her hand. "Even though it is manifestly ungentlemanly. Your father would be aghast."

As Silvester remembered it, his father had been utterly infatuated with his brilliant, creative wife. When the duke passed away, the dowager sank into gloom so deep that they all feared she would never recover. If that wasn't love, what was?

"You mustn't let it ruin your life," his mother said. "Just remember that you'll need a son at some point."

"You needn't worry about an heir," Silvester said.

His mother nodded and said encouragingly, "There

will be a new crop of ladies next Season. You'll find someone much better than Lady Yasmin."

Silvester murmured something. He wasn't particularly worried.

He had an ace up his sleeve.

CHAPTER TWENTY

An Ancient Roman Fête
THE DUKE AND DUCHESS OF TRENT'S TOWNHOUSE

𝒯he Duchess of Trent greeted Stella and her aunt in the entry of the ducal townhouse, hands outstretched. "Mrs. Thyme, this is such a pleasure. And Stella, darling!" she cried. "I adore your toga. Why *should* they be white, after all?"

"I cannot claim credit," Stella said, kissing her cheek. "You sent me to Quimby's Costume Emporium, and Mrs. Quimby herself suggested green."

"'Green' is not a sufficient descriptor," Merry said. "That toga is the color of ferns in spring and sets off your hair so beautifully! I only wish that I'd invited some eligible gentlemen."

"I am very glad to hear you have not," Mrs. Thyme said. "I cannot like the fact that my niece's arms are entirely uncovered. Moreover, Roman ladies may have worn their hair falling down their back, but I consider it highly unkempt."

"May I offer you a toga, Mrs. Thyme?" Merry asked. "Until I learned of the Costume Emporium, we always used large kitchen cloths. My maid is an expert at pinning them so they drape elegantly."

With a near visible effort, Stella's aunt didn't shudder. "No, thank you. Am I to understand that no gentlemen have been invited?"

"Only my children, Thomas and Peter, who at ages of fourteen and eight are not yet men. My husband may join us if he returns in time, but he's at the House of Lords, and you know how crowded the streets are these days."

"In that case, might I leave my niece under your care?" Mrs. Thyme asked. "If you are *certain* that gentlemen won't join you."

"I invited only the Dowager Duchess of Huntington," Merry said.

That did it. Stella's aunt fell into a flurry of apologies that could be summarized as: *I will never willingly put myself in proximity to the dowager again.*

"Of course, you must pay a call to Mrs. Swan," Merry said warmly. "I shall send Stella home in our carriage, accompanied by a lady's maid."

"If Mrs. Swan is not at home, I may return for Stella, but if not, that would be very kind of you. Stella, do keep your bonnet on at all times. And don't forget to wear your gloves as well. You don't want spots on your hands," Mrs. Thyme said. Then she trotted out to her carriage, so eager was she to avoid an accidental meeting with the dowager.

Merry escorted Stella through the house into rear gardens that stretched down to the Thames River. High stone walls enclosed a generous lawn dotted with old oak trees. Beds of flowers and herbs lined the walls, and the scent of lavender and peppermint floated to them on the breeze.

A large table with a pale yellow tablecloth was set in the shadow of the house; two footmen were setting out pitchers of lemonade and two ice buckets containing champagne bottles.

At the bottom of the garden, next to the Thames, a whitewashed gazebo was planted with riotous clumps of purple and blue flowers. A cluster of children's heads could just be seen through the lacy struts of the gazebo.

"The family likes to play baseball," Merry said, pointing to some bare patches on the lawn. "I believe you call it 'rounders' over here. Basically, you try to strike a ball before you run in a circle. I'm quite good at pitching balls, if I say so myself."

If Silvester's lawn screamed prestige and money, this one was far more comfortable, a place to play.

"You have a lovely garden," Stella said, feeling wistful. She had never been allowed outside as a child, and she had never even tossed a ball. Mrs. Thyme would consider that extraordinarily unladylike.

"You must visit us in the country," Merry said. "I fancy myself a gardener. I even have a pineapple stove, though more recently it has been in use to hatch ducklings. Peter, my eight-year-old, plans to care for animals when he grows up, so we regularly gather eggs from around the estate, and he raises the fowl to adulthood."

"That reminds me," Stella said. "I hope you don't mind that I am accompanied by Specs."

Merry clapped her hands. "Of course I don't! I hoped you would bring your kitten. Is she in your pocket?"

"She has grown too large for my pocket, so I turned my sewing box into a traveling home." She took the strap of Specs's box from her shoulder. "I'm so glad to see your walls, because she will be happy to run about."

"I had a good two feet of stone added to the walls when the boys began to climb, so Specs will not escape. Children!" Merry hollered, cupping her hands around her mouth. "Come meet Lady Stella's kitten!"

Stella pulled off her bonnet and gloves and tossed them on the table before she crouched down and opened Specs's box. This wasn't a world where freckles mattered, any more than a velvety green lawn.

Three children shot across the lawn, togas billowing behind them as they ran.

Merry held out her hand, palm forward, as they skidded to a halt. "Greetings first."

Stella rose to her feet with Specs in her arms, smiling at the children's exclamations.

"Lady Stella, may I introduce Thomas, Peter, and Fanny?" Merry asked. Thomas, the future seventh Duke of Trent, bowed with confident grace, Peter plunged forward from the waist and sprang back up, and Fanny, who seemed to be around eleven or twelve, bobbed a curtsy.

"It is a pleasure to meet you," Stella said, curtsying in her turn. "May I introduce you to Specs?"

"She's *adorable*," Fanny breathed. "I've never seen a white cat with black stripes."

"May I hold her?" Peter asked. "I never imagined a pet cat. Does she scratch you? The cats in our stables are wild and don't like us very much."

"That's because you used to pull their tails,"

Fanny said. She was cooing at Specs and stroking her ears.

"Specs is very friendly," Stella explained, "perhaps because I found her when she was a kitten. She's half-grown now."

"Please, may I hold her?" Peter asked again.

"Of course," Stella said, handing Specs over. The cat promptly climbed up to his shoulder and wrapped her tail around his neck.

Peter's face lit with pure joy.

"Perhaps you would care for her this afternoon?" Stella asked. "Someone must make certain that she doesn't get trampled during the battle."

"She'll be safe in the gazebo," Peter said. "George is there. I don't like battles, so I'm going to read. Specs can come with me." He pulled a book from under his toga and showed it to Stella.

"*A Narrative of an Expedition to Explore the River Zaire,*" she read aloud.

"They saw any number of interesting animals," Peter reported. "But they were rather foolish. They had three baby lions, but after they fed them soaked bread, the cubs died. You don't give Specs bread, do you?"

"No. Specs is fond of giblets," Stella said.

Peter nodded. "Mice have giblets inside them."

"No, they don't," Fanny retorted. "Giblets come from birds."

"We need to begin the battle," Thomas cried. He was hopping from foot to foot, slashing his sword in the air.

"Specs will like George," Peter said, heading across the lawn, a careful hand steadying the kitten.

"Who is George?" Stella asked.

"Our ancient bulldog," Merry said. "George is like the biblical Noah, living three hundred and fifty years after the flood. Peter doesn't stray too far away from him these days."

"I like your toga," Fanny said to Stella. "I wish I had a colored toga, Mama."

"*I* should like to win the laurel wreath that your mother told me about," Stella said, smiling at Fanny and Thomas. "What are the rules?"

"I should be very happy to explain them, Lady Stella. The gazebo at the base of the garden is the *domus*. I don't suppose you—"

"The family home," Stella said.

"Darling, Stella likely knows more Latin than all of us put together," Merry told her oldest.

"No one can attack in the *domus*," Fanny put in.

"The battlefield is open territory," Thomas said, waving at the lawn. "Two blows from a sword means you're dead. No one can attack without shouting an epitaph in Latin."

"The most important rule is that although warfare involves violence, no one is allowed to hit very hard," his mother added.

"Right," Stella said. "Since I am unused to battle, I'm going to form an army. An *exercitus*." She turned to Merry. "You can be my first conscript."

"Is that fair?" Thomas asked dubiously.

"*Omne pulchrum est in amore et bello*," Stella said.

"All is fair in love and war," Thomas translated.

"I'll be your brigadier!" Fanny cried, moving to stand beside Stella.

"That's not fair!" Thomas objected.

"I'm no ordinary foot solider," Merry said, ignoring

her son's complaint. "I'll be your lieutenant general, Stella. The dowager, when she arrives—"

Which was when Her Grace arrived.

She wasn't alone.

"Huzzah!" the dowager duchess called, marching across the lawn, her stout form wrapped in a toga.

Accompanied by Silvester.

He was wearing a toga too. It draped from his right shoulder down to his waist, leaving a good part of his heavily muscled chest open to the air. Not to mention a bare arm. His toga was as long as theirs, but it was made of light fabric that did nothing to disguise brawny thighs clad in tight silk breeches.

"Goodness me," Merry muttered.

"*He* can be my lieutenant general!" Thomas exclaimed, running toward Silvester.

"I'd be happy to conscript the duke," Merry said with a ripple of laughter. "If I wasn't married, of course."

Halfway across the lawn, Thomas stopped short before the dowager and her son, bowed, and then began chattering.

"Fanny, we'll definitely need you to be our brigadier," Stella said. "Thomas is stealing both new guests, unless I miss my guess."

"Probably that man is going to win," Fanny observed. "He has very long arms. Perhaps I'll play with the kitten instead."

"Never give up just because the enemy seems formidable," Stella told her.

Merry shot a mischievous look at Stella. "I must say, I find myself far more interested in ancient Rome than I could have imagined."

Silvester in the ballroom was one thing: he gleamed like the gold-plated aristocrat he was. But here? Wearing little more than a sheet, his burly chest undisguised? His nose seemed twice as bold and fierce.

And his eyes? Those gray, piercing eyes that could look so charming?

His coats must be cleverly cut to disguise his breadth, just as his charming smiles disguised the fierce desire to win every battle, important or otherwise. Stripped of his embroidery and lace, there was no mistaking who stood in the middle of the garden, wearing a swath of cloth and spinning a wooden sword while he listened intently to a young boy.

A warrior.

A man who ruthlessly manipulated currency markets for his own good—and incidentally to prevent the collapse of England's finances.

"He's a little scary," Fanny said. "I'm just going to see how the kitten is doing." She ran off toward the gazebo.

"His Grace is beautifully proportioned, isn't he?" Merry commented. "Who would possibly believe that the charming, civilized Duke of Huntington could turn into muscled Roman god?"

Stella tore her eyes away from Silvester and frowned at her friend.

"We *are* thinking Zeus, aren't we?" Merry pretended to fan herself.

"The Roman version is Jupiter," Stella said, retreating into facts because . . . she didn't know what to make of Silvester.

Silvester without clothing.

"In a ballroom, he seems the consummate aristocrat.

My husband glowers at the side of the room, bored, while Silvester flaunts his grace and distinction. The perfect manner and all that charm, though I am starting to think it is not as accidental as I assumed."

"I don't believe there's anything 'accidental' about the duke or his presentation," Stella said.

"Young men look to him to learn the best placement of a jewel or knotting of a cravat."

Stella snorted.

"That's what I just surmised," Merry exclaimed. "Fascinating! I'm so interested by people who are indifferent to society, and I would guess that the duke is one of them, all appearances to the contrary."

"He *is* his mother's son," Stella pointed out.

As they walked across the lawn, she saw that Silvester's chest was formed from solid slabs of muscle rather gracelessly put together. His arm had a wide pad of muscle at the shoulder that led to another powerful bulge and finally to a veined forearm.

No wonder he had picked her up and held her suspended in the air without groaning.

Fascinatingly, there was *hair* on his chest, which was something she'd never imagined. Her own chest had no hair, thankfully. His was the color of the hair on his head and glinted gold in the sunlight.

It didn't help her suppress a wave of longing when Silvester bent his head to talk to young Thomas, his powerful neck uncovered. Hunger coursed through her, setting her skin on fire. Why, why should a neck be so erotic? Perhaps that was why men wore cravats.

Or was it because most noblemen had necks like chickens that they disguised with layers of starched cloth?

Somewhere in the back of her head, Stella registered that her aunt would have a fit of vapors, were she to return unexpectedly. An unclad male neck would be shocking, but a bare chest and arm?

She caught Merry's arm. "My aunt," she murmured.

"I'll warn my butler to keep her inside, should she return," Merry promised.

Silvester was looking over Thomas's head at the two of them. Stella was suddenly aware of the hair pouring down her back, all of it brightly red. If only she'd braided it around her head. The toga disguised her bosom somewhat, but it certainly didn't make her look any taller.

Nothing could make her look taller.

"Good afternoon!" Merry cried as they reached the dowager and her son.

Silvester bowed and kissed first Merry's hand and then Stella's. They weren't wearing gloves, so his lips touched her skin. Merry didn't seem to notice, but Stella—did.

"I like that toga," the dowager said approvingly to Stella. "Mrs. Quimby is creative, isn't she? You must return and acquire a more flattering wardrobe."

Stella winced inwardly.

"Lady Stella's wardrobe is fine," Silvester said. "Personally, I like the gown that you claimed made her look like Holofernes."

The dowager rolled her eyes. "You're looking as her friend, not her suitor. She needs to find a husband so she doesn't have to endure another season on the marriage mart. A new wardrobe is essential, as I already informed her."

Stella was feeling hideously embarrassed. "Your toga is quite creative, Your Grace."

The dowager's toga would have been a crowning achievement for a Roman *modiste*, made as it was of gleaming white silk that fell to a hem of thick gold embroidery.

"Personally, I feel that wearing a toga over numerous petticoats has given my mother the outline of a *blancmange*," the duke remarked. "The fancy kind that has a stack of blackberries on top."

The dowager swatted him, clearly unperturbed by his sartorial criticism. "Never listen to male comments about your apparel," she told Merry and Stella.

"My husband never offers any," Merry assured her.

"It's probably just as well that he's not here this afternoon. He might have taken it amiss that my son is in *dishabille*," the dowager told her. "I assure you that Mrs. Quimby sent over a complete costume."

"Unfortunately, the undergarment ripped when I put it on," Silvester explained. "However, my understanding is that togas were worn without a shirt or breeches. I compromised."

"It's lucky that you are unchaperoned, Lady Stella," the dowager remarked. "Mrs. Thyme wouldn't have survived the shock."

Stella agreed with her.

Silvester didn't look or sound as if he'd lost weight from heartbreak, the way the Earl of Lilford had in Yasmin's absence. In fact, he looked remarkably healthy and not haunted by regret in the least.

Though, of course, he was the last man who would reveal genuine emotion.

Stella couldn't stop sneaking glances at him. His

arm and chest made heat swirl through her blood, tingling in her fingertips. If she wasn't careful, he would guess that she was besotted.

"I shall join the ladies' army," the dowager announced.

"Young Thomas informed me that he and I are two warriors fighting four bloodthirsty Amazons," Silvester said, twirling his sword in a way that suggested years of fencing instruction.

"Death comes with two blows of a sword," Thomas reminded them. "And no cheating, Mother! She likes to leap from behind trees and take a man down when he isn't expecting it," he explained to Silvester.

"Is there a rule against hiding?" Stella asked.

"It's not manly," Thomas said, glancing up at Silvester. "Gentlemen never attack from behind."

"A gentleman never fires first," Silvester agreed. "One must defeat the enemy, but that doesn't mean you should be a boor about it."

"Luckily, we are not men," Stella pointed out.

"There *is* one other important rule," Silvester said, raising his eyebrows. "No blows below the waist."

"Nonsense," Merry said. "I always aim for a whack on the bottom."

Stella couldn't imagine whacking anyone's bottom, let alone Silvester's, but she nodded. *"Omne pulchrum est in amore et bello."*

Silvester's mouth twitched. "All is fair in love and war, eh?"

"Certainly," Stella stated.

"I shall remember that," he said, his mouth curving into that lopsided smile Stella had never seen in a ballroom. He turned away. "Thomas, whether or not our enemies break the rules of gentlemanly combat, we shall remain true to our better instincts."

"Right, sir! I mean, certainly, Your Grace."

"I can't run terribly fast," the dowager said, suddenly appearing to be pitifully elderly. "I think you'd better concentrate on conquering the other Amazons, Master Thomas. I may not survive a blow from your sword."

Thomas bowed. "Of course."

"Our army will begin next to the gazebo and the other by the house," Merry announced. "I'll fetch my daughter." She ran off, waving her sword.

"I'll take your arm," the dowager said to Stella. She cast a minatory look at her son and Thomas. "The battle doesn't begin until I reach that structure, obviously."

Interestingly, her stroll was slower than it had been when she was plowing through river water. "Silvester is back in London, as you see," the dowager said without preamble. "I imagine you know that Lady Yasmin has agreed to marry that earl who was courting you. Perhaps she already has. I gather a special license is required."

"There is genuine feeling between them, so I'm happy for them," Stella said.

"Well, at least you aren't weeping into your tea," Her Grace said. "Silvester was so glum this morning I had to drag him along with me."

Stella winced. She hated thinking of Silvester longing for Yasmin. Or feeling desolate because he had been jilted.

"I can't think how I managed to raise a son with such a puling attitude toward the opposite sex," the dowager continued. "He told me he wants to be *in love* with his wife! Can you imagine anything more foolish?"

"I expect he will fall in love with someone else," Stella suggested, her heart aching at the thought. Silvester would have to be terribly lucky. Yasmin was the most exquisite woman in all England, or so people said. There weren't many Yasmins.

"I hope not," his mother said, somewhat surprisingly. "Love makes a fool of a person. Oh, not at first, but afterward. I wish better for my son."

"He will recover," Stella said. Of course, she'd known Silvester would be hurt by Yasmin's choice. But knowing wasn't the same as hearing from his own mother that his heart was broken. Her chest felt hollow.

The dowager flashed a look at her that was so akin to one of her son's that Stella blinked. "It's not possible to reason with him on the subject. I tried."

Thankfully, they finally reached the gazebo. Stella peeked inside and found Specs lying on her back on Peter's lap, her paws and legs stretched out blissfully as he stroked her stomach.

"Look how funny your kitty is, Lady Stella," Peter cried. "She's not in the least afraid, not even of George!"

George was bristled with white hair and snoring loudly as he twitched in his sleep. He didn't look like much of a threat.

"Specs is a shrewd cat," Stella told him. "She knows you're a friend."

Fanny was conferring with her mother. "Does everyone have their Latin epitaph ready to go?" she demanded. She had clearly appointed herself their general.

"The vicar gave me mine," the dowager said enthusiastically. *"Oderint, dum metuant."*

"We learned that one last year," Fanny said. *"Let them hate as long as they fear!* Do you know Mr. Addison?" she asked Stella.

"I don't."

"He's an American, and frightfully good at this game," Fanny said. "He beat Thomas."

"Sic semper tyrannis!" Fanny shouted. "Down with all tyrants."

Stella started to correct her, and stopped herself. Precision wasn't the point. This was a game. In fact, it was probably the first game she'd ever played, other than chess.

"Lady Stella?" Fanny asked.

"Semper primus!" Stella supplied. And then, in response to Merry's questioning glance, "Always first."

"Short but meaningful," Merry said approvingly.

"Now, here's our strategy," Fanny said. "Remember, they can't strike us until we strike them because they're boys. So your first blow *has to land.*"

Stella tightened her grip on her sword. She could imagine swinging it through the air. She simply couldn't imagine hitting a person with it.

"We'll run at them in pairs," Fanny continued. "All we have to do is poke them with both our swords, and they'll be dead."

"Very bloodthirsty," her mother said approvingly. "Your Grace, may I be your comrade-in-arms?"

"Sic," the dowager said. "That's 'yes' in Latin, by the way."

"Here's our strategy," Fanny said to Stella. "We'll take on the duke. He's old, so he won't run as quickly as

Thomas, and besides, Thomas will be afraid to hit the
dowager duchess with his sword. He's silly like that."

"Well, she is an elderly lady," Stella pointed out.

"But she's fierce," Fanny said. "Just look at the way
she's holding her sword. Mother shouts a lot, but she
hardly ever hits anyone with her sword. That's why
Thomas always wins the laurel wreath, except that
one time when Mr. Addison played. He swatted everyone, including Mother."

"We must win," Stella confirmed.

Fanny nodded. "The dowager is going to take
Thomas down, and our job is to kill the duke."

"I am ready," Stella said, practicing a few swings
with her sword. If she thought about the way that Silvester stared longingly across the ballroom at Yasmin,
she could definitely thwack him.

"Lieutenant general, are you ready?" Fanny shouted
at her mother.

Merry took the dowager's arm and then raised her
other arm in the air, waving her sword. *"Non ducor,
duco!"*

"Let's go!" Stella cried, grinning at Fanny. "I'm behind you!"

With a bloodcurdling scream, Fanny sprung out of
the shadow of the gazebo. Stella ran after her, sword
in hand, feeling her hair streaming behind her like
a Valkyrie. Out of the corner of her eye, she saw the
dowager tottering across the lawn, looking as if she'd
lost twenty years in the last ten minutes, leaning heavily on Merry's arm but flourishing a sword with her
other.

Fanny dashed forward and tried to poke Silvester
from behind with the point of her sword. He whirled

around from talking to Thomas and blocked her sword.

"*Noli me tangere,*" Silvester growled.

"I know what that means, and I'll tread on you if I want to!" Fanny cried, darting in to try again.

Thomas knocked her sword aside, and the siblings began energetically whacking away at each other, shouting in Latin.

"*Semper primus,*" Stella said, clearing her throat as she pointed her sword at Silvester.

Silvester's eyes seemed to be intent on her toga, perhaps due to the fact that only the shortest stays worked with the design.

Her aunt's insistence that lust unsettled male minds could be useful. Stella moved a step closer, and then another, until she was so close that she could smell snowy rain. And starched linen.

"Stella," Silvester said, his voice deep. "I missed you in the last month."

"You missed chess?" she said, raising an eyebrow. "So did I." She took another careful step. She was almost close enough to poke him. "I was very sorry to hear that your heart was broken."

"What? Oh, yes. Quite."

She took a final step and gave him a lavish smile, swinging up her sword and poking him in one leg. "Number one!" she called, leaping out of reach.

He narrowed his eyes at her. "Don't count on victory. As Thomas's lieutenant general, I can't let him down."

Stella danced from foot to foot, realizing she was grinning like a fool and not caring. Silvester didn't look as if he were heartbroken. Surely heartbroken men didn't have that greedy look in their eyes.

"How in the bloody hell am I supposed to strike a woman?" he asked.

Thomas clearly had no such qualms; behind Silvester's shoulder he scored a point against Fanny, who started screaming at him in English, not Latin.

The dowager drifted closer to the two children, held out her sword, and spanked Thomas on the legs. "Strike one!" she observed when Thomas spun about.

"Ha!" Fanny shouted, and the dowager, Merry, and Fanny surrounded Thomas, moving in a circle like the three witches in *Macbeth*.

Thomas managed to whack his sister on one leg. "You're dead!" he shouted.

The dowager chortled. "You are soon to die!"

Stella looked back at Silvester. "In my opinion, Thomas will soon fall to the sword, so to speak. Your team will lose."

"Only if I believe that as a lady, you cannot be exposed to my sword."

Stella narrowed her eyes at him. "Was that a randy comment?"

His grin was perfectly wicked. "*I will live in thy heart and die . . . in thy lap.* That's Shakespeare. As schoolboys, we memorized all the naughty parts."

"My heart is not available, and neither is my lap," Stella said briskly. He was circling her, holding his sword up. She couldn't stop looking at his chest, the power and grace of it. The way those muscles seemed chunky from afar but lithe and supple up close. The inherent strength that his shoulder displayed.

Why should a shoulder be erotic?

It was like a neck. Just a body part, no more than a body part, but the blood was racing through Stella's body as if they were back at the striped tents and she'd drunk three glasses of champagne.

Silvester was coming too close so she hastily circled to the right. He wouldn't slap her with the sword, so he'd have to trick her into allowing him to come close.

From behind her, she heard a cacophony suggesting that Merry had taken two blows.

"You're out, Mother!" Thomas bellowed.

"Retreat, retreat!" Merry called.

Silvester always wants to win, Stella reminded herself. That fierce light in his eyes? She wasn't entirely sure how to interpret it, but she'd seen it any number of times when she was closing in on checkmate. Or he was.

The Duke of Huntington wanted to win, even if the weapons were wooden swords and the army led by children.

The problem was that if she didn't let him come close, she couldn't strike him with her sword either. So she had to lure him close enough so that he gave her a blow, which meant she could give *him* a blow, and then he'd be dead.

She lowered her sword and watched him prowl around her, only turning to keep her front to him. "You'll have to come closer," she observed. "You might hurt me otherwise."

"Carpe diem, quam minimum credula postero."

"Seize the day," Stella said, frowning. "What's the other half of it mean?"

"Put no trust in tomorrow."

"What does *that* mean, in the context of this particular battle?"

"I will do my best to find a wife today, as I have little hope of tomorrow."

"What does that have to do with anything?" Stella asked. "Are you referring to losing Yasmin?" She had her eyes fixed on his sword. It hung loose from his hand but she was certain he could tap her with it if he lunged.

She had to welcome death in order to bring death.

CHAPTER TWENTY-ONE

"It has nothing to do with Yasmin," Silvester said, sliding sideways. He recognized the sneaky look in Stella's eyes. She got just that expression when she was about to attack in chess.

But that wasn't all he read in her eyes. The drumbeat of awareness between them, the way his toga was (thankfully) disguising his erection, the pink rising in Stella's cheeks . . .

She felt it too.

His desire wasn't one-sided.

As afternoon entertainments went, this one was proving sartorially challenging. It wasn't a matter of keeping his toga on. *Stella's* toga was the problem.

The breeze kept blowing it back, flattening silk against her bosom until he could actually see the lines of the corset she wore over her chemise. And everything else. All the generous curves and dips and valleys.

He forced himself to move to the right, his hand tightening on his sword. *Sword!* What in the bloody hell was he supposed to do with a blunt instrument besides make dirty jokes about it?

"Run to the tree, Stella!" a voice suddenly shrieked, bringing him back to the realization that they were silently circling each other like duelists.

Stella turned and ran away from him. Silvester was horrified to discover his muscles tightening, not wanting to let her go. This bloody *craving* was absurd. He never felt this for Yasmin.

But he'd been in love with Yasmin—or next best thing to in love with Yasmin. He adored her. Truly.

He didn't adore Stella. He craved her, like water in a desert. He'd never actually tried to kiss Yasmin, whose touch-me-not air made her aversion to intimacy obvious. But Stella? The first damn time he got her in private, he couldn't stop himself from pulling her into his arms, dead mouse or no dead mouse.

The memory of their kisses was like the beat of a drum in the back of his mind. So it was a damn good thing that Yasmin had dropped him for Giles.

He tightened his grip on his sword and padded after Stella, who had dashed behind a tree to confer with Merry, Fanny, and his mother.

"Sir, sir," Thomas said, running up out of breath. "How many times have you been struck, sir?"

"Once," Silvester said. "You?"

"Once. They don't play fair at all. I had to run like the blazes to get away from the dowager duchess, which is *not* the way someone like that is supposed to play!"

"How should she play?" Silvester asked.

"Well, she's *old*. And a duchess. She should be dignified. She's a lady."

"My mother never believed that rule, even when she was young."

"Oh, that's right, she's your mother. I apologize."

"*Your* mother won't be dignified at that age, either," Silvester pointed out. "She's also a duchess."

"Look, they've decided something," Thomas said, whirling around and backing close to Silvester's chest.

Silvester could smell sweaty boy and mown grass. It was surely imagination that made him detect the faint perfume that clung to Stella's skin as well.

The four women strolled out from behind the tree. Silvester's body flared to life at a glance from Stella. Merely a glance.

This was a disaster.

"Careful," Thomas warned. "Your mother may be the only one left alive, but I expect all four of them will try to ambush us. It's cheating!"

Silvester glanced down at the small, indignant general at his side. "Lady Stella is still alive. Your sister and mother have put down their swords, so they aren't cheating."

"We must separate," Thomas declared.

"Lady Stella is the most dangerous," Silvester told him.

Thomas blinked up at him. "She is?"

"Absolutely. My mother is, as you said, rather elderly."

"Lady Stella is a fast runner," Thomas conceded.

"I'll chase her away from the others, and you concentrate on taking out the dowager. I can't strike Her Grace, as she's my mother."

Thomas threw him a skeptical glance, presumably due to being the veteran of many battles with *his* mother. But he nodded. "I'll draw them to the right, and you can fight Lady Stella. Don't let her confuse you, sir."

"Confuse?"

"Girls have ways of doing that," Thomas said darkly.

"I shall do my best."

With that, the two Roman warriors split left and right, running toward the opposite army, swords in hand.

Stella took one look, turned, and fled.

Silvester could have caught her immediately. Her legs were short, and his were long. But what was the fun of that? Especially when the chase left so much to be enjoyed.

Stella's hair billowed behind her like a silk sheet, and when she turned to look at him over her shoulder, her freckles stood out like cinnamon sugar. Like something that needed licking. Kissing.

He loped after her, herding her to the end of the garden, until she dashed behind the gazebo.

Silvester strode around the structure, sword at the ready, peacefully ready to die.

Which was exactly what happened.

Stella had jumped up to stand on the edge of the gazebo floor, which protruded beyond the rails. When he rounded the corner, she poked him in the shoulder.

"You're dead," she whispered.

"Did you lose your voice due to shouting in Latin?"

Stella put a finger to her lips and pointed inside the gazebo. A boy was sprawled on his back, fast asleep, with an ancient bulldog draped over his stomach and Specs nestled in the shelter of his neck.

"That is adorable," Silvester said, coming closer.

She frowned at him. "Don't use that word. I loathe it."

"Why?"

"Overused and misunderstood." She dropped her sword to the grass and then sat down on the edge of the gazebo, putting her just at his eye level.

She was a little sweaty, and her hair appeared to have doubled in size: curls and waves billowed around her shoulders. Her freckles stood out as if they'd been gilded deeper gold by the sun.

"You're dead," Stella repeated, twinkling at him through her adorable spectacles. "We should return and inform the others that my army has triumphed."

"I must pay obeisance to the winner first. I gather you will receive a crown of laurel, although I'm not sure about a purple, gold-embroidered toga."

"Exactly. So—"

He swallowed her protest with his mouth, since her eyes were not protesting. Sure enough, she opened her lips and melted toward him. She tasted like grass and salt and *Stella*.

"Hell," he muttered sometime later, his voice ragged. She had one arm around his neck, the other caressing his bare shoulder. He had stopped himself from groping her only by flattening his palms on the floorboards to either side of her. "I really did miss you in the last month."

It was only because he was looking right into her eyes that he saw a flicker of . . . something. She pulled back. "Let me down, please."

Instead he crowded closer, pushing her legs apart. "No. What did I say wrong this time? I missed you."

"You didn't miss me except as a chess partner," she replied. "You left the city with Yasmin, remember? You might also remind yourself that I *know you*, Silvester."

"What does that mean?"

"You're not overly bothered by ethics when you want something. At this moment, I have allowed you to kiss me, against all prudence and common sense. You want me. So you'll say anything to get what you want."

Silvester froze. "That seems unnecessarily harsh."

She tapped him on the chin with one finger. "But true. You cut corners, Silvester. You buy gold and then invoke the gold standard. You play games that you know how to win, whether in a scavenger hunt or in kissing me."

"Are you a game? Because if you are, I don't know how to win, Stella."

"I suppose kissing is the game." She didn't seem to realize that one of her hands had returned to caressing his shoulder. "Which, by the way, you clearly know how to win."

"I like this game," Silvester said, grinning at her.

"Men do, don't they?"

He leaned in and dusted her lips with his. "Women like it as well."

His tongue ran along her lips with a silent question. She opened her mouth and their tongues tangled in a caress that sent molten heat down his legs. His cock was urgently pressing hard and hot against his breeches.

"Like it or not, gentlemen generally don't play this game with unmarried ladies," Silvester growled a while later. "Although, in case you're wondering, I am not a gentleman, Stella. Not a scholar either. Your vocabulary is much better than mine."

"I don't care about that," Stella said huskily.

"I *pose* as a gentleman," Silvester insisted. For some reason, he wanted to make sure she knew the truth.

"I know!" Her eyes were both amused and hungry.

"You're a fraud, a ducal fraud. A pirate hiding in plain sight. A Roman warrior in silk breeches."

Silvester tried to interpret her expression. "Is that a good thing?"

She sighed. "Kiss me again."

So he did.

"Do you hear shouting?" Silvester asked later. He was hanging on to propriety by the skin of his teeth. Stella's hands were ranging over his shoulders, slipping up his neck, even arrowing into his hair to tug him closer. But so far, he'd kept his fingers gripped around the wooden edge of the gazebo.

Everything in him wanted to surround her with his body, snatch her to him with all the desperate possessiveness he felt.

Stella's eyes were glazed. She shook her head, leaning in to kiss his chin.

"From the sound of it, Thomas managed to score a blow against my mother. But only one so far. Most of the shouting is Merry and Fanny." The next sentence came out without forethought. "I want to marry you, Stella."

She made a sound, a gasp, and pulled away. "What did you say?"

"I want to marry you."

It was his first marriage proposal. He hadn't imagined her eyes would respond with shock followed by horror.

"Because Yasmin is marrying, you must follow suit? Some odd kind of exchange, where Giles won the woman you want, so you will take the woman he didn't want?" Her voice grated with hurt and anger.

"No." He growled the word.

Behind her shoulder, the ancient bulldog snorted in his sleep.

"Are you saying this because I allowed you to kiss me?" Stella's jaw was tight, her eyes narrowed. "You have no need to offer a proposal on such slender grounds."

"I asked because I want you," Silvester said, making no bones about it. "I want you in my life and my bed. Even though you know all my worst characteristics, and you don't think highly of me."

"You don't think well of me," she pointed out.

"Not true. I love talking to you. I cannot stop touching you. You are intelligent, loyal, and kind when you wish to be. I also believe you tolerate me, that is, the way I look. And I don't mean my nose."

Stella scoffed, folding her arms over her chest. Which made her breasts plump in a way that sent lust ripping down Silvester's spine once again. "You know perfectly well that you are considered the most handsome man in the ton, nose or not. I can't imagine why you think that my opinion would vary from that of all the other women in London."

Silvester nodded. "On the surface I am, yes."

"Well?" she demanded, her eyes fiery.

"Most of it is good tailoring. I meant the parts that no one knows. I ripped the undergarment to this toga deliberately so you could see my chest."

"You are very odd," Stella said.

"I wanted to know whether you would be put off by my shape. My physique is not to all women's tastes." He cleared his throat. "A woman once called me brutish."

"You do simulate elegance well," she murmured,

her eyes flicking over his broad chest and down to his legs.

"It's gilt, not gold. Stripped of my garments, I am burly, hairy, somewhat immoral, lustful, undereducated, and fond of money. I was never interested in book learning, other than mathematics. I don't think I'll ever take up my seat in the House of Lords. The idea makes me feel faint with boredom."

"That *is* dismaying," Stella said, but Silvester could see a tinge of humor in her eyes.

"We would have a good marriage. I like being around you."

Stella hopped down off the gazebo. "No."

Silvester frowned at her. *"No?"*

"Exactly." She must have caught his confusion because she explained. "I like you, Silvester, even given your shady ethics. But I want what you gave to Yasmin, what you felt for Yasmin."

"What was that?"

"Love."

"I am not heartbroken. I care for Yasmin. A lot."

"Yes, well," Stella said, turning away from him and pushing her hair behind her ears. "I want to be cared for. *A lot.* Whatever you want to call that expression you had on your face whenever you looked at her."

Silvester felt a prickling of uneasiness. "What expression do I have when I look at you?"

"That's irrelevant."

He scowled at her.

"All right, you look at me as if—with the expression you have when you look at my breasts."

Silvester grinned at her. "That's right."

"I'm not marrying a man for lust," Stella said flatly.

"According to my aunt, I can get that anywhere. I want a man who isn't in love with another woman. I didn't realize it before, but that's my sole qualification. No husband of mine will stand beside me, casting longing gazes across the ballroom."

"I can promise that," Silvester said. "No longing glances unless I'm looking directly at you."

She snorted.

"What?"

"You don't adore me."

Silvester opened his mouth—and shut it. He didn't feel the same thing for Stella that he had for Yasmin. Yasmin was . . . *adorable*.

"Yes, she was adorable," Stella said crossly, obviously reading his expression.

Stella was irritating and exciting. She was unbearably luscious, and he couldn't wait to go to bed with her. He never worried too much about bed with Yasmin: she was beautiful, so it would be . . . fine. Great, even.

Now he thought about it, his disinclination to kiss Yasmin signaled a problem. Their marriage would likely have been friendly but tepid.

But Stella?

With her spectacles, and her freckles, and all that red hair, and curves, and scowling eyes? The way she pouted, and looked right through him, and scolded him for unethical behavior? She *knew* him, all the parts of him that he'd hidden from the moment he entered Eton.

He no sooner looked at her than a groundswell of lust and possession swept through him. Bedding Stella would be profound. Perhaps even a little frightening.

"I'm going to share something with you," Stella said, breaking the silence. "Then we shall return to the garden and pretend this conversation never happened."

He'd be damned if he'd ever pretend that he hadn't proposed marriage for the first time in his life, but he waited. He could be gentlemanly when he had to.

"The *game* you're playing is with your mother, not me."

"What are you talking about?"

"Your mother pulled me into the river before she summoned you to rescue her. She made certain you saw me drenched in water."

Silvester frowned. Damn it. Stella was likely right.

He had inherited his dislike of losing from his mother. Clearly, the dowager had only pretended to give up the idea of his marrying Stella, *her* choice for a duchess. But in reality, his mother had been scheming to make just that happen.

"I like the dowager," Stella continued, "but I won't be party to her maneuverings, even if it would get me a dukedom. I don't care about your title, Silvester. I didn't care about Giles's, either, and I would have refused his hand had he proposed."

"I see," Silvester said. Ever since he reached his majority, he'd been accosted by artful women with a grating determination to "win" a coronet. Until he met Yasmin, who, like Stella, showed no interest in his dukedom.

He had only himself to offer, but that wasn't what Stella wanted either.

"I will find a man who adores me, or I'll buy a

house next to a bookstore and live happily by myself," she concluded, shaking out her skirts. "Now, if you'll excuse me, Your Grace, you are dead, and I am very much alive, so I shall inform my army that we have won the battle and the laurel wreath."

CHAPTER TWENTY-TWO

Stella emerged from the shadow of the gazebo onto the lawn, forcing herself to march, although her knees felt wobbly. She had walked away from Silvester bravely enough, but inside she felt like a bowl of jelly.

He had proposed to her.

Silvester, Duke of Huntington, had offered to marry her.

If someone had asked her a day or a week ago, she would have said that marrying Silvester was the dearest, secret wish of her heart. But marrying him when he'd just been rejected by the woman he adored?

When he couldn't even sum up a lie and *pretend* that she, Stella, was adorable?

No.

He must have lost his mind. Or he was bent on saving face. Or he was ruled by lust. Likely, she thought, the latter. Having lost at love, he'd decided to propose due to lust instead.

A cluster of people, including two footmen, were gathered around the dowager duchess, who was leaning back in a chair as if the battle had exhausted her. Stella had serious doubts about that.

"Oh, there you are!" Merry called. "We had to call off our game, as Her Grace grew quite tired."

When Stella reached them, she discovered the dowager was smiling in a way that suggested she had won a more significant game. "You and my son were out of sight for a considerable period of time, Lady Stella," she said cheerfully, straightening with all the energy of a forty-year-old. "Unchaperoned, I might add."

"His Grace and I had an interesting discussion about the celebratory practices of Roman empires," Stella said. "According to him, I am due not just the laurel wreath but a purple, gold-embroidered toga, because I did give him a second blow with my sword, which means the battle is over."

The dowager narrowed her eyes.

Stella smiled at her. "We were ably chaperoned by Peter, of course."

"We won!" Fanny screamed, realizing what happened.

Merry clapped her hands. "Champagne!"

At the other end of the garden, Silvester strolled out of the gazebo, Specs on his shoulder and Peter carrying the elderly bulldog. The dowager's expression fell.

They sat down to glasses of champagne or lemonade. Specs dashed about the lawn, followed by Peter. At some point, George toddled over and leaned against Stella's leg until she lifted the chunky dog into her lap. He draped his white muzzle over one of her knees and fell asleep.

"He sleeps most of the time these days," Merry said. "Your toga will be covered with white hairs."

"I don't mind," Stella said, petting George's head as he slept. She listened quietly to the dowager sparring with Merry. Silvester was silent too.

After a while, the Duke of Trent appeared and sat

down beside his wife. He had always seemed frighteningly austere to Stella, but the expression in his eyes when he looked at his wife? And at his children, cavorting on the lawn in grass-stained togas, Fanny wearing a laurel wreath tipped over one ear?

It confirmed Stella's decision.

She wanted what Merry had, what Yasmin had. She'd spent her entire life playing second fiddle to perfection. She'd spent her life never being loved for being herself.

She'd be damned if she accepted a lifetime of the same.

Now that Silvester recognized his mother's manipulation, he would drop his unlikely courtship, if you could call it that. No man wanted to marry the woman his mother shoved in his direction. Especially once he realized that the dowager had chosen Stella on the basis of bad eyesight and height.

Back at home, Stella dabbed her face with the cream Blanche had given her, disguising her renewed freckles before going down to supper.

Mrs. Thyme greeted her cheerfully. After spending the afternoon with friends, she was feeling more sanguine about the Earl of Lilford's defection. Apparently, rumors suggested that Lady Yasmin might be carrying a child.

"Reprehensible," her aunt said. "But the truth is, dearest, now everyone will know that he wanted *you* to be his countess, although he had to marry the woman with whom he had consorted. Lady Yasmin is not just his mistress, after all. She is a lady, albeit a scandalous one."

"A possible child is not why the earl asked Lady

Yasmin to marry him," Stella said. "He is in love with her, Aunt. You said so yourself, after the picnic by the river."

"That will make their marriage pleasant, if unusual," Mrs. Thyme agreed. "My point is that *your* reputation will be untouched, in fact, somewhat enhanced since he bedded Lady Yasmin and then didn't ask her to marry him until a child was on the way. I shall send a letter to your uncle immediately. He will be so relieved."

Mr. Thyme was still in the country, overseeing the all-important work of gardeners as they turned his gourds toward the sun, morning and afternoon. In Stella's opinion, he didn't give a fig for his niece's reputation or even her marital prospects.

Three days later, Stella and her aunt were at breakfast when their butler entered and announced, "The Duke of Huntington has sent in his card, Madame." The butler would never be so gauche as to raise an eyebrow, especially where nobility was concerned, but his tone made it clear that he disapproved of a call paid far too early.

Mrs. Thyme looked up from her plate, puzzled. "Why on earth? Might he have left something here?"

"I doubt it," Stella said slowly. She had an unpleasant feeling in her stomach.

Silvester did not like to lose. Ever. No matter how important or unimportant the matter at hand was.

She put down her teacup. "Why don't I greet him in the drawing room, Aunt? You might—"

"I hope you don't mind if I barge in like this," a deep, urbane voice said. Silvester strolled into the room, exquisitely dressed in gray silk with black embroidery at the cuffs, his pantaloons cut close and worn with shining boots.

Without tassels, Stella noted.

He was up to something, a conclusion she reached not merely because he was wearing full dress, but because he was wearing his "Duke of Huntington" expression, radiating charm and dominance. As well as wealth, she noted sourly, seeing an emerald shaped like an insect pinned to his cravat.

Presumably, one of his mother's lucky scarabs.

Their butler drew himself up with an affronted air upon realizing that the duke had entered the house without invitation, but he visibly relaxed when Silvester gave him one of those beaming smiles he held in reserve, full of charm and a touch of mischief.

"I consider myself a friend of the family, but even so, I know that I am in breach of decorum," he admitted.

"Your Grace, we are not prepared for callers at this hour," Mrs. Thyme said, waving her hand to send the butler out of the room. "May we assist you with something?"

"I wish you good morning, Mrs. Thyme, Lady Stella. No, please don't rise." His bow was a masterful display of masculine elegance.

Stella took a deep breath. "My life is not a game for your amusement."

"What did you say, Stella?" her aunt asked.

"I could wait no longer," he said soulfully.

Stella started to her feet, rage filling her body. "Don't you dare!"

"Dare what?" her aunt said confusedly. "Are you here to play chess, Your Grace? While I know how much you and my niece enjoy a game now and then, we have calls of our own to make this morning."

"I am here because I have found the woman with whom I wish to spend my life in happy union and felicity, and for whom I possess the particular affection and esteem requisite for conjugal happiness."

Mrs. Thyme's mouth fell open.

Stella rolled her eyes.

"In short, I come to ask for your niece's hand in marriage," Silvester concluded.

"No, he has *not*!" Stella interjected. Before he could answer, she said, "If you repeat that trumpery sham again, the answer will still be no."

Mrs. Thyme was clearly in the grip of strong emotion: confusion, pleasure, suspicion . . . All of it chased across her face. Decorum won. "My niece will entertain no offers of marriage without her uncle's permission," she stated, adding, "Even from a duke."

"I would expect no less," Silvester said, bowing again. He drew a folded sheet of parchment from his breast pocket, handing it to Mrs. Thyme. "I would have allowed your husband's missive to reach you through the Royal Mail, but for the fact that *love goes toward love, as schoolboys from their books*." He flicked a twinkling glance at Stella.

Stella's temper detonated. She flattened her hands on the table and leaned toward him. "I suggest we alter Romeo's lament. I'd propose *'Love goes toward Yasmin as schoolboys from their books.'*"

"Stella," her aunt protested. She was still reading her letter. "Your Grace, am I to understand that you visited Mr. Thyme at our country estate?"

"Certainly," Silvester said. "After being overcome

by emotion at the Duchess of Trent's Roman Fête, I felt I had to express the violence of my emotions, but naturally, decorum was foremost in my mind. I left for the country, as I could not wait until Mr. Thyme returned to London."

"How romantic," Mrs. Thyme said, frowning as she tried to decipher her husband's handwriting. "Mr. Thyme writes that he has acquired a pineapple stove, hoping heat will increase the size of his gourds."

"I was pleased to be introduced to the pineapple stove, after which Mr. Thyme agreed to allow me to propose to Lady Stella," the duke confirmed.

Stella felt like howling, a little dizzy with anger. Having been warned her entire life that as a redhead, her temper would easily flare out of control, for the very first time, she felt a Medusa-like fury springing from her hair. Or her brain.

Mrs. Thyme suddenly snapped upright like a hunting dog on the scent. "Your Grace, you were at the garden party? I was informed there would be no male guests."

"The Duchess of Trent had no idea that I would accompany my mother," Silvester said, a nicely judged note of apology in his voice.

"The *dowager*," Mrs. Thyme exclaimed, her expression changing from suspicion to stark misgiving. "I forgot . . . that is, I had not taken Her Grace into account."

"You should have, Aunt," Stella remarked. "The duke is such a dutiful son. Imagine all the marvelous family gatherings we might have in the future if I accepted his proposal. Which I shall not."

"Your happiness is my only concern," Mrs. Thyme said without conviction.

"I don't wish to marry His Grace. In fact, I refuse to marry him. Under any circumstances, as it would make me very unhappy."

"Oh, but Stella, you'd be a duchess," her aunt pointed out.

"Better a happy spinster than an unhappy duchess."

Silvester dropped his elegant stance, squared his shoulders, and leveled a molten stare at Stella, made of a brew of primal masculinity and ducal outrage. "I assure you that *my* duchess will be happy."

"You will not be in control of her emotions," Stella retorted. "Any more than you were able to control your love for Yasmin, or hers for the earl."

"Enough of Lady Yasmin," Mrs. Thyme said, putting the letter to the side and rising from the table. "Your Grace, I shall allow you ten minutes to make your proposal in private while I decipher whether my husband is writing about gourds or his niece. I trust that you will act like a gentleman. Stella, you may escort him to the drawing room; leave the door open, if you please."

Stella bobbed a curtsy, unable to bring herself to look at Silvester's face. She walked down the corridor and then moved to the side to allow him to open the door to the drawing room. Which he promptly closed behind them.

"My aunt will fear the worst," she said stiffly, not meeting his eyes. "She has strong feelings about appropriate behavior for betrothed couples, let alone those who are *not* betrothed, like ourselves."

"Stella," Silvester said, his voice a deep rumble, utterly unlike the light sophisticated tones he had used a moment ago. "Would it be so terrible to be married to me?"

"Have you lost your mind?" Stella inquired. "I understand your wish to win every battle, Silvester. But this is *madness*. Truly. Next Season you might meet another Yasmin, and what then? You'd be tied to me for life."

"I am not interested in finding another Yasmin," Silvester said, folding his arms over his chest. "I want to marry you. It has nothing to do with winning. If anything, I am resigning myself to the fact that my mother will crow about her better judgment for the next thirty years or so. You are right: she decided you'd make a marvelous Duchess of Huntington from the moment she met you. By proposing to you, I am losing a familial battle."

"I feel as if I've walked into someone else's story," Stella said, after the silence between them stretched too long.

The pirate was peeking out from the aristocrat: Silvester's burly shoulders were straining his silk coat, and his jaw was set in a manner that would startle polite society. Actually, terrify most of them.

"I can make you happy," he said stubbornly, his eyes fixed on her face.

They were going to have to talk frankly. Stella turned around and walked to a chair. He followed her and seated himself opposite.

"Perhaps you might sit on my lap?" he asked, his eyes practically sparking with provocation. "I'm fairly certain I can convince you at close quarters."

Stella didn't sigh. "One doesn't marry for lust," she stated.

"My—"

"Please don't repeat that flummery you babbled at

my aunt." Her hands were gripped together so tightly that her knuckles were white. Stella forced herself to relax before she looked up. "I refused you at Merry's garden party, Silvester. I said no."

"I don't accept your answer."

"You must accept it. You can't just have your way all the time, simply because you're a duke!" Stella knew her voice was rising and couldn't stop herself. "You cannot force me to marry *you*, a man in love with another woman! You can't ruin my life simply because you want to win. Or because your mother told you to. Or because you want to bed me. Whatever foolish reason you have!"

"My reason is you."

"That's absurd." Stella couldn't sit still and listen to this drivel. She jumped to her feet and walked to the window, trying to control the tears rising in her eyes. "You are my *friend*, Silvester. Almost my only friend." She wound her arms around her body and pretended to look out at the street. "When I refuse you, my aunt will be so disappointed. She will be devastated. Couldn't you have pictured how difficult refusing you will be for me?"

Silvester moved to stand behind her, his large body just there. If she turned around, he'd catch her into his arms. He'd kiss her until she—

"You are my friend," he said.

"Then don't *do* this," Stella said, her voice breaking despite herself. "Please, please don't do this. I can't marry you. Tell my aunt you had a momentary delusion."

Silence.

Then: "I can make you happy." In his voice was the

deep obstinacy of a man who has never been thwarted. "Give me a chance."

Before Stella could answer, he turned her about, stepping both of them sideways so her back was against the wall. She looked up and frowned, startled by the expression on Silvester's face. He didn't look stubborn. He looked . . . She didn't know what that gaze meant.

His palms slammed into the wall on either side of her shoulders. "Damn it, Stella, do you really think that I would marry someone because my mother told me to?"

The pirate was in full evidence now. Silvester was glaring down at her, his gray eyes black, his jaw clenched. He loomed over her, not frighteningly, but like a bulwark against the world.

"No." Stella shook her head, not letting herself be tempted.

"So you think that I would *marry* someone just to win an argument?"

"Perhaps," she said honestly.

His face came closer. "Look into my eyes, Stella. Do I look idiotic enough for that?"

"No?"

"I'm on fucking fire for you," he rasped. "For you, Stella. You are mine. I need you. And in case you're wondering, betrothed men and women do *not* feel like this normally."

Stella couldn't bring herself to nod, because what did she know?

He took one more step and picked her up. In what felt like one smooth movement, her back was flattened against the wall, his body pressed against hers. He tugged up her skirts and hitched her even higher. Her legs curved around his hips as if they'd been made for the purpose: not too short . . . just the right length.

Sensation burst through Stella's body. She instinctively tilted her hips, and Silvester let out an agonized groan, the hand holding her left leg pulling her even closer. Stella's lips moved in a curse that would have shocked her aunt.

Silvester's expression wasn't cheerful or sophisticated or all the things he looked in the ballroom. His gaze was hungry, pinned on her face, full of desire.

For her.

His mouth closed over hers, ravishing her until she couldn't do anything but wind her arms around his neck, letting him swallow the whimpers she couldn't suppress. Dimly, she thought about whether lust was enough to carry a marriage. Obviously, her aunt and uncle didn't share that emotion, though her uncle when he looked at a prizewinning gourd . . .

When they kissed behind the gazebo, Silvester hadn't touched her. But now one hand was gripping her bottom, holding her up against the wall. His fingers flexed, sinking into the curve of her arse. The other was stroking one of her legs. Her aunt would *die* if she entered the room.

"You're mine," Silvester growled, his breathing choppy. His hips arched, just enough so that their bodies snapped together like puzzle pieces.

She thought it was meant as a declaration, but there were undertones of a curse. Whatever this was between them, it had caught him by surprise as well.

"It's just lust," Stella managed.

"Not just, though that's part of it." Making an obvious point, one of his hands rounded her breast, eyes caught on hers, nodding when she trembled, and her nipple beaded to a point in his palm.

"I want to marry you," Silvester said, his voice velvet dark. "I want you, and you want me, Stella. I don't *adore* you. I'm not kneeling before you. Although I can think of occasions on which I might."

His thumb moved, and Stella shuddered all over. "Might what?" she whispered, not following.

"Kneel before you." His voice was everything wicked and seductive that he wasn't, in general. His hips pushed close again.

"Kiss me," Stella said, because heat was burning through her, fogging her brain. She wanted more, more of that rocking pressure, the slide of his tongue against hers, the desperate flex of his fingers on her bottom.

Thankfully, Silvester was more rational than she was, because two minutes later, when Mrs. Thyme burst through the door, clucking with irritation to find it was closed against her *express* wishes, he had already set Stella on her feet. They were standing shoulder to shoulder, staring out the window at the street.

Stella turned around, praying that her hair didn't look too rumpled. "I'm sorry that the door was closed, Aunt, but as you see, nothing untoward happened. The duke has been a perfect gentleman. He has offered his hand in marriage once again."

Her aunt didn't look convinced. Stella glanced to the side and found that Silvester had put on his ducal facade. It would take a stronger woman than her aunt to accuse him of impropriety.

"I see." Mrs. Thyme seated herself and waved at the

sofa opposite her. When they were all sitting down, she asked, "Stella, what do you wish to do?"

"I have refused the Duke of Huntington's proposal," Stella stated. "I think he is suffering from delusions."

Silvester flashed her a look. Obviously, temper was not merely the provenance of redheads.

"Your Grace, perhaps you might court Stella," Mrs. Thyme suggested. "This has all been remarkably sudden! I am not surprised that Stella is shocked by your attentions."

"Actually, my attentions are not sudden," Silvester said.

"Yes, they are," Stella said. "You were known throughout London as Lady Yasmin's foremost suitor only a month ago."

"Ah, but *two* months hence, I accompanied you to your bedchamber."

CHAPTER TWENTY-THREE

When playing whist, Silvester loved holding a trump card. When he had a card powerful enough to triumph over all suits, he hugged it close and played it judiciously.

Now?

Hearing Mrs. Thyme's hysterical cry?

Meeting Stella's betrayed gaze as her aunt collapsed backward in her chair?

He should not have played that card.

"When?" Mrs. Thyme gasped.

"It was when Specs placed the mouse on my pillow," Stella said, rubbing her aunt's hand. "And *nothing happened*, Aunt!"

"I feel a spasm coming, such a fluttering as I've never experienced!" One of Mrs. Thyme's hands clutched Stella's, while the other pressed her right breast, which she apparently understood to house her heart.

Stella leaned closer. "His Grace has exaggerated the situation. We never approached the bed."

Mrs. Thyme was visibly trembling, head to foot. "I warned you, Stella. I told you and told you that men are at the mercy of their lusts. Now you've been ravished, and it's my fault. I never should have allowed him to accompany you upstairs. This is *my fault*!" She began sobbing so hard that she didn't seem to be breathing properly.

Silvester was struck by the conviction that even for a woman who suffered from nerves, Mrs. Thyme's reaction was unusual. Most women would celebrate a daughter who snared a duke by luring him into a bedchamber.

In fact, he had the feeling her emotions had little to do with Stella, who had pulled out a handkerchief and was blotting her aunt's tears. "I was not ravished," she said soothingly. "I'll bring you a cup of hot tea, and you'll feel better."

"My heart is beating as if it might burst from my chest," Mrs. Thyme cried. "Where are my smelling salts?"

"I'll return immediately," Stella said. She kissed her aunt's cheek, rose to her feet, and walked through the door without a glance at Silvester.

No matter how much he wanted to marry Stella, Mrs. Thyme's distress was so real and deep that he had to withdraw the trump card. Silvester slid into Stella's place and took Mrs. Thyme's hand. "I would never ravish a woman. Never."

"I kn-know," she hiccupped.

"I cannot allow you to believe that I deflowered Lady Stella. I did not."

"I see," Mrs. Thyme faltered.

"I offered her no violence." He kept his voice deep and calm. "My father raised me to have the greatest respect for the female sex." That was certainly true. And what his father hadn't said, his mother had enforced.

"Of course, you *are* a duke," Mrs. Thyme said.

No title ever prevented evil, but he nodded.

By the time Stella returned to the room carrying a cup of tea, her aunt had calmed, although she was still clutching her bosom, air sawing in and out of her lungs. Silvester moved back to his seat on the sofa. Stella coaxed her aunt upright with practiced ease, handing her tea, a fresh handkerchief, and a vial of smelling salts.

Silvester watched silently. On the one side, he felt sorry for arousing Mrs. Thyme's fears. But on the other? He had the distinct feeling that if he left the building, Stella would refuse to ever see him.

She was *livid*. She hadn't met his eyes, but every bit of her body signaled indignation, if not hatred. Stella would never play chess with him again, or waltz with him, or argue with him. She wouldn't let him woo her.

That was . . . unacceptable.

In fact, the very idea felt like a knife to his chest. Somehow, without noticing, he'd become attached to the idea of marrying a pint-sized vixen.

When Mrs. Thyme was calmer, he said, "I wish to assure you once more, Madame, that I maintained decorum throughout my brief visit to Stella's bedchamber."

"You must think me a veritable hysteric," she quavered, blotting her eyes again. "My doctor says I am a delicate woman, prone to allowing fear to overcome my rational senses. I should have known you would behave with the utmost propriety."

"You see, Aunt? You have nothing to worry about," Stella said.

"I mentioned that event because of my growing

conviction that our mere visit upstairs was improper," Silvester said, crafting a tone that was concerned yet ducal. "I am compelled to propose marriage after such a breach of decorum."

Stella finally looked at him, but only to roll her eyes.

"I see," Mrs. Thyme said uncertainly. She took the handkerchief away from her swollen eyes and peered at his face.

"I was taught that a duke must maintain the highest propriety. My conscience has anguished over that visit upstairs with your niece."

Stella rose to her feet, put her hands on her hips, and hissed, "You are a fraud, *Your Grace*. I suggest you stop speaking immediately."

"In mentioning that I accompanied Stella upstairs, I meant to emphasize that my attraction to her was obvious far earlier than a month ago," Silvester said, ignoring his irascible almost-betrothed. "Most of London believed I was courting Lady Yasmin, but in truth, I was coming here to play chess nearly every morning."

"That's because you thought of Stella as a little sis—" Mrs. Thyme broke off, her mouth forming a comical circle. "You didn't?"

He shook his head. "Never."

Stella was watching, arms folded over her chest. "Perhaps you might leave now, Your Grace."

Silvester kept his eyes on Mrs. Thyme. "I didn't debauch your niece, but we have kissed."

"Stella!"

"Several times."

"Traitor," Stella hissed.

"If she doesn't agree to marry me," he said

steadily, "the next time we are kissing, I *will* caress her inappropriately."

"That's easily solved," Stella said. "No more kissing! You warned me about men, Aunt, and—"

This time her aunt interrupted. "His Grace showed restraint, if I understand him appropriately."

"Which nearly killed me," Silvester said. "Only my father's precepts stood between me and disgrace. My disgrace, I hasten to add."

Mrs. Thyme's eyes fired.

"No!" Stella gasped.

"You are compromised," her aunt announced. "We'll keep it to ourselves, naturally. But you will marry the duke, Stella."

"I don't wish to."

"Then you shouldn't have kissed him." A hard edge came into her aunt's voice. "While I am happy that the duke was able to show a restraint that few men can muster, I know you, Stella. Had you not welcomed those kisses, you would have boxed him on the ears. Tell me that you were an unwilling participant, and this shall go no farther."

She was incorrigibly honest, his little Stella.

To his horror, her eyes filled with tears.

Silvester's heart sank as if weighted with lead. "Is it such a dreadful prospect to marry me?"

"It will be an adjustment," Stella said, her voice breaking. "I've adjusted before. If you'll excuse me, Your Grace, Aunt, I wish to retire to my chamber."

"Stella!"

She turned away without another word and walked rather blindly toward the door. Silvester's muscles tensed, instructing him to leap after her, to catch her in his arms and kiss those tears away.

A hand patted his arm. "Let her go," Mrs. Thyme said. "Marriage is a shock for a woman as independent as Stella."

"I do not plan to take away her independence."

"How will you not? A lady has nominal control over her future, though we pay obeisance to the idea with kneeling, jointures, rings, and so on."

Silvester was silent.

"Lady Yasmin chose her spouse," Mrs. Thyme said wryly. "Few other women are so lucky."

"I didn't mean to—" He stopped and began again. "I asked your husband for the right to propose to her."

"But you made certain the marriage would occur by offering my niece clandestine kisses. I must say, you are lucky that Lady Yasmin changed her mind and chose the earl. If I understand you, Stella has kissed you—I gather, several times—in the midst of your courtship of Lady Yasmin, which might well have ended in betrothal. After all, you are—"

"I am a duke," he said hollowly.

"Exactly. The lady's choice of a lower title is unusual."

Silvester was trying to think, but he felt dazed and incoherent. One side of him was jubilant. For good or ill, he wanted Stella in his life more than he'd ever wanted Yasmin, or gold, or anything else he'd pursued.

But the other side of him recoiled from the desperation he'd seen in her eyes.

"I have to speak to her," he said hoarsely. "I have to persuade her."

"Not yet," Mrs. Thyme said. "I know Stella. She is nothing if not rational. If you give her time, she will understand. When she first came here as a little girl, after her parents died, I was afraid she wouldn't speak again."

"Wouldn't *speak*?"

"She didn't speak for three days, probably the longest days of my life. She simply stared at me, completely mute. I had no idea what to *do* with a child, let alone one who wouldn't talk. Mr. Thyme and I had already concluded that our lives were best spent apart, so obviously children were not an option."

"I see," Silvester said, his heart aching for small Stella.

"I see now that I should have marched out to the stables and picked out a kitten," Mrs. Thyme mused. "Instead I left her in the nursery."

"Surely she had a nanny?"

"Of course, but the woman was new, as the previous one refused to travel to London. Nanny Price came down every afternoon and reported that the child hadn't said a word, refused to allow her hair to be brushed, and wasn't sleeping.

"Then on the fourth day, Stella emerged from the nursery, that mad cap of hair braided, and said, 'Good morning, Aunt Thyme.' After that, everything was fine."

It didn't sound fine to Silvester. He would have stayed in that nursery and read stories to his niece until she fell asleep.

"She has always been a dutiful girl. She will accustom herself to the new state of affairs," Mrs. Thyme said. "You will now be her lord and master, to quote the *Book of Common Prayer.*"

Apparently seeing the revulsion in his eyes, she smiled and patted his arm again. "I don't expect your mother paid much attention to that description?"

"No."

"Fair warning. I doubt that Stella will either."

CHAPTER TWENTY-FOUR

Stella was curled up in bed with a purring cat under her chin when a man broke into her bedchamber. He came over the slate roof of the conservatory, just as Mrs. Thyme had prophesized, pushed open the sash, and slung a leg over the windowsill.

Even seeing no more than a dark outline against the haze of a London night told Stella who was intruding. It was the broad-shouldered, oh-so-ethical duke, supposedly tormented by the mere memory of climbing the stairs with her.

Stupidly, her heart sped up. Her body tingled at the sight of Silvester, no matter how much her stomach clenched with anger. "If I had a glass of water, I'd throw it at you," she said by way of greeting.

"You could throw your cat," Silvester said. "I can hear Specs purring like a small motor."

Specs opened her eyes, luminous in the darkness, before she collapsed back into sleep. Stella dropped a kiss on one silky ear. "You must leave. I'm in bed, in my nightdress. You're not supposed to see it until our wedding night. Which, by the way, my aunt has decreed will not take place for six months or more."

Rather to her surprise, Silvester didn't move toward

the bed. Instead, he leaned back against the window-sill. "It's too dark to see much of you."

"I'm not wearing my glasses. Now you know what it feels like. Leave."

"I have to speak to you."

She stroked Specs's ear. "Why? You know, and I know, that I am hoist by *your* petard. You blew up my plans for my future. I have no choice but to marry you."

Silence.

Then: "I had no idea that your aunt would feel as strongly as she did. I apologize."

"My aunt's response is irrelevant. You wanted what I would not grant you. In case you are wondering, I know why."

In the dim light of the single candle burning on her dressing table, she saw him fold his arms over his broad chest. She didn't like Silvester very much at the moment. But for some damn reason, she desired every hairy, muscled inch of him.

"You do? Why is that?" he inquired, his voice expressing no more than polite interest.

"Yasmin is in love with Giles. You could have compromised *her* and forced her to marry you, but you would never do that."

A sound that was suspiciously like a growl came from the window. "Tell me, why is Yasmin exempt from my evil designs?"

"You adore her," Stella said. "I watched the two of you together. I didn't know what I was seeing at first, but now . . . Now I do understand. I saw Yasmin swat you after you addressed her with an endearment. I'll wager anything, all the gold you have, that she never allowed you to kiss her."

Silence, then: "I never tried to kiss her."

"Which is why you wouldn't compromise her," Stella said, a wave of exhaustion breaking over her head. "You adored her as a being above such menial emotions as lust. When you lost the object of your adoration, you settled for desire. Which I do have. For you."

She didn't allow her voice to be defiant. Women had the right to feel lust, just as much as men did.

"It's possible that you think a man has to choose lust or love," she said, spilling out everything that had gone through her head since she walked out of the drawing room. "You are wrong, by the way."

"Interesting."

He was clearly enraged, speaking through clenched teeth. But then Silvester never liked being corrected, did he? It went with the coronet, with the condition of being a swollen bullfrog.

"Merry's husband adores *and* desires her," Stella said. "I would guess he courted and seduced her."

Silvester snorted. "He did more than that. Their wedding was notorious. He stole her from his own brother."

Stella swallowed hard. She was happy that her friend had the experience of having a man adore her so much that he stole her. Merry deserved it. She was lovable.

"Don't you see, Silvester? You could have that too. You are behaving irrationally, in the aftermath of Yasmin's rejection of you. You are giving up too soon." She hesitated. "We could explain away your proposal. No one knows except my aunt."

Silvester walked across the room and bent over her

in the dark. Specs hissed and leaped from the bed. "You're a fool."

"Charming," Stella said, trying to stop her heart from speeding up.

"Do you want to know why I played my trump card, why I told your aunt I'd kissed you?"

"I know why. You're not evil," Stella said, feeling a wave of sadness. "But you are used to getting your own way. Far too used to it. You're a swollen bullfrog, in Merry's words. I understand."

"No, you don't. I want you so badly that I will do *anything* to have you, Stella. *Anything.* So put that calculation into your little witch's brew of incorrect assumptions." He leaned closer until his lips almost touched hers, his arms braced on either side of her head. "You think Yasmin's kisses would have been so damned heady that I would ignore a dead rodent?"

Stella swallowed. "How would you know, if you never kissed her?"

"I never *wanted* to kiss her!" he growled. His tongue swept across her bottom lip. "I don't just want to kiss you, Stella. I want to ravish you."

Stella couldn't stop herself from kissing him back because his voice was impassioned, and domineering . . . and maybe, just a little uncertain.

Next thing she knew he was lying next to her, kissing her so deeply that there didn't seem to be a beginning or end to their bodies. She was surrounded by heat and passion, desire flooding her veins. Silvester's hand curved around her cheek, and he was murmuring things in a voice so low she couldn't pay attention to them.

About desire, about her lips, about the way she kissed, about her eyes, about . . .

"You may not ravish me," she said.

He pulled his head back. In the dim light, he resembled a hawk, a predatory animal with grace and murder in its grip.

"You are mine," he retorted.

Stella was tired of the whole conversation. Her heart was bruised, but honestly? She had no chance of escaping being a duchess, not after Silvester fixed his gaze on her.

She wouldn't get what he gave Yasmin, but she would have something Yasmin never had.

That was important, right? They could build on lust.

"All right," she said with a shaky sigh.

Silvester rolled her flat on her back and then draped a heavy thigh over her, presumably to keep her in place, though Stella had no thought of leaping from the bed. "All right, you'll marry me?"

She nodded.

"We're getting married." He caught up her left hand and shoved something cold down her second finger.

Stella didn't bother to look at her hand. Knowing him, the ring was gold and studded with invaluable gems, the kind that queens squabbled over.

Instead she looked at his shadowed face. "You're going to bully me."

"You'll bully me right back," he said instantly.

"Did you return home to fetch that ring or were you carrying it this morning?"

"I had it this morning. I thought of coming to you immediately, but my pantaloons would have split, climbing the wall, and I was afraid your aunt might order a groom to shoot me as an intruder. So I went home and glowered at my mother until she threatened to retire to the country."

Stella ran her fingers down Silvester's cheeks to his chin, realizing he wasn't wearing a cravat. His neck was muscled and strong. "Did you wear the scarab this morning for good luck?"

"My mother insisted. Before you get around to telling me that my mother dictated my choice of wife, it didn't make a damn bit of difference to me that she likes you so much."

Stella crooked a knee, which pulled tight the frail linen of her nightgown so she could feel exactly what was pulsing against her thigh.

He let out a muffled groan.

Inside, she was exhilarated—and terrified. How would she survive the moment in the future when her husband looked across the ballroom and saw a woman who was as delicate and gossamer as Yasmin? One who would put that expression on his face, that *adoring* expression?

Her heart felt as if it might crack at the thought.

"My aunt spent a good deal of the afternoon celebrating your extraordinary restraint in the face of my imprudence."

"Imprudence?" He cupped her face, angling it so he could kiss her deeply.

Imprudently.

"You did a reasonable job of playing a Holy Willy tormented by the memory of walking a lady up a staircase," Stella said, when she was able to talk again.

He dipped his head so that his forehead met hers. Then he said in a husky voice, "I am gifted at playing a role, Stella. It hardly matters to me which it is. I've never bothered with self-righteousness, but if you want me to transform into a prissy duke, I can do so."

"Hmmm." She tilted her head to capture his lips again. She was marrying a chameleon, but as long as she could see his eyes, she would know what he was thinking. The pirate shone out of them, no matter what stories people liked to weave about His Grace's genial manners.

Everyone likes him, her aunt had said.

Silvester's elbows were braced at either side of her head, that big body of his stretched over her, practically forcing her to arch against him because . . .

Because she had to.

"Don't," Silvester said, the word dark as midnight.

Stella arched again, and wiggled against him for good measure.

A groan broke from his throat. "You're never going to obey me, are you?"

"Absolutely not. You could have chosen a docile woman, but you didn't," Stella said, feeling irrationally cheered by the thought. "I'm going to beat you in chess for the rest of our lives."

"I've beat you a few times," he muttered.

He nipped her ear. Stella's hands tightened on his thick upper arms, as if he might try to get away from her.

"Once," she whispered. "You beat me once."

He bit her ear again, making her tremble. "Do you like this?"

"We can't do this, Silvester," she whispered. "I couldn't face my aunt if I let you seduce me."

His head reared back, and he frowned. "Speaking of your aunt . . ."

"Something terrible happened to her, I think,"

Stella said, telling him something she'd never mentioned to another soul. "Not my uncle. He truly cares only for gourds."

"I got that impression when he dragged me around the bedding gardens before he allowed me to mention you," Silvester said dryly.

"For obvious reasons, they never had children."

He kissed her senseless again before he whispered, "We will have children, Stella."

"They'll be half-blind, like me," she said, clearing her throat.

Silvester shrugged. "I like your spectacles. I'm hoping they have your freckles too."

"Short and stocky, like me." She told him the truth. "Everyone is going to be shocked that you courted a woman as beautiful as Yasmin only to marry me, Silvester. Their surprise will be hard to bear."

"They only have to observe us together to know the truth. I can't stop looking at you," Silvester said, his voice hoarse with truthfulness. All pirate. No duke. "For God's sake, Stella, you can't doubt how much I desire you."

"Ladies like Blanche will believe that you need my dowry. If you had married Yasmin, they would have believed the marriage was forged for genuine reasons." Exhaustion caught her unawares. "I don't suppose it matters. No one would ever imagine that my marriage would involve romance."

He moved sharply, and she added, "I'm not whining about it, Silvester. Well, I suppose I *am*, but I oughtn't to. I'm so lucky."

"Yes, imagine," he said, his voice dry. "You are being forced to marry a duke."

Stella sighed. "They'll all see it the other way around, believe me. The only question will be what forced you to do it."

"Does it matter? You'll be a duchess."

"Does it matter?" She shook her head at him. "My aunt told me that no one in society dislikes you, Silvester. *You* ask that, you who have crafted your entire life around what other people think of you?"

His eyes narrowed. "I suppose you might see it that way."

"I *do* see it that way, but I'm not . . . it would be hypocritical to say that I wouldn't have done the same, if I had your charm. I occasionally rub white lotion on my face to cover my freckles. I have contemplated taking my spectacles off and blundering around the ballroom."

"I like your freckles." He dropped a kiss on her nose.

"Those are shallow things," Stella said impatiently. "If I had the allure that you have, I might well have flaunted it. I can't stop myself from asking the wrong kind of questions and volunteering the wrong sort of information."

"One of the things I like best about you is that you're interesting," Silvester said, splattering kisses on her face like a spring rain shower. "Don't worry about what society thinks."

"Says the man whom everyone loves," she said dryly. "In a perfect world, I would like society to think that my fiancé had chosen me over Yasmin. Not *instead* of Yasmin."

He was silent for a moment. "Your aunt told me that I was lucky she didn't accept my hand. My mother said the same, emphatically and repeatedly. I didn't choose you instead of Yasmin, though I understand that it looks that way."

Stella was constitutionally prone to making the best of things. Her whole childhood had been a lesson in that particular art: for example, her mother's terror of her freckles had led to her love of reading. Obviously, there were huge benefits to marrying Silvester, namely: being a duchess and going to bed with Silvester. She just had to focus on those things.

She wound her arms around his neck. "I suppose I'll get used to being married to the most beloved man in London."

"You're exaggerating." He brushed his thumbs over her forehead and down her temples. "Do you have freckles everywhere?"

The raw note in his voice made blood throb in her veins. "Yes, I do. They're . . . My mother loathed them."

"I don't."

Silvester meant it. Stella could hear truth in his voice. He liked the fact that she was speckled as a hen. Or even worse, as speckled as a toad, a charming phrase she'd overheard in a ballroom one night.

"More than anything, I want to strip this gown off you and caress every freckle, every curve," Silvester muttered. "With every part of me."

In case she didn't understand the implication, he rubbed that part of himself, the rigid, large *cock*, against her thigh.

"No!" Stella squeaked, alarmed by the sweet heat that made her want to curl her legs around his hips. "I mean it, Silvester."

He groaned. "Will you marry me by special license?"

"Absolutely not!" She could just imagine Mrs.

Thyme's reaction to that. Special licenses were only for disreputable unions. "My aunt is considering a Christmas wedding."

He shook his head. "We're calling the banns this Sunday."

She probably should complain, except Silvester was sliding down the bed, pulling up her nightdress as he went. "What are you doing?" Stella demanded, raising her head and gaping down at him.

"Kissing you."

She was going to protest: *of course* she was going to protest, but she didn't have time to formulate the words. Silvester nudged her legs apart and settled himself there while she was still trying to get over the erotic sensation of his callused hands touching her inner thighs.

"I don't—"

He blew on her most intimate part, and she broke off with a gasp.

"You're exquisite," Silvester breathed.

"It's dark. You can't see me," Stella objected.

"I don't need to see you. You're soft. You smell like honey and flowers." He licked her inner thigh. "Hello," he crooned, pushing her legs a little farther apart and dropping his head between her legs. "I don't need to see you to lick every delicate petal."

Stella slapped her hands over her eyes and let her hips arch toward him, asking silently for more. Begging for the broad finger that slipped inside her. The second finger that joined it. The relentless rasp of his tongue that tingled down her legs.

His pumping fingers made her shake, made pleading sounds tumble from her lips, turned her from a thinking human being into a mindless, raging fire. Sensation swept down her legs, swamped her body.

Stella opened her mouth to scream just as one of Silvester's hands covered her lips. Heat ripped through her, curling her toes. Just as she calmed, he did something with his fingers, together with a lick and a gentle bite, and the sensation raged down her legs once again.

Afterward she lay flat, panting. Silvester yanked down her nightgown, shifted up, and even in the dim light and without her glasses, she saw his triumphant grin. "I win," he whispered against her lips.

Stella thought about responding to that blatant provocation, but what was the point? If he thought she cared whether he won *this* particular game, he was out of his mind.

"I don't mind losing," she managed, shocked to hear the rasp in her voice.

He braced himself over her, his eyes sparkling with piratical pleasure. "You can win at chess, and *I* will win at this."

Stella's eyes shifted down. She couldn't see the front of his breeches, but when she put her hand down and cupped him . . . He threw back his head, leaving the cords of his powerful neck visible in the moonlight.

"Perhaps we should drop the idea of mastery in the bedchamber," she suggested, tightening her hand into a caress. "We could both win."

Silvester rolled off the bed and stood up. Stella had the sudden conviction that Silvester didn't know how to live without competing. Without winning.

"You're not marrying me because I can beat you at chess, are you?" she asked.

"Don't be a fool," he growled, *not* something that the elegant Duke of Huntington would say.

Stella couldn't stop herself from smiling. Polite society could keep their oh-so-perfect duke as long as she got the shamelessly unsaintlike man standing at her bedside, looking at her with a burning intensity that suggested he might beat a nightly thoroughfare over her uncle's greenhouse and through her window if she didn't stop him.

"You may not come to my bedchamber again," she said, making that into an order. He didn't have to obey her always, but if their marriage was to be successful, he had to listen to her sometimes.

"First banns this Sunday," he growled. "Marriage after the third week of banns."

"That will cause a scandal," Stella murmured, not caring much, but feeling she ought to point it out.

Silvester shrugged. He bent down and kissed her, then headed for the window. "Goodbye, fiancée," he said, satisfaction palpable in his voice.

Damn it.

The bullfroggish duke had got what he wanted again.

CHAPTER TWENTY-FIVE

Blanche was eating breakfast when her mother yelped and tossed her favorite gossip sheet across the table. "Look! Just look at this!"

"Lord and Lady Pettigrew have returned from their wedding trip," Blanche read, after plucking the page out of the butter dish. "Yes, I know. Lydia sent me a note this morning."

"Not *that*, below! The announcement!"

"Oh." And then: "*Oh*."

"That betrothal will set the cat among the pigeons. They all wanted the duke. Or they wanted to be his duchess, which is practically the same thing, isn't it? And polite society, at least the female half of it, spent a great deal of the Season tearing down Lady Stella before he chose her over all the rest. They'll say he needed her money."

"I doubt that," Blanche said, thinking of the Duke of Huntington's assured air.

"So do I."

"Do you see the note below? The Dowager Duchess of Huntington, together with Lady Stella and Mrs. Thyme, welcome morning callers. That's a show of force designed to counter unpleasant conjectures."

Blanche rose. "If you'll excuse me, Mother, I should answer Lydia. She would like to meet."

"Sit down."

She sat. Lady Boodle rarely used that tone of voice.

"This would be an excellent moment to sever the connection with Lydia."

Blanche's mouth fell open. "What?"

"You have been friends since you were young girls in seminary," her mother said. "You have been admirably loyal. Now Lydia is married, so it will be easier to let the connection go."

"But why should I?"

"Let me ask you this, Blanche. Who in all society has uttered the most unkind remarks about our newest duchess-to-be?"

"Lydia," Blanche said reluctantly.

"And you."

Blanche swallowed. "I did apologize to Stella after I said something unpleasant."

"Lydia brings out the worst in you," Lady Boodle said dispassionately. "She doesn't care whom she injures. You *do* care, but you get drawn in. You imitate her."

"How could I drop Lydia?" Blanche protested. "I was her only friend in seminary. The others made fun of her because her father took his life. It was so unfair."

"I am proud of you for not succumbing to such a callous impulse, but it is possible to honor Lydia for your girlhood friendship and yet not be drawn into her circle once again. She is married now. She'll be making friends with young matrons, flagrantly unfaithful ones, most likely."

"But—"

Her mother leaned across the table. "Blanche, a

friend in Belgium sent me a letter detailing Lydia's indiscretions while she was on her *honeymoon*."

"Oh," Blanche said weakly.

"She created a scandal, flirting with a ramshackle Frenchman in her husband's presence."

"Poor Lord Pettigrew," Blanche murmured, picturing the mild-mannered gentleman. Though she wasn't surprised. As the daughter of an earl, Lydia had always considered herself above the rules that dictated ladylike behavior. "She enjoys thumbing her nose at society."

"My point is that Lydia Pettigrew is likely to become truly scandalous as a married woman, rather than merely imprudent and unkind. I do not wish you to be associated with her, nor to imitate her in behavior or attitude."

"But I'm her only friend. They were *awful* to her in school, Mother."

"That may explain why Lydia behaves badly, but it does not excuse her cruelty. More importantly, Blanche, you are a follower. To be blunt, I believe one of the reasons you have been disappointed as regards marriage proposals, collecting them only from manifestly unsuitable men, is due to the fact you ape her mannerisms. Men are afraid of cruelty. They back away."

Blanche felt herself turning pale. "I never meant to be cruel."

"Lady Stella will soon be one of the most powerful women in London. How many unkind jests have you made about the future duchess, while striving to be clever?"

After a moment of silence, Blanche said, "Too many."

"If Stella had remained the least powerful woman in high society was your behavior acceptable?"

Blanche felt shame washing over her. "No. No, I've been despicable."

"Send Lydia a message saying that you cannot meet her, as we plan to visit the Dowager Duchess of Huntington, the better to congratulate her on her son's betrothal." Her mother rose to her feet.

Blanche nodded.

"Naturally, you will greet Lydia politely when you encounter her in a ballroom. But no more private meetings. She may well drag you into shameful behavior, and you are without the protection of a husband."

"Lydia is not *truly* scandalous," Blanche said in one final protest. "She merely kisses young men now and then. I would feel disloyal if I drop her."

"In my opinion, you must choose between being disloyal and unmarried." Her mother swept from the room.

Blanche sat staring at the butter-stained gossip sheet. When girls in seminary were mean to Lydia due to her father's suicide, she and Lydia had retaliated with unkind jokes. In the hothouse environment of a girls' school, witty put-downs felt retributory. Justified.

They weren't justified any longer. She had been unkind to Lady Stella. She had spread malicious gossip and even called her names behind her back.

Why?

Most often, to make Lydia laugh, because then Blanche felt as if the two of them were the cleverest women in the room. Examples of her own petty behavior flooded her memory, moments when she had uttered facile, mean jests.

Shame made her feel sick, not because of missed proposals, but because she had behaved just like the girls from seminary that she had loathed.

She had become them.

Her mother popped her head back in the room. "Your maid is waiting for you, Blanche. I should like to be the first of the dowager's callers. I'm sure most of society will beat a path to her door."

Blanche felt even sicker at the idea of greeting Stella. She would deserve it if the future duchess gave her the cut direct. Not that Stella would ever do such a thing, which was probably why Stella, short, eccentric Stella, had won the hand of the most eligible bachelor in London.

"You will find Her Grace in the drawing room," the ducal butler told them when Blanche and her mother arrived at the Duke of Huntington's mansion. "We expect a crush, and she would prefer to greet her guests personally, in lieu of formal pronouncements."

When Blanche and her mother entered the drawing room, the first person she saw was not their hostess, but Lydia. She was standing in the middle of the room, eyes glinting, chin high. Stella and the dowager were facing her, and Mrs. Thyme was standing to the side, clutching her smelling salts.

No one noticed their entry.

"I merely said what everyone was thinking!" Lydia remarked with a shrill titter.

Future duchess or no, Stella looked exactly the same. Her spectacles were firmly on her nose, she hadn't bothered to cover up her freckles, and she wore no lip color.

"That's just it," Stella responded. "Everyone was

not thinking such unkind thoughts, Lydia. *You* were thinking them—and saying them aloud. I must ask you to restrain yourself."

Blanche was astounded by how brave Stella was. Even when Blanche thought Lydia had gone too far, she had never dared criticize her. Fear would slosh around in her stomach like sour sherry until the impulse passed.

"Nonsense!" Lydia snorted. "I only remarked that the Duke of Huntington must be grateful for your large dowry, Lady Stella. That's a fact. Any man would be grateful for such a bountiful gift."

"My fiancé has no need for money," Stella said.

"That's right," the dowager chimed in, scowling at Lydia.

"I'm afraid that you must brace yourself for more queries," Lydia cooed. "As Stella knows, Blanche and I did our best to refine her appearance." She eyed Stella head to toe. "The match will be seen as a mystery, for obvious reasons."

"My son is desperately in love with Stella," the dowager declared.

"*Is* he? I was under the impression that he adored my sister-in-law, Lady Yasmin."

Stella's cheeks had turned pink, but she held her head high. "Silvester likes my freckles and spectacles. Your advice was not necessary."

"Not when an unchaperoned carriage ride could do the work for you," Lydia said unpleasantly. "One must commend the duke for his adherence to the rules governing honorable behavior."

To Blanche's surprise, Stella smiled. "He would agree."

"After my niece refused His Grace's offer, he insisted that a simple kiss had compromised her virtue," Mrs. Thyme put in. "He would not take no for an answer."

Lydia raised an eyebrow. "A *duke* considered himself compromised by a kiss?"

Stella's smile widened, but she didn't respond.

"You're mighty priggish for someone whose honeymoon was apparently quite eventful," the dowager duchess said.

Lydia's eyes flared.

Blanche winced. Lydia enjoyed a battle of wits, which boiled down to her firing a volley of insults. But when the tables were turned? If she fell in a rage, she threw all restraint to the wind.

"At least Lord Pettigrew married a woman. He won't find me mucking about with an oily engine, pretending to be a man!"

Mrs. Thyme audibly gasped.

"Stop it," Stella ordered, her deep voice filling the room.

Lydia narrowed her eyes.

Stella raised her hand, palm forward. "*No.*"

She may be small and round, but Blanche suddenly realized that Stella had something Lydia didn't have: strength of character. Her steady, calm eyes regarded Lydia through her despised spectacles. "You may not be rude to Her Grace under her own roof. I must ask you to leave."

Lydia scoffed. "As if *you*—"

"She speaks for me," the dowager said cheerfully.

Lydia tossed her head. "I suppose you hope to rule the ton because you've jumped up through marriage. We'll see about that. I am an earl's daughter."

Mrs. Thyme moved to stand beside Stella. "I am a marquess's daughter," she said in a grating voice, utterly unlike her usual flighty tones. "My bloodline goes back to William the Conqueror. I would be ashamed to act as you have. To *be* who you are."

"We are all overset," Stella said as she put her arm around her aunt's waist. "It would be best to forget this conversation. I am sure you are tired by your sea journey, Lady Lydia."

"I am not such a ninny!" Lydia's eyes traveled from the dowager's face, to Mrs. Thyme's, to Stella's. "I did no more than repeat what everyone is saying. I suppose you all hope I will fall to my knees in tears, proclaiming myself a horrid person."

"You have no need to proclaim it, when so many other people can do it for you," the dowager retorted.

Lydia curled her lip and turned away. "Blanche, come. I fancy a lavender ice from Gunther's. I found the Continent shamefully impoverished in culinary matters."

"No," Blanche said, without need for a prompt from her mother.

"You dare." Lydia's voice was flat.

Blanche had never noticed how fishy and cold her friend's eyes were. She imitated Stella's stance, squaring her shoulders, folding her hands. "Goodbye, Lady Pettigrew."

Silence held in the room as Lydia walked through the door and down the corridor, snapping something at the butler, her voice fading.

"Well," the dowager duchess said briskly, "there's a woman who is incapable of kindness, even at knifepoint."

Stella drew in a deep breath.

Her fingers were trembling. She had finally stood up for herself. Or rather, stood up for the dowager, but most importantly, she had fought back.

One of the reasons she had decided to refuse Giles's proposal, if he had made it, was because she could not bear Lydia. Would she have had the courage to fight back without the shadow of a dukedom at her shoulder?

As if she heard that thought, her aunt spoke up. "You are already a duchess, Stella. I've always scolded you for being blunt, but on this occasion I applaud it. My sister would be so proud."

All she had to do to gain Mrs. Thyme's approval was force a bully to a standstill?

Lady Boodle and Blanche had been frozen before the door, but now Lady Boodle stepped forward and dropped a curtsy. "Good morning."

"Lady Boodle, I apologize for the fact you witnessed such an unpleasant encounter," the dowager said briskly. "I shall ring for tea. Vitriol always makes me thirsty."

Blanche caught Stella's hand before she could turn away.

"I want to apologize. And not because you're going to be a duchess."

"You didn't say anything; Lydia did."

"I have in the past, and I'm ashamed," Blanche said bluntly. "I should have stood up to her the way you did. Instead, I joined in. I ought to have been brave, like you."

Stella gave her a wavering smile. "I don't feel brave. Actually, I feel rather sick."

"Many times I didn't like something Lydia said or

did, but I never had the courage to tell her so. I made it worse by imitating her. I am afraid that we made your Season intolerable."

"You tried to help when you gave me the face paint," Stella pointed out. She took a deep breath. "Why should I care if people think I don't deserve the rank? Or the husband? Lydia will say what she wishes."

"Miss Boodle, Stella, come join us," the dowager called from the couches.

"The dowager duchess addresses you by your first name," Blanche said. "I wouldn't have thought . . . She's so brusque."

"Her Grace is very nice if you chat with her," Stella said.

"I wouldn't dare *chat* with a duchess."

Stella blinked. "She's just another person, like you and me."

"No, she's a duchess."

"I'm going to be a duchess too. Yet I'm the same person I was: freckled, and bespectacled, and prone to dropping wineglasses and saying the wrong thing. Lydia is right: I don't have style, taste, or beauty."

"Yes, you do," Blanche said. "Lydia was wrong, and so was I."

When they joined the others, Mrs. Thyme was fretting about Lydia. "That young woman will say unpleasant things about my niece. We have to stop her somehow."

"That would be difficult," Lady Boodle said, sipping her tea.

"I shall ignore her," Stella said. "I don't care what she says."

"She's right," the dowager put in. "Unkind blather has force only if the person affected listens. You can't imagine all the things that have been said about me over the years. I don't give a damn, and I suggest you follow my lead, Stella. When you walk down the aisle, they'll all be whispering nasty tidbits, no doubt."

Stella groaned silently. A wonderful prospect for her wedding day.

"Everyone is naked under their clothes," Blanche said, unexpectedly.

Mrs. Thyme cast her an appalled look.

"One of the facts that we don't care to think about," Blanche clarified. "It doesn't make it less true. If someone is mocking you, imagine her naked. Or him."

"That is *not* the action of a lady," Mrs. Thyme said, clearly appalled.

Stella laughed. "I can do that."

CHAPTER TWENTY-SIX

A few weeks later, polite society crowded into a cathedral to watch a woman in spectacles walk down the aisle toward the most handsome and most eligible man in London.

Lillian Thyme could scarcely believe it. After all the anguish and fear she'd experienced since her sister died, her orphaned niece—her short, freckled niece, spectacles and all—was marrying a *duke*.

Lillian kept reeling between joy and terror, unable to stop herself from worrying that people would be unkind. From the first moment she met her mute, plump little niece, she had silently promised her sister that she would do her very best to marry Stella to a good man.

But she never expected a *duke*.

Even now, the nave was crammed with whispering women entertaining themselves by coming up with more and more fanciful reasons why the Duke of Huntington was stooping to marry Stella.

According to Mr. Thyme, the betting book at White's was coming down hard on the idea that His Grace had lost all his money, but the claim that Stella had managed to compromise him was a strong contender. Lillian had overheard Lydia Pettigrew suggesting that Stella's rounded figure concealed a ducal heir on the way.

She rarely gave set-downs, but she had swept down on the tittering group like an avenging fury.

As Stella entered the cathedral on Mr. Thyme's arm, everyone rose, turning to gawk. Her gown was fashioned from thick, pale pink silk. It draped low, tightly clinging to her bosom before falling to the ground. A cape of gold lace hung from her shoulders and swept behind her. Her hair was caught up with gold pins that glinted in the light from the cathedral's chandeliers.

Lillian couldn't help smiling. Her niece was *beautiful*.

"Look at the groom," the Duke of Trent said quietly to his wife. As Stella's dearest friend, the duchess and her husband sat in the front pew beside Lillian. "That's the way I looked at you, terrified you would run away before I could claim you."

Merry, as Stella called her, chuckled and reached up to kiss her husband's cheek, which made Lillian think about how quickly the world was changing. The rules that she grew up with didn't seem to apply any longer. She could scarcely believe that her own niece regularly addressed a duchess by her first name.

Her mother would have been horrified had anyone offered such an affront, but these days even Lillian caught herself thinking of the Duchess of Trent as Merry.

The Duke of Huntington—Silvester—was known throughout society for his pleasing manner: his easy flow of language, agreeable address, self-possession, and charm. Now he wore an intent expression that Lillian had never seen on his face, paired with a tension that made his body look twice as large as normal.

To her mind, he was already unfashionably big. Thankfully, her husband was slight and hardly taller than she. Mr. Thyme bowed to His Grace and left his niece at the altar, returning to sit at Lillian's right.

When the duke said his vows, his voice was not a sophisticated drawl, but deep and almost rough, his eyes fixed on Stella's face.

It wasn't until the new couple were walking back down the aisle together that Lillian again saw the duke she recognized, a gallant, sophisticated man sauntering along, smiling at all the guests.

"He is keeping an arm around her," Merry observed.

The Duke of Trent looked down at his wife with a smile. "I was just as relieved walking you back down the aisle. I had been terrified that you would run out of the church screaming."

Merry leaned into his side, beaming up at him. "Instead, I created a scandal by kissing you."

He dropped a kiss on her nose. "Exactly what I hoped for from my American Duchess."

Lillian pretended not to notice. Manners may be changing, but *she* would never countenance such an exhibition of inelegant breeding.

All the wedding guests emerged from the shadowy cathedral into bright sunlight, to find the new duchess laughing as her lace cape billowed in a light breeze.

Instead of the ducal barouche, footmen in velvet were leading forward a snow-white horse that had to be nine hands tall at least. It had been fitted with a saddle of silver leather with velvet trim and silver tassels, its reins shining in the sun.

Stella was giggling so hard that she dropped her bouquet of flowers in the street. Lillian couldn't help sighing when the duke placed Stella carefully on the saddle and vaulted up behind her. It was like a fairy tale: all she could have wished for her niece.

Stella's lace cape caught under her husband's leg, and His Grace plucked it free, tossing it to a footman. Her hairpins fell out, and red ringlets spilled down her shoulders. Normally, Lillian would have shuddered at her niece's disarray, but all around her, guests were remarking on Stella's delightful hair.

"You did well, Mrs. Thyme," her husband said in his quiet way. "Our niece is now one of the highest in the land."

Lillian smiled at him, noticing he had distinguished streaks of white hair over his ears. They were both growing old, but now that Stella was taken care of, it wouldn't matter. "I think my sister would be happy."

A group of scruffy men, gossip columnists, stood on the opposite side of the street, scribbling madly on scraps of paper. Behind them, liveried grooms held back hordes of Londoners, who had gathered to see the new duchess.

The duke's coachman walked with magisterial slowness to his master, hoisting a large canvas sack in the air. Silvester pulled small velvet pouches from the sack and began tossing them to the excited crowd of Londoners.

"Those velvet bags are a step up from tossing a handful of coins, the way most bridegrooms do," Lillian whispered to her husband.

"That should squash the rumor that Huntington married Stella for her money," Mr. Thyme responded. "This is all very shrewd of the duke. A woman carrying a child cannot ride a horse. His Grace would never endanger his heir, so this is an efficient way of quelling the claim that our niece is *enceinte*."

"He managed to crush the idea that he had lost his money *and* counter the claim that Stella is carrying a child," Lillian said, awed by the duke's forethought.

When the bag was empty, His Grace put an arm around Stella and pulled her against his chest. She waved at Lillian and blew her a kiss. When they took off at a canter, the tears Lillian had been suppressing rolled down her cheeks.

"She's go-gone."

Mr. Thyme handed her a snowy white handkerchief. "Not for long."

"She caused me such grief," Lillian said, trying to explain. "But without her . . . there's nothing in London without her."

"Then come to the country," Mr. Thyme said. When he smiled, his eyes crinkled in a kindly fashion. "The duke promised to bring our niece for a visit."

Lillian had never considered leaving the city, but in contrast to the brittle, gossiping people who surrounded her, Mr. Thyme suddenly seemed like a safe harbor.

"Kittens had just been born when I left," he said.

"Oh," Lillian managed, blotting her cheeks.

"Red as Stella's hair," he added.

CHAPTER TWENTY-SEVEN

Stella's teeth were just beginning to feel rattled when Silvester rounded the corner and drew up next to an imposing barouche, shaped like one of her uncle's gourds, albeit with an escutcheon painted on its bulbous side. Grooms, dressed in the normal Huntington livery rather than white velvet, dashed toward them.

"That was a short ride," Stella remarked, turning her head to look up at Silvester.

"Hello, wife," he said, just touching her nose with one finger before he jumped down and held up his arms.

Stella leaned forward and allowed him to pluck her from the saddle. She was filled with emotions that she couldn't identify. She felt like babbling, which she never did. She felt nervous, and excited, and loving, befuddled, besotted . . . all kinds of embarrassing words that she had vowed to herself she would never utter aloud, and wished she wasn't feeling.

"As you know, our townhouse is filled with guests," Silvester said, as Stella climbed into the barouche and sat down. It was lined in midnight blue velvet, and a silver bucket containing ice and champagne was affixed to the wall.

"I am aware of that," Stella said, pushing her wind-tousled hair behind her shoulders as the carriage took off. "My aunt and I penned the invitations to the wedding breakfast."

Silvester leaned forward, plucked her off the carriage seat, and popped her on his lap. "Huntington Grange, on the other hand, is empty. That's our country house."

Stella couldn't bring herself to meet his eyes. It was all too embarrassing. Silvester nudged her head to the side so he could kiss her neck. "Oh," she said lamely.

"I plan to make love to you in every room," Silvester said, the words coming out with burning intensity. "In every damn room, Stella. I mean to strip your clothing off in the library and have my way with you on the manuscript table."

Stella gulped. "I, ah . . ."

"I summoned all the footmen to London for the wedding breakfast. Wickford insisted on leaving a few maids in the country, or I would have emptied the whole place."

"No cook?" Stella inquired, somewhat alarmed.

Silvester's mouth settled over hers without answering. His arms surrounded her with passion and heat that burned through her clothing. *This* emotion she understood.

For whatever reason, the Duke of Huntington was wild with desire for her. She sank into his kiss, swamped by need and the way Silvester's hands were ranging up and down her back, slipping up to her breasts, shaping them in a rough caress that made her tremble.

But there was something she had to ask. "Why . . . Why the white horse?" she managed, once he shifted his mouth to her jaw.

"Horse?" Silvester's voice was thick. He was licking the hollow at the base of Stella's neck in a way that made her shift in his lap. His hands tightened, and a sound came from deep in his throat, next thing to a grunt.

"The horse," Stella persisted. "The white velvet and gold reins?"

"Matched your veil," Silvester said, his lips drifting down to the edge of her bodice. "Your lower lip is so plump and soft, Stella. I love your mouth."

Stella shook off the sensual undertow of his voice, the way his wintery scent seemed warm and enticing up close. "It was a *performance*," she insisted. "Why?"

"Had to silence that damned Lydia Pettigrew," Silvester said, raising his head. "I can't stand the woman."

"You staged a production after our wedding because of Lady Lydia's scorn? You needn't have. I already made it clear to her that she was *persona non grata*."

"No, because I'm your husband," Silvester said.

Husband. The word knocked about in Stella's head. She was tied, vowed to stay with Silvester.

She wiggled again, enjoying the way that Silvester's body jerked in response. "Well, husband, are we not attending our own wedding breakfast?"

"No, because I kidnapped you from the church on my white steed." He kissed her. "My mother and your aunt know, by the way." One hand slid from her hip to her breast.

"Am I going to lose my virginity in this carriage?" she inquired.

"No."

Stella was under the impression that Huntington Grange was at the very least a two days' journey.

"We will sleep in The Swan tonight," Silvester said, his lips running along her bodice. She had the distinct impression that any moment he would pull down that delicate silk so he could kiss her breast.

"No," she said.

His eyes met hers, amused, impassioned. "No to The Swan?"

"No to whatever you're planning to do to my bodice. I could not possibly enter a coaching inn wearing a ripped wedding gown."

"We could do things that would keep your gown intact," Silvester said, his hand running up her leg again.

"Are you referring to The Swan, not far from Notley Abbey?"

"Yes," Silvester said, the word rumbling from his chest.

Once they cleared the city, The Swan would be only an hour's drive outside London. It was a most elegant inn, graced with a French chef and surrounded by gardens of lavender and purple iris.

Stella clamped a hand down on Silvester's, just as his fingers began to slip around her inner thigh. "I can't enter The Swan with a crumpled gown either."

Her husband threw her a mock mournful look.

She shook her head.

He laughed. Stella was shocked to hear the happiness in his voice. Silvester was . . . *happy*. Happy to be married to her.

She had never expected that from any man. She'd always pictured a husband choosing her because he needed her dowry or a hostess or just a wife. She hadn't imagined happiness would be part of that picture.

Stella drew in a deep breath that she hadn't known she needed. Then she scrambled off Silvester's lap and seated herself opposite, winding her hair into a coil and putting it over one shoulder.

"I'm fairly sure that a woman addressed as *Her Grace* shouldn't play the hoyden in a carriage, even with her new husband."

Silvester's eyes traveled over her slowly. "Your wish is my command. Though I should tell you that I reserved the entire inn for the night. You will be greeted by the innkeeper and his wife, with no other guests to witness our arrival. I ordered meals to be brought to our rooms."

Stella rolled her eyes. "I suppose that level of extravagance befits a duke."

"That level of privacy does," Silvester said promptly. "I had to fire our butler yesterday, after he provided one of the papers with a detailed account of our wedding night, down to the menu I requested."

"How on earth did he learn the details?"

"From my valet. So, no valet. I fired him as well."

Stella's eyes rounded. "Do I still have a maid?"

"Your maid follows in another carriage, but only because I hesitated to tell Mrs. Thyme that I would act as your lady's maid." His smile was positively wolfish.

"You are so unlike your reputation," she exclaimed.

Silvester leaned back. "True. For good and ill."

"Ill?"

"My mother finds it extremely annoying that my pleasing manners are artifice."

"Pleasing manners are always artifice, are they not?" Stella asked.

"Refinement is learned," Silvester said, nodding.

"My father never bothered. My mother does not consider it a necessity."

"But you do."

He nodded. "My childhood was punctuated by my parents' eccentricities. I decided as a boy that my life would be improved if polite society welcomed rather than gawked at me."

Stella forced herself to say what she was thinking. "I am awkward, and my aunt would be the first to say that I possess no refinement. I ask the wrong questions, am interested in the wrong things, am likely to turn the wrong way in a dance, and regularly drop wineglasses. My aunt has told me a hundred times that the object of conversation is to amuse, which I regularly forget."

"I married you because you are mine, Stella. *Mine*."

Stella considered that sentence thrilling and extremely unhelpful. She raised an eyebrow.

"I've crafted most of my life to parameters set by polite society," Silvester added, folding his arms over his chest. His mouth looked definitely mulish.

"The better to win," Stella prompted him.

"There's nothing to be won by being sociable," he scoffed.

She smiled at him. "The title of most desirable, most affable, most charming. All of which covered up the battles you were winning on the side, which had to do with currency, as I understand it. Perhaps more."

A moment's silence, and he said, "I might have something to do with the way banks handle their debt."

"Hopefully, you haven't yet opened your own bank?"

"I have no interest."

"Yet the Bank of England desperately needs you to think for them."

Silvester moved his shoulders restlessly. "Those fools don't understand the danger that they risk. I'll be unsurprised if there's another run on the bank in a year or two, leaving a mere five thousand sovereigns in the vault. Who will they turn to, then?"

"You," Stella said, grinning at him. "They'll turn to you."

"I suppose I'll inject some sovereigns into their holdings if need be," he grumbled.

"All this . . . this *cover* allows you to do just as you wish. It seems to me that your duchess ought to be an extension of the way you have chosen to live your life."

He frowned at that. "I don't follow."

"You staged a theatrical production in front of the cathedral in order to convince society that you wished to marry me."

"You could say that," Silvester said, his eyes wary.

"No matter how much money you spend on me," Stella said flatly, "I will never be an adequate partner in your theatrics."

His eyes lightened, and he gave her that crooked smile that she was irrationally fond of. "I know."

Stella winced inside. Yasmin would have been a perfect party to his machinations. But was there any point to bringing up her name? Silvester had failed to win Yasmin's hand. After which, he went the opposite direction.

"This marriage will be very good for me. Being as I'm a swollen bullfrog," Silvester said. "Just look how many times you've said no to me in the last half hour."

"If that's my role, I will do my best," Stella said demurely. Then she sat upright. "Where's Specs?"

"She's following in the carriage with your maid and sufficient provisions. I had to send the cook at the Grange to London, as the staff there is not used to the influx of guests anticipated for the breakfast we are not attending." Silvester glanced out the window. "We're almost at The Swan."

Stella gulped. There was one question she had to ask him, because it had been beating in her mind since the moment she woke up. "Have you ever deflowered a virgin?"

Silence.

Then a roar of male laughter.

CHAPTER TWENTY-EIGHT

Silvester couldn't stop snorting with laughter, even though his bride frowned at him when he wouldn't stop chortling. He swept Stella into The Swan, not giving her a chance to admire the lavish gardens surrounding the inn.

Happily, his wife overcame her irritation enough to greet the nervous innkeeper's wife with a smile before she stalked up the stairs.

He followed. That's what husbands did, didn't they? They followed indignant spouses wherever they went, enjoying the way said spouse's hips swayed as she climbed the stairs. He couldn't help it. He was focused on one thing, the very thing she had inquired about.

In a vulgar parlance that no one in society would believe him capable of: the old in-and-out.

The belly bump.

The marital polka.

With a wife who seemingly had doubts about his prowess in the bed.

He managed to be patient as the innkeeper's wife raved on about the built-in bathtub with its privacy screen, the small room *with* a door that housed a privy, the bed made up with the duke's own bedding, including a mattress, which had been delivered the day before.

Stella rolled her eyes at that detail, and he shrugged, unrepentant. He'd be damned if he and his wife caught bedbugs on their first night in Cupid's Alley.

In Lover's Lane.

While deflowering a virgin.

Finally, the innkeeper's wife realized that his eyes were burning into her back because she pointed out the uncorked wine delivered from the Huntington cellars and skipped herself out the door and down the stairs.

"Where do you suppose my maid is?" Stella asked, drifting over to peer out the windows over the gardens, not meeting Silvester's eyes.

"An hour or two behind us," Silvester said promptly. "Perhaps more."

Stella sat down to one side of the fireplace, looking entirely composed. Though when he looked closer, a delightful flush warmed her cheeks. Silk puddled around her feet.

"May I give you a glass of wine?"

Her brow puckered as she looked about her. "I had better not. I wouldn't want to spill wine on my gown. I have trouble judging the distance between myself and a side table, so I often drop glasses."

"Easily solved," he said, rising and walking across the room to a small table positioned before the window. He tossed the lace doily on a chair and carried the table to her, placing it next to her armchair.

Her smile made Silvester feel distinctly giddy. He poured out wine and gave her a glass before taking a huge gulp from his own.

He was figuring out how to bring up the fact that he was on the verge of leaping on her like a frenzied satyr, when she asked, "Have you made love to many women?"

He had thought brides felt fear. Panic. Stella was peering at him through her spectacles with a curious expression.

"A few."

She raised an eyebrow.

"Not many." He took another hearty swallow of wine. "No virgins, before you ask again. My mother was characteristically forthright about her opinion of men who 'deflower' women without marrying them. She not only made her opinion clear: she dragged me and my sisters through an orphanage, once we were old enough to understand what we were seeing."

"How many women is 'not many'?"

"Seven."

"That seems like a great many lovers to me. Do most gentlemen rack up larger numbers than that?"

"I've heard men boast of one hundred or more."

Her brows knit. "At what age does a man become active, so to speak? How many mistresses could one support in a given year?"

"One might visit brothels for an hour or a night," Silvester explained. "Brothels in which one pays for the privilege of a night's encounter."

"I forgot about that," Stella said, rather surprisingly.

"I would have thought that Mrs. Thyme would keep knowledge of such establishments far from her innocent charge's ears," Silvester said, pouring Stella a little more wine. He felt like a horse straining at the opening gate, longing to scoop her up and pin her to the bed.

"I read about them," Stella explained.

That was interesting. "What have you been reading?"

"Have you read anything by Thomas Nashe?"

Silvester had never heard of him.

"We have a great many books in the library at home that are bound in vellum and leather, not plain cloth. My aunt has always made the mistake of judging a book by its cover." Her eyes ranged over him, a smile curling her lips. "As do so many."

Silvester's heart was thudding in his chest. "I would guess that Mrs. Thyme believes that a book describing a brothel would be bound in cloth?"

"If not cardboard," she said, nodding. "Aunt has formed the inaccurate belief that tawdry creative works are always clad in cardboard. Miss Austen's *Sense and Sensibility*, for example, appeared in paper-covered board with a paper spine."

"I am fairly certain that Miss Austen does not portray a brothel. My mother proclaims that she has no time for fiction, but she makes an exception for Miss Austen. Based on scenes she has read aloud at the dinner table, the stories are irreproachable."

"Not so," Stella said, her eyes sparkling at him. "In *Pride and Prejudice*, for example, the heroine's sister lamentably runs away with a man—whom she doesn't immediately marry. Learning of that detail led my aunt to ban clothbound books from the house."

Silvester nodded, eyeing his new bride. Stella wore an expression of innocent virtue that he entirely mistrusted. Those eyes hid sauciness. Audacity. Mrs. Thyme hadn't had a chance of stopping Stella from reading whatever she wished.

"I find it hard to believe that you have not read

Pride and Prejudice, given your knowledge of the plot."

"Luckily for me, it was re-published a few years ago in three volumes bound in calf leather with gilt titles on the spine," Stella told him. "The set has a positively Shakespearean air."

"Let's return to Thomas Nashe," Silvester said.

"You haven't read *The Choise of Valentines*?"

"No, I have not. The title seems innocuous."

She nodded, her eyes dancing. "I own a delightful edition with lilies worked into the velum cover."

"Positively Biblical," Silvester observed.

"The subtitle is *The Merry Ballad of Nashe His Dildo*," she said, adding: "It was written in the early 1600s, as I understand, and the subtitle does not appear on the cover."

Silvester choked. His wine went down the wrong way, and he ended up coughing so hard that Stella put down her glass and came over to pat his back—which allowed him to pull her into his arms.

"May I remove your spectacles?"

She nodded.

He carefully unthreaded them from her ears and set them to the side. *"Dildo?"*

She nodded, eyes laughing. Not only did his bride appear fearless, she seemed . . . naughty. Desirous. Not at all discombobulated by the idea of her imminent deflowering.

Silvester cleared his throat. "Was the said dildo the subject of the ballad?"

"Not exactly. You see, after experiencing financial difficulties, Nashe's lady love removed herself to a brothel."

"I'm not certain what the proper response would be to that revelation."

"He paid her a visit, of course."

Silvester held up his glass of wine.

Stella nodded, and he carefully brought it to her lips, watching intently as she licked a drop of wine from her lower lip.

"Perhaps we ought to remove your wedding dress," he said huskily. "As you pointed out, it wouldn't do to stain it."

"My maid can't be more than two hours behind us."

Silvester could have sworn his expression didn't change, but it must have, because she giggled.

"I gather you'd rather not wait for my maid?"

"Good God, no," he said. "The carriage might have lost a wheel. The coachman may have stopped for a drink."

A pucker appeared between her brows.

"Not that he would do such a thing when he was granted responsibility for Specs," he said hastily.

"I certainly hope not," Stella said. She took the wineglass away from him and sipped, eyeing him over the rim. "Do you have any other questions about the plot of Nashe's ballad? It is a narrative poem."

"Why did Nashe pursue his beloved to the brothel, since presumably he would now have to pay for what he had received for free?" Silvester asked, tugging gently at his wife until she was leaning against his shoulder. From there he could see the tip of Stella's nose and a constellation of freckles that spread like pale cinnamon across her cheeks.

Which reminded him that they spilled down her breasts as well, down her stomach, perhaps even her legs. Perhaps there was a constellation of starry spots that he could trace with his tongue as he found his way around her body.

"Nashe followed her to the brothel," Stella said, "because she was his *beloved*. Not a mere acquaintance."

Silvester was so struck by Stella's eyelashes that he didn't follow what she was saying. Her lashes were a feathery pale color, a beauty that no one could see except for him, hidden as they generally were behind her spectacles.

"What happened during his visit?" he managed.

"He joined his lady love in bed," Stella said. She glanced at him. No timid virgin's look, hers. Her eyes were bright and roguish. His heart kicked in his chest.

"Oh?" He casually put a hand on her calf.

Stella had more knowledge of intimacy than he would have guessed. She certainly could identify the long, thick ridge that was throbbing against her rear end, to put it inelegantly.

"He wasn't able to satisfy her," Stella said, throwing him a sad look.

Silvester's hand was sliding up her leg, but it stopped. "No?"

"Thank goodness, she brought her dildo with her when she changed establishments."

Silvester choked, and his fingers curled into the soft curve of Stella's thigh. "Indeed?"

"As she told him, her dildo never bent or folded, but always stood as stiff as if made of steel."

"This was written in the *1600s*?"

Stella nodded. "Is your surprise related to her resourceful use of a specialized tool, or the historical pervasiveness of the problem?"

Silvester laughed. *"Historical pervasiveness?"* His left arm tightened around her. "It's not a problem I've experienced. May I prove it to you?"

Stella tipped her head back to meet his eyes. The heavy mass of her hair fell over the side of his armchair. Her hair was redder than he had thought, closer to dark mahogany.

He caught up a silky lock. "Your hair is darker than I knew."

"My aunt prefers me to pull it back and wear a light powder to dull the color," Stella said calmly.

Anger thudded through Silvester's gut. "She doesn't like your freckles, or your reading, or your spectacles, nor your hair either?"

Stella looked at him with evident surprise. "It's not really Mrs. Thyme's fault. After I was orphaned, she was forced to confront dreams she had buried, about having a daughter of her own."

"So?"

"I was not what she would have hoped for. My mother and her sister were known as the two lilies when they debuted. They were both very elegant. Deportment and distinction were important to my mother." She gave him a mischievous grin. "She would have liked you."

Silvester's arms closed around her like a vise. He had a sudden vision of how he would feel if a small, befreckled daughter of his was treated unkindly by the likes of Mrs. Thyme. "If your aunt were a man, I could challenge her to a duel," he said, his voice coming out with grim intent.

Stella chuckled. "Don't be silly!"

"I'm not." He said it flatly.

"My aunt was never cruel to me," Stella said. "She was always kind, and so was my uncle, though I believe he thinks of me as a gourd that has taken too long to ripen."

"How is it kind to treat you like a green gourd?"

"Kindness is allowing me to wear spectacles though my aunt abhors them. Respecting my decision not to paint my face. Not complaining too much when I break things because of my imperfect vision."

"Hmm."

"Allowing Specs to stay in my bedchamber even though my aunt dislikes animals. Though not, it turns out, kittens."

"That's not kindness. That's sufferance."

"I wouldn't have been their choice, their first choice," Stella said.

The words hung in the air between them. She hadn't been *his* first choice, either, and they both knew it.

Banishing the thought, Silvester tipped up Stella's face and caught her mouth in a kiss. He tried to say with the stroke of his tongue what he didn't seem to be able to articulate: what he felt for Yasmin was nothing like the driving, raw desire he felt for Stella.

Yasmin *had* been his first choice.

But a first choice is not always the right choice. The day would come when Mrs. Thyme understood how lucky she was to have a niece who loved her enough to understand her terror and tolerate her hysterics.

Silvester didn't express the thought, though, because he had Stella's luscious, curved body in his arms. He wanted to make love to her more than he had wanted anything in his life. Desire slammed into his mind as he tried to communicate the wild craving that was ravaging his body.

"All right," she gasped, a while later.

Silvester lifted his head, feeling dazed.

"You may unclothe me."

He stared at her mouth, hearing the words but making no sense of them.

"Time to deflower a virgin," she clarified.

Silvester stood up, placing her on her feet. "Right."

She poked him in the chest. "Not that you'll be using the skill hereafter, Duke."

He shook his head. "We took vows. Yours. Till death do us part." Lust seemed to have diminished his coherence.

Stella nodded and then turned around. "Buttons first . . ."

For the rest of his life, Silvester never forgot the experience of desiring his new wife so desperately that his hands shook as he removed garment, after garment, after garment. "I hate women's clothing," he muttered, when he finally began unlacing her stays.

At last, Stella stood before him wearing nothing more than a translucent chemise. Plump nipples stood against the delicate fabric. Freckles spread like a splattering of gilt down her neck, over the curve of her breast, disappearing behind the lace that edged her chemise.

"As I told you, they're everywhere," she said, apparently following his eyes. She stuck out one elegant foot, which had its own collection of freckles.

Silvester swallowed hard. He wanted to sip her like a fine whiskey. His mouth actually tingled, thinking of licking her from her ankle up.

"Your clothing?" his wife asked, cocking her head, pulling his mind back from madness to near sobriety.

CHAPTER TWENTY-NINE

Never having been unclothed before anyone but a maid or a *modiste*, Stella felt wretchedly awkward. She was trying to appear calm, but inside, her stomach was in knots.

Her chemise had been designed to be worn under her wedding dress. It was fashioned of transparent cotton, in the same pale pink color, with a low neck and a gold ribbon threaded just under her bosom. If she had had slim hips, the fabric would have drifted to her ankles.

But as it was, the swell of Stella's hips pulled the cloth tight in that area. Supervising her dressing that morning, her aunt had moaned, asking whether Stella had eaten excessively since she was first measured, a question to which Stella had no answer.

Silvester didn't seem to mind. His gaze devoured her from head to foot, but kept pausing and returning to the shadow of red hair visible under the taut fabric.

As if he could read her mind, he said hoarsely, "That chemise is a marvel."

Happiness sparked in Stella's chest. "Truly?" She smoothed her hands over her hips, pulling the fabric down so it didn't bunch. "It is somewhat ill-fitting."

A ragged groan tore from Silvester's lips. "It's *per-*

fect. I've been dreaming about your curves, but the reality is more lush than I imagined. Please, wear only that garment for the next week."

A surprised laugh sparked from Stella's chest. "Don't be absurd!"

"We'll banish your maid to the Dower House when she isn't needed. Just think of all the washing that won't be required, because you'll wear your chemise and only your chemise." His hands were curled at his side, as if he didn't trust himself to touch her.

Stella blinked at him. Mrs. Thyme had taught her that maids were needed every moment, in every circumstance.

"Remember, I plan to debauch you in every room," Silvester stated, as if his sentence was entirely reasonable. Meeting his hungry eyes made heat bloom between her thighs.

She cleared her throat. "Perhaps you might unclothe now?"

With a rough sound of acquiescence, Silvester shed his bridal garments, tearing off his heavy coat, the embroidered waistcoat and breeches. Curiosity and desire battled for precedence; Stella had to stiffen her knees so that she didn't sink onto the bed as her instincts suggested she should.

He was beautiful. That was a given.

But when the body he had described as brutal emerged from starched linen?

A wild craving surged through her at its clean lines, the strength signaled in every lineament, from his flexing back muscles to his Roman nose.

"May I ask whether you own a toy such as that celebrated by Nashe's lover?" Silvester asked. His voice was rough and throaty, his eyes fixed on hers as he pulled down his smalls and threw them away. His staff bobbed against his stomach.

Stella nodded. She couldn't make herself speak. It wasn't that the illustrations in the book were inaccurate . . . No, they *were* inaccurate. Undersized.

She cleared her throat. "Nashe's lover calls it her 'little dildo.' I presume mine is the same size. It might not be lifelike."

He looked down, as did she. His thick, heavy length was straining toward her. Heat pooled in her body as their eyes met.

Silvester surged toward her and pinned her to the bed, all that delicious male weight holding her down. Stella wasn't entirely sure where to place her hands.

On his shoulders? That was safe. Those long muscles that she'd glimpsed when he turned to throw his breeches on a chair: Could she caress those? His arse?

"I need to know the rules," she gasped.

"There are no rules," Silvester said instantly.

So she wrapped her arms and legs around him, pulling her chemise tightly between their bodies. He rocked against her, and a desperate whimper broke from her throat.

Silvester drew back, taking his weight away from her. He put his hands on the hem of her chemise, meeting her eyes with a silent question. When she nodded, he slowly pulled it upward, revealing first her legs, then her hips, her waist. She sat up and allowed him to pull it over her head.

He looked at her for long minutes until she could feel herself turning red.

His eyes gleamed hungry, even desperate. "I want

you," he murmured. "Exactly as you are, every curve, every freckle—everything."

Stella had already realized that. Her embarrassment wasn't about him; it was about *her*. Sensation was searing through her in an entirely unladylike fashion. Her limbs were trembling, and she could feel unladylike heat pooling in her body.

It wasn't that she hadn't experienced desire; she had. But desire in the presence of another person? Moreover, the very man whom she used to imagine making love to her, and now he was here in the flesh?

It was *embarrassing*. She could pretend to be unmoved so that he wouldn't guess. But was that the right thing to do?

Stella was trying to stop herself from gracelessly panting with desire. Trying to stop herself from speaking so she didn't start pleading with him to lie on top of her again.

Silvester's hands hovered over her breasts. His gaze asked a question that Stella answered by arching toward him. As callused hands palmed her nipples, she sucked in a breath.

He lavished attention on her breasts, his tongue painting a streak of fire that left her breathless, lapping her nipple until she started shaking, sweat prickling her neck.

When a moan broke from her throat, he gave her a wicked grin and then slid farther down, tracing freckles on the curve of her belly before he rubbed his cheek against her private hair and licked. His warm, wet tongue made her feel slippery and soft, as if stars were streaking through her veins. Like drinking starry wine, intoxicating wine.

With a sigh, Stella gave in. She pushed away the idea that Yasmin would have been more ladylike, the fact that Yasmin's stomach wouldn't have formed rolls.

Silvester was *hers* now. She peered down at the gorgeous, muscled male body that lay sprawled between her legs. Naïve or no, she could read the rigid tension in his shoulders, going down to the curve of his back that rose into a muscled arse. He was here with her, and she'd be a fool to discount that.

He did something with his thumbs that made her squeak. Her head fell back as she let herself simply *feel* how swollen and sleek she was under the rasp of his tongue.

"No rules for this," he murmured, raising his head a few moments later.

Stella's hands were entwined in his hair, just in case he tried to move. "I have a rule: don't stop."

He laughed, reached up, and pinched one of her nipples.

She gasped, and sensual fire washed over her again and again, smashing through her idea of what desire was like. Even of what orgasms were like, because those she gave herself with her dildo were in a different category.

A different universe.

The heat subsided, and then Silvester did something with the thick fingers he'd thrust inside her, and she spilled into fire again, panting, gasping, crying out, her hands pulling his hair.

Finally she subsided with a muttered curse.

Silvester reared back, his hands moving to grip her thighs. Stella peered at him through her lashes. His smile was devilish, satisfied.

"Bullfrog," she muttered, surprised by the hoarseness of her own voice.

"I own that," he said promptly. "I'll croak proudly about giving my wife pleasure."

Her eyes flew open. "Silvester!"

"No, I won't," he said. "But here, in this bedchamber, between us? Damn right, I am proud."

"Humph," Stella said, relaxing into a warm puddle of satisfied woman again. "I suppose I'll allow your superior smirk under the circumstances."

He crawled over her on his hands and knees, dropped his head, and devoured her mouth. At first Stella felt too *melted* to engage, but then he lowered his body slowly onto hers, and everything in her woke up again, her skin tingling.

"Am I too heavy for you?" Silvester murmured, his voice gravel in her ear.

"No," she said honestly. She wasn't grasshopper delicate. Her body relaxed under his weight, and she felt lush and perfect, rather than awkward and heavy. This close, she didn't need glasses to read his face.

"I like your face," she muttered, palming it.

"I like everything about you," he said throatily.

"Especially your ducal nose." She kissed it.

His expression was hard to read. "Ducal nose, eh?"

"Yes, *Beaky*," Stella said cheerfully. "I got that right, didn't I? Or was it Duckbill?"

He shook his head.

"Did the nickname bother you?" Stella said, realizing suddenly that she might have raised a painful subject.

He scoffed. "If we must stay with waterfowl, I'd rather you didn't call me a lame duck."

She frowned.

"As was poor Thomas Nashe."

Stella shifted teasingly, letting one thigh rub against his erection. "As you assured me, that doesn't seem to be a problem you share."

Silvester shuddered and then pulled back, one hand pushing her legs farther apart. The thick, round head of his shaft eased forward, sliding over her sleek folds before easing into her body, bringing with it a pleasure so keen that she gasped.

She tilted her hips, her fingers curling into the muscle of his shoulder. Silvester was sweaty, his chest heaving. She pulled at him. "Come closer."

Silvester's jaw was clenched. "Have to go slowly. *Virgin.*"

"*Dildo,*" she hissed, and yanked at him again.

Her husband barked with laughter, and braced himself against the bed, pulling her underneath him. Stella arched up with a shriek as Silvester surged forward, his hard warmth coming to a space that seemed to have been made for him.

Her legs curled around his hips as he rocked forward. Rumpled locks of hair fell over his forehead as he whispered, "Is it painful?"

"No," Stella said flatly.

His eyes flared with raw desire.

She bumped up, inelegantly but urgently.

He kissed her with a scorching promise, holding both their bodies still, his weight pinning her to the bed, and then he began moving, pulling back and thrusting, burying himself inside her again and again. Feeling pulsed through her, as ferocious as the thrusts of his body.

"It doesn't hurt?" Silvester rasped sometime later.

Stella was clinging to his muscled forearms, pressure building in her slowly as she chased a spark that threatened to become an inferno. She'd never felt anything like this when she played with her dildo, making up stories in which a duke kissed her on the dance floor.

"God, no," Stella cried. She arched against him. "It's not quite enough, if that makes sense."

A bark of laughter broke from his throat.

"Are you supposed to be merry at this moment?" Stella asked, blinking at him.

"Never have been, with another woman," Silvester told her. He adjusted, clamped a large, callused hand on her right hip and pulled her body toward him, just as he thrust forward.

The sound burst from Stella's chest without volition: a raw, scorched cry.

"There," he said, his own voice thicker and dark, not laughing.

"Again," she breathed.

"Like this?"

"Harder."

"Goddamn, I was so lucky to marry you," Silvester whispered.

He began thrusting so hard that the bed slammed against the wall. Thankfully, he didn't stop, just kept driving forward again and again, his eyes searching hers except when he pulled her into a scorching kiss, never losing his rhythm.

Before Stella knew it, she was careening toward another climax, this one threatening to be so powerful that she felt a little afraid and clung tighter to him.

Which made him slow down and whisper ragged words in her ear.

She didn't listen to them, but they sank into her anyway, a blessed flow of language broken by hoarse gulps of air. Always his hips kept up that even rhythm until she bit his lower lip. "Harder!"

That did it.

Silvester lost control, his face contorting, jaws clenched. There was nothing civilized about his face now. Sweaty with a red streak on each cheek, his eyes glittering through lowered lids, an instinctive grunt slipping from his lips every time he flexed his hips.

Stella looked at him, saw the pirate, saw the Roman warrior, saw the man she married and loved, and abruptly felt fire sweep through her. She clenched on him inwardly, a cry exploding from her lips.

Silvester groaned and ground his pelvis down on hers, shuddering, his hips jerking inelegantly over and over as he spasmed, spilling himself inside her.

And collapsing.

He caught himself on his elbows, his sweaty forehead touching hers. He looked as if there was no civilization in him. Sure enough, when he opened his mouth, a guttural sound came out.

Stella giggled.

Silvester shook his head. "You."

She waited, but he let his head fall to the sheet. True, he had worked hard. A sheen of sweat spread over his back and his arse. She picked up the corner of the sheet and dried him off.

"Sorry," he mumbled.

"I like it," she whispered. "I love the way you smell."

Sweaty. Real. Not scented. Not that I don't like your soap, because I do."

"Chatty." He was clearly reduced to single words.

Stella *did* feel chatty. Happiness had burst inside her and was still drenching her with joy. She loved it when her articulate chatty husband was reduced to words like "virgin."

Not that she was a virgin any longer.

"We can make this marriage work," she whispered.

Silvester eased backward, away from her, and then reached for the linen cloths hanging against the wall. "Damn right." He returned to the bed. "Spread your legs, wench."

"*Wench?* Is this what I should expect of the duke I married?" Stella cried, unable to stop giggling. But she spread her legs.

He patted her dry. "No blood."

"Dildo!" she reminded him, giggling even harder. "Honestly, I wasn't sure we could make it work. Because, well, because you had that Yasmin problem, and we don't match, do we, and if I don't have my glasses on, how am I to see what's happening in your eyes?"

"What are you talking about?" Silvester said, pausing in his patting to frown at her.

"The pirate you," Stella explained. "You play the placid, amiable duke very well, but the haughty, real duke is always there in your eyes. I thought I had to have my glasses to see, but I hadn't been thinking about how close we can be, as married people."

She slid backward and sat up. "Like this." She reached out and cupped his face, bringing her own as close as she could without their noses bumping. "No charming duke to be seen," she whispered.

"Half the time I don't know what you're talking about," Silvester said. "Is that a problem?"

"Your mother suggested I could find a man with a better vocabulary," Stella said, smiling so hard that her cheeks hurt.

"She would." Silvester groaned and sprawled onto his back beside her, one arm falling above his head. "It's not a question of vocabulary."

Now that she was sitting up, her stomach overlapped in a way that would horrify her aunt. Not that it horrified Silvester, proven by the fact he wound his arm around her waist and hauled her against his hip.

She leaned over him and kissed his nose. "Then why don't you understand me? I assure you that I strive for clarity."

"'Pirate me'?" Silvester said, not opening his eyes. "Who knows what you mean by that?"

"Mmmm," Stella replied, dropping a kiss on his lips. "The pirate side of you illicitly buys gold."

His eyes popped open. "Oh, God, I'm going to have to run my investment decisions by you, aren't I?"

Stella hadn't considered it before, but . . .

"Absolutely."

He shut his eyes again. "Bloody hell."

"I don't have to be prissy, you know," Stella said, tracing his temples with her fingers. "I can learn to walk on the wrong side of the law. I'll be your partner in crime."

"I told you, no law forbade my purchases."

"On the wrong side of ethics, then," she amended. "Why not? Perhaps we could rob the rich to give to the poor, like that old story."

"I don't rob people," Silvester objected. "Are you always this chatty after an orgasm?"

"No," Stella said brightly. "But I find that the orgasms I gave myself and those you gave me don't deserve the same name."

"Where did you get your dildo anyway?" Silvester said, his eyes opening again.

"The Pantheon Bazaar," Stella said.

"I don't suppose you were shopping with your aunt at the time."

She shook her head. "Absolutely not. I asked a shopkeeper for a dildo. That was somewhat embarrassing, but he was most helpful."

"Enterprising," Silvester murmured.

"It was practical, honestly. There was pleasure to be had, it seemed, and I could not count on receiving it from a husband, if I ever had one. Just look at my aunt and uncle. They prefer not to live in the same county, let alone share a bedchamber."

"That will never be your fate."

"It could have been," Stella pointed out. "I've been courted by loads of men this Season who would describe me as freckled and fat."

His eyes snapped open. "Who?"

"No one," she said hastily—and untruthfully, since she'd overheard just that unkind phrase from a disgruntled suitor.

The pirate was in full ascendance, and she didn't want to visit her new husband behind bars. "My point was that back in the 1600s, Thomas Nashe said that a woman couldn't count on a man for her pleasure, and I believed him. As soon as we moved to London for the Season, I visited the Pantheon. It only took one discreet question before I was directed to the right shop."

"Excellent," Silvester murmured, closing his eyes again. "I will do my best to satisfy you, just so you know. But if I happen to be away from home, I'm happy to know that you will be satisfied in my absence."

Stella was rather surprised to see that his tool had lengthened and thickened again. She slid down to lie beside him and then allowed Silvester to pull her partly on top of him.

"I like the parts of your body that society dislikes," she told him, satisfaction leaking into her voice. "Your nose." She kissed it. "Your ungentlemanly chest." She wiggled downward and kissed it. "Arm muscles."

"Biceps," he murmured.

He sounded uncaring, but she knew him. To him, *this* mattered, more than the easy deceptive charm he wore like armor. His muscles were her freckles.

"I like these parts best," she whispered, running her fingers over his waist, lean hips, powerful cock that rose to her hand. "So soon?" she asked huskily.

"Is your source of information the lamentable Thomas Nashe?" Silvester inquired, his eyes glinting at her under heavy lids. "The man was clearly not at his best."

Stella tightened her hand and rolled her wrist experimentally. Silvester made a ragged sound in the back of his throat but didn't move, letting her play. She pulled herself to a seated position, her bottom settling onto his legs, and enjoyed herself, tracing the iron-hard slabs that covered his chest, the way he trembled when she lightly scored her nails down his arms.

She returned again and again to his staff, as

Thomas Nashe called it. Each time she touched him, encircled him, Silvester's hips arched into the air as if he couldn't control the tiny movement, even pinned down by her weight.

She loved it. *I am not as was Hercules the Stout,* she murmured, *"That to the seventh journey could hold out."*

Silvester's eyes glittered at her. "More Nashe? Seven journeys? Try me."

Abruptly, Stella realized that she'd set the rules of a game, and Silvester *had* to win, but this kind of winning . . .

He beat Hercules, naturally enough.

CHAPTER THIRTY

Stella's maid didn't arrive at The Swan until the morning, at which point Silvester reluctantly strolled into the adjoining bedchamber so his wife could have a bath.

But when he stopped hearing splashing noises, he walked back into the room, banished her maid, and carried Stella over to the bed, pulling the toweling from her body as he went.

"What are you doing?" Stella asked. "Shall I give Specs to my maid?"

Silvester glanced over his shoulder. "She's crawling into my boot."

He was flooded by need, a primitive, base lust. "You must be sore," he said, kissing Stella's throat. Her skin was the color of milk.

Stella ran her hands down his back. "No, I am not," she whispered, arching up so she bumped against him.

He slid a hand between their bodies and sank his fingers into the slick heat between her legs.

"I thought about you during the bath," his wife admitted, dragging him into another kiss.

Silvester sank into her slowly, instructing himself to let her body adjust. But his body moved without permission, responding to her heavy eyelids and the way she sucked in air.

He braced his elbows on either side of her, so they could keep kissing. Words kept tumbling out of his mouth, words he never thought he'd say to anyone, let alone to his wry, funny wife.

He wasn't supposed to feel this way. Their marriage was . . .

It was about passion, physical passion.

Not muttering words that tumbled over on each other, "perfect," "soft," "perfect," "mine."

Ridiculous drivel that didn't feel ridiculous, but necessary, as if the words were spilling from his heart, a thought so absurd that he recoiled and briefly came back to logic. Just long enough for pleasure to wash over him again, reducing him to an animal who only spoke in single words. They finished in slow silence, eyes clinging to each other.

Silvester left the bed, legs feeling oddly shaky. Specs strolled out of his boot and jumped in his place, giving him a glowering look.

After he dressed, the words that spilled from his mouth when he stamped into his boot, discovering that the leather was warmly wet, albeit rapidly cooling?

Blasphemous.

But then he saw his wife sitting on the bed, having pulled on a wrapper. She had her legs crossed, red hair tumbling over her shoulders. Specs was in her arms, cradled like a furry baby.

He dropped onto a chair. "That bloody cat peed in my boot."

"What did you say?"

Stella looked up at him. Her lips were swollen from

his kisses, a flush still high on her cheeks. He knew that between her legs, she was wet for him, wet from him, and the feeling that overpowered him didn't allow for irritation.

"Specs," he said. "Peed in my boot."

"I suppose she was angry at being left behind." Stella looked at the cat, who batted her nose with a paw. "You mustn't pee in people's boots, Specs. It's like leaving a mouse on a pillow. Just not done, especially to such a high-and-mighty personage as the Duke of Huntington."

Specs batted her nose again. Stella rubbed her lush lips over the forehead of the kitten, whose purring could be heard across the room.

If he knew how to purr, he'd be doing it, wouldn't he?

Instead of purring, Silvester got another erection, which made him glad that he didn't have a valet any longer.

A man didn't care to lose control like this under a valet's watchful eye.

CHAPTER THIRTY-ONE

Once in the carriage, Stella fended off her husband's inappropriate caresses, which meant she was looking out the window when the carriage bowled through a set of tall iron gates and set off down a hill, giving an excellent view of the ducal estate.

If Silvester's townhouse was impressive, this was . . .

Not.

The word that came to mind was "ridiculous." Also: "Absurd."

The manor was an ill-designed, shabby pile of stone, one chimney tilting at an angle that suggested imminent collapse, the turret missing stones so that it resembled a mouth that had lost a few teeth, the lawns segmented by strange black lines.

"The Grange is . . . large," Stella observed.

Silvester glanced out the window. "Ugly, isn't it? All the parts are grafted together, more or less, though the roof leaks where the newer parts join the original castle. It was damaged by Cromwell, but rather than tear it down, the family just built on, everything from crenellations to lancet windows."

Stella nodded.

"If you look closely, you'll see a few gargoyles. There was a spire, but it snapped off in a storm and wiped out the priest's house, which dated back to the 1200s. Luckily, my father believed too much religion is bad for the brain, so the house was unoccupied at the time."

She could just make out the medieval castle in the center of the Grange. Successive dukes had slapped on new wings, and outbuildings sprouted haphazardly to the left and right.

Just as startling, there was a locomotive parked before the front door. "Does that machine include your mother's chimney?" she asked.

Silvester didn't bother to look. "All the locomotives have her chimneys. In fact, that is true across England. Hers is the chimney with a bend in it, at the front."

"What does this particular locomotive do?"

"It runs around the property on cast-iron rails."

"Like the Oystermouth Railway?"

"No, that is drawn by horses," Silvester said. "Ours can take a few passengers around the estate. It is actually the first passenger railway drawn by a locomotive."

Stella had seen drawings of locomotives in the *London Times*, but the machine was larger and fiercer than she had imagined. It had a round cylinder for a body and a chimney that curved from one end and jutted into the air, with three wheels per side and some rods sticking out here and there.

"Does it traverse the entire estate?"

Silvester nodded. "Huntington Grange is three hundred acres and, yes, it goes through most of it. We'll go for a ride tomorrow."

"I believe that Scotland will authorize a passenger

railroad next year, possibly the year after," Stella said. "That would be a better investment than ill-gotten gold."

"My mother would like that," Silvester said amiably. "A tribute to her chimney."

Her husband lounged opposite her, still all pirate. Since he had no valet, the clothing he'd changed into that morning was unremarkable. Unducal. Just a plain coat, breeches, boots that suited the challenging look in his eyes.

A gleaming, hungry challenge that suggested two bouts before breakfast had not been enough.

Stella's heart ricocheted around her rib cage. "I don't know how to be a duchess," she blurted out. The carriage was slowing down.

"There's not much to know," Silvester said, that wicked smile curling one side of his mouth. "In the normal course of things, servants would line up outside the front door, ready to curtsy."

"But you sent them all to London."

"Hawtree, our country butler, was needed there, to replace the butler I fired. We do have a maid or two, enough to light fires in the morning. A few grooms who will act as footmen. The people who work in the buttery, the stables, and the ironworks are still here, but without a butler, they won't assemble for the new duchess's inspection."

The coach pulled to a halt, a spray of gravel striking the undercarriage.

Silvester shoved open the door and jumped out, reaching back and lifting her out of the carriage. "Welcome to the Grange." His smile was rueful.

Stella stood beside him, looking in silence from the

deformed turret to the mismatched wings. Off to the side was a gothic ruin that was obviously only a few decades old because it looked as fake as her Egyptian crown.

Even the grass wasn't velvety green, like that at the London townhouse. Where it wasn't weedy, it had been cut through by the iron tracks laid for the railroad. A sharp odor of burning coal and smoky oil hung in the air.

Silvester caught up her hand. "I might as well warn you that my mother has no interest in domestic matters. One year we discovered the drawing room draperies were rotten when they crashed to the floor in a cloud of dust, feathers, and an ancient bird's nest."

Stella raised an eyebrow.

"Birds do tend to make their way in because the front doors are so large. We hadn't realized that a pair nested there. Presumably they raised their children and the family flew out a window with no one noticing."

Where was the housekeeper? Stella kept that thought to herself.

The front door was massive, clearly dating back hundreds of years. A tarnished brass knocker jutted from the left side. When Silvester hauled on it, the door swung open silently, letting out a puff of musty air.

"You know how archaeologists are rooting around in Egypt, opening up tombs?" Silvester asked.

"Looking for vulture crowns," Stella confirmed.

"The Grange isn't quite that old, but there are similarities." He kicked a stone in place to hold the door open before leading her in.

The echoing entrance hall was more fitted to a castle than a country mansion. The blackened beams of the ceiling were at least twenty feet over their heads, the corners gray with cobwebs. Stella walked over to a stone fireplace, its cavernous opening taller than her head. "Is that *moss*?"

Silvester joined her, putting a hand on her waist and then most inappropriately letting it slip to her arse. "It appears to be," he said, poking at the growth with his other hand. "When my sisters and I were growing up, the front doors were always open, even when it rained. One time a wild hog wandered in. The butler cornered it. Since the kitchen fireplace wasn't large enough, we roasted it here. See, the spit remains."

"It must have taken several trees to cook such an animal."

"My parents never bothered to heat the entry, so that was probably the last time this fireplace was used. We invited everyone from the nearby squires to the vicar."

"Did they all fit in the dining room?" Stella asked. "Did the hog fit on a platter?"

"Most of them didn't come because they disapproved of my parents," Silvester said, taking up her hand again. "As for the platter, it arrived in the dining room on a door, held high by four footmen. With a starched ruff around the hog's neck and a Juliet cap on its head."

"A Juliet cap?"

"Velvet ornamented with pearls and silver beads, with a tiara perched on top. My mother thought it was frightfully funny."

"A tiara?"

"The vicar took offense, thinking that my mother was mocking the queen. Which, to do her credit, she wasn't: my mother just thought the velvet cap and tiara were amusing on a hog's head. The vicar never deigned to dine with us again. But the leftover hog made enough pork sausages to get the entire village through the winter."

Stella nodded. She was starting to get a clear idea why Silvester had decided young to become so polished and urbane. "Did your parents mind the vicar's disapproval?"

"Not at all. They were not particularly devout, and felt his indignity allowed them to stop attending church on Sundays. One of my sisters became convinced that the devil would attend our deathbeds, but luckily her certainty had waned before my father passed away. May I show you a few more rooms?"

Silvester shoved open doors here and there while barking labels. "Map room, Guardroom, Chapel, Garderobe, Solar."

"Why is there so little furniture?" Stella asked. She was feeling slightly dizzy.

"Most of it was sold in lean times," Silvester said. "The hog's tiara is no longer ours, for example. My father's passion for steam engines was a constant drain on the estate. My mother's chimney design actually made money, but even so, she has shown little interest in replacing the furniture."

He pushed open the door to a room that contained nothing more than a sofa minus a leg. The windows were stone-mullioned with pretty lacework, but the glass was covered by ivy, so it was gloomy as well as empty. "The yellow drawing room," Silvester said.

Stella squinted, trying to see if the walls had once been yellow. They seemed a dingy brown.

"Named after the settee and chairs that used to be here," he clarified.

He didn't say anything more, and neither did she. He led her into a newer—but by no means new—area, the North wing, and started opening doors. "Breakfast room, library, my mother's study, another drawing room, a sewing room. Shall we rest before visiting the other wing, let alone the kitchens? I should warn you that they are best described as medieval."

"Perhaps we could see the South wing tomorrow," Stella said, feeling overwhelmed by the pure size of the Grange along with its dirt and shabbiness.

Not to mention the way Silvester's hand kept slipping down to her rear and squeezing. She could whip around and frown at his impertinence, but every time their eyes met, she was seized by an all-consuming *lust* for her husband.

That was the only word for it.

"Ungodly," Mrs. Thyme would call it. "Depraved." That was before her aunt even heard about the coroneted hog.

And yet Stella couldn't suppress the pulse of desire that kept going through her. The comforting thing was that Silvester's eyes were hard and hot. She wasn't in the grip of this cyclone alone. The two of them were both there, whirled by desire.

Returning to the castle at the heart of the Grange, he drew her up the sweeping stone stairs leading from the entry. "There are two bedchambers on this floor, and then the nurseries above. Of course, there are a great many bedchambers in the South and North wings. Servants used to live above the nursery, but they rebelled long ago and now they are housed in the South wing."

"I would like to see the nursery," Stella said. It was absolutely clear to her that Silvester's goal was not the bedchamber, but the bed. Not that she didn't share the idea, but they would likely be there for hours.

Her husband nodded and drew her up another flight of stone steps. "This floor was designed as a set of interconnecting rooms, all reached through the nursery." He pulled open double doors. The enormous room held an empty bookcase and a rusty trunk along a stone wall. "We spent most of our time out-of-doors, but we used to have a rocking horse," Silvester said, as if he wasn't describing the most dismal childhood imaginable. "And a few books, of course."

"I gather they were sold?" Stella asked faintly.

He shrugged, and led her back to the steps. "I suppose so. Beyond that room is the nanny's chamber and a night nursery."

Stella couldn't even imagine the work that would have to happen before the castle was habitable.

Back down a flight, he pushed open another set of double doors. "Our bedchamber."

"*Our* bedchamber?" she echoed, blinking at him as he drew her inside.

Silvester closed the door and backed against it, as if she might try to escape. "My parents always slept together."

Stella's eyes rounded as she looked about. Unlike the other chambers, this room was charmingly decorated and smelled of lemon polish rather than dust. The walls were papered, and the windows cleared of ivy.

"Your father and mother shared this room?" She couldn't imagine the dowager snuggled up to a man.

Silvester nodded. "The chamber has been completely renovated, including a new bed. I turned the duke's dressing room into a water closet. The Dower House has also been renovated, as my mother will live there when she pays us a visit. I waited to renovate the rest of the Grange, thinking that my wife would wish to direct the work."

Stella's heart plummeted to her feet.

Of course, the room had been renovated.

He had been preparing for a wife: Yasmin.

Stella looked around her, rather blindly. Petals blew across the four walls as if in a brisk wind, collecting in creamy eddies. The scene continued from wall to wall, as lovely and unique as Yasmin herself.

"It's beautiful," Stella said, her voice coming out with a hoarse edge, despite herself. She cleared her throat. "Is this an example of Chinese wallpaper?"

"Actually, I heard of some artists in Versailles who paint paper, rather than wood-blocking it. They came last summer to install it." Of course.

French, just like Yasmin.

"We put them up in the South wing, but my butler reported they complained a great deal about the leaking roof." Silvester's voice was noncommittal. "I had hoped they would paper more than one chamber, but they returned to France in high dudgeon, so the other chambers await a duchess's eye. My mother may have had a hand in dispatching them: she likes the Grange as it is."

Stella was trying to digest the fact that the dowager duchess could like this ruin of a house. "Couldn't you have fixed the roof in the South wing?" she asked.

"My mother has been unwilling to accept interference. We decided that I would have free rein with the London townhouse, until the point when I planned to marry. After that, she agreed to move to the Dower House and accept that my wife would oversee renovations."

An enormous bed was pushed against one wall, covered with snowy white linen and more lacy pillows than she'd ever seen in one place.

As if the wallpaper suddenly came into focus, Stella realized that the petals on the walls were jasmine. Delicate jasmine petals everywhere she looked.

One emotion seared into Stella's bones: she could not, she simply *could not* sleep with Silvester in the exquisite nest he designed for Yasmin.

"We could always rip out the wallpaper," he said, as her silence went on too long. "Do you think it's too frivolous?"

"That would be a desecration. The paper is a true work of art," Stella said. She had never imagined anything like the playful way the petals swirled and eddied, sweeping across all four walls. It belonged in a museum.

Silvester walked toward her slowly, as if she were a kitten that might startle and run away.

"Shouldn't Specs have arrived by now?" Stella asked hurriedly. They had consigned the cat to her maid's carriage after she hissed at Silvester, who had expressed a strong desire not to be urinated on. Specs had clearly decided that Silvester was responsible for Stella's absence.

"Their carriage followed closely after ours," Silvester said. He moved to stand just in front of her and jerked his head toward one of the tall windows that presumably looked over the ducal lands. "I asked them to put a box for her on the balcony."

"I'm not sure we should sleep together," Stella said carefully. "My aunt would be—"

"Your aunt's opinion is irrelevant to our marriage."

Silvester didn't interrupt often, but Stella had to admit he had a good point. His eyes were searing a question into hers.

"Privacy is important," she blurted out.

He frowned.

"Privacy," she repeated, fidgeting. "A woman's privacy."

He transformed before her eyes from a demanding husband to the endlessly courteous Duke of Huntington. "I apologize. I was being thoughtless."

Profound disappointment washed over her because she was so stupid that she wanted him to argue over a rule that she'd just established.

He took a step toward the door. "I shall send your maid to you as soon as she arrives. And Specs, of course."

"Where will you sleep?"

"In the other bedchamber," Silvester said. "I'm afraid my clothing has been placed in the dressing room, but my valet—" He stumbled, likely remembering that he had no valet. "I'll remove my garments now."

He strode across the room to a door cleverly set into the wallpaper, the outline scarcely visible in a cloud of jasmine petals, and emerged with an armful of clothing that he placed on the bed. "There are a few more odds and ends." There was nothing resentful in his expression as he turned away again.

But Stella felt terrible. Silvester had dreams about

marriage. Presumably, he had imagined sharing this charming, lovely room with its stupid French wallpaper with Yasmin.

He'd slotted Stella into the place where another woman belonged, but she didn't fit.

"Why don't you stay here, and I'll go to your bedchamber?" The words burst out of her mouth.

Silvester appeared from the dressing room with a stack of starched cravats.

"That's a much better idea," she said, ladling enthusiasm into her voice to cover up the abject mortification she felt. "You created this lovely chamber, and you should stay here. Your clothing is already here!"

Her voice sounded strained even to her own ears.

"Certainly not, although I thank you for the offer." Silvester's entire face was set in lines of genial courtesy. "The other bedchamber has not yet been renovated. The water closet here has one of the new Lewis Commodes."

"Silvester!" In contrast to her courteous spouse, her voice was filled with frustration. In fact, she growled at him.

"Yes?" He placed the cravats neatly beside the clothing and turned toward the dressing room, but he pivoted back to her.

It was miraculous, the way his eyes could shine with geniality and be so utterly false. Under all that charm, he was cross. She knew he was cross because Silvester liked to make a plan and have it work out.

He saw himself sleeping in this room with his wife, and she was thwarting him.

Just look at the way he'd run after her when Yasmin refused him. He didn't wait five minutes, simply threw himself at another woman. Not just *any* woman: the woman whom Giles had been courting.

She wasn't just second choice: she was second best.

A realization that didn't make Stella feel any better.

Silvester arched an eyebrow, and she realized that she was staring silently at his face.

"When you disagree with me, it would be best if you could share it," she pointed out. "As regards our marriage, I mean."

"I will. *If* the disagreement is in an arena where I have the right to an opinion. Your privacy is sacrosanct, and I should never have assumed that the messy living arrangements that my parents reveled in would be agreeable to you."

Stella didn't know what to say. He was right, wasn't he? She'd never heard of a lady living in the same room with her husband. It simply wasn't done.

Silvester disappeared into the dressing room once again and returned with a few more shirts. He picked up all the clothing and gave her the charming smile that she hated.

Loathed.

"May I trouble you to open the door for me?"

She folded her arms over her chest and glared at him.

Silvester looked at her and then returned the pile to the bed. "I gather we should discuss the situation further. Shall we be seated?"

Stella marched over to a couple of spindly, ornate chairs, picked out with gilt paint. Likely imported from Paris. She sat down and crossed her arms again. Then she waited.

She knew her husband. He did not like disapproval. Why else would he fabricate such an elaborate shield against the world? She let her frown deepen, to make her point.

He followed her and sat down. After a few minutes of silence, his urbane cheer fell away, and Silvester started to look more sincere, which in this case meant irritated. His brows drew together. "I'm just trying to make you happy. You are my wife."

"Husbands and wives *talk* to each other."

"Not about things like this!"

"Why not?"

He looked at her, incredulous. "You suggest that I try to talk you out of a response to the idea of living in close proximity to me that was . . . that was so visceral that I *saw* you recoil? You looked pleased when you first walked into this chamber, and then you realized I would share it with you, and you looked horrified."

Oh, dear.

He had caught the moment that she realized that the chamber had been designed for Yasmin.

"You misunderstood."

It was his turn to wait. She couldn't tell him the truth. It was too humiliating, and besides, there was nothing either of them could do about it.

"I'm not sure that I'm as needful of privacy as I thought."

His mouth tightened.

"What would it be like, if we shared a room?" she burst out. "Would you be here when I took a nap? When I took a *bath*?" Despite herself, her voice did sound somewhat appalled.

"Only if you wished." His voice had changed from courteous to wry and teasing. "We napped together yesterday."

"That was because . . ."

"*That* is part of married life. Will be a regular part of *our* married life no matter where you are sleeping."

The horrifying thing was that now Stella couldn't think of anything other than *that*. His body was branded in her memory, even the rough hair that shadowed his chest muscles, thickening into an arrow over his stomach. He hadn't shaved in the morning so short rough hairs, invisible except in the sunshine, had prickled her inner thighs.

When he buried his face between her legs . . .

It was hard to keep her mind on why she didn't like this room.

"We might consider sleeping together in the other room," she suggested. Her hands curled around the arms of the delicate, pretty chair, Yasmin's chair. She was lucky it didn't creak and fall to pieces when she sat in it.

She had to hold herself back, or she would launch herself at him like a lustful dairymaid. Two people in one of these chairs? It would smash to the ground, just like the rotten draperies downstairs.

Silvester looked utterly nonplussed. "You don't like this chamber?"

"I would like to look at the other room," she said, getting to her feet. She walked over to the door without looking back. "Is it to the right?"

The corridor was wide and lined with mullioned windows. Deep shadows stretched between windows since the sun couldn't make it through the dirty glass. Stella reached out and swiped one dingy brass lamp as she passed. Her finger came back brown with dust.

Silvester took her hand without comment and rubbed the dust off with a handkerchief. "I have to warn you that the other bedchamber was last decorated for a royal visit."

He pushed open another set of double doors. A huge bed jutted from one wall, surrounded by crimson velvet draperies and, oddly enough, a picket fence. In the center of the room was a second bed, marooned in empty space. Around the walls gilt chairs were arranged in double rows.

"The royal visit was some time in the past," Silvester said apologetically.

"Did the visiting monarch need to be penned like a disobedient chicken?" Stella asked, stunned. She gasped. "Was it King George? I've heard his mind is disturbed, but do they fence him in?"

She took a step back. The very idea of sleeping in a room where a king had been imprisoned was distasteful.

"No, no," Silvester said. "The fence marks the private area, which was, as you can see, not very private. It isn't meant to fence in the monarch; it prohibits those of lesser status from approaching the monarch."

"Oh. Did the king's attendants sleep there?" Stella nodded at the central bed.

"Presumably so. The royal personage in question was Queen Elizabeth. Family lore has it that she traveled with hundreds of courtiers, who bedded down everywhere from the buttery to the parapets. One of them was nearly beheaded when the family claymore fell off a wall. He was apparently sleeping on a chest in the armory."

"A claymore?"

One side of his mouth hitched into a teasing smile. "Didn't you read through the letter C in the encyclopedia?"

"I gather a claymore is a sword of some sort, but the encyclopedia overlooked it," Stella told him.

"A two-handed sword that definitely could have cut the man through to his spine if it had fallen point first," Silvester said.

"If that was one of Queen Elizabeth's men, does that mean this room has been unused since the 1500s?"

"Elizabeth was the only queen who has ever showed the faintest propensity to have anything to do with the Dukes of Huntington, let alone pay a visit to the Grange. My parents' reputation for eccentricity was exceeded by that of my grandfather. Moreover, the family always blamed her royal visit for our impecunious financial situation. Housing all those courtiers for a month was ruinously expensive."

She frowned, and said with certainty, "The family is no longer impecunious."

"No. You are free to redecorate as you wish."

Of course, her pirate had made a fortune, or several fortunes, the moment he was old enough.

"Well, this chamber is perfect!" Stella said briskly. "I have always admired Queen Elizabeth. I shall enjoy thinking of myself as royalty."

"It might well be the same mattress she slept on," Silvester said dubiously.

Stella walked over and poked at it. "It's a husk mattress covered by a feather bed," she reported.

Before she could turn, her husband moved to stand just behind her, pressing his body against her back and plopping his hands on the mattress, which responded with a puff of dust. "We should lie on it to make certain that it's acceptable. The bedding, I mean."

A gasp escaped Stella's lips. His cock was informing her silently exactly how they would test the mattress.

"The sheet is gray with age," she pointed out.

Silvester pulled away, turning her around. "I don't suppose you'd like to return to my bedchamber?"

Yasmin's bedchamber?

She shook her head. "You said there were a few maids left on the grounds. Might one of them change this bedding?"

"I can ask. The few who remain refused a trip to London," he said. "I'm afraid that my mother's lackadaisical view of domestic chores means that the household staff are accustomed to doing as they wish, when they wish."

"I can see that," Stella said.

"Should I apologize?"

"The state of the house is not your fault." She couldn't help wondering what Yasmin would have made of it, though. She struck Stella as extremely fastidious. "Let's find the maids."

Silvester started. "The Dowager House! We can spend the night there. It is fully renovated."

"Including furniture?"

He grinned at her. "Yes, with new beds and bedding. I ordered that the house be outfitted from top to bottom. Animals had made their home there, so everything was torn down to the studs and rebuilt. It took almost a year."

Exactly what would have to happen to the Grange, Stella thought grimly, only renovation was likely to take a decade.

CHAPTER THIRTY-TWO

Showing Stella through the Grange made mortification settle on Silvester's skin like a greasy film. When he was a child, he had racketed around happily, darting in and out of the castle, running down to the kitchens for a boiled egg when he was hungry. Meals were irregularly served, since no nanny would stay in service. In retrospect, he knew they were likely unpaid.

No one put him and his sisters to bed, at least until he was old enough to realize that little girls were supposed to sleep when night fell. After that, he began doing it himself. As well as fetching tea and boiled eggs for the girls' tea.

They were neglected, but not unloved.

The dowager loved all three of them fiercely. But she shared her husband's passion for locomotive engines. When they weren't traveling around the country meeting other enthusiasts, the two of them often worked late into the night, utterly absorbed by the fascinating process of engineering a new kind of machine.

When his mother remembered their existence, she would summon her children to the drawing room and give them lessons in deportment. She taught them to dance, and the girls to embroider, holding an embroidery frame with fingers blackened by soot and engine oil. They all learned exquisite manners, the better to cut up their boiled eggs.

Far more frequently, she would bustle them off to the machine shed and illustrate how to sketch a design using a ruler, with crucial parts identified as Fig. 1 and Fig. 2. Silvester still remembered sketching a design for an improved link-motion for steam engines, though he never knew exactly what it was meant to do.

Stella walked silently beside him out of the castle. Silvester didn't fool himself about his wife's reaction to the Grange. She was appalled. Of course, she was appalled. He felt a stab of guilt. He could at least have sent a team down from London to have the cobwebs and dust swept away.

"The Dower House was designed by Sir Christopher Wren and built around a hundred years ago," he said as they walked through the neglected gardens. He made a mental note to hire gardeners.

Stella murmured something.

He led her off to the left, through a gap in the high hedge. In sharp contrast to the Grange, the Dower House was symmetrical in design. There were five windows on the upper floor and two on each side of the door. Two dormer windows jutted from the roof.

The brick gleamed in the afternoon sun, having been recently pointed and cleaned. What's more, a wisp of smoke came from the chimney, suggesting that such maids as remained could be found here.

Sure enough, when he opened the door, three women came trotting from various parts of the house and dropped into curtsies, congratulations bursting forth.

Stella beamed, greeting each one and asking about their responsibilities.

It didn't take long to walk around the ground floor of the Dower House, since it had only two drawing rooms, a dining room, a study, and a small parlor lined with empty bookshelves.

"I love that chaise longue," Stella remarked when they entered the parlor.

It was upholstered in cherry-colored velvet and positioned before a window to catch the best light.

"The color?"

"Yes, and it's so blissfully close to the floor," Stella said. "Even I couldn't spill my teacup from that height."

"We can move it to the Grange," he suggested.

"The room couldn't do without it. The cherry is designed to complement the gray wainscotting."

"I employed the same company for the Dower House that worked on the London townhouse," Silvester told her. "We can hire them for the Grange, and you may have a chaise longue in every room, with legs that scarcely clear the floor, if you wish."

He escorted her upstairs to inspect the bedchambers, trying to pretend that his skin wasn't prickling. That his whole body wasn't taut with desire. That he was interested in inspecting the new water closet.

Stella, on the other hand, was fascinated by Bertha's explanation of how water was heated before it reached the bathtub. Silvester stopped listening and watched his wife's arse as she bent over to open the tap.

"There's hot water in the nursery on the floor above as well," Bertha reported.

Disappointingly, Stella straightened. "Why is there a nursery, if this was designed as a dower house?"

"No idea," Silvester said. "My mother will probably turn them into workrooms." He led her from the water closet through an adjoining door into the largest bedchamber. It was furnished with more bookcases and comfortable chairs positioned before a tiled fireplace. It wasn't ducal, like the chamber the Frenchmen had designed, but it was comfortable.

Stella beamed. "Your mother has marvelous taste."

He followed her gaze to another chaise longue, upholstered in dark purple velvet.

"My mother had nothing to do with it," Silvester said. He jerked his head, and Bertha backed out of the room, closing the door behind her.

Stella was chattering about wainscotting when Silvester lost every fragment of patience he had left in his body, scooped her up, and brought her over to the bed. Luckily, she began giggling, so he felt free to pull out her hairpins and start the elaborate process of unclothing his wife.

"Didn't you promise that you would wear only a chemise for the first days of our marriage?" He rolled her to the side so he could tackle some irritating laces.

"*You* suggested that," Stella said. She smiled at him as he eased her gown from her shoulders. She was blushing, but her eyes were happily desirous. How had he even considered sleeping with other women, given that no one had looked at him with this expression, this precise combination of desire and curiosity?

"I meant it," he told her.

"You imagined me running down corridors in the Grange wearing a chemise? I'd be mistaken for a ghost! Not that there's anyone to scream, except you."

"I wouldn't scream," he promised. His heart was

beating in his throat so hard that the words scarcely emerged. She let him remove her glasses, and her lashes swept her cheeks. He wanted to lap her up, taste her, bite her, make her his. He ripped her chemise, but thankfully it wasn't *that* one, the one that caught on her hips and made him feel dizzy with lust.

When she was finally naked, he pulled her to the edge of the bed and spread her legs wide so he could admire every perfect, private fold. Stella being Stella, she didn't squeal in ladylike horror, but arched her back in silent invitation. Silvester took in one ragged breath before he dropped to his knees and buried his head between her legs.

She tasted like sweet spice and honey. He meant to tease her into incoherence and then bring his cock into play, but watching desire chase ecstasy across Stella's face kept him where he was, his hands wrapped around her thighs, fingers sinking into her yielding flesh.

He didn't let go until she began gasping, pleading for more. Then he worked two broad fingers inside her tight, hot core, pumping into her until she sobbed with need, pushing back against his fingers, shivering at the stroke of his tongue, begging him to come inside her.

He held back, denying the ravaging desire to take his wife, until he had driven her into an orgasm so powerful that he felt her body clamp around his fingers.

When Stella settled, boneless and sweaty, Silvester had to fight not to come as he crawled over her on all fours. One touch of her hand and he would cover her breasts with his seed.

She opened her eyes, pleasure-drenched, and caught

him by the shoulders. "You didn't obey me. I wanted you."

"No." Silvester didn't bother to tell her that he never would obey her in the bedchamber.

Stella gave him a mischievous grin and bent her knees, planting her feet and arching up until her slick, soft folds rubbed against his throbbing cock. "There's more than one way to win," she whispered.

A deep sound wrenched from his chest before he pushed her knees higher and sank into her heat. Her fingernails pricked his shoulders as she pulled him closer. Their lips met in a devouring kiss, stealing his ability to think, but he managed two words. "My. Wife."

Sometime later, he was flat on his back, panting, drunk with pleasure, when Stella surprised him again. She had been lying beside him, eyes closed, a dreamy expression on her face that made him foolishly proud of himself.

Then she sat up and said, "I don't want to be the duchess of the Grange, Silvester. I want to be the duchess *here*."

Silvester was drifting, blood sparking as if he'd been hit by lightning. His cock had just made it known that it was preparing for another round. He was thinking about that, and the fact that the Dower House's cook had not left for London but was down in the kitchen preparing a meal. He didn't remember hiring a cook for the Dower House, but he was very glad she existed.

"Here?" he repeated. "In the country, you mean?"

"No, I want to be a dowager."

"We've only been married two days," he pointed out, running a hand down her arm. Her skin was silky smooth. "I'm not ready to shuffle off this mortal coil."

"*Hamlet*," Stella exclaimed. She clapped a hand over her mouth. "I shouldn't have said that."

"Why not?"

She fidgeted. "It is ill-bred to show knowledge of a quotation. Clearly, you already knew the source, so I was simply trying to impress you."

"Were you?"

Stella was turning a delicious shade of pink. "What?"

"Trying to impress me?"

"No. I just . . . I enjoy identifying things. Facts. It's like a game, but an insufferable one, as my aunt has told me. I should keep useless facts to myself."

"I like it," he said lazily, taking her hand and bringing it to his mouth. "I was force-fed all sorts of ridiculous phrases as a boy, before I left for Eton, so I can keep you guessing. We couldn't retain tutors—they wanted to be paid, the poor sods—so my father would read aloud at night and then quiz us the next day."

"That doesn't sound so terrible," Stella said. "I wish I had more memories of my parents."

He turned her hand over and planted a kiss on her palm. "It was, and it wasn't. One of my sisters can still recite most of Lady Macbeth's lines, but as she pointed out, unless she marries badly or becomes unexpectedly familiar with royalty, her education had no purpose."

"I never considered plays to offer patterns for living," Stella objected. "Even if your sister did come to know His Majesty, she needn't arrange for him to be murdered."

"Exit, pursued by a bear," Silvester offered. "That might be useful, if we take to leaving the front door of the Grange open. Or not. I found most of Shakespeare terrible tripe. What play is that from, wife?"

"The Winter's Tale. No Bard for our children?" Stella asked teasingly.

The words shot through him like silver lightning. "We'll have children, won't we?"

She nodded, then leaned over and poked him. "Sooner rather than later, with the way we're carrying on. I'm hungry. How about you?"

"Did you say that you want to live *here*, in the Dower House?" He propped himself up on his elbows.

"Yes, I did. Your mother loves the Grange, so why shouldn't she continue to live there?"

"Because I am the duke?"

Stella shrugged. "Does anyone truly care where the duke lives? You said yourself that the nearby gentry have nothing to do with your family. It's not as if we'll be inviting them for Christmas dinner."

Silvester let himself slip down to lie on his back again. "I always pictured myself living in the Grange, restored to its former glory."

"It is true that most of the ton would leap at the chance to break bread with you," Stella said with a distinct note of dismay in her voice. "I suppose that was the way you imagined 'winning' when you were a boy."

"Yes," Silvester said, thinking about it. "I wanted all the people who snubbed my parents to long for an invitation to the Grange."

"Your parents didn't care," Stella reminded him.

"*I* cared."

Stella moved to lie partly on top of him, just enough so she glazed his mouth with a kiss. "Would you find it shameful to live in a less-than-palatial building? This is a normal house. Just the right size for two people and a few children."

"Footmen, maids, cook? The servants' quarters are limited."

She shrugged. "If they can't be housed here, surely they could run over from the Grange? The cook we just met seemed very capable, and I like Bertha."

"I hired a French chef for the Grange."

He saw her eyes harden.

"No."

"You dislike French food as well as French wallpaper," Silvester guessed.

She shook her head. "That's not it. Though I am glad not to marry your cousin and open a laughing gas salon in Paris."

"I don't like Harold."

"Why not?"

"For one thing, I don't care for the way he looks at you," Silvester said, his voice roughening. "He gobbles like a turkey, thinking French is the language of love."

Stella laughed, which brought his attention to her lips, swollen from his kisses. He licked and kissed her mouth some more until his cock was throbbing against her leg.

She broke free and said, breathlessly, "Silvester, I want to live here, in this house."

Silvester's mind boggled. He'd never imagined living anywhere other than the Grange, the house where his ancestors going back generations had lived. Lived uncomfortably, it's true.

Silence fell as he tried to think it through. Stella had been orphaned, so of course she wouldn't care about an ancestral home.

"I can see that won't work," Stella said, dropping a kiss on his nose. "Then I suggest we move to Queen Elizabeth's chamber. I can't live with the jasmine wallpaper."

"What wallpaper?"

"Jasmine. The jasmine petals blowing around the walls."

He blinked at her. "I didn't tell them to do that."

"You must have told them the name of your future wife."

Remorse tore through Silvester's chest. Of course she didn't want to be reminded of his idiocy. "We'll rip out the paper," he promised. "You'll never see it again. Would we live in the Dower House forever?"

He wanted to make her happy, but the squeaky little boy inside him was protesting. He was a *duke*. He was supposed to be *ducal*.

Of course . . .

Being *ducal* to an eight-year-old boy had meant clean rooms with shining furniture, fireplaces without soot, meals that were served on time. All of which could be had in the Dower House far more comfortably than in the Grange.

"We can stay here," he said, before Stella could answer. "My mother would be happy to continue living in the Grange. I notice that she has become protective of any room or object that reminds her of my father."

"I would love that," Stella said, leaning down to nip his lower lip. "Thank you. And no, you are not ripping out that paper. Guests will be dazzled by it."

Silvester wound a hand into her hair and pulled her in for another kiss. "Harold cannot pay us a visit," he said thickly sometime later. "I won't have him ogling you while singing."

She giggled at him. "You're absurd."

"No, I'm not. He wants you."

"I'm married. And I'm hungry, husband. Since I do not want to dress and go down to the dining room, would you please reach over and pull that cord?"

"Would you like a boiled egg?" Silvester laughed at her confused expression, but he'd always fetched food for people he loved.

The thought made him blink.

Love?

People he was *fond* of. *Living* with. Family!

Yet Stella was his family now.

So he would always bring her boiled eggs and toast. But of course he didn't love her. That would be absurd. He was fond of her. In time, he certainly would love her.

But not romantically, just in the warm, affectionate way that happy couples . . . loved each other.

CHAPTER THIRTY-THREE

The Duke and Duchess of Huntington returned to London two weeks later. Specs traveled with them, since Silvester had managed to win back the kitty's favor through frequent gifts of cheese. At the moment she was upside down in his lap, playing with the strings that laced his shirt at the neck. Since they would be traveling all day, Silvester was wearing a loose linen shirt and no cravat.

"She looks like an upside-down furry caterpillar," Stella remarked. "When we first met, I thought you smelled like winter. Now we're married, you smell like cheddar."

"Not very ducal," Silvester said, giving her that wry smile that she saw only in private. He ran a finger over Specs's head, and the cat instantly turned and started wrestling with his hand. "She's my favorite caterpillar."

Stella cleared her throat. "So I gather that the townhouse was renovated fairly recently?"

He nodded. "Our chamber has an adjoining water closet with a separate Lewis Commode."

"Is there a balcony for Specs?"

"There isn't, but even if there was, we couldn't allow her onto it. A large tree grows close by the window, and from there she could flee into Hyde Park, just across the road."

Specs didn't show any signs of wanting to escape. Right now she was purring as Silvester stroked her tail. "Where will we put her box?"

"In the fireplace for the moment," Silvester said. "We'll figure out a better location when it grows cold."

Specs flicked her tail out of his hand, her eyes closing. "Perhaps we ought to put her down and amuse ourselves." He raised an eyebrow suggestively.

In the end, the cat slept, nestled on a linen cravat, while the duke and duchess indulged in marital pleasures.

After spending the night at The Swan, the barouche arrived at the London townhouse in midmorning. Stella was ceremoniously introduced to each and every servant, including those who would be returning to the country, after which the housekeeper, Mrs. Briggs, gave her a tour of the townhouse, punctuating her commentary with useful information. Apparently, there was no keeping a housekeeper at the Grange.

"It's the dowager's fault," Mrs. Briggs whispered, opening a floor-to-ceiling closet containing towering stacks of immaculate linens. "She won't have it when they suggest changes, not even getting rid of tattered sheets. She won't even take the nasty spit out of that huge fireplace in the entry, all because of some memory she has with the duke as was, her husband. Something about a wild hog, which speaks for itself, doesn't it?"

"They must have loved each other very much."

"I am fond of Mr. Briggs," the housekeeper said

with magisterial emphasis. "I assure you that his passing will not affect my housekeeping."

At luncheon, the dowager greeted them cheerfully. Apparently, Harold had shelved his plans for a laughing gas salon and moved into a suite in Germain's Hotel. "I have kept myself busy planning my next event, which is designed to please not merely a small list of invitees but all of our neighbors."

"Oh?" Silvester asked. "I find myself exhausted by our journey and shall need to retire to my bedchamber after luncheon."

Luckily, his mother didn't see his wicked twinkle or the fact his hand crept onto Stella's knee.

"I plan to have Italian acrobats capering on the townhouse roof at night."

"Who will see them?"

"That's just it: I discovered that they regularly juggle lighted torches at Vauxhall!"

Silvester's hand abruptly disappeared. "We'll be treated to the spectacle of our house burning down."

"I plan to pay a visit to Quimby's Emporium tomorrow afternoon," Stella said hastily.

The dowager's eyes lit up. "Is there a costume ball in the offing?"

"Not that I know of," Stella replied. "I plan to order a new wardrobe fit for a duchess. I know that *modistes* generally visit duchesses' houses, but my understanding is that Mrs. Quimby operates from her emporium."

She had made up her mind to order an unfashionable wardrobe that would flatter her figure. If a duchess truly could set a style, as her aunt believed, then she meant to do it. And if she didn't set a style, *c'est la vie*.

The dowager duchess clapped. "No more ruffs. A duchess shouldn't look like John the Baptist on a platter."

"My wife has no resemblance to any historical male, John or Holofernes," Silvester said, his gaze slanting over Stella's breasts. "I might agree to Cleopatra. I could imagine Stella on a chaise longue, being fed grapes by a devoted servant."

Which is just what he had done the evening before at The Swan. Stella couldn't stop herself from smiling at him.

"Egyptians wore gowns that looked remarkably like chemises," he added helpfully. Under the table, his knee bumped hers, although his expression was blamelessly thoughtful.

"Since Cleopatra did not wear a ruff, I have no argument with ancient Egypt," his mother announced. "I shall join you. Clearly, Mrs. Thyme had all too much influence over your sartorial choices, Stella. I advise a dash of originality."

The dowager's current costume, which appeared to have been designed for a military man, was certainly original, and it didn't have a ruff. Stella had formed a dislike for the word, let alone the embellishment.

Quimby's Costume Emporium was a prosperous-looking establishment with a striped awning proudly declaring that they were *Purveyors to Drury Lane Theatre & More.*

The dowager halted on the sidewalk, staring at a window displaying a blue silk gown with a low bodice. Soft pleated material wrapped the dress form, creating a natural waist marked by a pearl-embellished belt.

"Look at that," Her Grace exclaimed, catching Stella's arm. "That gown is for you!"

"The ensemble is designed for a masquerade ball," Stella objected. "See the crimson cloak trimmed in ermine? I suspect it is the costume for a princess."

"Humph." The dowager stumped up the steps to the Emporium.

They walked into a large antechamber furnished by a low box before a mirror and a cluster of sofas to one side. Three seamstresses were seated there, sewing tin stars on a red gown.

The two curtained enclosures to the other side presumably allowed ladies to change their clothing. When Stella had visited the Emporium to order a toga, there had been no question of undressing. The toga was designed to be worn over a morning gown, so measurements were taken over her clothing, and the garment delivered to the house the next day.

Presumably, now that she was ordering gowns, she would need to be measured in a chemise, which suggested she would have to unclothe herself in one of those enclosures. Mrs. Thyme would faint at the mere prospect. A male customer might stroll through the door at any moment, with nothing more than a curtain to protect the lady's chastity.

Mrs. Quimby herself came to greet them. She had the confident swagger of a woman who owned her business. "Your Graces!" Mrs. Quimby exclaimed, dropping into a curtsy. "It is a true honor. May I offer my sincere congratulations on your recent nuptials, Your Grace?"

"Thank you very much," Stella said. "The white horse at my wedding was a charming surprise. My husband credited you with the design." She held out her hand.

"He asked for a fairy tale, and I gave it to him," Mrs. Quimby said, chuckling. She took Stella's hand. "A few years ago, I would have shook all over at the very idea of shaking a duchess's hand."

"I have never shaken hands," the dowager remarked, "but I have no particular dislike of the idea. We must all change with the times, eh?" She took Mrs. Quimby's hand and moved it up and down vigorously.

"May I introduce two of my seamstresses, Mrs. Peebles and Miss Prewitt?"

The women dropped into curtsies, while Stella practiced the gracious nod she'd copied from her friend Merry.

"As an unmarried lass, my daughter-in-law relied on *modistes*," the dowager said. "Just look what that did for her."

Everyone stared at Stella's gown. The bodice was formed from red and white vertical ruffles extending from a high neckline to a high waist. The *modiste* had posited that vertical ruffles would add height and disguise Stella's bosom.

From Mrs. Quimby's dubious expression, she was as unconvinced as Stella.

"She looks like a barber's pole," the dowager added.

All eyes moved to Stella's chest.

"I am not straight up and down like a barber's pole," Stella acknowledged. "I should like a new wardrobe that takes account of my curves. The Duchess of Trent assures me that you will be more observant to my figure than to fashion."

"I can't be too particular about fashion when I have

to make every leading lady look her best, can I? They come in all shapes and sizes." Mrs. Quimby gave Stella an impish smile. "Although I do assure you that I see the illustrations that *La Belle Assemblée* will publish before anyone else in London."

"If you would be so kind as to take that blue gown out of the window and put it on my daughter-in-law, Mrs. Quimby," the dowager announced. She walked over to the couches without waiting for an answer.

Stella smiled ruefully. "You needn't tell me that the gown is designed for someone much taller and slimmer. Perhaps we might look at some illustrations?"

"Actually, the gown is fashioned with a simple lacing in the back," Mrs. Quimby said. She waved at one of her seamstresses. "We create a few gowns hoping to inspire theater folk, without knowing which actress might wear it. If you wouldn't mind retiring with Mrs. Peebles, Your Grace, I can have the gown off the mannequin before you're down to your chemise."

Once Stella was in the curtained enclosure, it was no more embarrassing undressing with Mrs. Peebles than with her maid. Back in the anteroom, the dowager was demanding a gown covered with tin stars.

"This gown is designed for a theatrical performance, to catch the attention of an audience member in the back of the theater," Mrs. Quimby said doubtfully.

"I shall enjoy that," the dowager stated. "I am a duchess, after all. Why shouldn't I be visible from the other side of the ballroom?"

Mrs. Peebles pulled the lacing in the back of the blue gown until pleated silk clung to Stella's body. The bodice was so low that Mrs. Thyme—

She pushed her aunt's opinion out of her head yet again and walked out of the dressing room.

"Exquisite," Mrs. Quimby cried, darting over to tweak her skirts after Stella climbed on the wooden box. "We call this color azure. What do you think of the pearl ornament?"

The neckline came to a point between Stella's breasts, ending in a brooch with three dangling pearls.

"Those aren't real," the dowager observed. She was walking around Stella, peering at her from all sides. "We can't have a duchess in sham jewels."

"We can certainly substitute real ones," Mrs. Quimby said, standing back, arms crossed over her chest. "The white edging sets off Her Grace's freckles in a charming fashion."

"She looks taller with her neck and bosom bared," the dowager said. "Will you be able to make up the fabric in the back?"

Humiliatingly, Stella could feel cool air where the sides of the gown didn't meet, although the lacing held it in place. The skirts were too long, and cloth puddled around her feet.

"I shall remake the gown for Her Grace," Mrs. Quimby said, looking offended. "While the Emporium creates costumes, we also pride ourselves on being as exclusive as any *modiste* in London, if not better. Her Grace may be assured that no other lady in all society will have a gown made to this pattern."

"Or on the stage either," the dowager said. "I don't want to see Juliet entertaining Romeo in my daughter-in-law's gown."

"Certainly not," Mrs. Quimby assured her.

"In that case, you'd better make three or four in this

shape, in different colors, of course," the dowager said, waving her hand.

Stella plucked the folds clinging to her body. She thought Silvester would love the gown, as it wasn't unlike his favorite chemise. It had little resemblance to the airy concoctions that ladies wore to drift around the ballroom floor.

"You're a duchess now," her mother-in-law said, apparently guessing what she was thinking. "You may wear whatever you wish. You look delicious in that gown. Can't you see it?"

Stella could. But she could also hear her aunt's faint scream as she toppled into a faint.

"We need a wardrobe that's suited to *you*, not to a stalk of grass hoping to catch a husband." The dowager turned to Mrs. Quimby. "Design the rest of the wardrobe in this fashion. You can see what she looks like."

Stella flinched, but the dowager kept talking.

"Make her as pretty as she is. Her carroty hair would look well with almost any color. And then there's her bosom. You'll want to make the most of *that*. All her curves, in fact."

Stella had never heard her hair referred to appreciatively. None of the assembled seamstresses were looking at her figure or her hair with distaste. In fact, they looked excited.

The experience was a stark contrast to her memory of visiting *modistes* with Mrs. Thyme before her debut. The French seamstresses had been as dismayed as her aunt, suggesting that she swill vinegar and avoid cake.

"Make her look like Cleopatra. That's what her husband wants," the dowager concluded.

Mrs. Quimby turned to Stella. "What do *you* want?"

Stella blinked at her, nonplussed. She had come to the Emporium because she didn't want to look like Holofernes, but she didn't know more than that. "I'd like to feel more attractive," she said, finally.

She almost blurted out that she wanted to look pretty. That would be a humiliating revelation. But what she really wanted was to *feel* attractive, never mind the fact her face and body didn't match society's ideas of beauty. She wanted to *feel* brave.

"How do you feel in this gown?"

Stella looked at the glass. Facing her was a lady whose cheeks were pink with embarrassment. But that lady was . . .

More than just attractive. She had ample curves, and the azure gown celebrated each one. Freckles scattered over her nose and down her breasts in a way that drew the eye, and white edging enhanced them rather than trying to hide them.

Her mother had been wrong about her freckles. Her aunt had been wrong about her breasts. Neither were disgusting.

"I feel like a duchess," she said.

"I would suggest a round robe of blossom-colored crepe with a demi-train, gathered in the rear with puckered white satin," Mrs. Quimby said thoughtfully. "I can shape it to fit Her Grace like a glove. Mind you, the design leaves the back and bosom uncommonly exposed."

"I don't mind low bodices," Stella stated.

She was a married woman now. Her husband appreciated her bosom.

"Then you may leave the rest to me," Mrs. Quimby

said, beaming. "Unless you would like to have a hand in choosing fabric and designs, Your Grace?"

Stella shook her head. "I would not." Time spent examining illustrations from *La Belle Assemblée* was time she could be reading. Or dallying with her husband, for that matter.

"An excellent decision," the dowager stated. "I always leave such matters to those who are experts. I can't say that has always worked out in the household, but my husband never complained."

Back in the carriage, Stella couldn't stop herself. "Did your late husband, the duke, truly never complain about the condition of the Grange?"

She held her gaze steady when the dowager frowned. She couldn't allow herself to be turned into a doormat by her brusque mother-in-law. "Because I would describe it as unfurnished and rather dirty," she added.

"It didn't used to be."

"Did Silvester tell you that I would prefer to move to the Dower House, if you don't mind staying in the Grange?"

"He did. As I told him, I would be happy to live among my best memories," the dowager said, unsurprisingly. "I did promise Silvester that he could begin renovation whenever he wishes. I won't live forever, so someday, you'll have to move there. The Dukes of Huntington have always lived in the Grange."

"For the moment, the Dower House is very comfortable," Stella said.

"I've never been able to care much about comfort," Silvester's mother said. "Not when there were so many interesting things to do. Even now, although I have no chimney to work on, I feel as if I'm expiring when I listen to a housekeeper prose on about linens. Who cares if a sheet has a hole or two?"

Stella cared.

But the dowager's throat bobbled as she swallowed. "I don't care, and neither did the late duke. We were partners in something far more important than the . . . the society foolishness that seems to amuse my son so much."

"Did you stop working on locomotives when His Grace passed away?" Stella asked.

"Naturally," the dowager said, slumping back into the corner. "He died suddenly. We were working on a regulator for the engine, just sketching it out, when he collapsed. He was gone by nightfall."

"I'm sorry."

"I missed him so much, and then by the time I woke out of my grief, the men who had been working with us had scattered to the winds." She shrugged. "He and I together could do such things. But a woman, by herself? Never. Now I just create entertainments."

From working on a steam engine to sewing duck's hats? That was a downfall. Moreover, the dowager had clearly loved her husband passionately. No wonder she often had a desolate air.

"I don't understand why you are unable to work on engine designs," Stella said. "Who is stopping you?"

"The men won't pay attention to me."

"Then hire men who will. Or pay them enough that they can't stop themselves from paying attention."

The dowager snorted. "It would cost a fortune. You

have no idea how condescending inventors can be. Quite a few of them still pretend that my husband designed that chimney, rather than I."

"Then pay a fortune. Silvester has more money than he knows what to do with. A few weeks ago, he was talking about shoring up the Bank of England if they approach a breaking point."

"I'm years behind." But there was a trace of hope in the dowager's voice.

"Travel about and learn what other inventors are doing," Stella said briskly. "You don't have small children to keep you at home. Afterward, you can design a new chimney, a better chimney."

A flicker of shame crossed the dowager's face. "We weren't . . . we weren't perfect parents. I couldn't keep a nanny in the Grange, but I told myself that the children were fine."

"They *were* fine," Stella said. "Your children are grown, healthy people."

"Silvester raised the girls," the dowager said. "I suppose he raised himself as well. I turned around, and my son had turned into this . . . this *perfect* gentleman, polished from head to foot. Beloved by polite society." She snorted. "His father never bothered to court the admiration of fools."

Even his mother was not allowed to insult Silvester in Stella's presence.

"Your son made up his mind as a child that he would be respected and admired for the man he is, not merely for the title he inherited. He also decided to build a fortune that could weather future generations of Huntington inventors. He has succeeded in every possible measure."

The dowager narrowed her eyes, and Stella narrowed hers right back.

Her Grace burst out laughing. "I deserved that. I suppose *we* deserved that, my husband and I. Thank goodness Silvester didn't marry that foolish twit he was in love with. Yasmin never would have dared to contradict me. She would have ruined him. Tasseled boots and brocades for the rest of his life, without a sensible thought between them."

A searing pain went through Stella's heart at the mention of Silvester's love for Yasmin, but she didn't allow her expression to change at all. "That's not fair. Your son was courting Lady Yasmin at the same time he saved the English monetary system by moving it to the gold standard."

"Oh that." The dowager waved her hand. "Silvester can't help liking numbers; he inherited it from both of us. But that golden-haired gal? She would have ruined him."

"I like Lady Yasmin," Stella said, though it made her feel ill to admit it. "She's tremendously kind."

"I'm not!" the dowager said, with another bark of laughter. Then she pointed at Stella. "Neither are you. Whether my son agreed with me or not, I knew you were the one for him. You'll make him into a man, not a milliner."

Stella cleared her throat.

"That boy never does a thing when I order him to do it," his mother observed. "Don't think he married to oblige me. I've seen him looking at you, like a beggar with a crust of bread. I had nothing to do with that."

"How lucky," Stella managed. She laced her hands

in her lap and tried to arrange her features into a casual expression.

"Lust *is* lucky." The dowager cocked her head. "When I married, my husband had a carriage draw up to the church. Then he sent it around London for a few hours. When I arrived at the breakfast, I wasn't a virgin any longer."

Stella smiled. "I trust it was a happy drive?"

"I hardly knew the man," the dowager said, her eyes softening. "You didn't, in those days. All I knew was that he had legs like gateposts and a fondness for mathematics. That wasn't fashionable, you know. He was supposed to like hunting. Luckily for him, I like men with thick legs, and he liked my shape as well."

She lapsed into silence for a moment and then roused. "He would have abhorred all that foolishness my son spouted, moaning that he wanted to be in love with his wife!"

Stella's heart thudded against her ribs with a sickening thump.

"I told Silvester he was a fool, because you and he are suited to each other. As was I to my husband. No flummery between us, but plenty of old-fashioned lust."

"I'm glad to hear it," Stella said. She was fighting a horrible rush of misery. She *knew* Silvester hadn't chosen her first. She *knew* he had been in love with Yasmin. Nothing that his mother was saying was particularly fresh.

So why did she feel so cold and miserable?

"You can build on lust," the dowager was saying. That seemed to be the end of her marital advice, so they sat in silence while Stella gave herself a lecture.

She wasn't in love with Silvester. She refused to be in love with Silvester. He wasn't in love with her. That was . . . *fine.*

She simply had to keep her equilibrium. Stop sneaking looks at him. Romantic love was a fantasy, and besides, he'd given what he had to Yasmin. She'd take whatever the dowager and her duke had. The love that came from years together, from loyalty and passion.

As long as she kept her dignity, she would be fine. No embarrassing Silvester or herself. She couldn't start hanging on him, like a lovesick ninny.

"My eyesight is worse than it used to be," the duchess said suddenly. "How would I manage the details of a design, the figures and so on?"

"Spectacles," Stella said flatly. "I'll send for the man who sold me these. He'll come to the house with a box full of them. You'll try each on until you find the pair that corrects your vision."

"The queen doesn't like to see women wearing them," the dowager said.

Stella shrugged. Whether or not Her Majesty approved of her spectacles was very low on the list of things she cared about.

"*You* are a real duchess already," the dowager said, pointing at Stella again.

Stella managed a smile. "I'm not certain that is a compliment."

"Why should I care what Her Majesty thinks?" the dowager said to herself. "She's never approved of my chimney. In fact, I don't think she's ever mentioned it to me, just complained about my monocle. How on earth could I have designed a chimney while holding a lorgnette?"

"I have wondered the same about reading," Stella said with feeling. "If I were to hold the lorgnette in one hand, how could I hold a book *and* turn the pages?"

"Even if I weren't given to unladylike pursuits," the dowager said, nodding, "I could scarcely hold a child along with a lorgnette, could I?"

Stella found it difficult to imagine her mother-in-law peering at a baby through her monocle, but she nodded.

"I shall introduce you to the queen," the dowager announced.

Stella frowned. "I was formally presented at one of the Queen's Drawing Rooms. Her Majesty wasn't impressed by me the first time, though I gather now that I was lucky to escape without a comment about my spectacles."

"What did she say about you?"

"Homely and plump, as I heard later."

"Heard? From whom?"

Stella hesitated. "A friend."

The duchess snorted. "No true friend would say that. I doubt it was true. I've known the queen since we were both girls. Her Majesty exclaims about the Season's diamonds but doesn't dish out insults on the rest of the gals."

Stella managed a wavering smile. Lydia might have invented the royal insult, but Silvester had admitted to commenting that Stella didn't care about her appearance, which was just another way of saying she was homely.

"I shall wear spectacles, and you shall wear that blue gown," the dowager announced. "Then you shall sing for the queen, Stella. My governess would have the vapors if she heard me use your forename. You don't mind if I address you as Stella, do you?"

Stella shook her head.

"Like shaking hands and spectacles, I must move with the times." The dowager was sitting bolt upright, looking far more energetic and happy than Stella had seen her other than when waving a wooden sword. "I shall inform Her Majesty that I plan to design a better chimney."

The upshot of this conversation was that three weeks later the Dowager Duchess of Huntington and the new Duchess of Huntington were bidden to a private audience with Her Majesty, the Queen.

After drinking several cups of tea, Stella sang in French for the queen and her ladies-in-waiting. When she sat back down, the ladies-in-waiting twittered and fluttered like tulips in a stiff breeze, until finally the queen roused herself and declared that she hadn't been so moved since Lady Merlin sang that ditty she wrote about love.

One of the ladies-in-waiting whispered something.

"Just so," the queen snapped. "I forgot the foolish woman ran off with a piano tuner. *You* don't have plans to run off with anyone, do you?" She glared at Stella.

Stella felt herself turning pink. "No, no, not at all."

"Of course, you wouldn't," Her Majesty said. "You caught the prettiest cock in the yard, didn't you?"

Stella couldn't wait to tell Silvester that particular comment.

"Sing me something else," Her Majesty declared. "I can't say I like your spectacles."

"If I didn't wear them, I couldn't read the music," Stella pointed out.

"I suppose I'll have all my ladies peering at the world through little circles of wire in the future."

The following week, Mrs. Quimby had to hire another seamstress, because three of Her Majesty's ladies-in-waiting visited the Emporium to demand gowns that were flattering rather than fashionable. Others demanded the same of their *modistes*, so waistlines across London promptly dropped a handbreadth.

As for society's view of the new Duchess of Huntington?

It was astonishing how quickly ladies forgot that freckles weren't attractive. Or spectacles. Or curves. Or lack of height.

By the end of the month, no French tutors were to be found in London for love or money. Every anxious mother with a young daughter was forcing the girl to practice singing in French so that when the new Season began, she could warble in the language.

SILVESTER WATCHED BEMUSEDLY as his new duchess became the rage. Every afternoon, the street before the ducal townhouse was crowded with carriages as footmen delivered cards in the hope that Her Grace would declare herself at home.

The same matrons who had snubbed Stella now adored the new duchess's witty comments and her gowns, so fresh and unconventional. It wasn't merely ladies. Gentlemen clustered around her, begging her to waltz, especially the French ones.

They wanted to gape at her breasts, in Silvester's opinion.

No one but his mother realized that while Silvester

had been unmoved by Lady Yasmin's suitors, he became distinctly grumpy when his young wife was whirled around the floor by any man other than himself.

"Stop staring at your wife like a beef-witted buffoon," the dowager hissed one evening, as Stella circled the floor with Harold—for the second time.

"My cousin is trying to seduce my wife," Silvester said through clenched teeth. He turned his back to the dance floor and met his mother's mocking gaze.

She snorted. "Harold? Harold is about as seductive as a mayfly. I thought that nothing could shake you free of that gentlemanly composure." She grinned at him. "As I told Stella, I was absolutely right to select her for your wife."

Silvester couldn't stop thinking about that revelation. His mother had told Stella about that long-ago breakfast conversation?

His mother's command had nothing to do with his marriage, as he had told Stella himself. But he found himself wishing that his mother had settled on Yasmin, and he had chosen Stella. It would have been . . . easier.

Still, his mother had been right about Stella, not to mention his buffoonish behavior, staring at his wife as she danced with others.

He asked the first woman he encountered to dance with him.

"Your duchess is so *original*," Lady Corbyn said, simpering at him.

"Yes, she is."

"Some foolish chits have started dotting their noses with a mixture of saffron power and water to give themselves freckles," she reported.

"Indeed."

"I suppose you have heard that the Earl and Countess of Lilford are visiting Bath. Lady Yasmin is reported to have taken the waters." She twittered, so presumably that was supposed to mean something.

He shrugged.

"As do women suffering from the effects of carrying a child," Lady Corbyn added, clearly irritated by either his ignorance or his apathy. "The paper reported this morning that they took lodgings in Bath for a month, after which they plan to return to London."

He didn't give a damn what Yasmin and Giles did.

But the news did remind him that it was his duty to create an heir. He should take his wife home and talk her into repeating last night's depravity, which had involved one of her favorite chaise lounges, a glass of brandy, and a handful of raspberries.

So he did.

CHAPTER THIRTY-FOUR

In the month that followed, Silvester came to an uncomfortable realization. He seemed to . . . to care too much for his wife.

It was disconcerting. He didn't like it.

Lust was one thing. Lust was to be expected after a lifetime of never-quite-satisfied desire. He had happily debauched Stella in every room in the townhouse, even carrying her downstairs in the dark of night so he could bend her over a chair in the drawing room that was the perfect height.

The problem was not lust. Stella greeted his proposals with shining eyes and outstretched arms, which was lucky, because in the grip of lust he was reduced to a few words, an unsettling experience for a man used to eloquence.

But truly disconcerting was the way he found himself searching out Stella for other reasons. What did she think of the latest decision by the Bank of England? Should he intervene now, or wait for the next bout of idiocy?

He had sunk a small fortune into a Scottish rail line, so of course he had to tell her when it was approved for its maiden journey with passengers. He could have waited until evening. Instead he strode into her dressing room and disturbed a flock of seamstresses with pins in their mouths.

He tripped over the threshold at the sight of his wife tightly wrapped in darkened purple silk, the color of a stormy sky without a fleck of sunshine. It draped low over her breasts and swathed her shape before belling out to a small train. The gown made her hair glow like coals burning low.

He felt his tongue withering when he looked at her.

Stella's face fell when he didn't compliment the gown, and finally he had to banish all the seamstresses and unwind her from the silk himself, scattering pins right and left before he convinced her that he approved of the garment.

The following evening they attended a *"fête avec danse"* hosted by his ridiculous cousin. These days Harold spent far too much time chattering in French with Stella, ignoring the fact he was supposed to be wooing an heiress.

It was enough to make any man grumpy.

Just now Stella was across the room, surrounded by Frenchmen, and Silvester was pretending not to care. He was talking to Lord Buckstead about the Bank of England's plan to start printing legal tender when Yasmin and Giles walked through the door.

Silvester's mother was serving as Harold's hostess, so the new countess promptly dropped into a curtsy before the dowager. Silvester was rather amused to find that the sight of Yasmin left him cold. She was as exquisite as ever, her gown doubtless in the very newest Parisian style, the outline of her slender thigh clearly visible through her gauzy skirt.

He'd never thought about it before, but he'd be

damned if other men could ogle *his* wife's legs. She offered his mother her infectious grin, which gave him a burst of cheer. He had missed Yasmin's friendship.

He glanced over his shoulder, but Stella was dancing with Fabrice Epagnard, one of the band of idiotic Frenchmen who clung to her petticoats.

Silvester shook off his dislike of Epagnard and strode across the room. When he reached his mother's side, Yasmin was charmingly explaining that she needed to sit down, as she was *enceinte*, which made her light-headed.

Ladies were never supposed to admit such a thing, but her bump was clearly evident in her light gown, and Giles's pride burst through his normally stern expression. She congratulated Silvester on his marriage, giving him that twinkling smile she had down to an art. He nodded, wishing the music would end so Stella could join them.

When the three of them sat down, Giles took up the question of whether the government should intervene and curtail the Bank of England's power to print currency.

Silvester forced himself to pay attention. Stella said that he cared only about making money, but that wasn't true. The question was more complicated than Giles seemed to think, so Silvester argued one side, and then switched to argue the other.

Where was Stella? Likely that Frenchman was still flirting with her.

He turned back from scanning the dance floor to find Giles looking at him with a raised eyebrow.

"You surprise me."

"Silvester is endlessly surprising," Yasmin said merrily.

"I could always count on you for a convincing account of whichever action would make you the most money," Giles said. "But now you acknowledge complexities. Perhaps next you will take up your seat in the House of Lords?"

"Unlikely," Silvester said. But he had the feeling that Stella might find those laws they endlessly debated interesting. He would take it up, if she wished it.

Finally, the damn dance ended, with Epagnard sweeping to a halt not far from where he was sitting. Stella turned around when he called to her and froze, just briefly, before she walked toward them.

The men rose, Yasmin offering a graceful apology for staying in her seat. Silvester could read hesitation in Stella's determined smile as she greeted the earl and countess. She dropped a curtsy and murmured her congratulations.

But before Silvester could take her hand and pull her down to sit beside him, she said that she'd promised to sing a duet with their host. Without glancing at him, Stella flitted away.

Silvester sat down again, irritation filling his chest. Giles turned away, engaging in conversation with Lord Boodle.

. Yasmin smiled at him. "I don't know your wife well, but I find her so interesting. Perhaps we could attend the theater together, before I must retire due to my condition?" She wrinkled her nose at him in that charming way she had. "Apparently I should remain invisible in the last months of my pregnancy."

Stella headed blindly for the other side of the room,

aware that she was taking in deep, shuddering breaths that she could not allow anyone to see. She forced her mouth to curve into a brittle smile, keeping her head high.

Harold's eyes lit up as she walked to his side, probably the same way that her husband's eyes had lit on seeing Yasmin. Stella's stomach roiled. Luckily Harold was capable of carrying on conversations entirely by himself, switching from French to English every few minutes.

"Don't you agree?" he asked now.

Stella looked at him blankly. All she could think about was the way diamond pins in Yasmin's hair caught light from the chandeliers, highlighting her golden locks. The way her violet silk gown drifted around her slim body, whereas Stella's gown swathed her body, which suddenly made her feel dowdy.

The Earl of Lilford would never need to fake a romantic charade to tell the world why he married his wife. It had nothing to do with their baby, no matter how soon it arrived.

"The decorative value of buttons," Harold said painstakingly. "A man may have as many as a dozen useless buttons on his evening coat, black and almost invisible. If a thing is useless, it should be exquisite, don't you agree?"

Stella murmured something, her gloved hands tightening on her reticule. Was she useless? She wasn't exquisite.

"Buttons should be gilt, enamel, or inlaid metal," Harold proclaimed. Then, with a grand wave of his hand: "Otherwise, they have no reason for existing."

Before Stella could summon up a response for that

statement, Blanche shouldered Harold out of the way. She caught Stella's arm in hers. "Smile!" she hissed.

Stella smiled.

"If you'll excuse us," Blanche said to Harold, pulling Stella away.

As they walked through the door of the ladies' retiring room, Blanche gave the one woman resting in a comfortable chair a hard look, and the lady fled.

Stella could feel her face crumpling. Hot tears pressed the back of her eyes.

"No crying!" Blanche said fiercely. She turned to the table at one side and upended her reticule, scattering the belongings. "I'm going to powder your face. You'll put on lip color, and then you'll walk back into that room, picture every single person naked, and regard them as loftily as might a queen."

"I will?"

Blanche flipped open a powder pot. "I'll be *damned* if you are pitied by all those idiots out there."

Stella's throat was thick with tears. "It's nothing new. He loves her, you know."

"So what?" Blanche began expertly dusting Stella's face with powder. "Who gives a damn whom a man loves or doesn't love? My father loves French *prostituées*." She shrugged. "All we can ask is that these fools keep their entertainments to themselves. That is not too much to require."

"Silvester would never be unfaithful," Stella mumbled.

"You can believe that if you wish. But really, who cares? He humiliated you in front of your friends, in front of society. That is *not done*." Blanche's voice grated with fury.

The door slammed open, and the dowager walked in. She narrowed her eyes at Blanche. "You're not making things worse, are you?"

"She's not," Stella said. "She's . . . she's being very kind."

Blanche dropped the powder and picked up some lip salve. "I was just telling the duchess here that she is going to return to the room with her head held high. She will dance with every attractive man in the room, most of them twice, perhaps a third time if there's a pretty one on offer."

"My son is a fool," the dowager said, advancing just enough to wrap her arms around Stella's shoulders and give her a brief squeeze.

Stella stood still, made uncomfortable by the unfamiliar experience and grateful when the dowager stepped away.

"More than a fool, he's cruel," Blanche snapped.

"He's not cruel," Stella said, her voice choked. "He can't help himself."

"A grown man can't help himself?" Blanche said, at the same moment the duchess snorted loudly.

A huge lump was lodged in Stella's chest. She took a deep breath, telling herself again that dignity was everything. "I suppose I can't call for my carriage?"

"Absolutely not," the dowager said. "You will dance the night away. My nephew Harold is a worthless fellow, but tonight his *penchant* for you is useful."

Blanche was painting Stella's lips dark crimson; Stella caught sight of it in the mirror and shuddered, thinking of Mrs. Thyme. If she were in London, she would be horrified by Stella's new wardrobe, let alone this bold lip color.

Her aunt's weekly letters were thick with advice drawn from ancient books of etiquette. Surprisingly, Mrs. Thyme's weekly letters never mentioned a wish to return to London; mostly she wrote about her kitten, Sparks. But Stella could read between the lines.

In her own way, Mrs. Thyme loved her.

Unfortunately, "in her own way" was the only way anyone ever loved Stella: as second choice, second best. Not that Silvester loved her even second best, because if he did, surely he wouldn't blithely humiliate her. Stella felt like an orphaned girl once again, her throat so raw with tears that she couldn't speak.

"All right," Blanche said. She stepped back. "Did you know those Frenchmen out there refer to you as a *Vénus de poche*, a pocket Venus?"

Her accent was perfect. Stella cleared her throat. "Didn't you tell me that you could scarcely remember how to say hello in French?"

"Of course I can speak French; I've had years of lessons. But I refuse to admit it. My father is maddened that I can't speak the language. He loves everything about the country, including, obviously, the women."

"Stop shaking, Stella," the dowager ordered. "I've had a life full of humiliations, and while this is embarrassing, my son will not return home with Yasmin. As I informed him long ago, she doesn't share his absurd adoration."

"Obviously, since she chose a man of lower rank," Blanche agreed.

Stella took a deep breath. She'd made a fool of herself, thinking that shared pleasure in the bedchamber would make a difference to Silvester's feelings. Love wasn't like that. It wasn't logical.

"He has never lied to me about his feelings for her," she said, her voice cracking despite herself.

"My father has never hidden his conviction that French women are the most delightful creatures to walk the earth," Blanche said. "But at least he doesn't flaunt those women in front of my mother. He gives her that much."

The dowager nodded. "Order my son to be a better actor. Or I will tell him."

"If you'll excuse me, Stella needs to lay down the rules of their marriage, not you," Blanche said. "My mother has kept her head high because in the first week of their marriage she directed my father to keep his Frenchwomen in the outskirts of London, or she would scratch their eyes out."

She met Stella's and the dowager's eyes with a shrug. "I've known my whole life that marriage requires backbone."

"You have backbone," the dowager said, looking rather fascinated.

"Not really, but I am learning to have one," Blanche replied. "I am trying to change my ways."

"All right," Stella said. "I will inform Silvester that he can't show his emotions so plainly now that he's married."

She felt as if her heart was cracking. Her husband was a consummate actor, capable of hiding every emotion. The fact he didn't manage to, in this particular case, was evidence of the strength of his feelings for Yasmin.

She *refused* to think that it was due to disrespect for

her, for his wife. Silvester did respect her. She was certain of it.

He just loved Yasmin . . . that much.

Stella squared her shoulders.

Blanche finished painting her own mouth and nodded at her. "You are a duchess. *Be* a duchess."

"Thank you," Stella said. She hesitated. "I really mean it. I was close to tears out there, thinking I was a useless button."

"I've been a *pouffiasse* to you in the past," Blanche said. "But if you'll give me a second chance, Stella, I can be a true friend. I promise."

"I would like that," Stella said.

"Come along, you two," the dowager said. She eyed them. "I suggest you get rid of that green ruff," she said to Blanche. "It looks like a wilting head of lettuce."

Blanche paused, then she gave the duchess a smile. "Nonsense," she said, holding open the door. "I look beautiful."

"I shall address you as Blanche," the dowager announced. "I am startled by my own modernity."

Blanche curtsied. "I should be honored, Your Grace."

Thankfully, a crowd of young Frenchmen surged toward them when they returned to the ballroom. The expatriates had turned Stella into their mascot, their *petite duchesse.* Stella glanced to the other side of the room just long enough to see that Silvester was still seated beside Yasmin.

She danced the next two sets, including a perfectly executed quadrille, after which Harold begged her to sing another duet.

Stella shook her head, but Blanche appeared beside

her and hissed, "You're going to sing, Stella. It's what you do best."

"I can't," she whispered. "What if my voice shakes?"

"I'll sing with you." Blanche grabbed the sheet of music Harold had in his hand.

"Your father is on the other side of the room," Stella pointed out.

"I haven't been a good friend. I mean to change." Blanche smiled at Harold, showing all of her teeth.

Not being entirely foolish, he flinched and said, "A trio!"

Blanche's smile grew. "We have a lovely surprise for you," she called, clapping her hands. She waited until guests broke off their conversation. "This song was written by Madeleine de Scudéry over a century ago. She dedicated it to *les amoureaux*. The lovers."

Her French accent was flawless. Stella saw her father's mouth fall open.

"L'eau qui caresse le rivage," they sang. Harold's voice supported from below, and Blanche's beautiful soprano arched over Stella's husky tones. *"Tout dit qu'aimer est un plasir."*

Everyone says that love is a pleasure, or so Madeleine de Scudéry claimed.

Stella didn't agree. But singing? Despite her sadness, she felt a wash of pleasure at their three-part harmony. Blanche smiled at her as they launched into the second verse about two lovers.

Harold's guests were utterly silent. Silvester was still seated by Yasmin, but his eyes were riveted on Stella. She forced herself to look away.

When the song finished, the room broke into wild applause. Blanche wound an arm around Stella's waist. *"Merci beaucoup,"* she told the room. "We are happy to have given you such pleasure."

I am worth loving, Stella told herself. *I am not a useless button.*

I am worth loving.

CHAPTER THIRTY-FIVE

"**I** had no idea that Stella could sing like that," the Earl of Lilford remarked.

"Nor Blanche Boodle!" Yasmin exclaimed. "I'm surprised she hasn't accepted any proposals, but I would guess there will be a line in front of her father's study tomorrow."

"An exquisite soprano," Giles agreed.

Silvester gave him a ferocious look. "No one sings as beautifully as my wife," he stated. It wasn't just Stella's husky voice either. Her red lips, and her curves, and her joy as she sang?

He'd never be free of those Frenchmen now.

"Of course not," Yasmin chirped.

Silvester liked her; he truly did. But how did he ever think he could put up with all that sunshiny cheer, day in and day out?

"Our marriage would have been disastrous," Yasmin said, guessing what he was thinking.

"Because he's a damned fool," her husband growled, drawing her to her feet. "It's time for you to rest."

Yasmin smiled again. "Good evening, Silvester."

Silvester stood up belatedly, thinking about the fact that he genuinely liked Yasmin, but the emotion wasn't love. He might well have been influenced by the fact that Giles wanted her. Perhaps their marriage would have been disastrous.

But his with Stella would not be.

One thing was clear. He had to convince Stella that he chose *her*.

That he would choose her next time, the next day, the next year, in another life. That she was the only one he ever truly wanted, and the only woman he could have lived with.

That they were *not* golden girls and boys, as the Shakespeare verse had it. They were sweaty and testy and *real*. Laughing in bed. They were so damned lucky.

Set upon his plan, he was blindsided when he escorted Stella into a carriage only to discover that his wife was furious. She sat on the opposite seat, her eyes hard, her arms closed over her chest.

For his part, he looked at her wrapped in her pelisse, and desire rose thick and hot in his body. Normally, he would catch her in his arms and bring her to his lap, and then amuse them both by kissing her with such carnal intent that they would stumble from the carriage and straight to the bedchamber.

Not tonight.

"What's the matter?" he asked cautiously.

"The matter?" Her laughter had an acidic edge. "What could possibly be the matter?" Her wide eyes usually met his with a glint of shared desire. Now they were steely cold.

"I don't know."

"For all your faults, you are rarely unkind."

He frowned. "Are you referring to when I compared you to a hammer?"

Stella leaned toward him. "Unkindnesses are not

merely spoken. Your true love walks into the room, and instantly you trot to her side. You don't think *that* was unkind?"

"I didn't *trot to her side*. You were dancing."

"Yes, I was dancing. You couldn't wait to greet Yasmin until I was free, knowing that the world was watching to see your reaction? Not even to spare me that humiliation?"

She dashed away a tear with a jerky movement, and Silvester's gut screwed into a sickening knot.

"I didn't think of it that way."

"As everyone surmised. You saw Yasmin, and she was all you thought about, so you went directly to her side. I might have expected it, but I didn't anticipate that you would show the world. *You*? The man who lies every day about who you are? *You*, who created that romantic charade after our wedding? You couldn't be bothered to put up a bit of a facade when it came to Yasmin?"

Silvester choked. He was never without words, except in the grip of emotion. "I didn't think. I'm sorry."

"I'll get over it," Stella said, her voice cracking. "I didn't expect . . . Well, that's not fair because I didn't think ahead. But I would have thought that you didn't want people to know that you're still in love with her. After all, Yasmin is married to Giles. You lost that contest."

Her words were whipping past his head so fast that he could hardly make sense of them. "It wasn't a contest." But then he remembered his own conclusion about his courtship. "Perhaps my courtship of Yasmin was a contest, but I'm not in love with her."

She rolled her eyes. "You're the only one who believes that. Your mother gave me a hug. Your mother! Also she said that you were a fool."

"My mother said that?"

"Astonishing, isn't it? For all she loves to scold, you are her golden boy. She adores you. Do you know how many sympathetic glances I received tonight, not to mention outright expressions of sympathy—along with an indecent proposal, given that *your* lack of interest is so clear that men feel you don't give a damn what your wife does?"

Silvester's back stiffened. "I give a damn."

"I know you do. I also know you won't be unfaithful. You did nothing that I shouldn't have anticipated. But in the future, I would ask you to hide your emotion."

"I scarcely chatted with her," Silvester said, stunned. "I was talking to Giles about banking regulations. Stella, you have to believe me. I don't give a damn about Yasmin being back. It was nice to see her, that's all. I like her smile—"

He instantly realized he'd made another mistake.

"She has a lovely smile," Stella said evenly. "Truly lovely. We'd better stop talking now, don't you think? It's hard enough making my way in this marriage without enumerating Lady Yasmin's best qualities."

The carriage drew to a stop before Silvester could marshal words. What were the right words? Being around Stella seemed to strip away his sophisticated rhetoric, leaving him in a jumble of words punctuated by "mine," which was entirely unhelpful.

Silvester pushed open the door and, once on the ground, turned to give Stella a hand. She flicked a glance at him and ignored his hand, missed the step and plunged down with a faint scream. Silvester caught her just before she hit the pavement.

"Thank you," she said with frigid emphasis.

He put her back on her feet and followed as Stella greeted their new butler, handing him her reticule and assuring him that it had been a most pleasant evening.

Pleasant?

Silvester felt as if he'd been flayed. She walked directly into their bedchamber, but the dowager jerked open a door farther down the corridor and glared at him.

He obeyed her silent command and walked toward her, bowing. "Mother."

"You fool."

She slammed the door in his face.

CHAPTER THIRTY-SIX

Stella put her spectacles to the side before she scooped up Specs and sat down on the edge of the bed, burying her face in warm fur. Her cat broke into a purr like the rumble of a tiny locomotive. At least one person loved her best.

Though perhaps a cat didn't count as a person. She really had to stop being so sorry for herself. She was a duchess in love with her husband. That should be enough.

Silvester walked through the door, his face wiped of all expression. Without speaking, he leaned over to pull off his boots.

"I would like to sleep alone tonight," Stella said, knowing her eyes were glossy with tears that she couldn't allow to fall. Her throat ached with sorrow.

Her husband dropped one boot on the floor. She knew he was about to launch into an argument meant to convince her that he had done nothing wrong. Silvester hated criticism.

"I am not punishing you," she said, clearing her throat. "Tomorrow, I promise that I shall be entirely back to normal. We have no need to speak about this evening ever again."

"I am not in love with Yasmin," Silvester said. "I never was." He dropped his second boot.

"That's marvelous," Stella said, not believing him for a moment. "That will make it easier for both of us as the years pass, I'm sure. Please, Silvester. I'd like to be alone."

He walked across the room and threw open the sash, staring out into the dark trees, all that was visible of Hyde Park at this hour. "I don't want to sleep apart from you. May I say again that I never loved that woman?"

Stella looked down at her cat, wondering how Silvester could utter those words, when the evidence was so clearly against him. She took a deep breath. "I'm tired. Please, please can we just—"

"I need to—" He turned to face her and started again. "I need to explain."

Raw panic clawed at Stella's throat. She didn't want to hear his explanation.

"I want you to understand."

"I do understand," Stella said quickly.

Silvester had that stubborn look that suggested he would refuse to give up.

Fine. She had offered him a civilized silence, and he had rejected it. "I understand that my husband adores another woman. I also understand that he is an honorable man, who will not betray me. Do you think that fact makes me feel better?"

"I just said—"

"I don't care," Stella cried, dashing away tears that insisted on falling. "You'd think I'd be used to being second choice, but *I'm not*. I looked at you snuggled on the couch beside Yasmin, and I felt so angry I couldn't even breathe."

"I was not—"

She took a deep breath. The bleak feeling in her gut? She had to live with it. Get through it. But she couldn't stop herself. "You forced me to marry you, even though I warned you that you might feel differently after Yasmin returned to London."

"I don't feel differently!"

Her words tumbled out. "Well, I do! I realized in the carriage that marrying you took away *my* chance to find a man who loves me that much. There might have been a man out there who would think I was enough. I could have been his first choice. But now I'll never know, will I?" Her voice broke.

Silvester had an appalled expression.

Of course, he didn't want to hurt her feelings. He was an innate gentleman, even when overcome by reverence for another woman.

"I do think you're enough. More than enough."

Lovely. Just what every woman wanted to hear from her husband.

"I'm talking about a man who would choose me *first*," Stella said, choking out the words. "I'm not sure I can forgive you for that. Even if I had ended up an old maid, the way my aunt feared, I would have known that I had held out for the best."

"You'd rather be an old maid than married to me?" His voice was thick with emotion. Disbelief, maybe.

Silvester clearly couldn't believe that every woman wouldn't choose to marry him. Another swell of anger rose in her chest at his arrogance. "Of course I wouldn't. But you . . . you took that from me too, didn't you?"

"Took what from you?"

"The love I would have given that man!"

"The hell you'll give love to any other man," Silvester said, his voice dropping as he stepped toward her. "You're mine, Stella. I don't give a fig for Yasmin. Nothing. And I never did."

"Hogwash!" Stella retorted, glaring at him. "What about that telling bit of cruelty, when you told me of Yasmin's lovely smile?" She felt her heart crack again, saying the words. She buried her face in Specs's fur, another sob rising in her throat. "All I wanted was a cottage next to a bookstore. I never wanted to be a duchess."

"What you're saying is that you never wanted me as a husband." Silvester walked a few steps to a chair and dropped into it with an audible thud. "You wanted a cottage?"

"Next to a bookstore," Stella said, her voice thick. Tears shone on Specs's white fur. She knew Silvester wouldn't like what she was saying, but she said it anyway. "If I did marry, it would have been to someone who put me first, not like my aunt. And to be blunt, not like you either."

"I do put you first." He sprang forward and wrapped his arms around her, sitting back down on the bed. Specs gave an irritated meow and jumped to the floor.

Stella turned her face into his chest, her body shaking with sobs. He smelled so good, so much like the man she loved. The man she *adored*.

She loved his wry smile as much as he loved Yasmin's luminous one, a truth that bit into her heart. Part of her wanted to cry out that she hated to quarrel. To pretend that he didn't hurt her, because did it matter? It didn't. They were married.

"I didn't know what love was when I was courting her," Silvester said hoarsely. "My feeling was no deeper than the icing on a cake, and just as treacle-sweet."

That was all very well—but by running to Yasmin's side, he told all of London just how shallow his feelings were for his wife. Thinner than icing, apparently.

Stella curled more tightly against his chest. A night breeze swept through the room, bringing with it the sleepy chirps of London sparrows.

"My so-called love was made up of flirtatious glances and shared laughter," Silvester said. "The truth is that a good deal of my so-called emotion sprang from the way other men looked at her, especially Giles."

"It was a competition," Stella said shakily. "I understand." She *did* understand. Her husband could not resist a contest.

"Then you also know that I wasn't truly in love with her."

He had thought he was, and wasn't that what mattered? She didn't answer.

"You can't have it both ways, Stella. Either I wanted to win a competition for Yasmin's hand *or* I was genuinely, desperately in love with her. Do you truly believe the latter?"

"Yes."

"Remember, I was coming to play chess with you every morning while wooing her. I was kissing you in your bedchamber. No man in love kisses another woman. I never kissed Yasmin, by the way."

"But you were wooing *her*."

"I couldn't get out of it at that point, could I? I

had to let the courtship play its course. I knew Giles would overcome his fear and marry her. He genuinely wanted and loved Yasmin, and I didn't. But I was stuck playing out the game until he finally got his ass going."

A stifled sound escaped from Stella's mouth, almost a giggle, at the upright, august earl described in such rude terms.

"If you'll excuse my vulgarity," Silvester added.

"Gentlemen don't say things like that," Stella said against his shirt, her voice rusty with tears.

"I'm not a gentleman. I'm your husband. Your pirate." He tightened his arms, and she could tell he was kissing her hair. He loved her hair. And her freckles. Why wasn't that enough for her? It had to be enough.

Silence fell in the room, broken only by the scratch of branches blowing against the sill.

Silvester sprang up, dropping Stella on her feet. He spun in a circle. "Where's Specs?"

"What?" She looked about confusedly.

Silvester strode over to the window, took one look outside, and launched himself into space.

Stella let out a little shriek. "What are you doing?"

But he was gone.

CHAPTER THIRTY-SEVEN

Silvester hadn't climbed down this particular tree since he was sixteen years old, but the skill hadn't left him. He swung along the branch, hand over hand to the trunk. He saw no sign of Specs; she must have fled downward.

"Silvester!"

He had already moved down several branches, but he paused and looked up.

Stella was leaning out the window. She'd grabbed her spectacles, and red curls tumbled over the windowsill. "What are you doing?"

He felt dull pain in his chest at the sight of her. He'd hurt her. Made her cry. Because he was an idiot. "Specs went down the tree," he said. "Don't worry. I shall fetch her." It was the least he could do.

"No, she didn't." Stella ducked away and reappeared with Specs in her arms. "I'm sorry to say that she peed in your boot again. When I pulled her out, the odor was unmistakable."

Silvester let out a curse that would have shocked the "polite" inhabitants of London. He reached to the branch above and hauled his body up.

"I love how strong you are," his wife said, conversationally.

He froze and looked at her. His heart squeezed.

"All your muscles," she clarified. "The problem, Silvester, is that I love more than your arms."

He pulled himself up another branch until he was level with her.

"Stay there," she ordered. "This is easier to say at a distance."

Silvester's heart was beating faster than it ever had during a boxing match. "What else do you love?" His voice was hoarse, without a trace of a noble accent, but he didn't care.

"You," she said, aching sadness in her voice. "I love you, Silvester. It's like some sort of curse, to love a man who adores another woman."

Silvester took a desperate breath of air, but as always, words didn't come quickly.

"I'm telling you so that you never hurt me again as you did today," Stella told him. "Perhaps your love for Yasmin is a thin layer of sugar. I need you to respect me enough so that you hide the icing."

Silvester stared at her. "I do respect you," he said, forcing the words out from a throat that felt as if it had been sliced by knives.

Even in dim light, he saw the apologetic smile on her face and the embarrassed flush on her cheeks. "Of course you do. I know it. I just . . ." She turned to the side and tipped Specs out to the floor. "I'm merely asking that you continue the charade that you enacted after our wedding. That you pretend in public that you . . . that you feel more for me and less for her. *Please.*"

Curse words echoing through his head, Silvester swung himself at the window. Stella fell back as he slung a leg over the sill.

"There was no charade," he barked.

She looked not only unconvinced, but disappointed. "All right."

"I love you." The words cut through the room. "You smell like cat piss, and I love you. You smile at me and frown at me, and I love you. You're beautiful, but I don't care. I love your secrets."

"'My secrets'?" Stella repeated, sounding stupefied.

Silvester pulled the window shut, just in case Specs did decide to jump out, and took a step toward his wife.

"The way your glasses hide your lashes. They curl, did you know that? The way you love my hairy chest, rather than my chin or my title. The way you love with such bravado, defending your aunt and uncle, loving them despite absurdities and—and gourds. I love the shape of your arse, and your mouth, and your eyes. I *adore* how intelligent you are, and the way you try to hide it with wry comments."

Stella clapped a hand over her mouth, but after all these weeks of marriage he could read her eyes. He saw hesitant joy.

"I love the way you say 'No' to me," he said gruffly. "The way you say 'Yes' to me. No other woman would take me as I truly am."

"That may be true," Stella said, a germ of laughter in her voice.

"They like me for the suit of armor I fashioned as an apprehensive boy of eight years old. You like me despite my armor."

Stella took one step forward. "I *love* you despite the armor."

"I truly don't give a damn about Yasmin. I was irritated that some damn Frenchman was flirting with you because it turns out that I am ridiculously posses-sive of the wife I love. Then I started talking to Giles and trying to be the man you want me to be."

Her eyes were swimming with tears again. "You were?"

"I argued against my own interests. Giles conde-scended to say that I should take up my seat in the House of Lords."

She shook her head. "You'd hate that."

"I thought I would . . . if you wanted me to. But not as a competition. Not to win."

"No?"

"Yasmin was a prize in a competition that I never should have entered. If there was one thing that you taught me, Stella—and there have been many—it's that I have to stop throwing myself into any competition that presents itself. I *could* and *did* make another fortune by buying gold before Britain was informed that it was moving to the gold standard."

"I know," she murmured.

"Should I have? Likely not. Probably not."

He saw agreement in his wife's eyes.

"My love for you didn't stem from competition," he said hoarsely, cupping her face in his. "You are the only person in the world for me. You are the most beautiful woman in the world, and the most sensual, and the most intelligent, and the funniest—"

He stopped because her mouth covered his lips.

He could say it all again, later.

Many times. For example, late that night when they stole down to the kitchens. After toast and hot chocolate, when Silvester pulled open his wife's wrap-per and uncovered the body that fired him with lust.

When he tipped her back on the kitchen table, the better to ravish her. To whisper his love against her bare skin.

"You *are* a hammer," he said when they were back in bed, his voice gruff from exhaustion and contentment.

Stella draped herself over him, silken hair falling like a curtain around his face. "More insults?"

"You smashed all my preconceptions and beliefs, about myself and society."

"Hmmm," she said. Her eyes smiled at him.

"You left me in a strange world."

"As long as you're with me, I don't care what world we're in," she whispered.

It wasn't until they stopped kissing that Silvester clarified the new world in which they both lived: one that had nothing to do with titles, but was built around love, fidelity, loyalty, and honor.

But mostly love.

EPILOGUE

Three years later
LONDON

Stella smiled at the footman guarding the entrance to the Earl of Lilford's family box in the Theatre Royal.

"Your Grace," he said, dropping into such a low bow that he almost let fall the velvet curtain he held open.

She walked into the darkness. At the front of the deep box, Yasmin and Giles were seated beside each other. Yasmin was giggling, tapping her husband on the shoulder with a fan. Her golden hair was piled high on her head, her neck glinted with jewels, her shoulders gleamed in the box's candelabras.

Most of the audience would be ogling the countess, but that didn't matter a pin to Stella. To her, Yasmin was not a leader of the ton, but one of her closest friends, as beloved as Merry and her mother-in-law.

"One smile and that poor sod of a footman went weak at the knees," a deep voice said in her ear. "Why am I here again?" Silvester's hands settled on her waist as he pulled Stella back against him just enough to ensure she understood that he'd prefer the bedchamber to the theater.

Stella turned her head to smile up at him. "Because you love me, and I love plays, and Yasmin is expecting again, and I want to know how she's feeling."

Silvester nipped her ear. "You had tea with her two days ago. You know how she's feeling. Tired, according to Giles."

"Benjamin is naughty," Stella informed her husband. "He *still* wakes up at night. We're lucky that Leo is such a contented baby."

Silvester's arms wrapped around her as he kissed her neck. "Leo is perfect. Almost as perfect as his mama."

At that moment, Yasmin turned around and caught sight of them. Her face lit up. "Stella!"

Silvester's arms slid away, and they walked to the front of the box.

"I found this delightful shawl for you," Yasmin said once they were all seated. She held up a confection of gossamer silver lace. "You must wear it with that rose-colored morning gown we ordered last week."

Stella laughed. "You are a darling," she said affectionately. "You'll never turn me into a fashionable lady like yourself, but thank you." She leaned over to kiss Yasmin's cheek. "How are you feeling?"

"Nauseated half the day and exhausted the rest. Like an *imbécile*," Yasmin groaned. "Benjamin is finally sleeping. Why, why did I let this happen? Another child? Why?"

Stella glanced over Yasmin's shoulder at the earl. She liked Giles much better now than she had when they were supposedly courting. The Earl of Lilford's deep ethical stance was obvious, but he smiled and even laughed sometimes. And always he watched his wife with deep, true love in his eyes.

She raised an eyebrow at Yasmin. "Do you really want me to answer?"

Yasmin sighed ruefully. "How is Leo? Sleeping soundly?"

"Yes," Stella confessed. "He's a sociable babe, so he tries to stay awake, but he can't manage it."

"Whereas Benjamin is so much older, and still wakes at dawn, if not during the night," Yasmin groaned.

Silvester leaned forward. "If there's an *imbécile* in this box, it's your husband after that absurd debate at the House of Lords yesterday."

"It wasn't absurd," Stella cried, swatting her husband with her fan. "*I* thought you offered a brilliant compromise under the circumstances, Giles."

The earl's somber face eased into a smile. "Thank goodness someone appreciates me."

"Silvester and I will never join the chorus. You already think too much of yourself," his countess laughed.

Then the curtain rose, and the play began. None of the four of them paid any attention to the audience who ogled their every move, envying their friendship, their sparkling laughter, their beauty . . .

Thinking they were like the gods living on Mount Olympus.

Yet unlike those bad-tempered Greek gods, no one ever suggested that the duchess or countess or their husbands had feet of clay.

They were always kind.

Which is the only compliment that really matters.

The Next Evening

"**Y**our mother is a hammer."

The future Duke of Huntington was fighting to stay awake as best he could. Every time his head fell back on his father's arm, eyes drifted shut, he started awake. He obligingly tried out the new word. "Mer. Mer."

"No, a hammer." Silvester was sitting in the nursery rocking chair. "She just published another article arguing that steam engines will soon power ships."

The little boy's eyes closed.

A soft voice came from the door to the corridor. "You are teaching our son to insult his mother?"

Silvester touched his son's nose with one finger and then grinned at his wife. "Teaching him to admire her."

Stella laughed, then picked up their son and sat back down on Silvester's lap. Happiness unfurled in his chest as he wrapped his arms around the two people he loved most in the world.

"After all, his grandmother is in the same mold," Silvester pointed out. The Dowager Duchess of Huntington's innovation of a cog wheel driven by twin cylinders embedded in the top of a center-flue boiler had revolutionized British-built locomotives.

Possibly, no one would have paid attention except the young duchess's very first article for the *Times* had explicated her mother-in-law's remarkable achievements, after which engineers beat a road to the Grange.

Stella tipped her head back against Silvester's arm and smiled. "If I'm a hammer, you are too," she whispered. She traced his bottom lip with the tip of her tongue. "You smashed all my ideas about who I was and what I wanted."

"You didn't want to be a duchess," Silvester said. "Intelligent woman that you are."

"I don't mind as long as you are my duke. If you hadn't smashed up my beliefs . . ."

"And claimed you," Silvester put in, with deep satisfaction.

"I'd be living next to a bookstore right now," Stella said, twinkling at him.

"As opposed to turning this entire house into a library. We have more books than the Bodleian. Our son can't even eat with a fork yet, but he has a shelf of books. I fully expect that by the time renovation of the Grange is completed, we'll have to build an addition just to house your collection."

"A point in your favor," his wife conceded. She picked up his free hand, the one that wasn't cradled around her back, and dropped a kiss on one finger. Then wrapped her lips around that finger.

Which led to His Grace surging upright, placing her safely on her feet, taking their son and walking him through a connecting door.

"All yours," he said to Nanny Grey.

"There's my sweet baby," Nanny said, cuddling the little duke. She glanced at the duchess. "You'll want an early night, Your Grace." Without elaboration, she took the baby into the night nursery.

Silvester wrapped his arms around Stella. "I admit that all that hammer smashing is tiring, but is there something you need to tell me, dearest?"

"You love my secrets, remember?" Stella replied, joy gleaming deep in her eyes.

The duke threw back his head and laughed, his large hand slipping down to rest on his wife's stomach.

In the duchess's womb, a little girl was tumbling about, not ready to greet the world—but once she did arrive, squalling at the top of her lungs, she would put on her spectacles, tie up her red curls, and devote herself to smashing up every lingering preconception about how a lady should act.

Polite society would never be the same.

A NOTE ABOUT STEAM ENGINES, SPECTACLES, AND RED-HAIRED GIRLS

I grew up in a farmhouse full of books, the oldest child of two eccentric, creative parents: my father was a poet and my mother a short story writer. A couple of miles away, down a few dirt roads, was a small Minnesota town . . . where I never fit in. I was too weird, too addicted to reading, too plump. Like Stella, I was no good at disguising who I am. Thankfully, unlike Regency England, no girl is forced to attend the junior prom. I stayed home and catalogued my romances, practicing skills that would make me an English professor—and a romance writer.

In *Not that Duke*, I leaned on my past. The dowager duchess is wry, loving, and brilliant, but that doesn't mean she's always an excellent parent (though we never ate boiled eggs for supper). Stella bravely wears spectacles, but that doesn't mean she isn't battered by self-doubt. Silvester almost makes the fatal error of marrying a woman because the world desires her, not because he desires her. Blanche tries to be clever, and ends up being mean.

It took me a long time to shake my experiences in

middle school. Stella was shamed for her freckles, her reading, and her girth. Silvester created a suit of armor to offset his boyhood shame. Luckily, Silvester and Stella find their way together to a different way of being in the world.

So this book is dedicated to my husband, Alessandro.

When he fell in love with me, I felt like the most beautiful, intelligent, and desirable woman in the world. Love isn't about reality, but perception, and I'm so grateful to have spent half my life looking through his eyes.

Discover Eloisa James'
captivating romance series,
The Wildes of Lindow Castle

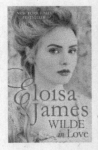   

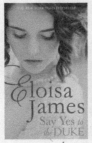